TO ED
FOR ALL HIS HELP IN BRINGING THIS BOOK TO
FRUITION
AND HIS UNWAVERING
ENCOURAGEMENT AND SUPPORT

* * *

AND TO MY AMAZING FAMILY
THEY PROVIDED THE CHARACTER TRAITS
FOR THE PERSONALITIES WITHIN THIS STORY

* * *

THE CHARACTERS ARE BASED ON REAL LIFE PEOPLE
BUT THE EVENTS ARE PURELY FICTITIOUS

CHAPTER ONE

IT WAS JULY, 1956. THE ARKANSAS SUMMER was typically hot and humid. Occasionally a gentle breeze would create a soft wave in the tall grass, which covered most of the slope running about thirty yards from the farmhouse down to a log fence bordering the dirt road. A few dandelion puffs broke free from their stems and floated languidly into the air while honeybees gathered nectar from the flowering bushes growing next to the house. The faint sounds of a barking dog in the distance were barely audible to the four youngsters who were quietly passing time in the yard at their grandparents' home.

Geneva, who would turn eighteen the following month and her sister Loretta; almost sixteen, were searching for four-leaf clovers in an area of mowed grass in front of the house, which stretched almost a third of the way to the road. Their brother Johnny, who had just turned fourteen was swatting at honeybees as they circled the flowers. The youngest of the four siblings, twelve year old Gary was sitting on the steps of the porch, deep in thought. The family visited this set of grandparents every other summer. They were the children's paternal grandparents; Grandma and Grandpa Austin.

Gary was wondering about his uncle Romey, who lived with the grandparents. He had never really given his uncle much thought before. He had merely taken him for granted. Uncle Romey had been around for as long as Gary could remember. The children had always enjoyed playing games with him as if he were one of them. Now Gary was wondering how old his uncle was. He looked sort of like a grownup and he had to shave every day, but he was shorter than the other grownups,

1

and he usually hung out with the kids. He had his own playhouse, which was full of comic books and toys that he would gladly share with anyone who wanted to spend time with him.

It was noontime and everyone was resting for an hour; Grandma's orders. Gary, Johnny and Loretta had complained extensively about having to rest, but Grandma had laid down the law that everyone must be quiet and keep still during this hottest part of the day. She said that if the children ran and played, Romey would want to play too and he would become overheated and possibly suffer a heatstroke. She had Romey lying down in his bedroom with the fan next to his bed circulating the air around him.

The screen door opened behind Gary, and his mother, Lula Mae stepped out onto the porch. Her smile expressed her general good nature and added to her natural good looks. She looked much younger than her thirty-three years. Her honey-blonde hair hung free, almost touching her shoulders and her blue eyes showed a kindness that was inherent within her. Her appearance had not changed much since she was the fifteen year old bride of Guy, a man ten years her senior. At fifteen, she already looked very much a young woman and over the years she had maintained her youthful appearance; not as a result of any effort on her part, but merely good genes. Being young and athletic had resulted in a quick recovery from four pregnancies and she had experienced very little trouble in regaining her figure after each one.

Lula Mae was one of the older children in a large family and her parents relied heavily on her for help in caring for her younger siblings. When her own children came along so early in her life, this past experience provided her with the knowledge she needed to be a skilled parent.

Wearing Khaki shorts and one of Guy's white dress shirts with the sleeves rolled up and the tail tied at the midriff, she carried a tray holding four glasses of fresh lemonade. She set the tray on a small table next to a rocking chair, and carrying one glass of lemonade, sat next to Gary and offered him the glass.

"What are you thinking about Son?" she said. Then without waiting for Gary to answer, she called to the others. "Geneva, you and Loretta and Johnny come and get some lemonade."

Gary eagerly accepted the glass his mother was offering him and took a sip of the cool beverage before asking, "How old is Uncle Romey?"

Johnny and Loretta rushed past their mother and brother in an effort to be the first at the lemonade. A brief pushing match ensued and then they each grabbed a glass and drank deeply from it.

Geneva stood facing Lula Mae. "Look," she said, holding out her hand, palm up. "I found two four-leaf clovers. I'm going to press them in a book." Without waiting for a response from her mother, she made her way to the porch swing and sipped her lemonade. Geneva was not opposed to sitting and being quiet. She felt that she was too old to play childish games with her brothers and sister and she preferred to sit and read.

"Well good, Geneva," said her mother. "Those will bring you good luck."

Johnny and Loretta, having finished their drinks jumped from the porch and onto the lawn where they each began to attempt to trip the other by putting a leg behind their opponent and pushing against his or her shoulders. Loretta cried out in frustration as she lost her footing and fell backwards from Johnny's lucky shove. Johnny laughed loudly and scoffed at her failure.

"Now you kids stop that. Romey will be resting fifteen more minutes and then you can play." Lula Mae stood up to go back into the house. She was trying to be lighthearted with the children, but it was difficult for her. She did not like all the rules that her mother-in-law generally placed upon everybody, and she was a little on edge, fearing that the children would cause their grandmother to display her ill temper.

"Mama!"

"What, Son?"

"How old is Uncle Romey?"

"Oh…" Lula Mae brushed back her bangs, which hung over one eye. "I don't know for sure Gary. I think he's either twenty-four or twenty-five years old. Why?"

"Is something wrong with him?"

This question took Lula Mae by surprise. Romey's atypical characteristics were rarely discussed, and when they were discussed, the conversations were hushed and covert, and consequently resulted in varying opinions about his condition. She had never heard of the term

Down's syndrome; she had only heard the rumors that her mother-in-law had done something to try to abort the fetus when she was pregnant with Romey. Lula Mae had no intention of discussing this with her twelve year old son.

Johnny and Loretta were still roughhousing and this gave Lula Mae an excuse to turn away from Gary and avoid the subject. "Johnny and Loretta stop that!" she said through clenched teeth. "If you two get your grandma started I'm going to take a switch to you both. Now go around to the back of the house and get a bucket and go down to the barn and get it full of potatoes for dinner. And be quiet!"

Johnny and Loretta were only too happy to oblige. They were both full of energy and could not wait to leave the *serenity* of the front lawn. Lula Mae, relieved that she had successfully dodged Gary's questions about Romey, picked up the tray and Johnny and Loretta's empty glasses and went back into the house.

Gary turned his attention to his oldest sister, for whom he had a great deal of admiration. He watched her for a while as she sat with one foot tucked beneath her and the other gently touching the floor as she pushed the porch swing back and forth. Gary thought that she looked very grown-up; reading one of her movie magazines, chewing bubble gum and occasionally blowing bubbles. To him, she looked just like the actresses in her magazines, with her dark hair pulled up into a ponytail and her turned up shirt collar.

Of course, their grandmother did not approve of the way Geneva and Loretta dressed. She had repeatedly said to their mother, "Lula Mae you should be ashamed of yourself; letting those girls dress like little harlots. Lord knows they're gonna wind up in trouble." Gary did not understand what a harlot was or why his grandmother thought his sisters were going to get into trouble. He liked the way they looked. He turned and looked out over the front yard as he sipped his lemonade.

Lula Mae did not pay much attention to her mother-in-law's unsolicited advice on how she should raise her children. In the eighteen years that she had been married to Guy, she had learned to stand up to the woman; unlike the naïve young girl that she was when she first came to this house. Even then, she had to use a lot of self restraint to keep from talking back to her new husband's mother. She had always been self confident and independent and would have challenged Mary's domineering rule, but her devotion to Guy and her ideal of having a happy harmonious marriage kept her from it for a while.

When she had married Guy, he had very little money and was still living with his parents. The couple spent their first six months as man and wife living in this house with Frank, Mary and Romey. The atmosphere, which prevailed, forced Lula Mae to make quite an adjustment in her attitude towards family life. She was accustomed to living in a household where the family members showed love and respect to one another. Frank and Mary's household was desperately lacking in these values.

Frank and Mary were both stubborn, dominating people who had little regard for polite pleasantries. At that time, however, Frank had been the stronger of the two, which left Mary frustrated and angry. She was unable to wield much control over her husband, and being partial to Guy, she was usually pleasant to him. That left Romey and her new daughter-in-law as targets of her ill temper and dominating authority.

During those first six months Lula Mae realized that married life was not going to be the loving affectionate life that she had envisioned. She became accustomed to dealing with bickering, complaining, and ultimatums. She adjusted, and began standing up to her mother-in-law. By the time she and Guy moved into their own place, she had established herself in the family structure and exhibited strength and resistance to her mother-in-law's demands.

She did, however still resist the urge to lash out at Mary. She felt that when she was in her in-laws' home, that she should show them respect. And she also hated the inevitable squabble that would result in challenging Mary's authority.

Several minutes had passed since Lula Mae had gone back into the house. Geneva and Gary were still sitting on the porch. Romey was up from his nap and he was sitting in the living room. All was peaceful and quiet; then suddenly...

"Oh my Lord-o-mercy!...Oh my Lord-o-mercy!"

At the sound of their grandmother's cries, Gary and Geneva jumped up from where they sat on the porch and rushed to the screen door. They peered through the screen as the previously sedate scene inside the house turned to chaos.

"That old mule is gonna kill her!" Mary yelled as she stood waving the skirt of her apron in front of her and looking out the side window of the living room.

"Loretta!" Lula Mae yelled as she followed behind Guy who burst through the screen door slamming it against the side of the house, popping the spring that was used to pull it shut. Geneva and Gary watched as their parents flew past them, bounding into the yard without touching the porch steps.

In three seconds, Guy vaulted over the fence that surrounded the pasture; with Lula Mae right behind him. The two of them ran in the direction of the barn a quarter of a mile away. Geneva and Gary, having followed them to the fence, stopped there and watched while Mary continued with her "…Lord-o-mercy's…" from the window and Frank and Romey stood on the porch watching.

Bolting in the direction of the house was Frank's old mule with Loretta on its bare back. She was hanging on to its mane for dear life; her bright red hair flying out behind her and her feet kicking out in front of her. She was bouncing from side to side somehow managing to stay on top of the animal.

Guy had his hands raised in the air in front of him as he and Lula Mae ran toward the mule and their daughter. The mule slowed its pace and came to an abrupt halt when it reached the two of them, practically throwing Loretta over its head. Guy grabbed the mule's mane to hold it steady while Lula Mae pulled Loretta safely to the ground.

Running some distance behind the mule was the other redhead of the family, Johnny. He and Loretta; true to the belief about middle children were forever getting themselves into one fix or another. Johnny slowed his pace and switched to a casual swagger upon seeing that his sister had been rescued from the runaway mule, which he had slapped on its flank after persuading her to sit on its back. He was in no hurry to face the consequences of his actions and he had assumed his usual attitude of nonchalance, hoping to save face and veil his sense of dread.

By the cool of the evening everyone had pretty much forgotten the incident with the mule. Johnny and Loretta, having completed their prescribed punishment of sitting on the front porch for not such a long time, had been allowed to join the rest of the family.

Supper was over and the children and Romey had been ushered out of the house so that Guy and Frank could listen to The National Farm and Home Hour on the radio. Lula Mae and Mary had begun cleaning up in the kitchen and doing the dishes. Usually, Geneva preferred not to join the other youngsters in their frolicking, but since it meant getting out of doing the dishes she was very agreeable to going out to play.

Working in Mary's outdated kitchen made Lula Mae appreciate her own kitchen and its modern conveniences; not that she had difficulty in this kitchen, she had learned years earlier how to work without the luxury of running water. There was a well just off the back porch of the house, where in the past, water had to be pulled up manually with a bucket. The recent installation of the water pump at the sink had been a great improvement. There was also a new gas range, which was fueled by a butane tank about fifty feet from the back of the house. The gas range made heating water much easier and faster than the old wood burning stove that it had replaced. The old stove, however, remained in the kitchen next to the new one. The smell of burning wood and the heat that it gave off made the winter months so cozy that Frank and Mary refused to get rid of it.

The house was basic, but comfortable. The forty acre plot, which it sat on, had been a wedding present from Frank's father and mother nearly fifty years earlier. With his father and brothers' help, Frank had built the original house so that he would have a place to live with his bride, Mary. Back then it had consisted of only two rooms; a kitchen and a bedroom. The original bedroom was now the dining room. Over the years, neighbors and family members had helped him add two downstairs bedrooms, a living room, the large front porch and four upstairs bedrooms.

To the chagrin of the visiting relatives, Frank had never built indoor bathrooms. The only indoor water supply was the hand pump at the kitchen sink. Bathing was done in the kitchen or in the shed down by the henhouse. The brushed aluminum bathtub was about three feet in diameter and about one and one-half feet deep. It could be easily carried from one point to the other when it was empty.

The house had been equipped with electricity about ten years prior. The large console radio that Frank and Guy were listening to was one of the first electrical appliances that Frank and Mary had ever owned. Frank had purchased it along with their first electric lamp. It was one of their most treasured possessions.

The commentator's voice from the radio carried softly throughout the house and out onto the front porch giving the women in the kitchen and the children outside a sense of calm.

The evening was one of those ideal summer evenings that are remembered for years to come. The warm night air was filled with the sweet aroma of the fragrant flowers, which grew in profusion around the house. The cicadas were beginning to play their nocturnal symphony, occasionally accompanied by a few crickets warming up for their night's performance.

Geneva, Gary and Romey sat on the front porch, examining Romey's assortment of toys that he had collected from boxes of Cracker Jacks. Geneva was unconsciously doing one of her Julie London impersonations as she lined up her favorite toys on a small table, which was illuminated by a lamp from inside the house. Gary and Romey were quiet as they went through their own piles of toys, picking out their favorites. They were enjoying Geneva's performance as much as any of Julie's audiences had ever enjoyed hers.

"Look!" interrupted Loretta as she walked up the steps of the porch. "I'm engaged!" She stood in front of the others and held up her left hand and showed them her ring finger. There was a faint golden glowing line around it. "Come away from the light and you can see it better." She jumped off the steps of the porch and ran into the darkness of the yard. Geneva and Gary followed her into the yard with Romey (who was not quite so quick) right behind them.

"What is that?" asked Geneva.

In the dark, the band of light around Loretta's finger was much more obvious. "Lightning bugs."

With the darkening skies, the fireflies were becoming more noticeable. As the youngsters looked out over the yard and beyond, they saw scores of pinpoints of light as the tiny beetles blinked their abdomens on and off.

A voice came out of the darkness, "Look at me." Johnny appeared with a crude glowing cross on his forehead. "Can you see it?" he asked.

"How are you doing that?" asked Geneva.

"Like this." Johnny took Geneva's hand and began rubbing his thumb around her finger. Gary and Romey moved in closer to get a better look.

Johnny had a firefly between his thumb and forefinger. He pressed the back half of the bug against Geneva's finger and circumvented it, leaving behind a glowing line.

"I want to try," cried Gary.

Romey kept silent. He did not know what to think of what the others were doing. It was exciting to him, but he was afraid that it might be something he was not supposed to do.

Johnny moved deeper into the darkness and began swiping the air with his hand. "When they light up, grab them; then you rub their little butts on you and it lights up."

"You're not supposed to say that," said Gary. Getting the typical unresponsiveness from his older brother for his criticism of his language, Gary quickly joined the others as they began spreading out and swiping their hands through the air trying to catch the fireflies.

Half an hour later the screen door slapped against its frame as Lula Mae walked out onto the porch. She looked around the darkened yard trying to see the children. "Kids, where are you?" she called. There was no answer. "Geneva!" Still no answer. The screen door opened and closed again.

"Where are those kids, Lula Mae?" Mary was wiping her damp hands on her apron as she walked to the edge of the porch. She put the palms of her hands on her backside and called out. "Row-meee!"

The two women saw Geneva crossing the yard. "What are you doing in that tall grass?" said Lula Mae. "Where are the other kids?"

"They're coming." Geneva turned to assure that the others were behind her. In the faint light cast from the lights within the house, Mary and Lula Mae saw Loretta emerging from the darkness with Romey in tow and Gary following a few feet behind them. Romey was breathing heavily as Mary rushed down the steps of the porch and approached him and Loretta.

"Good Lord-o-mercy, Loretta Fay; if your mama has any sense at all she'll whip you good for this." Mary took Romey's hand and led him towards the house, scowling at Lula Mae as she passed her. "These kids of yours have about killed him. Look how he's breathing."

"Are you okay, Romey?" asked Lula Mae as he passed by her, being pulled along like a child.

Romey held up his free hand to Lula Mae. "Look, I'm engaged," he said breathlessly, but with a wide grin.

Mary led Romey up the steps and into the house, muttering as she went. "You kids just wait until I tell your daddy what you've done. If your mama won't make you mind, I bet he will."

Lula Mae turned toward Geneva, "Where's Johnny?"

Geneva pointed toward the porch. Lula Mae turned to see Johnny, who, under the cover of darkness had sneaked behind his mother and grandmother when they walked into the yard, and was now sitting on the steps trying his best to look innocent. He had a Mason jar full of fireflies.

"You kids all knew that Grandma would have a fit if you took Romey out into that grass."

"But that's where the lightning bugs are." Johnny held up the Mason jar filled with fireflies.

"Where did you get that jar?" Johnny did not answer his mother. "Damn it Johnny! That's one of Grandma's canning jars. She's going to be even madder when she finds out that you've been in the cellar." Lula Mae looked around at Gary and the girls. "You kids all know how she is. Why do you have to do things to get her going?"

The screen door opened and shut with a bang. Guy walked onto the porch and stood beside Johnny. He jerked upward on the hair at the back of Johnny's neck.

"Ouch," cried Johnny, accustomed to this act of discipline from his father and resentful of the intent to humiliate him.

"Get in the house, god-damn it," said Guy.

"Oh leave him alone," said Lula Mae walking back to Johnny. She reached for the jar of fireflies. "Give me that jar."

"No!" Johnny pulled the jar close to his body.

Guy slapped Johnny on the back of his head.

"Will you stop?" Lula Mae said to Guy. "Give it here." She pulled the jar away from her oldest son.

"Mamma, don't," pleaded Johnny.

Lula Mae ignored his pleas as she unscrewed the lid to the jar and set free the insects. "You kids get ready for bed."

"Mamma it's too early for bed," said Geneva.

"It's not too early. You kids just have to show yourselves. You all know how your grandma is."

"We didn't do anything," whined Loretta on her way into the house.

"You've been told there are snakes in that grass. What if Romey had been bitten?"

"There aren't any snakes out there," growled Johnny as he followed behind Loretta.

Guy looked accusingly at Lula Mae as they ushered the children inside. "Just let them go to bed," she said to him. "They didn't really hurt anything."

"The hell they didn't. Mamma's in there fretting over Romey right now. She said they almost killed him."

"Oh for crying out loud, you know your mama fusses over Romey too much. He was just playing. It don't hurt him to get a little winded."

"Yeah, you know it all don't you?"

"I know that if your mama can cause trouble between you and me she will. And you know it too, so just shut up." Lula Mae let the screen door slam shut behind her as a final comment and ushered the youngsters into the kitchen to wash up and brush their teeth.

"Johnny what is that all over your face?" she asked when she saw him in the bright light of the kitchen.

"Lightning bugs," said Gary.

"Well good God, don't you kids know that's dirty?" Lula Mae pumped well water into the white enameled wash basin. She then lifted the tea kettle off the stove and poured hot water into the basin and set it on the kitchen counter. "There, you kids get ready for bed."

She left her children in the kitchen and went into an adjoining room that was Romey's bedroom. She didn't think that Romey was in any danger, but she just wanted to make sure. She loved Romey very much and she would hate for anything bad to happen to him.

Romey was seven years old when Lula Mae first met him. She remembered thinking that he acted younger than the average seven year old. As she watched him grow older, it was evident to her that he had trouble learning things that most children picked up readily. She had noticed, however that there were other areas in which he seemed to function normally. Nowadays there were times when he conducted himself in a very adult-like manner, but Mary seemed to discourage this behavior in him. She doted on him like she was a mother hen and he was her only chick. Lula Mae could not help but feel that Romey was capable of doing much more on his own than Mary would ever allow him to do.

As she entered the room she saw Mary in her usual stance with her hands on the back of her hips watching Romey, who was sitting on the chamber pot.

"Are you okay Romey?" Lula Mae asked.

"You don't need to be in here. You just go on out," said Mary.

"I just want to make sure Romey's okay."

"Well if he was left with those kids too long he wouldn't be. They wiped those nasty bugs all over him."

"I'm okay Lula Mae," said Romey, belying Mary's claims of his less than well being.

Lula Mae bent over and kissed Romey on his cheek. In many ways he was still very child-like. He seemed to have no more inhibitions or sense of embarrassment than a five year old as he sat on the chamber pot while his mother waited for him to finish.

"Well then, good-night Hon."

"Good-night, Lula Mae."

Lula Mae turned to leave the room.

"Tell Guy not to forget to come and kiss his mama good-night," said Mary.

Her bedroom adjoined Romey's and she usually left the door ajar so that she could hear if he called to her in the night; as if he were a child. Lula Mae suspected that her mother-in-law wanted her and Romey's bedrooms to be downstairs so that she would be aware of what was going on in the main part of the house at all times. This also gave her an excuse to tell everyone else when to go to bed. She would claim that it was so that Romey could sleep.

Lula Mae returned to the kitchen where the four youngsters were still washing up. They had been barefoot for most of the day, so she reminded them to also wash their feet. "And when you get upstairs go straight to bed and be quiet."

"Mama, it's too early to go to bed," said Geneva.

"You can stay up and read if you want to; just be quiet."

Lula Mae had said many times that she felt like she was always "walking on pins and needles" when she was visiting her mother-in-law. She was constantly afraid that she was going to lose her temper with Mary, which would invariably lead to an argument between her and Guy.

She left the youngsters in the kitchen and walked through the living room. She stood at the screen door looking out at Guy, who was sitting on the front porch. After eighteen years, the sight of him still aroused her. The light from inside the house fell across his bare shoulders and accentuated the well defined muscles in his back, left bare by the white underwear shirt he was wearing.

He turned and leaned against the porch railing when she walked outside. He looked her up and down as she approached and stood next to him. "I like those Betty Grable shorts," he said, reaching up and rubbing the back of her bare thigh.

"According to your mama, they make me look cheap."

"Come here." Guy took Lula Mae by the hand and pulled her downward. He directed her to sit on the steps between his legs. With her back against his chest, he put his arms around her and pulled her closer. He nuzzled her neck and kissed her ear. "Mama don't mean nothing, Honey; she's just old fashioned."

"Lula Mae did you tell Guy to come kiss his mama good-night?"

Guy released his wife at the sound of his mother's voice behind him. She was standing at the screen door looking out at them.

"If you two want to act like ruttin' pigs you should find someplace private. Lord-o-mercy, what if one of your children was to walk out here. Guy you never saw me and your papa acting like that. I had more respect for myself."

Lula Mae stood and walked into the yard without saying a word. She pulled a pack of cigarettes out of her shirt pocket. Guy stood and went to his mother. He opened the screen door and kissed her on the cheek.

"Come kiss Romey good-night. He won't go to sleep until you do." Mary turned and went back to Romey's bedroom.

Guy looked back at Lula Mae who remained with her back toward him. He watched her as she lit her cigarette and exhaled deeply, while looking up at the night sky. He wanted to say something comforting to her, but he was at a loss for words; so he turned and obediently followed his mother.

After a while, Geneva, Loretta, Johnny and Gary had finished in the kitchen. Geneva and Loretta were climbing the stairs behind Gary.

"Where's Johnny?" asked Geneva.

"He had to pee," said Gary.

During the nighttime, when the male members of the household needed to relieve themselves, it was a common practice for them to go a short distance from the house and urinate on the ground. The outhouse was a good distance from the main house so they would not bother to go all the way to it.

"Look what I got." Johnny was coming up the stairs behind his siblings. The others stopped halfway up the staircase and turned to see what he was talking about. He was carrying a battery operated tabletop radio, which was a little larger than a loaf of bread.

"I got it out of Romey's playhouse. We can listen to *Tales of the Macabre*."

"Oh boy!" said Gary.

Geneva and Loretta were also very pleased. They all hurried up the stairs to listen to one of their favorite radio programs. The program consisted of dramatizations of strange occurrences, always suggesting the supernatural.

Their grandmother had kept them from listening to it the previous night as they and Romey had all huddled around the large radio in the living room. She had come out of the kitchen where the adults were having coffee, and after listening for a few moments, went to the radio and changed the station to a religious program. She said that what they were listening to was about Satan's work, and that God fearing Christians should not want to hear those things.

The room where Johnny and Gary slept was the farthest away from their grandmother's bedroom, so in hopes of keeping her from hearing them, the four youngsters took the radio there. They adjusted the dial until they found the right station and waited for the program to begin. In the meantime rock-and-roll music was playing. They kept the volume low while Loretta and Gary practiced all the latest dances.

Within the past year, Loretta had become very aware of her blossoming sexuality. She had been a tomboy her whole life, but when her breasts began to develop and she noticed the attention she was getting from the boys; she began to see the power she had over them. She had yet to understand how to use that power, but she loved wearing makeup and dancing a little provocatively. It was all just a game to her and she took none of it seriously. She was a very good dancer and she had found that this ability also added to her popularity with the other girls at school, so she practiced every chance she got.

Gary was her standby partner. He loved dancing almost as much as Loretta, but he was too shy to dance with anyone other than family members. They were disheartened at their grandmother's edict that there would none of that *vulgar dancing* in her house, but they disregarded her rule when she was not around.

Presently the music ended and they all huddled around the radio and turned out the light in order to create a spooky atmosphere. After a moment their eyes adjusted to the faint glow spreading over the room from the crescent moon outside. Their favorite program began:

The sound of leaves rustling in the wind, and the eerie hooting of a lone owl set the scene as being outdoors at nighttime. The rhythmic click-clacking from a woman's high heeled shoes echoed off a sidewalk.

The steady, measured clacking of the footsteps stopped abruptly.

A woman's voice was heard. "Is somebody there?"

Silence.

The sound of the footsteps resumed; now the pace was a little faster.

The hooting owl was heard again.

The rhythm of the footsteps picked up.

The menacing noise of a wolf howling in the distance carried over the wind.

The woman's breathing became faster along with her still quickening footsteps.

The footsteps stopped again. "Who's there?"

Silence.

The footsteps began once more, quickly breaking into a run. The woman's breathing became louder and faster.

A wolf howled again; this time it was closer.

Keys rattled together and the echo of the footsteps halted.

The keys could be heard being inserted into a lock. The lock turned. A creaking door opened quickly and slammed shut.

The quiet measured breathing suggested to the listener that the woman was safe as the wind continued to moan outside.

A chain was pulled to turn on a lamp. The woman screamed loudly, only to be drowned out by a long sinister laugh, followed by the pronouncement; "Tales of the Macabre," uttered by a deep sonorous male voice.

Loretta grabbed Gary by the shoulders, "Gotcha!"

Gary let out a yell and jerked out of her grip.

"Shut-up you guys," said Geneva. "If Grandma hears us she'll make Daddy come up here and turn the radio off."

Geneva's warning was heeded and the four sat quietly for the next fifteen minutes as the story unfolded. The tale was about a young woman who went to a fortuneteller at a carnival. While having her fortune told in the old woman's trailer, the young woman inadvertently glimpsed a deformed boy who was chained to a post behind a curtain. The old fortuneteller became very upset over the fact that the boy had been exposed. She said the young woman should never have seen the boy; that she was now cursed and she should go straight home.

As the commercial played, the brothers roughhoused and the girls speculated about what would happen next.

The second half of the story told of the young woman becoming disfigured and taking on the same physical characteristics as the boy behind the curtain. She soon mutated into something half animal and half human, and fled into the forest to escape the expressions of horror that she saw on people's faces when they looked at her. The narrator of the story told his audience that the legend stated that she now roamed the forests every night; more monster than human, searching for youngsters to feed upon.

"There she is!" shrieked Loretta, pointing toward the window.

The others jumped in fright! Johnny and Gary quickly turned their fear into retaliation and began pushing Loretta, making her stagger from one brother to the other.

"You better put that radio back where you got it," said Geneva. "You'll get a whipping if Mama and Daddy find out you took it out of Romey's playhouse."

"I'm not going out there," said Johnny. "What if the monster woman is out there?"

"She'll eat you for dinner." Loretta pushed Johnny and ran to her and Geneva's bedroom.

"You better put it back Johnny." Geneva left the room too.

"Come on let's put this back." Johnny motioned for Gary to follow him.

"No…I'm not going outside."

"Oh dummy; there's no such thing as a monster woman." Johnny got a sly grin on his face. "Except maybe for Grandma."

"Take it back by yourself. I don't want to go."

"Scaredy-cat!" Johnny left the room and without attracting attention from the adults, successfully made his way to Romey's playhouse and back again. He returned to the bedroom and he and Gary played checkers for a half-hour or so, until their mother came into the room.

"Okay boys its time to get to bed. Gary you go pee first." Gary had a history of bedwetting.

"I don't have to go."

"I don't want you wetting the bed. Now go pee."

"I don't do that anymore," protested Gary.

"What? You don't pee anymore?" Johnny laughed.

"Gary Ray, do what I say. Now go."

"Tell Johnny to go with me."

"Go with him Johnny."

"Scaredy-cat." Johnny picked up the flashlight on the nightstand and reluctantly proceeded to descend the stairs with Gary behind him. Romey's bedroom was next to the kitchen and he had already gone to bed. The bedroom door was left open for air circulation. Mary did not want the kitchen light turned on because it might wake Romey, so that meant that there would be no light spilling out into the back yard.

Once outside, the two boys stood on the porch. Johnny held the flashlight, directing the beam into the back yard, giving Gary a lighted path to a point far enough away from the house to pee. Gary stepped cautiously to the edge of the porch. He hesitated as he scanned the area of darkness before him.

"Shake the flashlight and make the batteries touch, so that it will shine brighter."

"You big baby…go on." Johnny gave Gary a push.

Gary staggered a little from the push, but immediately regained his balance; then he slowly stepped off the porch and began making his way into the yard, trying to avoid any rocks or stickers with his bare feet. He stopped and turned to his brother. "Come with me."

"Oh you little baby." Johnny put the flashlight on the floor of the porch. "I'm going back inside." He went inside, leaving Gary alone.

"No!" Gary whirled about and still trying to avoid stepping on sharp objects, hurried back to the porch. He picked up the flashlight and started to go inside, but then hesitated; he really did have to pee. He would never make it through the night if he went to bed without urinating, and there was no chamber pot in his and Johnny's bedroom. If he didn't go now, while some of the household were still awake, he would have to be back out here later on when everyone else was asleep. It was some comfort for him to know that at this moment, if he needed help, it would be readily available.

He turned toward the yard and fanned the light back and forth through the darkness. There was nothing out of the ordinary…no reason why he should not go ahead and pee. He laid the flashlight back down on the porch with it pointing in the direction, which he wanted to go. He would need both hands to insure that he didn't dribble on his briefs; the only clothes he was wearing at the time. It was a great relief when the stream began to flow.

Modesty dictated that he stand with his back toward the house, just in case somebody were to walk out. As his eyes adjusted to the darkness, he began to make out forms lighted faintly by the moonlight. The fireflies were still popping up here and there. A short distance away there were two, which were rather large and not moving. Gary gazed at them while he finished up. Then a chilling awareness came over him. They weren't fireflies at all. He was looking into a pair of eyes, which

18

were reflecting the light from the flashlight. His throat tightened as he pulled his briefs up. The eyes disappeared. He began backing up, slowly moving toward the porch. He had heard that there were bears out here at night.

Suddenly there was a quick break in the beam cast from the flashlight. Something had crossed between Gary and the porch. Gary turned sharply and thought he saw something moving next to the house. He could not help himself…he began to scream. He stood where he was and screamed at the top of his lungs.

"What is it?"

"Gary is that you?"

"Romey?"

The voices could be heard throughout the house. The kitchen light came on and the screen door flew open. Frank rushed out of the house, pulling the strap of his overalls over one shoulder and holding a shotgun in the other hand.

"Frank, put that gun down." Mary was right behind her husband.

Guy and Lula Mae came running out of the house followed by the rest of the family. Lula Mae went to Gary who immediately grabbed his mother around the waist and held on. He was trembling and buried his face against her.

"What's the matter? What happened?" asked Lula Mae.

"Something tried to get me." Gary kept his hold on his mother.

"God-damn." Guy stood on the porch and shook his head.

By this time Johnny and Loretta were standing on the porch snickering to one another. They often entertained themselves by frightening Gary. Although they had had nothing to do with this incident, they did not once consider that there was anything in the yard other than Gary and his vivid imagination.

"What Gary…what tried to get you?" Lula Mae pried Gary's arms from around her waist and put him at arms distance so that she could see his face now illuminated by the light spilling out from the kitchen.

"I don't know what it was." Gary looked around the darkened yard.

"Well if there was anything out here it's been scared off," said Lula Mae. "It was probably old Skipper." Skipper was the neighbors' old hound dog. He was free roaming and all of the residents in the area were familiar with him. It was not unusual to see him prowling around at night.

"Unh-uh," said Romey, standing on the porch in his boxers. "Old Skipper is out chasing raccoons. Listen, you can hear him."

There was a distant sound of a dog baying as if it had trapped something up a tree.

"Aw it wasn't nothing," said Guy. "He just imagined it." He let the screen door slam shut behind him as he went back inside.

"Take the boy back inside Lula Mae," said Frank as he sat down in the ladder-back chair he had carried from the kitchen. "I'll sit out here for a while and see if anything's roaming around."

Lula Mae ushered the kids back inside and went as far as the bottom of the stairs with them. "You kids get to bed. I don't want to hear anymore out of any of you." Geneva had already gone back upstairs. She had returned as soon as she saw that Gary was okay. She, like the others, was accustomed to Gary's excitable nature.

"Scaredy cat." "Cry baby." Johnny and Loretta were getting a lot of enjoyment out of tormenting their younger brother as the three of them climbed the stairs.

Lula Mae went back into the kitchen and stood at the screen door looking out onto the porch. "Do you think there's anything out there Frank?"

"I don't know Lula. You go on to bed. It was probably just an old polecat or something."

"Well, good-night." Lula Mae left her father-in-law and went up to bed.

The night was still and quiet as Frank shifted his position in the chair.

"Turn that light out!"

Frank bristled at the sound of his wife yelling at him from her bedroom. He got up, went into the kitchen and picked up a kerosene lantern. He lit the lantern and pulled the chain hanging from the ceiling light, turning the light out. Then he carried the lantern outside where he placed it on the porch next to his chair as he sat down.

It was not unusual for Frank to be sitting out on the back porch late at night. He had quit any serious farming a few years earlier, and he no longer had to get up at four a.m. to go to the fields. With his old age pension and the revenue, which he received from his sharecroppers, he had been able to retire. He, Mary and Romey now lived a comfortable life. They raised pigs and chickens and had a couple of milk cows and a mule. They still worked a small portion of the land; just enough to grow vegetables for their own use.

Retirement had resulted in Frank having a lot of free time on his hands. He was no longer involved in the things that had basically defined him as a person for most of his life. He had always been a farmer. Now he was not quite sure what to do with himself.

Not working in the fields meant that he was around the house more; and Mary was not happy about this. The acrimony between them had gotten worse. They tolerated one another; but there was no real intimacy or gestures of love between them. They merely went through the rudimentary motions of being married.

Mary begrudgingly claimed to anyone who would listen to her that the only thing Frank was interested in was their daughter, Jesse Mae. Jesse Mae lived in Pine Bluff, which was about thirty miles from the farm. She was recently widowed and lived alone in a large house that had belonged to her late husband before she had married him.

With Jesse Mae the only girl in the family, and the youngest child for fourteen years, it was not unusual for her to be her father's favorite. It was a typical father-daughter relationship, but Mary resented it and felt slighted and excluded by her husband and her daughter.

Frank had always been genial towards the boys in the family, but not as demonstrative in his actions towards them as he was towards Jesse Mae. He got along very well with Harold, their oldest son who lived with his family in Dumas, a town about ten miles from the farm. Harold was married to Louise and they had a ten year old son named Scotty.

Frank's relationship with Guy, who was the second child, was not always harmonious, but there had never been any serious rifts between them.

Romey, of course was loved by everybody. Frank would have shown him more attention, but from the day he was born, Mary monopolized him to the point of doting. She discouraged anyone else's involvement in Romey's upbringing; making every decision for his welfare hers alone.

Mary's discordant relationship with her husband and daughter caused her to be more demanding of her sons for their affections. This had resulted in them showing her more attention and giving the appearance that they favored her over their father, but Frank was not bothered by this. He appreciated the fact that his sons showed their mother respect. He had a good relationship with them, and they did not show any sign of resentment for his closeness with Jesse Mae.

Since he no longer had to work from sunrise to sunset, Frank had more time to interact with his children. He was getting to know them better and he enjoyed all of them, but he was especially fond of having Jesse Mae around. Her visits always lifted his spirits. She flattered him and behaved as if he were important. She was considerate of him, and he always looked forward to seeing her.

Now as he sat in the glow of the kerosene lantern and gazed into the darkness surrounding him, his thoughts drifted back through time. He could not help but feel a sense of sadness for what he and Mary had lost; the closeness, which they had shared when they were young. Their relationship had always been turbulent, but their lost intimacy was often on his mind and he regretted it; but they had been estranged much too long to try and go back. He sighed deeply and resigned himself to a life of bickering and hatefulness.

He felt his old age creeping up on him as he stretched his tired back; and he found himself wondering how much longer he had on this earth. 'Don't be a sentimental old fool,' he thought, then reached into the pocket of his overalls and pulled out his pipe. He cleared his mind of his unhappy marriage and his advancing age, and felt grateful that all of his children and their families would soon be gathered together here with him for the holiday. He pressed tobacco into the bowl of the pipe and put a lighted match to it as he sucked in. The glow of the tobacco and its sweet aroma soothed him as he leaned back on the chair and expelled the smoke with a sigh.

CHAPTER TWO

GARY AWOKE THE NEXT MORNING TO THE smell of frying bacon and the sounds of his grandmother's hymns rising to the second floor from downstairs. He was grateful that the sheet beneath him was still dry.

He looked at Johnny, who was sleeping soundly next to him and decided that it might be fun to disturb his brother's slumber; just for kicks. Unfortunately the kick, which Gary got from the little tickle with a feather under Johnny's nose turned out to be a swift kick to Gary's shin as Johnny mumbled something and turned away from his bothersome younger brother. Not wanting to engage in a scuffle at the moment, Gary scurried out of bed and slipped his Levis on. Johnny would sleep for another half hour or more. It was vacation time, so Guy and Lula Mae allowed their children to sleep in as late as they wanted.

As Gary walked down the stairs, he thought about the night before and wondered what it was that had been with him in the darkness; that thing, which had been circling him for reasons unknown.

"Good morning", said Lula Mae when Gary walked into the kitchen and stood next to her, resting his hand on her shoulder. Lula Mae was standing at the kitchen counter peeling potatoes. "Did you wet the bed?"

"No," said Gary indignantly.

"Wash your hands before you touch anything in this kitchen!" Mary was standing at the kitchen range with one hand on her hip and a fork in the other. She was turning bacon in a frying pan.

Gary remained next to his mother, paying little attention to his grandmother's commands. It seemed she was always yelling for someone to wash his or her hands. He and the other kids had learned to tune her out.

"Gary come over here and churn for a while." Geneva was sitting on a small three legged stool. Between her knees was a ceramic pot, about thirty inches high and ten inches in diameter. She had a wooden rod in her hands, which she was rhythmically pushing down, then pulling back up through a one inch hole in a wooden lid, which covered the pot. The fresh cream in the churn made a sloshing sound as the wooden cross on the end of the rod churned the cream into butter.

"Don't stop churning, Geneva," said Mary. "You've got to keep going or it won't turn to butter."

"I'm tired Grandma. He can churn for a while."

"I've got to go to the bathroom," Gary said, as he headed outside, grateful for the bodily function that helped him avoid the drudgery of the churn.

"Don't slam that door!"

Gary's grandmother's cries were punctuated by the sound of the screen door as it slammed against the door frame. It was only seven-thirty but the sun had already dried the dew from the grass and plants. It was going to be a hot Independence Day.

The area behind the house, which was considered the back yard, was primarily bare dirt with scattered patches of crabgrass, thistles, dandelions, and other hardy weeds. It measured approximately fifty feet wide by ninety feet long. It stretched from the back of the house to the henhouse and bathing shed; behind which, were the cow's shed and a small grazing area. The sides of the yard were bordered by Romey's playhouse, the smokehouse, the pigsty and the outhouse.

Several chickens were scratching in the dirt and searching for small insects as Gary inspected the area where he had seen the eyes of whatever it was that had been stalking him the night before. He decided that if there had been any tracks, the chickens had erased them with their scratching and pecking. He heard voices in the distance and looked past Romey's playhouse toward the barn where he saw his father and grandfather walking through the grass carrying shotguns; probably going hunting for rabbits.

Gary was not allowed to go hunting with them. Two years prior, during the previous vacation here, Guy had taken Gary and Johnny on their first rabbit hunt. Guy seldom participated in any kind of recreation with his children; it seemed he was always too busy when they were home. Being on vacation and in a benevolent mood, he decided to spend some time with his sons. He felt that hunting was something that every boy should know, and it was an enjoyable pastime, which he and his own father had shared when he was a boy. He wanted to pass along the tradition, so he had roused them from bed and brought them along with him and their grandfather on an early morning hunt.

After about forty five boring minutes of walking through the brush, Johnny and Gary had been wishing they were back at the house reading comic books with Romey. Suddenly a large jackrabbit bolted from a thicket nearby and raced into the clearing ahead of them. Guy raised his shotgun to take advantage of a sure shot and show his sons what an excellent marksman he was. Unfortunately in the excitement of it all, Gary, who had been concentrating on kicking at dirt clods, spotted the rabbit, and feeling a true hunter's surge of adrenalin, forgot about the guns his father and grandfather were carrying and made a run for the rabbit in an attempt to overtake his prey and bring him back alive; thus putting himself in the direct line of fire of his father's shotgun. Guy had very little patience with his children when their behavior was not to his liking, so needless to say, after a loud round of profanity and scolding, Gary was sent directly back home on his own.

This morning, as Gary passed Romey's playhouse; unbeknown to him, he was being closely watched by two sets of eyes. Loretta and Romey had been playing checkers when they heard the screen door slam shut.

It had not taken much effort for Loretta to convince Romey that it would be fun to frighten Gary while he was in the outhouse. "He's probably still shook up over his imaginary monster from last night," she said. At fifteen years of age, Loretta was full of mischief and bombarding hormones. She seldom sat still for long and she loved to play jokes on people. And her little brother was just so easy.

Romey was always extremely happy when Guy and Lula Mae and their kids would come to visit. Being surrounded by other adults most of the time, he was ordinarily very quiet and well behaved, but when there were children around and Mary would let him play with them, he would become childlike and mischievous. After a moment of telling Loretta that she shouldn't pester her little brother, he succumbed to his zest for a good time and agreed to go along with the prank.

Romey had a bearskin rug, which Frank had given to him when he was a child. Frank had shot the bear and skinned it himself and Mary had made a rug out of the pelt. Loretta threw the bearskin over her head and she and Romey went to the outhouse where Gary was inside. Romey began scratching on the door and growling like a bear and Loretta opened the door a few inches and Gary saw what he thought was a bear trying to get at him. In his panic to get the door closed against the bear, Gary lost control of his urine stream and sprayed urine over the toilet seat and floor of the outhouse. Laughing loudly, Loretta and Romey ran back to Romey's playhouse and returned the bearskin rug and headed to the house for breakfast; leaving Gary to clean up the outhouse.

Loretta and Romey charged into the kitchen. "Don't slam that door!" called out Mary as the screen door slapped closed, sending a cracking sound throughout the kitchen. Loretta bounced to the kitchen table and took a seat, anxious to begin breakfast.

Romey slowed his pace in the presence of Mary. He walked to the kitchen counter where the enameled wash basin sat next to the sink. He dutifully said, "Loretta you come over here and wash your hands."

"My hands are clean," chimed Loretta.

"Lula Mae, tell your daughter to get over to that sink and wash her hands." Mary continued to cook the breakfast meal, spouting edicts almost without thinking about them; not even bothering to divert her attention from the frying pan. After all the years that Guy and Lula Mae had been married; Mary still tried to treat Lula like a child.

"Loretta, get up and wash your hands," said Lula Mae.

"Oh cripes." Loretta rose and stomped toward the basin.

"Good Lord, Lula Mae, what are you teaching these girls? Such language coming from a fourteen-year-old girl."

"What? All I said was cripes. And I'm fifteen, Grandma."

Mary stopped flipping bacon and turned to face Loretta. "I'm going to tell your daddy to wash your mouth out with soap."

"Can I stop churning now?" lamented Geneva.

Mary went to the churn. "Let me see." She removed the wooden lid to the churn and put one finger into the butter. "Okay, it's butter."

"Did you wash your hands?" Loretta, still standing at the wash basin, imitated her grandmother's stance with her hands on the back of her hips as she spoke.

Mary looked at Lula Mae. She was unsuccessful in her attempt to suppress the small grin on her face. She wanted to be stern, but she found herself being amused at her youngest granddaughter's cheekiness. Remembering her own indomitable spirit as a child; she could not help but appreciate the similarities between herself and Loretta. In spite of her constant attempt to remain stoic and dogmatic, she sometimes found it difficult, not to enjoy her grandchildren.

Mary's haughtiness and pushy attitude were character traits, which she had developed as a child as a defense mechanism against her own controlling mother. Later on when she married, those traits were honed even further, due to a volatile relationship with a husband who could be extremely demanding and tyrannical if allowed. She and Frank were locked in a continual struggle; one always trying to control the other.

The couple made no attempt to conceal their displeasure with each other; but of course, divorce was never an option. They were both comfortable in the home that they had made together. They had each learned to put up with the other, and both of them obviously loved Romey and would do anything they could to keep from hurting him. Over the years, the position of power had blurred. As they grew older, Frank had become more submissive and Mary had become more aggressive. Mary now stood in equal footing with Frank in his attempt to rule the household.

"Grandma that sausage smells good." Johnny had walked into the kitchen and sat at the table. His auburn hair was standing up on one side of his head.

"Go wash your hands!" Loretta slapped the back of Johnny's head and a scuffle ensued.

"Gosh-darn it!" Lula Mae grabbed Johnny and Loretta by their shoulders and pulled them apart. "Straighten up there and eat your breakfast."

"She started it." Johnny continued to push at his sister, resisting his mother's attempt to hold them apart.

"And I'm going to finish it. Don't make me go out there and get a switch off of one of those trees."

"Go get a switch Lula Mae." Romey was easily swayed from one alliance to the other. He was also easily excitable and had a strong desire to be co-operative with the adults in the household. He did what he could to receive praise for being a "good boy".

Neither Johnny nor Loretta believed that they had pushed their mother to the point of whipping them, but they did feel that they should pull back a little; she seemed very serious at this point. "Oh they're going to behave their selves, Romey," said Lula Mae as she released her hold on them. The two squabbling siblings obediently directed their attention to breakfast, and the unruliness was forgotten.

Slam!

The group was startled as the screen door once again slapped hard against the door frame. Gary stood just inside the kitchen; his hands on his hips and a sullen look on his face, making his best attempt to command attention and display his displeasure with Loretta and Romey. There was a moment of silence while the group waited for Gary to explain his exaggerated posture.

"You better pull your lower lip in before you trip on it," said Geneva with a smile. This was a common phrase used by the family to placate Gary when he was angry about something.

"What's the matter Son?" asked Lula Mae.

Loretta grinned broadly, struggling to suppress her laughter. Romey looked at his plate and chewed quietly.

Honk. Honk.

A car horn blared outside; redirecting everybody's attention to it, including Gary's. Mary, lifting a pan of biscuits from the oven, stood up and looked out of the kitchen window over the sink. "Here's Harold and Louise." She put the biscuits on the top of the stove and wiped her hands on her apron as she walked to the back porch.

"Don't slam that door!" Loretta called out.

Lula Mae raised her hand in a mock threat to Loretta. Mary paid no attention as she stepped onto the porch to greet her oldest son, Harold and his wife, Louise and their ten year old son, Scotty.

Romey rushed past Mary, who was now on the back porch displaying her characteristic arched back stance with her hands on the back of her hips. Romey was very fond of Harold and his family. He waited in the yard as the car approached. The car had not quite come to a complete stop when the rear door opened. Scotty jumped from the car a little too soon and almost stumbled on his face. After gaining his balance, he ran to Romey and threw his arms around him in a bear hug.

"Walter Scott, I told you to wait till the car came to a stop!" Louise's admonishments were virtually lost on her son as the others filed out of the kitchen to greet the newcomers.

"You're just in time for breakfast," said Mary, keeping her position on the porch.

Before arriving at the farm two days earlier, Guy, Lula Mae and their four children had stopped in town to visit Harold and Louise and Scotty for a few hours. They had all been looking forward to re-uniting at the grandparents' home for a Fourth of July celebration.

Lula Mae walked to meet Harold and Louise at their car. After all the years she had known them, she was still amazed at the differences in her brother-in-law and his younger brother, Guy. They were both almost six feet tall, but Guy was lean, muscular and macho, whereas Harold was on the plump side, a little hyper and overly animated.

Harold seemed the perfect complement for his wife, who was an attractive woman of Italian heritage; standing five feet, two inches tall, with dark short curls on her head and a somewhat rotund figure. She had a no-nonsense attitude and a solid sense of fairness, mixed with a stalwart character governed by compassion and integrity.

Louise got out of the car and she and Lula Mae greeted one another with an affectionate hug. They were very fond of one-another. Lula Mae now felt that she had an ally here in the Austin's household. Harold was busy retrieving groceries out of the trunk of the car. Lula Mae, after greeting him, also with a quick hug, joined Louise and him in carrying groceries into the house.

Romey went to the trunk of the car and reached for a bag of potatoes. Mary saw Romey and yelled, "Romey don't you be lifting anything heavy out of that car you'll get a hernia."

"Mama!" said Romey, standing at the back of the car with the bag of potatoes in his arms. He was annoyed that she was being her usual overbearing self. He felt really happy about being with his brothers and their families and he wanted to be a part of the activity.

"I mean it. You put those potatoes back in that car." Mary looked at her oldest son. "Good Lord, Harold, don't let him go and hurt his self."

Harold walked back to Romey, who had put the bag back in the trunk. He reached into the bag of groceries that he was carrying and pulled out a loaf of bread. "Here, Romey, carry this bread for me. It was about to get smashed in this bag with this other stuff."

With a smile of resignation, Romey took the loaf of bread and followed Harold into the house.

Louise pitched right in and joined Mary and Lula in their kitchen duties. Frank and Guy would be back from hunting soon, so they wanted to get Romey and the children fed and out of their way so that they could get breakfast started for the adults. They gave Harold a cup of coffee, which he took into the living room, and then they fed the youngsters and ushered them out of the kitchen.

Harold had brought a newspaper with him, which he was reading as he sat in the living room. Romey went into the living room and sat next to him on the sofa. Harold gave him the comics, which Romey was unable to read, but he still enjoyed looking at the *funnies*, as he called them; and more than that, he just wanted to be close to Harold. Geneva went to the front porch with one of her movie magazines, and Johnny, Loretta, Gary and Scotty went out to Romey's playhouse to play.

Louise and Lula Mae were washing and drying the children's breakfast dishes and re-setting the table. Mary was frying up more bacon and sausage.

"I talked to Jesse Mae last night," Louise said. "She said she would be here sometime this week."

"Well, I'm sure her papa will be glad to hear that," said Mary. "She's the only one he really cares about seeing. His 'little girl' he still calls her."

"Oh Mary, I'm sure Frank is enjoying having his other kids and grandkids around," Louise said with a hint of annoyance in her voice.

"All I'm saying is that I'm just glad that I have Romey here to watch those two when I'm alone here with them. They're always whispering and sneaking around, and when I come in the room they shut up. I don't trust them."

"Well good grief, Mary," said Lula Mae. "What do you think they're talking about?"

"They're talking about me! Trying to figure out how they can get rid of me. *The old battleaxe.*"

"Get rid of you?" At the refrigerator, Lula Mae poured fresh cow's milk from a pail into a pitcher.

"They tried to poison me 'bout a month ago."

Louise and Lula Mae stopped what they were doing and looked at one another.

Mary looked up from stirring the sausage. "You think I'm lying? You ask Romey. I was sick for two days." She turned her attention back to the skillet on top of the stove. "They just didn't figure on me being as strong of constitution as I am. I don't let Jesse Mae do the cooking any more."

"Oh Mary, Jesse Mae wouldn't try to hurt you. You're her mama." Lula Mae sat down at the table and sipped her coffee.

"Yes, I'm her mama and she's my only daughter, but that woman is mean. And you've both seen Frank's temper. She takes after him, not me."

The two younger women smiled at one another. They found their mother-in-law's accusations absurd. It was true; they had seen their father-in-law's temper. He could be very abrasive and almost violent, and Jesse Mae did indeed take after her father, but there was no way that they believed that the two had conspired to try and poison Mary.

Louise had finished setting the table and sat down to join Lula Mae with her own cup of coffee. "Mary you know they didn't try to poison you. You may have gotten food poisoning from some bad meat or something. I hope you don't talk like that in front of Romey."

"You just never mind how I talk in front of Romey. I take care of him; nobody else."

Outside, the youngsters could be heard talking to Frank and Guy, who had just returned with a couple of rabbit carcasses. They were hanging them up in the smoke house, where they would later skin them and prepare them for cooking.

Louise called into the living room, "Harold, here's Guy and your papa. Come on in to breakfast."

Harold and Romey came into the kitchen. Harold sat at the table, bringing with him his nearly empty coffee cup. Romey stood next to him as if he wanted to stay. Lula Mae was sitting at the table next to where Romey stood. She reached up and put her arm around Romey to give him a hug. She was a very tactile person and this was her way of conveying her affection for him.

"Go on Romey," said Mary. "The adults are going to eat now."

"Mama, I'm an adult," Romey responded crossly.

"Of course you are Son," soothed Lula Mae."

"Don't you take that tone with me; and Lula Mae stop babying him. He has a mama, he don't need you. You take care of your own kids. Lord knows they're enough to keep you busy. Go on Romey; tell your papa and brother to hurry up, breakfast is getting cold."

Begrudgingly, Romey left the kitchen, being careful to close the screen door gently. He walked to the smoke house to give Guy and Frank the message. By the time he reached them, his resentment toward Mary had passed and his interest was focused on the rabbits being hung in the smokehouse. He was one who lived in the moment and his normal attitude was happy and loving.

After delivering the message and leaving the smokehouse, Romey joined the youngsters in the middle of the backyard where Geneva, having left the front porch, had recruited the others to help her build a fire in a shallow pit in the ground. A large black caldron hung from a metal tripod, spanning the pit. While the others had started the fire, Geneva had carried buckets of water from the well to the caldron. The caldron was now practically full of water, which was beginning to boil.

With no running water, the method of preparing a bath was to heat the water in the caldron and then transfer it into the aluminum bathtub. Geneva was the only one of the youngsters who wanted to take a bath, but the others were helping because they enjoyed building a fire.

Of course Johnny and Loretta had other reasons for wanting to build a fire. They knew that Gary had one firecracker in his pocket; all that was left from the cache they had brought from home. They would get the last firecracker from Gary and toss it into the fire and scare their older sister. Geneva had been complaining about them setting off the

32

firecrackers near her, so they thought that it would be fun to give her this one last fright.

With his usual expertise of manipulating Gary, Johnny pulled him aside and easily talked him into giving him this last firecracker. Just when Geneva dipped her pail into the boiling water in the caldron, Johnny tossed the firecracker beneath the caldron and into the fire. *Pop!* The firecracker exploded, causing Geneva to drop her pail into the boiling water.

"Gosh-darn you Johnny!" yelled Geneva, jumping back from the fire.

Laughing boisterously, Johnny and Loretta turned and ran towards the barn. They did not want to be around when their mother heard about their little *joke*.

Geneva, glad to be rid of her mischievous brother and sister did not bother to go inside and tell their mother of the incident. She continued her preparations for her bath. She fished the pail out of the water and enlisted the aid of Gary, Scotty and Romey to help her carry the hot water to the waiting bathtub in the shed down by the henhouse where she could have privacy for her bath.

After Geneva had shut herself away in the shed, Gary, Scotty and Romey went back to the fire, which was now barely burning. "That was neat when the firecracker went off," said Gary.

"Yeah, did you see all those sparks fly out," Scotty squatted next to the fire and poked it with a stick.

"I wish I had another one," Gary squatted next to Scotty. Romey struggled to squat next to them, but it was not so easy for him. His weight and compromised sense of balance resulted in him sitting cross-legged on the ground instead.

"I have lots!" Scotty beamed with pride as he stood and ran to his father's car. He opened the trunk and pulled out a brown paper bag about the size of a grocery bag. He returned to Gary and Romey and said, "I'm not supposed to play with these without my dad. He said we have to wait until tonight. But firecrackers are for the daytime." Scotty again squatted next to Gary and Romey. He placed the bag on the ground, so that Gary could see the contents.

"What's this?" asked Gary, pointing to an object inside the bag.

"That's a Black Snake." Scotty reached into the bag and pulled out a small, black, disc shaped object about one half inch in diameter and a quarter inch high. "You light one end and it grows into a long black curly snake."

Romey sat quietly. He was intrigued by all of these mysterious goings on. Scotty lit the snake and the three of them watched it grow and curl around on the ground. After a moment the snake ceased growing and a line of burnt ashes lay inert on the ground.

"That was neat." Gary looked into the bag again. "What else do you have in there?" Gary reached into the bag and pulled out a large firecracker. "Wow." The boys and Romey looked at the firecracker and then at one another. Gary said, "Let's throw this into the fire and see what happens."

"Okay," said Scotty, ignoring that little voice in the back of his mind reminding him of the stern warning from his father, and backed up by his mother, that he was not to set off any fireworks without one of them being present. Being an only child, Scotty was eager to please when he was in the company of other children, so his parents' warning had now been virtually forgotten amidst all the camaraderie and excitement of being with his cousins.

"Here." Gary handed the firecracker to Scotty. "Throw it in." Gary was not certain that it was a wise decision to throw such a large firecracker into the fire, but his hunger for thrills outweighed his better judgement. Besides, if Scotty threw it in, and it was his firecracker, how could Gary be blamed if anything went wrong?

With but a moment's hesitation, Scotty tossed the firecracker into the embers. Instinctively Gary got to his feet and moved back away from the fire. Scotty, as usual, followed Gary's lead.

"Romey move back!" Gary rushed to Romey and helped him to his feet. The three adventurers stood about ten feet away from the caldron and waited... Nothing happened.

"It's not going to pop," said Scotty.

"Stay back." Gary held his arms out from his sides creating a barricade between the others and the fire. They stood motionless. Suddenly the firecracker exploded, sending burning embers in several directions.

"Ahhh! Ahhh!" Romey began running wildly around the yard slapping at his ear where an ember had brushed against it on its way past his head. Gary and Scotty were running behind him, trying to get him to stop so that they could help him.

"Good Lord-o-mercy! They've put his eyes out!" Mary burst through the back door and raced toward Romey. In an instant, chaos overtook the back yard of the Austins' residence.

Frightened that they had blinded their Uncle Romey, Gary and Scotty turned and ran the other way, stopping in front of Romey's playhouse, out of reach of their grandmother. Romey continued to scream as Mary overtook him and stopped him from running.

By this time all the other adults were outside participating in the melee. Even Geneva was peeking through the partially opened door of the shed.

Mary allowed Guy to examine the extent of Romey's injuries. It only took a moment for Guy to see that Romey's eyes were fine and that he had a little blister on his right ear.

The hysteria being squelched, Harold turned his attention to his son, Scotty. "What happened?"

The look on Scotty's face told Harold that he was guilty. "Did you get into your fireworks, Scott?"

Scotty looked at his mother and then at his father. He knew that he was in trouble. Harold walked to Scotty and took hold of one of his ears. He bent forward so as to look Scotty directly in the face. "Didn't I tell you not to touch those fireworks? Those are for tomorrow night after supper. Where is…?

Harold's words were halted by a sudden high pitched whistling sound, as a twelve inch rocket shot along the ground towards the pigsty causing the pigs to squeal in terror, and run helter-skelter. Scotty's bag of fireworks was now engulfed in flames and with hisses and pops, the contents were all beginning to ignite.

"God-damn! Get in the house!" Guy began pushing his mother and Romey toward the house and waving his other arm, motioning for the others to run.

Pop! A firecracker exploded, followed immediately by several others. Something like a fireball shot into the sky in a spiraling trajectory, leaving a trail of smoke. Whistles and pops and streaks of fire shot in all directions. Geneva's cries could be heard from the bathing shed as the others ran for the safety of the house.

"Stay where you are, Geneva!" screamed Lula Mae as she dragged Gary toward the house. Once inside everyone vied for a position that would allow them to view the holocaust outside. After little more than a minute, the chaos subsided and the only activities in the yard were the sporadic squeals and grunts of the pigs and diminishing crowing and cackling of the chickens, along with some occasional sizzling sounds and the fading whistle of a Fountain of Fire as it died out.

The kitchen was quiet for a moment as the adults turned there attention toward Gary and Scotty.

"Go sit on the porch," said Guy, with a stern look at Gary.

Gary quickly walked toward the front porch; happy to leave the company of his elders. He turned to give Scotty a look of pity as he left. Scotty stood with his head down. Harold and Louise were both glaring at him.

"Now what are we going to shoot off tomorrow night?" Louise asked. "That was your whole supply of fireworks"

"They cost a lot of money," said Harold.

Scotty looked up at his parents with tears in his eyes. "Go on to the porch with Gary," said Louise. She felt that Scotty was feeling badly enough without any further punishment.

"And stay there until we tell you that you can get off it," said Harold, adding a little weight to his wife's light punishment.

Just then the screen door to the kitchen burst open and slapped against the kitchen wall. Johnny and Loretta rushed into the kitchen, letting the door slam shut with a loud crack.

"Wow!" said Johnny.

"What was that?" Excited amusement showed on Loretta's face.

"Where have you two been?" It had suddenly occurred to Guy that the possibility of his two middle children being behind the recent chain of events was quite plausible.

"We were down at the barn." Johnny looked at Loretta who was nodding her head in agreement.

Guy looked at the two children and decided that they were telling the truth. "Then go get Gary off the front porch and go out there and clean up that mess. Rake all those pieces of burnt wood back under that caldron."

"And be careful," said Lula Mae. "Don't burn yourself."

Johnny and Loretta did not protest. They had heard the noise from down at the barn and looked up to see all the smoke and sparks. They were dying to know what had happened. Gary filled them in on the details as the three of them made their way to the back yard. Scotty remained sitting quietly on the porch, feeling very remorseful.

CHAPTER THREE

B Y EVENING TIME, SUPPER WAS FINISHED AND the unfortunate incident with the fireworks was forgotten. Both the dining table and kitchen table had been cleared and Louise and Lula Mae were washing and drying the dishes while Mary sat at the kitchen table keeping them company. The men were on the front porch, smoking, and the five youngsters and Romey were in the living room, playing Monopoly. Romey did not quite understand the game, but Geneva was helping him and he enjoyed rolling the dice and moving his game piece.

At twenty-five years old, Romey had never spent a day away from Mary. When he was born, he had become her main focus in life. When she realized that there was something wrong with him, she became obsessed with his care. The local schools were not equipped to deal with a child with Down's syndrome so he never attended. Mary saw to his needs and almost seemed pleased to have someone depend upon her for his every need.

For the first few months of Romey's life, Mary's devotion to him put a strain on her and Frank's already imperfect marriage. Frank resented Romey at first, and tried not to love him. But over the years, he had grown to love Romey as much as Mary did. Romey was so innocent and childlike; it was hard for anyone not to love him.

"I'm looking forward to seeing Jesse Mae next week." Louise handed Lula Mae a serving bowl to dry.

Mary was shelling pecans and eating them as she spoke, "I'll bet Lula Mae isn't."

Lula Mae stopped drying the bowl and looked at her mother-in-law. "Well, Mary why would you say a thing like that?"

Mary continued directing her attention to the pecan in her hand and not bothering to look up. "You don't like Jesse Mae; you never have."

Lula Mae looked at Louise and then back to Mary. "Jesse Mae and I have had our differences in the past, but that don't mean we don't love each another."

"Oh, she don't love you."

With an incredulous expression on her face, Lula Mae returned her attention to Louise who just shook her head at Mary's statement.

"Well she don't." Mary finally looked up from her pecan. "She says you're jealous of her and Guy. She said that her visits with him are much better when you're not around."

Lula Mae did not know what to say. Mary had hit a nerve. The truth was that she was indeed jealous of her husband and his sister. She felt that they always treated her like she was simple minded or something when the three of them were together.

It was true that Lula Mae had only finished the sixth grade in school, but she had continued to learn on her own. Her math and reading skills were just as good, if not better than Guy's. She was the one who ran the household. She did all the budgeting and paying the bills.

The trouble she had when talking with Guy and his sister, was due to the facts that Jesse Mae had continued her education and Guy was out in the world, interacting with other people and ideas, while Lula Mae stayed home and took care of housework and four young children. When the three of them were together, Lula Mae knew nothing or very little about the subjects that Guy and Jesse Mae wanted to discuss.

Lula Mae shrugged her shoulders. "Well…" she said, and continued drying the bowl.

"That woman's a bitch, Lula Mae. Don't you trust her." Mary again directed her attention to the pecans.

"Good Lord, Mary; what's gotten into you; talking like that?" Louise waited for Lula Mae to put the bowl in the cupboard and then handed her a plate.

Mary, chewing the meat of a pecan, gave a superior shrug of the shoulders. "Eh."

"Jesse Mae might be a little hard on people," said Louise. "But she's okay. Look what she's trying to do for Romey."

Slam! Mary's hand landed solidly against the top of the table. "I'll be in my grave before that woman takes Romey away from me!"

Louise gave a sigh of exasperation. She was not the least bit intimidated by her mother-in-law, but it was not her style to bicker and quarrel when she could avoid it.

"What are you talking about? What's Jesse Mae trying to do?" Lula Mae directed her question to either of the other two women.

"There is a center in Pine Bluff that teaches retarded people how to function in society." Louise handed Lula Mae another plate.

"Romey is not retarded."

Louise ignored Mary's denial. "Jesse Mae wants to send Romey there for a couple of months to see if he can learn how to be independent. She's even offering to pay for it."

"Why shouldn't she pay for it?" said Mary. "Miss high and mighty! Married herself a judge, then probably did him in herself. She has enough money to support all of us."

"So then why don't you let her send him there?" Louise dried her hands on a kitchen towel.

"Because Romey is mine! I'm his mama. I'll take care of him. He don't need to learn to be independent. Would either of you let someone take one of your kids away?"

Louise sat down at the kitchen table so that she could look Mary in the eye as she spoke to her. "If it were for Walter Scott's own good to be sent away from me for a while; then yes, I would allow it."

Mary did not like the answer that she got from Louise, so she turned to Lula Mae. "How about you Lula, would you let someone take Gary away and teach him how to get along without you?"

Before Lula Mae could answer, Louise interjected, "Oh Mary, that's not a fair question. Gary is a child. Romey, whether you want to admit it or not, is a grown man."

"I'm not talking to you now. Lula Mae, answer me. Would you let someone take away one of your children?"

Lula Mae did not want to side with her mother-in-law against Louise, but she was a very honest woman and in this instance there was no question in her mind as to her answer. "Well, I may not be as smart as a lot of other people, but I do know how to take care of my kids. I couldn't imagine ever letting anyone take one away from me or tell me how to raise them." She placed the last dish in the cupboard.

"Oh good grief." Louise stood up and went to join the men on the front porch.

By ten p.m. everybody except Lula Mae and Louise had retired to their respective sleeping quarters. The two women had returned to the kitchen table and sat drinking coffee and talking. The conversation had reverted to the possibility of Romey attending the school in Pine Bluff.

"I guess it would be good for Romey to learn how to take care of his self." Lula Mae got up and poured hot coffee into the two cups on the table. Sitting back down, she continued. "I just don't know if he could be away from his mama that long."

"You know, I think Romey is a lot smarter than everyone gives him credit for. If the situation were explained to him, I think he might want to do it. Besides, Mary could stay with Jesse Mae. She could visit Romey. They even suggest that for severe cases of what they call separation anxiety, the person closest to the student, visit every day for the first week and then start skipping days until they visit only on weekends."

"Well…" Lula Mae stared into her cup; then, looking up she said, "You know she'll never allow it."

"Yeah, I know. It's a crying shame though."

Changing the subject, Lula Mae asked, "Sis, is everything okay between you and Harold?"

Louise registered a look of surprise on her face. "Yeah, why?"

"Oh, I don't know. Harold just seems a little depressed or something."

"Oh that."

Lula Mae waited for elaboration.

Louise leaned toward Lula Mae slightly, as if to suggest secrecy. "Well, you know Jesse Mae is planning to go to Paris, France."

"Yeah."

"So, in order for her to get her passport, she had to have a copy of her birth certificate." Louise took a sip of her coffee; then continued. "And you know Jesse Mae; she never could resist stirring up a hornet's nest where her mama is concerned. Anyway, while she was checking the county records and things, she decided…" Louise shook her head. "… and God only knows why she would even be interested. She decided to check her mama and papa's records.

"Now, Lula Mae, don't you tell another soul what I'm about to tell you."

"Okay." Lula Mae hated to be sworn to secrecy, but if there was one thing she was good at, it was keeping a confidence. Louise was aware of this as she continued.

"It seems that our sanctimonious mother-in-law was married only five months before she gave birth to her first child, Harold. Their wedding day; instead of being in the year nineteen-hundred-and-ten, was in nineteen-hundred-and-eleven."

Lula Mae's mouth parted and remained open in disbelief.

"Of course, Jesse Mae had to call Harold right away and tell him. She even mailed him a copy of the marriage license. She said he had a right to know, and I guess she's right; but it has him a little upset."

"Well, it don't change nothing. That was…what…forty-five years ago?"

"What it changes is Harold's respect for his mama. You know Harold was always the good kid. Guy and Jesse Mae were the ones who gave their mama grief. Harold never once went against her. He always had the highest respect for her…felt that she could do no wrong."

"Yeah, I guess that would be hard to learn something like that about your mama."

"And Mary is always so judgmental with everybody. Look how she's always telling you that your girls are going wind up in trouble."

"Oh, I don't pay much attention to those remarks."

"Well, Harold has always taken his mama's opinion as God's truth. You know he divorced his first wife because he found out that she wasn't a virgin when he married her?"

"No," said Lula Mae, trying not to let her eagerness for these juicy revelations show.

"Yes; and that was because of his mama! In fact she insisted. I don't know why he would discuss something like that with her, but he did. She told him that any woman who had relations out of wedlock was unfit to be a wife and a mother."

"Oh well that's just silly."

"He didn't think so. He divorced her. Now he finds out that his own mama had had relations before she was married. He denies it, but I think he's questioning whether he did the right thing with Judy; that was his first wife's name."

"You mean he thinks he should have stayed married to her?"

"No, he says they wouldn't have stayed married anyway. Says he never really loved her. He just felt it was time for him to marry and she seemed to have her sights set on him. Harold was never much of a lady's man. If I hadn't approached him, we wouldn't have ever gone out on a date.

"Anyway, he felt really bad about divorcing her like that; so quick I mean. Actually the marriage was annulled. She didn't want people to know why they were splitting up. They just both claimed they had made a mistake. He said that she was pretty unhappy about it. They never spoke again after that.

"He always felt justified because of what his mama taught him. Now all that guilt is dredged up again. He thinks he should have stayed married to her for a year or so and then divorced her; that way people wouldn't have talked about her the way they did. But most of what's bothering him is he's just angry with his mama. And he always feels guilty when he gets angry with her. He doesn't know if he should just pretend not to know and keep quiet or say something to her about it."

"How about Guy? Has he mentioned it to him?"

"I don't know. Last he talked to me about it, he wasn't sure if he would or not."

"You know Jesse Mae will."

"Yeah, I know. One way or the other, Guy will find out. How do you think he'll react?"

"Well, he loves his mama, but he don't have her up on a pedestal. I think he'll just think she was being foolish to keep it hidden."

"If you want to tell him it's okay."

"No, I think I'll let Harold tell him. Guy don't like to hear bad things about his mama from me."

Louise turned her head sharply and looked toward the dining room. "What was that?" She turned back to Lula Mae. "Did you hear something?"

Lula Mae listened for a moment and then shook her head. "No...I don't hear nothing unusual."

Louise got up from the table and walked toward the swinging door leading into the dining room. "Sounded like the front door closing." She pushed the door open and peered through the dining room and into the large living room. She walked to the front door of the house and opened it.

"What is it?" Lula Mae was right behind her.

Looking outside, Louise said, "Nothing I guess...must have been someone upstairs." She pulled the door shut and turned the deadbolt. "I'm going to lock it just the same. She stifled a yawn. "I think I'm ready for bed."

"Me too," said Lula Mae. "I'll wash up the coffee cups. You go on to bed. Good-night, Sis."

The two women gave each other a brief hug. Louise went upstairs and Lula Mae went to the kitchen.

Outside, the soft moonlight highlighted a head of tousled red curls just cresting the edge of the porch, followed by two big blue eyes, which had been pre-maturely accentuated with too much mascara.

"Are they gone?" Geneva asked, with her back pressed against the outside edge of the porch.

"Shhh," whispered Loretta as she continued to assess the situation. She waited for a moment more and then left her position at the edge of the porch and tiptoed up the steps towards the front door. She raised herself up on her bare toes in an effort to gain the height she needed to look through the glass window in the door. The living room was still dark except for the line of light, which was showing around the now closed door leading from the dining room into the kitchen. "Uh-oh," she muttered as she tried the door knob.

"What?" Geneva knew before she asked the question, what Loretta's 'Uh-oh' was all about. "It's locked, isn't it?"

Loretta stealthily made her way back to her sister's side. Once out of the line of sight from the living room she stood upright. "Yeah, it's locked, but Mama will be in bed by the time we finish. We can get back inside through the kitchen. They won't lock that door; not with the boys in Romey's playhouse." She pushed the switch on the flashlight and pointed it toward the ground. "Come on."

45

Geneva followed Loretta towards the side of the house where the night-blooming jasmine was growing. "I don't know if this is such a bright idea. If Mama and Daddy find out that we were out here in the middle of the night, they'll be mad."

"They're not going to find out. Quit being such a worrywart." Loretta was more accustomed to being disobedient than her sister. She very seldom worried about the consequences of her actions until it was too late.

As they rounded the corner of the house the pale glow emanating from the moon, which was just above the treetops provided them with a little more light. Geneva carried a penny and one of the four-leaf clovers that she had found growing in the front yard.

"This looks like a good spot," said Loretta. She knelt down next to the flower bed and began digging in the soft earth with a table knife.

"If Grandma finds out that we were digging in the dirt with one of her knives, she's going to skin us alive." Geneva knelt down next to Loretta.

Loretta continued to dig. "Oh quit being such a chicken about things. She won't find out. I'll wash it off and slip it back with the others later." She stopped digging and turned to Geneva. "Okay, put the four-leaf clover in first and then put the penny on top of it."

"Are you sure a penny will work?"

"Well, do you have any gold? A penny is made of copper. It's sort of like gold. Maybe you'll just find a boyfriend instead of true love." Loretta snickered at her own joke.

"Very funny," said Geneva, sarcastically. "This is probably just all superstition anyway." She put the clover in the small hole that Loretta had dug in the flowerbed and then placed the penny on top of it.

"No it isn't. Carol's mother did this before she met Carol's father. Of course the moon was full and she used a gold pin instead of a *penny*." Loretta emphasized the word penny with a mocking tone as she pushed the loose dirt back into the hole, covering the clover and penny.

"Oh shut-up. Let's..." Geneva stopped talking and turned quickly, looking out toward the sloping pasture. "What was that?"

Loretta stood up and looked in the same direction. "What? There's nothing." She knelt back down and held Geneva's hand and they began reciting the spell, which was to bring Geneva her true love.

Meanwhile, as Lula Mae exited the kitchen, she eased the back screen door closed so that it would not make a noise. She wanted to check on Johnny, Gary and Scotty before she went to bed. Light spilled out of the kitchen window, illuminating part of the back yard as she walked to the playhouse. The small building; about ten feet wide and twelve feet long, was more like a cabin than a child's playhouse. As she peered through the screen door, she could see Johnny lying on the cot reading a comic book and Gary and Scotty, lying on top of their sleeping bags on the floor, playing a game of Chinese checkers. She pulled on the door handle, but the door was locked with a hook and eyebolt. "Are you boys doing okay?"

"Ahhh!" With spontaneous involuntary yelps, Gary and Scotty both scurried across the floor, in the direction away from the door. Of course, Johnny, being as always, Mr. Cool, calmly looked up from his comic book without a word.

"Mama, you scared us!" Gary got up and went to the door and unhooked it to let his mother in.

"I'm sorry." Lula Mae hugged Gary, who now had his arms around her waist. "I just wanted to see if you boys were okay out here."

"Yes we're okay, Mama." Johnny tried to project an air of annoyance, but in truth, he was comforted by his mother's attention.

"Okay then; good-night." Lula Mae walked over to Johnny, still lying on his cot and bent over and kissed him. She turned and kissed Scotty and then started to kiss Gary when she suddenly stood upright. "What the hell?"

The sound of voices from outside came through the open door and windows of the playhouse. The voices were garbled at first, but they quickly became distinct and definitely frantic before erupting into well defined hysterical screams and yells for help.

Instinctively, Lula Mae burst from the playhouse, grabbing a baseball bat, which was standing against the wall next to the door. She had recognized the voices of Geneva and Loretta in fits of terror. Underneath the screams she could also hear what sounded a lot like the snorts and grunts of a pig.

"What's the matter?" called Lula Mae when she saw Loretta running towards her in the semi-darkness, immediately followed by Geneva. Both girls ran past their mother and into the playhouse. Lula Mae stood in the middle of the back yard looking about for any sign of a threat to the girls.

Voices could be heard from inside the house and then Guy burst from the kitchen door and into the back yard. Frank was right behind him with his shotgun, followed by Mary and Romey, who lingered on the back porch. Harold and Louise quickly appeared behind Mary and Romey and pushed their way past them and into the yard.

Guy approached Lula Mae as she stood looking about the yard. "What the god-damned hell is going on?" He saw her looking about and began looking about, himself, wondering what it was he was supposed to be looking for.

Ignoring Guy's outburst and the other family members, Lula Mae returned to the playhouse where Johnny, Gary and Scotty were crowded behind Geneva and Loretta, vying for a position that would allow them to see into the back yard from the safety of the inside of the screen door. "Are you girls okay?"

"Unh-huh," Loretta's eyes were still wide with fear.

"What was that?" muttered Geneva in a voice much younger and frightened than she would have preferred to express.

"What the hell is going on?" Guy stood behind Lula Mae.

Turning, she said, "Oh just calm down; the girls were scared by something."

"What the hell are they doing out here?"

The others from inside the house stood in silence, looking on at the unfolding scene between Guy and Lula Mae.

"And why do you have that bat in your hand?"

Lula Mae had forgotten about the bat. She relaxed her grip on it and made a motion with her other hand to encompass the area around the house. "There was something out here chasing the girls." She opened the screen door and placed the bat back inside the playhouse. With the screen door open, the girls slowly came outside while the boys chose to remain inside, watching from the safety of the playhouse.

Guy had been frightened by the screaming, which had awakened him from a sound sleep. At the realization that the commotion was nothing but his unruly children acting out, his fright had turned to anger. "What was chasing them?" He looked about the yard, where there was nothing except the other family members. "And why in the hell aren't they in bed?"

Ordinarily, Lula Mae would avoid a scene with her husband in front of others, but she was still shaken by what had happened and she was in no mood to be cross examined with such a lack of respect as that, which she heard in her husband's unsympathetic sounding voice. "You either stop cussing or just shut up! There is something out there that tried to hurt your daughters and if you don't give a damn then you can just go back to bed."

By this time the whole family was out in the yard gathered around Lula Mae and the girls. Mary stood with her hands on her hips. "Lula Mae what's got into you? And why are you out here this time of night anyway?"

"Well god-damn it; do I have to explain myself to everyone? There's some kind of wild pig out here or something and I'm trying to protect my children from it."

"Wild pig?" Mary's demeanor changed from accusative to concern. "You saw a wild pig?"

"Well...I saw something." With Mary's change of attitude, Lula Mae dropped her defensive stance. "I'm not sure what it was, but it sounded like some kind of pig."

Mary looked around at the group. "Good Lord, I've heard about that pig. I thought it was just a tall tale."

"What have you heard?" asked Guy.

"Oh, Bobby Dean, the letterman told me that some old lady a couple of miles from here was half eaten by one of her pigs. Said she was slopping the pigs when she got dizzy headed and next thing she knew she was waking up in the slop trough, screaming in pain cause the pigs were biting her. They thought they was going to eat her. Her husband heard her screaming and came running. All the pigs but one shooed away when he yelled at them and kicked them. The one old sow though, just wouldn't let go. She had hold of the old woman's leg. Blood everywhere. The old man was beating the sow with his fists and the sow let go of the old woman and turned on him. He got a couple of bites on his hands before he picked up the pail that the old lady had been using for the slop. He started hitting the sow on the head till she turned and ran through the gate that the old man had left open. The old lady nearly died from loosing so much blood. She ain't never been the same. The pig ran away and didn't come back. People say she roams around at night, looking for blood."

"That's the devil pig," said Romey standing close to Harold.

"Oh Romey, there isn't no such thing as a devil pig," said Guy. "Mama, you shouldn't be telling stories like that in front of Romey."

"Romey's old enough to know about stuff like that. He knows there's evil in the world."

Guy looked at Romey. "That's just some little pig that got out of his pen and he's rutting around looking for something to eat. He's scared of us; that's why he ran away." He turned to Lula Mae. He felt ashamed at the way he had just treated her. The girls' screams had frightened him and he realized that he had overreacted. He put his arm around Lula Mae's shoulder and rubbed her upper back. "Come on, let's all go to bed."

Lula Mae was glad for Guy's change of attitude. Being accustomed to his outbursts, she was not too bothered by them. She was happy to just forget about it. She turned to Geneva and Loretta. "Go on girls; back to bed." Turning back to Guy, she said, "I'll be up in a minute, I want to tell the boys good-night."

Guy, Frank, Mary, and Romey all turned and walked back to the house. Geneva and Loretta quickly scurried past them, and without a word, went into the house and up to their bedroom; relieved that all the commotion was over, and quite ready to go to bed and go to sleep. Considering that everyone seemed to have overlooked the fact that they had been outside when they were not supposed to be; they felt that it would be best if they were not seen or heard from for a while.

Harold and Louise stood outside the playhouse with Lula Mae. Lula Mae opened the screen door to enter and Scotty and Gary ran out and stood next to their mothers.

Louise hugged Scotty's shoulders with one hand while he stood next to her. "Go on back to bed, Scott."

"No, I don't want to sleep out here." Scotty looked up at her, imploringly.

"Oh don't be silly," said Harold. "You don't see Johnny and Gary being scared do you?"

Johnny stood just inside the playhouse at the open door. It would take more than some pig to frighten him. Gary however had been ready to tell his mother that he wanted to sleep inside the main house. Now he could not very well show his fear after his uncle had praised his courage. He suspected that his uncle Harold was being rather sly about the matter; but just the same, he said nothing.

"Give Mom a kiss." Louise bent down and kissed Scotty. She gently nudged him through the open door and he reluctantly made his way to his sleeping bag on the floor and crawled in. He knew that it would do him no good to protest.

"Good-night Gary and Johnny. Good-night Lula Mae," said Louise as she and Harold went back into the house.

"Good-night," replied Lula Mae. She walked with Gary into the playhouse and over to his sleeping bag. "You boys can use one of Romey's empty coffee cans if you need to pee tonight. I don't want you going outside." She tucked Gary into his sleeping bag and kissed him and Scotty on their foreheads. She stood and put her arm around Johnny's shoulders. They walked to the door and she kissed his cheek. "You hook the latch on this door after I leave. You boy's will be okay. Your daddy was right. That's probably just some harmless little pig out there rummaging around for something to eat."

As she walked back to the main house, Johnny hooked the latch and watched until she entered and turned off the kitchen light. This was too perfect for him to pass up. He loved playing tricks on his younger brother and cousin. He stayed at the door gazing through the screen. "I'll bet Romey was right. I'll bet that is a devil pig out there."

"Unh-uh," said Gary pulling his sleeping bag up around his neck.

"What's a devil pig?" Scotty's eyes were wide with fear, and he wanted to know all about the danger threatening them.

"It's a pig that came up from hell when the earth cracked open." Johnny turned to the two younger boys so that they could see his eyes, which he opened wide, in order to show the look of fear and knowing on his face. "There was a big earthquake a couple of years back and the ground cracked open. That's when he came up." Just at that moment, a low rumble of thunder sounded in the distance. Johnny narrowed his eyes to appear sinister. "They say that when he kills somebody, he makes a sound that sounds like thunder."

"Unh-uh," insisted Gary.

Scotty rose up on one elbow, but remained silent; his attention riveted to his older cousin.

"Johnny."

All three boys jerked back in fright and looked to the screen door where the voice had come from. Guy was looking into the playhouse. They could see that he was holding a shotgun. "Go to bed. I'll be out here for a while to keep an eye on things."

CHAPTER FOUR

"*UNDERTAKER TAKE IT EASY, UNDERTAKER TAKE IT slow...for the body you are carrying; oh Lord I hate to see it go...*"

Mary's singing was a familiar sound around the Austin's farm. Her repertoire consisted of mostly religious hymns and a few country-western favorites. Her voice carried from inside the kitchen, throughout the main house; and when she stepped onto the back porch to throw table scraps into the yard for the chickens to eat, it carried into Romey's playhouse. It was her way of waking the whole clan.

The funereal anthem was having its intended effect as it roused the three reluctant boys from their slumber. Gary got out of his sleeping bag and headed toward the outhouse to relieve his bladder. Scotty rolled over in hopes that a new position would help him go back to sleep. Johnny covered his ears with his pillow. "Shut up old lady," he muttered with no intention of being heard by his grandmother. The statement was mainly to impress his younger cousin, who really was not impressed. Scotty did not appreciate Johnny's comment any more than his grandmother's singing.

"Hey! Get up you lazy bones!" Loretta was standing outside the playhouse looking through the screen door; a quick stop on her way to the outhouse.

"Get out of here!" Johnny threw his pillow against the screen.

Scotty rolled over to take in the action. His hopes for continued sleep were now gone and he accepted the fact that it was time to get up.

Loretta walked briskly toward the outhouse. In meeting Gary on his return from there, (he was wearing only a pair of briefs) she teasingly said, "You better put some clothes on or that old rooster is going to run out here and peck your pecker."

Gary's jaw dropped at the audacity of his older sister in saying the word pecker. He was not quite sure, but he guessed that it meant his *thing*, which he had never really referred to as anything other than that. "Ahhmm...I know what that means. I'm going to tell," Gary said to Loretta's back as she continued on to the outhouse.

"Go ahead, tattletale. I'll just say I didn't say it." Loretta turned and looked over her shoulder giving Gary a smug look before entering the small wooden building and closing the door.

"What's a pecker?" were the first words out of Gary's mouth when he entered the playhouse. To his chagrin, his comment was met with nothing but boisterous laughter; not only from his older brother, but from his younger cousin. Gary decided to drop the subject. He slipped on his Levis and went into the main house for breakfast.

"Did you wash your hands?" Mary said to Gary as he sat at the table.

"Good morning son," said Lula Mae as she hugged Gary and kissed him on the cheek.

"Gary Ray?" His grandmother stood looking at him with her hands on her hips.

"Oh Grandma."

"Get up and wash your hands, Son," said Lula Mae. "Do you want some oatmeal?"

"Yeah." Gary walked to the counter to wash his hands in the wash basin. As he stood washing his hands, he could hear his uncle, father and grandfather talking in the living room.

"Do you think that old sow would hurt anyone?" asked Guy.

"Nah, she's just a dumb old pig," said Frank. "But if I see her roaming around here, I'll take care of her. We'll be having pork chops for dinner."

"You're not going to shoot that pig," said Mary in a loud voice. "That's Mrs. Slocum's pig. I don't want any trouble with her family."

"Ah shut up old woman," responded Frank.

Gary dried his hands and took his seat at the kitchen table. He looked at his mother. "Is there really a devil pig?"

Lula Mae dished oatmeal from the pan into Gary's bowl. "No Son; that was just an old ornery sow wandering around last night. She's not a devil pig. But just the same, you stay away from her if you see her."

Even with all the explanations and denials of the existence of a devil pig by the adults, the major topic at the children's breakfast table was the possibility of said phenomenon. After breakfast, the immediate goal of Johnny, Loretta, Gary and Scotty was to hunt down and capture the beast. Geneva was content to adjourn to the front porch swing and read.

With the kitchen table having been cleared of the children's dishes; Frank, Guy, and Harold were called for breakfast. As they sat down at the table, they were discussing Frank's sharecroppers, while the women prepared bacon, eggs, biscuits and gravy.

"Their lease is up at the end of the month," said Frank. "They been wanting to buy the land. I'm thinking I might just sell it to them."

"No one's selling my land." Mary placed a plate of fresh biscuits on the table.

"See what I have to put up with," said Frank, looking at Guy and acting as if Mary were not in the room. "There's no reasoning with her."

Mary opened her mouth to respond, but Frank put up his hand to shush her. "Never mind old woman; just fix us breakfast."

Mary gave Frank a look of disdain and then continued with the breakfast preparations.

Frank and Guy continued their conversation on business as the women finished serving breakfast and sat down with them to eat. Harold had contributed little to the dialogue; his pensiveness virtually unnoticed by anyone in the group except Mary. He had never been the most outgoing one in the family, and it was not unusual for him to take a back seat in the conversations when Guy was around. She had noticed, however that he was being unusually quiet.

As she watched him, she noticed a knowing look that was exchanged between him and Louise. Raising a piece of crisp bacon to her mouth and nibbling slowly, she glanced from Harold to Louise and back to Harold. "What are you two up to?"

Harold had not noticed his mother's attention focused on him. He was caught off guard; left vulnerable by his thoughts, which he had shared only with Louise. "What?" he said, with a mild look of guilt on his face.

"You heard me. What are you and your wife cooking up?"

Louise sipped her coffee; keeping her eyes directed toward Harold, as he looked at his mother and hesitated. Feeling that it was time to open the discussion of what was going on; she said to Mary, "Harold has something that he wants to discuss with you and Frank."

With Louise's statement, Guy and Frank stopped talking and everyone at the table looked at Harold. Louise reached across the table and took his hand, saying, "Go on Harold."

Harold looked down and reached into his shirt pocket. He pulled out a sheet of paper, and keeping his eyes lowered, began unfolding it. He glanced up; first at his father and then at his mother, and then he looked back at the paper in his hand. "A couple of weeks ago, Jesse Mae called me. She said that she had found out some interesting news." He laid the paper on the table. "This is a copy of your marriage license. It says here," he pointed at the paper, "that you were married in the year nineteen-hundred and eleven."

Mary had her coffee cup almost to her lips at this point. She held the cup where it was and looked quickly at Frank and then at Harold. "No Son, your papa and me was married in nineteen-hundred and ten."

"That's what I told Jesse Mae when she told me. I told her that she must have misunderstood the people at the records department. She said she had understood them perfectly. She mailed me this." He lifted the paper. "This is an official copy of your marriage license."

Mary replaced her coffee cup down on the table a little too hard. "Well that's just crazy. I told you that we was married in nineteen-hundred and ten. Someone in that records department just made a mistake, that's all."

Harold looked at Frank. "Is that right Papa?"

"Now Harold, why are you asking me some fool thing like that? I don't remember when me and your mama got married. What god-damned difference does it make, anyway?"

"I called the lady in the records office," said Harold. "She assured me that there was no mistake. She told me that you and Mama were married in nineteen-hundred and eleven."

Frank was holding his knife in one hand and his fork in the other. He lifted them in an expression of openness. "Well okay then! What if we was? What do you care?"

"I care because that means that I was conceived out of wedlock."

Frank lowered his utensils to the table and leaned back in his chair. He shot Mary an accusing glance, as if it were her fault that this was happening.

Mary searched the eyes of the others for a sign of empathy. "It wasn't my fault. I was just a young innocent girl." She glared at Frank. "I was manhandled!"

"Oh bullshit," said Frank.

"I was! Lord knows I wasn't brought up like that. I was a clean living Christian girl. You manhandled me. I didn't have a choice."

"Everything is always my fault, isn't it?"

"If it's something bad it is. You're just a nasty old man."

Harold rose from his chair and walked to the front porch. Louise also rose from her chair but she remained standing next to the table. "He's really upset by this. One of you needs to talk to him."

"Bullshit," said Frank. He looked at Mary. "Pour me some coffee old woman."

Mary stood up and moved toward the coffeepot on the stove. "I was manhandled. And that's all I got to say about it." She filled the cups of Frank, Guy and Lula, as Louise; frustrated with her in-laws, left the room to join her husband.

Noontime rolled around and everybody was *resting* once again. In view of the fact that the date of Mary and Frank's wedding seemed to have little interest to anybody but him, Harold had decided that he had probably overreacted to the whole thing and would do just as well to put it behind him and forget about it. By nature, he had an easygoing attitude and he would usually let go of ill feelings before long. Now as he sat across the checkerboard from Johnny, his main concern was figuring out how to take Johnny's last king.

Louise and Lula Mae sat at the kitchen table drinking coffee and talking quietly, so as not to disturb Romey in the next room.

Suddenly, the hushed sounds of the noon hour were broken by the loud blaring of a car horn. A bright red Cadillac convertible was making its way up the dirt road leading to the back porch of the house.

Louise and Lula Mae hurried to the back porch where Frank was sitting in a kitchen chair smoking his pipe. "That's Jesse Mae," said Frank.

"My Lord," said Louise at the sight. Lula Mae merely stared in silence. By this time all the children had made their way to the back of the house and were eagerly awaiting their aunt's arrival.

Jesse Mae brought the car to a stop next to the other cars. She stepped out of the car, wearing a pair of red Capri pants with white high heeled sandals and a loose fitting white sleeveless blouse that ended just below her bust line. On her head was a large red hat with a floppy brim and she carried a white leather purse with the strap slung over one shoulder.

Geneva and Loretta ran to her and embraced her, while the boys, stood watching her with a mild sense of awe. After greeting the girls, she bent her knees and stretched out her arms. "Look at these handsome young men. You boys come give your Aunt Jesse Mae a big hug." With her arms around Johnny, Gary and Scotty, Jesse Mae made her way toward the house. Frank walked out to meet her and she let go of the boys and embraced her father. "Hi Papa", she said.

Frank hugged his only daughter enthusiastically. "We didn't know you was coming today."

With their arms around each other, and surrounded by the youngsters, the father and daughter continued toward the house. "Well Papa," said Jesse Mae, "I wasn't going to come today, but I got to thinking that I'd rather spend the Fourth with my family, than with a bunch of people that I don't care much about."

By this time Guy had awakened from his nap in the living room and he was standing next to Harold on the back porch. The two brothers stepped down and joined their wives, who were already off the porch extending their greetings to Jesse Mae. Hugs were exchanged all around as the group made its way to the back door of the house.

Being given the lead by the others, Jesse Mae stopped at the bottom of the porch steps. She looked at her mother who was standing on the inside of the screen door, which led into the kitchen. "Hi Mama," she said with a slight tone of sarcasm.

"What are you doing here?" Mary remained behind the screen.

Jesse Mae shifted her weight to one leg and put her hand on her hip. "Can't you just say hi, Mama?"

"Well good Lord…Hi…now, what are you doing here?"

"I came to spend the Fourth of July with my family." Jesse Mae turned and looked at the others who were all waiting to enter the house behind her. She turned back to her mother and spotted Romey, who was standing behind Mary. "Hi Romey," she called with outstretched arms.

"Hi Jesse Mae," said Romey, enthusiastically as he peered at her from behind Mary.

"Romey's resting. It's too hot for him to be getting excited," said Mary.

"God-damn it Mary," said Frank. "Let him come out here and say hello to his sister."

Mary did not like giving in to Frank's demands, but she knew that he would become more aggressive if she did not quit being obstinate. Instead of sending Romey out; she pushed the screen door open and stood holding it for the group. "Come inside; all of you."

Jesse Mae entered first. She bypassed her mother and threw her arms around Romey. "Hi Son, how're you doing?"

"Don't call him Son. He's my son. I'm his mama; nobody else."

"Oh for crying out loud, Mama, that's just a term of endearment and you know it."

"Term of endearment?" Mary looked around at the others. "Miss high and mighty with her fancy words."

"Hi Jesse Mae," said Romey with his arms around her. Jesse Mae ignored her mother's sarcasm and walked into the kitchen with Romey, followed by the others.

Guy was right behind Jesse Mae and Romey. He motioned to a chair at the kitchen table. "Have a seat Sis." He turned to Lula, who was just entering the house with Louise. "Honey pour us some coffee."

Lula went to the stove and picked up the coffeepot without speaking. It irritated her that her husband acted like she was here to serve his sister. She had never gotten past being a little uncomfortable around Jesse Mae. She had difficulty accepting the attention that Guy showed her, but she had always felt that family was important and that the members should show respect for one another, so she made an effort to be agreeable.

"You know, it's really hot today," said Jesse Mae, removing her hat. "Do you think you could fix us all some iced tea instead, Lula?"

Lula Mae felt the muscles in her back and neck begin to tighten as she made a conscious effort to overlook Jesse Mae's slighting attitude toward her.

"Yeah, iced tea, iced tea!" The chant rose from the children.

Lula Mae turned toward the children with one hand raised as a gesture to quiet their voices. "Okay, I'll fix iced tea, but you kids go on out to play. I'll call you when it's done."

Jesse Mae blatantly overrode Lula's authority with the children. "Oh no, don't go out to play yet. I have some gifts for you kids. Johnny, there are some paper shopping bags in the back seat of my car. Would you go out and get them for me?"

Johnny immediately headed for the back yard where the cars were, with Gary and Scotty right behind him.

"Don't slam that..." Mary's words were too late as the screen door, once again slapped against the frame.

Lula put the tea kettle filled with water over the burner. Louise had resumed her seat at the table and moved Lula Mae's coffee cup from in front of Jesse Mae and placed it to her left, at the other end of the table.

Lula Mae sat down next to Louise. "Jesse Mae, I hope you didn't go spending a lot of money on the kids."

"Don't you worry about me spending money. Eugene left me very well off. I never have to worry about money again."

"You'll have to worry if you don't stop spending it like it's water running through a sieve," said Mary, taking a seat at the table.

"Mama, I've told you before; you have no idea how much money I got when Eugene died. I'd tell you, but you still wouldn't know how much it was. It's higher than you can count."

Mary disregarded the not so subtle insult, and retaliated with her own little dig. "Well, I should hope you got something out of marrying that nasty old man."

"I got a lot out of marrying that 'nasty old man' as you insist on calling him; who, by the way was not much older than you. I got respect, for one thing. When I go into a fine restaurant, they just fall all over themselves to make me feel welcome. Everybody knew Judge Burns."

"Miss high and mighty."

"That's right..."

The screen door slammed behind the three boys as they ran to the table with the shopping bags; interrupting the habitual bickering between mother and daughter. A sense of relief was felt by the others when Jesse Mae shifted her attention from her mother to the youngsters.

"Oh thanks boys. Just put them down here." Jesse Mae motioned for the boys to put the bags next to her. With the bags on the floor, she reached down and picked one up. "Now let's see what we have here." She reached into the bag and pulled out what looked like a small travel case with an electrical cord extending from it. She put the case on the kitchen table. "This here is for Romey. Harold, would you plug this in?" She held the end of the cord in her hand offering it to Harold, who was standing next to Guy. She motioned toward the outlet attached to the overhead light, which hung by a cord from the ceiling.

Romey stood next to Jesse Mae, intensely interested as Harold inserted the plug into the socket. Jesse Mae opened the case to reveal a phonograph. Romey stared at it with a look of anticipation. He had no idea what it was.

Jesse Mae took a forty-five rpm record from a pocket in the lid of the case and placed it on the turntable. She moved the lever to the 'On' position and the record began spinning. Romey's eyes widened.

Jesse Mae picked up the handle and placed the stylus on the spinning disc and sat back. There was a brief moment of silence and then the music began. *"Happy trails to you, until we meet again. Happy trails to you, keep smiling until then..."*

Romey was ecstatic. He began laughing as he listened to the music. Roy Rogers and Dale Evans were his two favorite western stars. He loved to listen to them on the radio. He had almost learned all the words to the song. He had also seen them in a couple of movies in town and he had several comic books, which featured them.

"Do you know who that is Romey?" asked Johnny.

"Of course he knows. Don't you Romey?" Lula Mae stood up to check the teakettle.

"Roy Rogers and Dale Evans!" Romey smiled broadly and looked around at the group.

"Now you can play their songs anytime you want," said Jesse Mae. "There are three more records in here too; one more by Roy Rogers and two by Gene Autry.

"Thanks Jesse Mae." Romey briefly put his arms around Jesse Mae and then turned his attention back to the record player.

Jesse Mae lifted the stylus off of the record and turned the lever to the 'Off' position. "We'll take this into the living room in a while and you can listen to all the other records.

"Okay," said Romey as he stood with his arms at his sides, patiently waiting to see what else Jesse Mae had brought. Frank reached up and unplugged the cord from the electrical outlet. He lifted the record player and said, "Come on Romey, let's find a place for this in the living room." Although he would have denied it, Frank was just as excited about the phonograph as Romey. The two of them hurried out of the kitchen to listen to the other records.

Jesse Mae reached for a larger shopping bag. "This bag is for Johnny, Gary and Scotty." The boys elbowed each other in attempts to be the one closest to their aunt.

"Now you boys will have to be very careful with these. You'll have to get your fathers to help you with them." Jesse Mae began removing very sophisticated looking fireworks from the bag, inspiring exclamations of wonder and appreciation from the boys with each piece as she pulled it out.

With the whole cache laid out on the table, the boys continued to marvel over them. Louise reached over and picked up one of the rockets. She held it up in front of her and looked at Scotty. "Walter Scott, you are not to touch any of these. You let your daddy handle them. Do you understand?"

"Aw Mom…"

"Do you understand me?"

"Yes." Scotty dropped his head to pout.

"Johnny, that goes for you and Gary too," said Lula Mae.

"We'll take care of them." Guy began collecting the fireworks and replacing them in the bag. His willingness to take on the supervision of the pyrotechnic extravaganza revealed more than a paternal interest in his children's entertainment. Harold's assistance in collecting the items also showed a high degree of enthusiasm.

The boys followed their fathers into the front yard. Guy and Harold began pulling the fireworks out of the bag and spreading them out on the lawn. The boys also began pulling items from the bag. Guy pounded a rocket stake into the ground and turned to the youngsters. "You boys go on and play somewhere else. Harold and I will set these up for you. It will be just like a real fireworks display."

"But we want to help," protested Johnny.

Guy picked up a box of firecrackers. "Here, go on and play with these. We'll set these other things up."

"But Aunt Jesse Mae gave them to us. Why can't we set them up?"

"God-damn it, Johnny; go and do what I told you."

"Go on Scotty," said Harold. "Me and your Uncle Guy will set these up for you."

With sullen faces, the boys walked away, resigned to the fact that they were to have no part in arranging the fireworks show for the night.

Meanwhile, back in the kitchen, Jesse Mae reached into the last remaining bag. "And now…," she said as she revealed another portable record player. "…this is for you girls. I also got you…" She reached into the bag again and pulled out a stack of discs. "…ten records."

Geneva and Loretta began sorting through the records. "Oh boy! Elvis Presley," cried Loretta. Geneva picked up a record. "And Julie London. Thanks Aunt Jesse Mae." The girls picked up the phonograph and the records and hurried upstairs to their room to listen to them.

They were barely out of the kitchen when Mary turned to Jesse Mae. "What do you mean; giving those girls that vulgar rock-and-roll music?"

"Mama, Julie London is not rock-and-roll music; and besides, there's nothing wrong with rock-and-roll. All of the kids are listening to it."

"Not in my house they aren't. It's all I can do to keep them from playing it on the radio. Now they can play it any time they want to. Why didn't you get them some nice gospel music; something to bring them nearer to their Lord?"

"You know, Mary," said Louise. "Elvis Presley was a gospel singer in his church before he started recording music."

"Is that so?" said Jesse Mae. "I didn't know that."

"Lula, is that water boiling yet?" Mary rose from the table and walked to the counter, turning her back to Louise and Jesse Mae. She realized that her argument against the music was weak and she did not want to pursue it.

Lula Mae got up and turned off the burner under the teakettle. She lifted a large glass bowl from underneath the sink and placed it on the countertop. She and Mary busied themselves with unwrapping tea bags and placing them in the bowl.

A brief silence filled the room. Mary turned and walked to the swinging door that separated the kitchen from the dining room. She pulled the door closed and walked back to the kitchen counter and resumed the preparation of the tea. Without turning around, Mary said to Jesse Mae, "I hear you've been nosing around at the county records office."

Jesse Mae shot a quick glance at Louise. Louise nodded her head slightly to let Jesse Mae know that the secret was out.

"I thought we might talk about that later…in private," said Jesse Mae.

"Private?" Mary twisted violently to face Jesse Mae, accidentally ripping one of the tea bags and spilling dry tea leaves over the counter. "There's nothing private in this house! Why did you tell Harold that me and your papa wasn't married in the year nineteen-hundred-and-ten?"

"He had a right to know." Jesse Mae looked defiantly at her mother.

Mary's anger was palpable. "I suppose you think you've got something on me now, huh?"

"This is not the time, Mama."

"Why? Why not?" Mary turned to Lula, who was cleaning the spilled tea leaves off the counter top. "Lula Mae knows." She turned back toward Louise and Jesse Mae. "Louise knows. Everybody knows!" She waved her hands up in the air and brought them down against her thighs. "Well no, not everybody. The young ones don't know." She leaned in towards Jesse Mae. "Unless you told them too. Did you tell them, Jess? Did you tell them how I was manhandled by your papa when I was a young innocent girl? How he forced me to do things I didn't want to do? Do they all know that I was with child when your papa and me got married?" Mary stood up straight and took a deep breath. Calmly, she said, "You think you got something on me; something that will shame me and make me humble. Well, you're wrong. I am a righteous woman. I was manhandled."

Mary looked up from Jesse Mae and her eyes widened in shock when she saw the open dining room door. "Good Lord-o-mercy! Loretta Fay you get back up those stairs."

Loretta, who was standing behind the partially opened door with her jaw hanging down, turned and ran to tell Geneva what she had just heard.

"Now that little blabbermouth will tell all the other kids. Romey had better not get wind of this."

"Now you just hold it right there," said Lula Mae. "Nobody is going to start calling my kids names."

"I'll call your kids anything I want to."

"Like hell you will."

"Don't you start using that foul language in my house, Lula Mae."

"Oh shut up; both of you." Jesse Mae stood up. "I think I'll go see how Romey is enjoying his records." She left the kitchen and went into the living room, leaving the swinging door closed behind her.

Mary resumed her seat at the table and Lula Mae turned her attention back to preparing the tea. It only took a moment for Lula Mae to finish placing tea bags in the bowl and pouring hot water in. She placed a cover over the bowl and sat back down at the table. There was a brief silence while the three women sipped their coffee.

"They're out there cooking something up," said Mary.

"What do you mean?" asked Lula Mae. Their words from a moment earlier were virtually forgotten. Accusations and threats were just part of the everyday dialogue in this family.

"They're cooking something up," Mary said again.

"Well, Mary, what do you *mean* by that?" Louise was still feeling a bit exasperated with her mother-in-law.

"They want to kill me," said Mary in a matter-of-fact tone.

"Oh Mary!" said Louise.

Lula looked at Mary with an expression of annoyed disbelief.

"You don't believe me, but I know they're plotting to do me in." Mary stood her ground.

"Who, Mary? Who's plotting to do you in?" said Louise.

"That old man in there and his daughter. They've tried to poison me before." Mary looked at her silent daughters-in-law. "Well they have. I heard them right here in the kitchen a month ago. Talking about putting something in my food. Said I wouldn't last the night after I ate it. Said everybody would be better off without me rutting around. Saying that they would have to keep it secret. Nobody else could know."

Lula Mae looked at Louise to get her reaction, which was of course the same as hers; disbelief. She looked back at Mary. "Did you hear them mention your name?"

"Well no, but they said they could put some kind of poison in '*her*' food. And since I'm the only other '*her*' around here; who else would they be talking about?"

"You're not the only '*her*' around here," said Louise.

"This was before you all came. When they said it; I was."

"That's not what I mean."

"Well, what then?"

"What about that old sow that roams around here?"

"Of course," said Lula Mae. "Frank's been wanting to get rid of that old sow. That's what they meant by rutting around."

Mary did not appreciate the simple solution that the other women had arrived at. She felt that they were not grasping the true situation. "You two don't know them like I do. When there's nobody else around, if it wasn't for Romey they'd gang up on me and do me in. I know it."

Lula and Louise looked at one another. They both knew that Mary had a history of accusing Frank of mental cruelty, but they silently concurred with a knowing look that she was carrying things a bit too far with this accusation.

"Do you think that tea has brewed long enough?" Louise said to Lula Mae.

CHAPTER FIVE

OWN AT THE BARN, JOHNNY, GARY, AND Scotty were looking for ways to keep themselves entertained. They had their pockets full of the firecrackers from Jesse Mae, and Johnny had a large box of matches, which he had snitched from their grandmother's kitchen. They were walking around the barn, directing their attention up under the eaves where they were tracking wasps, which were coming and going in a lazy routine fashion. An exciting idea occurred to Johnny when they spotted the wasp's nest. He considered himself to be a *Great White Hunter*. He had waged many a battle with various flying things, and he was ready to add these demons to his list of conquests.

Johnny turned to the other boys and said, "If we tie ten firecrackers together and then tie them to the end of a pole, we can hold the end of the pole up to that nest and blow those suckers to kingdom come."

Gary looked up at the nest and the dozens of wasps crawling on it. "But won't we make the wasps mad at us?"

"No, stupid; they'll be dead."

Gary was not so sure of his brother's plan. He looked at Scotty as if to ask him what he thought. Scotty merely shrugged his shoulders.

Johnny held out his hand. "Both of you give me five of your firecrackers."

"That's too many," protested Gary.

"I'll give you three," said Scotty.

"Yeah, three is enough," concurred Gary.

"Okay, give me three then." By this time, Johnny had begun securing his own share of the firecrackers into a bunch, using the kite string that he had pulled from his pants pocket. He took the other firecrackers from Gary and Scotty and added them to the bunch, tying them securely together. He looked around for a pole of some sort. His eyes rested upon an old pitchfork leaning against the wall; this would do nicely. He tied the bundle of firecrackers to one of the prongs on the pitchfork.

"Are you sure this is going to kill all of those wasps?" asked Gary.

"It will kill most of them. We can swat the rest of them." Johnny's adrenaline was already pumping at the thought of the battle.

Gary took a step back. "I'm not going to swat those wasps! Those things will sting you."

"I don't think my mom wants me to swat wasps," said Scotty, happy to be adhering to his mother's probable ruling on the matter.

"Oh you little babies! They're not going to hurt you. If they come at you run out of their way."

Gary and Scotty both knew that they were not going to get out of this confrontation with these aggressive insects. They quickly began looking around for weapons, with which to defend themselves. They each picked up a flat stick from a nearby pile of wood, and prepared to stand their ground.

"Go stand over there." Johnny pointed to an area about five feet from him. Gary and Scotty obediently moved to the spot. Johnny tossed the box of matches at Gary's feet and then he picked up the pitchfork with the mini-bomb attached to the end of it. He had twisted the fuses of the firecrackers together, creating a single fuse. He extended the pitchfork so that the firecrackers were within Gary's reach. "Okay Gary," he said. "Light the fuses."

Gary leaned over and picked up the box of matches. He laid his stick on the ground next ho his feet, took out a match from the box, and dragged it across the side of the box, creating a burst of flame. When the fire met the twisted fuses, tiny sparks erupted in every direction and the fuses began to burn rapidly toward the shafts of black powder. Johnny quickly lifted the end of the pitchfork towards the nest and held it there.

Pop...pop...pop...pop... Instead of one powerful explosion, the firecrackers exploded independently; failing to accomplish the intended objective. Also, Johnny had managed to get the firecrackers close to the nest; but not close enough to do any real damage. He had merely succeeded in irritating the nest's inhabitants.

In an instant the air was filled with angry *dive bomber* wasps. Johnny dropped the pitchfork and retreated from the nest as fast as he could. His hands were flailing around like a mad windmill as he slapped at the wasps, which were buzzing around his head as he ran helter-skelter.

Gary and Scotty ran first one way, and then the other; not knowing which escape route to take. It would be only seconds before the *Kamikazes* would discover that their attacker had two accomplices.

Scotty dropped his stick and screamed in pain as he slapped at an avenging warrior planting its stinger into the flesh of his exposed neck.

Gary ran from the drove of buzzing daggers, which were rapidly approaching him. He rounded the corner of the barn, hoping to escape from the wasps' line of vision. He was sure he had succeeded as he pressed his body against the wall of the barn, trying to make himself unnoticeable; but then Scotty rounded the corner behind him, followed by a substantial swarm of angry combatants.

"The root cellar!" screamed Gary as he broke from his position against the wall. He had seen the faded, rotting, wooden door to the old root cellar next to the barn. It looked to be embedded in the earth and had weeds growing over it, but he went for it anyway. He grasped the wooden handle and pulled. The door remained anchored to the ground. A small portion of dirt shifted around the edges of it, but it remained closed.

Scotty ran past Gary, slapping and screaming. A few of Scotty's attackers diverted their attention to Gary and began swarming and diving at him. Gary let go of the cellar door and dropped to the ground, squatting on his haunches, covering his head and neck with his arms as best he could.

A hard shove from Johnny toppled Gary over onto his side where he continued to hold his arms over his head as he watched Johnny pulling at the cellar door while the winged *torpedoes* aimed for any exposed targets. The door ripped up from the ground and flung open. Johnny jumped into the dark hole.

Gary crawled to the opening in the ground and looked in. He could see a set of wooden stairs leading downward. Slapping at the darting wasps around his head he quickly maneuvered himself into the opening and began his descent. "Scotty," he called as he felt the stairs beneath his feet.

Screaming and slapping, Scotty found the stairs and began climbing downward. With what seemed like one continuous motion, Johnny jerked Scotty off of the stairs with one hand and pulled the door closed with the other hand. They all fell backwards into the damp dark hole.

The three of them hunkered at the bottom of the stairs, struggling to catch their breath. After a moment, their breathing returned to normal and the cellar was quiet. Then...bzzzzzz...each boy tensed when he heard the unmistakable sound of the wasp or wasps, sharing the small confined space with them.

"What's that?" said Scotty.

"Shut-up, you know what that is," said Johnny. "Gary do you still have those matches?"

"No," said Gary in a small voice.

"Great," said Johnny with as much sarcasm as he could express.

"I have some," said Scotty.

"You do?"

"Yeah."

"Give them to me," ordered Johnny.

There was a moment before Scotty spoke. The other two could hear him reaching into his pockets.

"Where are you?" Scotty asked.

Johnny felt around and found Scotty's outstretched hand. He took the small box of matches, removed a match and then closed the box. The smell of sulfur reached the boys' noses as the match sparkled and burst into a small flame, which gave them a just enough light to barely see their surroundings.

An eerie sight presented itself to the boys. The cellar was about eight feet wide and ten feet long. The wooden ceiling was no more than two feet above Johnny's head, and it had roots growing between the planks; coming down from the plants, which grew outside. Against the back wall was what was left of some wooden shelves holding a few empty jars and a kerosene lamp with no glass halo on it. "Ow!" said Johnny when the fire reached his fingertip, and the cellar went dark again.

"Light another match," said Gary.

"Shut-up dummy, what do you think I'm going to do?"

They heard the match scratch against the sandpaper on the side of the match box just before the sulfur sparkled again and the second match ignited. Holding the match in one hand, Johnny quickly took the lamp off the shelf and shook it to see if it had Kerosene in it. When he heard the kerosene sloshing in the lamp base, he handed the box of matches to Gary. "Light another one." Gary lit another match and held it high, while Johnny dropped his burned out match and adjusted the wick in the lamp; trying to get it to soak up the kerosene.

"It's going out," said Gary, holding the match high.

"Light another one."

"Here, Scotty." Gary handed the box of matches to Scotty, while he held the burning match. "Light another one."

Scotty lit another match right before Gary's went out. Johnny set the lamp on the floor and grabbed the matchbox from Scotty. When he touched a burning match to the lamp wick, a small flame rose from it. The next moment the flame spread across the whole wick and the cellar was bathed in a faint orange glow.

The light from the lamp eased the boys' anxiety somewhat as they looked around their sanctuary with curious eyes. Then they detected the faint *buzz* of the wasps that had followed them into the cellar. The light had roused the insects, and they were now flying around in the shared space. Johnny picked up a thin piece of lumber, which had broken away from the shelving. "You guys get behind me; up against the stairs." Johnny would have his battle after all, and he was ready for it.

The lamplight flickered throughout the space. The small black spots moving through the air were Johnny's targets. Gary and Scotty stood motionless.

*Swash…*The piece of lumber cut through the dank air. The black spots continued to circle. *Swash…*Johnny swung again. Still the spots circled. He raised the board in the ready position again and waited. He realized that it was highly unlikely that he would connect with a wasp while it was in flight. If he could see one land on something, and stay there for a moment, he would have a better chance at hitting it. He just hoped that it would not be him or one of the others that the wasp would chose as a resting place.

Then his opportunity presented itself. He saw one of the wasps land on an empty mason jar lying on its side on one of the shelves. With lightning speed, he swung the board, crashing down on the wasp, the jar, and the shelf. The glass jar shattered beneath the blow. Also, the shelf, on which the jar had rested, broke in two under the force of the swing, causing the connecting rotten lumber of the shelving to collapse inward; bringing after it, chunks of damp soil.

The cellar grew quiet again. The boys stood still, listening for the surviving wasp; Gary and Scotty careful to keep out of the radius of Johnny's implement of destruction.

Johnny stood motionless with the piece of lumber in a raised position, ready to strike again. As he stood there, he noticed something odd. Where the planks of wood had broken away from the back of the shelving, there appeared to be empty space. He stepped closer, so as to get a better look. As he did so he relaxed and let the wood in his hands drop downward.

"What's wrong?" asked Gary.

Johnny laid the wood on the lower shelves, which had not splintered under the force of his blow. He leaned across the rotted, broken shelving and tried to see what was behind it.

"What?" said Scotty. He and Gary kept their positions.

Johnny, saying nothing, turned and picked up the lamp from the floor. He turned back and held the lamp close to the opening that the broken planks had left in the back of the shelving. The light showed that there was empty space behind the still attached planks. "Wow…'" he said softly.

Gary and Scotty scurried over to see what he was remarking about. Standing on either side of Johnny, they looked at the space between the planks. "What…?" said Scotty. "It's a hole."

"Yeah, but what's in it?" Johnny put his face close to the back of the shelves and tried to see behind them.

"Huh?" Gary did not know what his brother was getting at.

"I'll bet there's treasure behind here." Johnny set the lamp on a shelf and began pulling more planks away from the wall. The wood in the shelving was very old and rotten, and was easily broken.

"Treasure?" Gary immediately started helping Johnny disassemble the shelves.

"Oh boy," said Scotty, joining in.

It only took a moment for the boys to clear a space wide enough for them to get a good look inside the recess, which was about three feet in radius and went back into the earth about the same distance.

"Aw, there's no treasure," said Gary as he squeezed next to Johnny and peered into the hole in the wall.

"Well dummy, they wouldn't leave it uncovered." Johnny found a large piece of glass from the broken jar and leaned over the lower shelves. Reaching inside the recess; he began to scrape away at the soil on the bottom of the hollowed out cavity. The earth was dense and not easy to excavate. After several minutes, Gary and Scotty were beginning to lose interest in the process.

Deciding he had had enough, Gary said, "I'm going up if those wasps have gone away."

"Fine, but if I find a treasure it will belong to me."

"What about me?" said Scotty.

Johnny was also growing a little tired of the exercise, and decided to shift the workload onto Scotty. "You'll have to take your turn at digging."

"Okay." Scotty was not as easily discouraged as Gary.

Just then, Johnny's digging tool hit something solid. "Oh! Wait a minute." Johnny began scraping away at the dirt more vigorously.

"What is it?" Gary's interest had been renewed.

"I found something."

Gary and Scotty squeezed next to Johnny again in an attempt to see what he had found. "Hand me that lamp," said Johnny, elbowing them away from him, and then returning to his scraping. Gary and Scotty both scampered to retrieve the lamp. Scotty got to it first and handed it to Johnny. Johnny placed the lamp inside the recess so that he could see better, then the two younger boys pushed their way back beside him.

The object imbedded in the earth began to take shape as Johnny continued to scrape around it. The three boys fell silent and looked on with anticipation as the object was slowly being revealed; Gary and Scotty watching and Johnny digging.

Each boy refused to let his mind identify the object, which was becoming more and more obvious with each scrape of the glass shard. As Johnny scratched away at the soil the pale rounded shape became exposed; riveting the boys to the sight. With a little more scraping the eye sockets became evident. Finally; when the teeth were exposed there was no doubt in their minds of what lay before them.

Silence filled the space as the boys looked at each other, then to the skull and back to each other again. The faint *buzz* of the surviving wasp brought them out of their daze, and they all backed away from the recess. Without a word from any of them, they scrambled away from the hole and bolted up the stairs and out of the cellar, totally disregarding the still swarming wasps. They raced up the pasture to their grandparents' house, swatting at the few persistent insects that pursued them.

"Mama! Mama!"..."Mom, Dad"…"Mama." The boys burst through the kitchen door; out of breath and each determined to be the first to break the news.

Finding the kitchen empty, they ran, pushing and shoving each other through the house toward the front porch. Lula had heard the commotion and met them in the middle of the living room. Louise, Jesse Mae and Mary were right behind her.

"What's wrong?" asked Lula Mae.

All three of the boys started talking at once. None of the four women could comprehend what they were trying to tell them. What they heard was: "…skeleton…dead man…ghost…cellar…bones…" The women heard enough to alarm them. Lula Mae took Johnny by his shoulders and shook him. "Wait a minute! Wait a minute! I can't hear what any of you are saying. Johnny what happened?"

"We found…" started Gary.

Lula put her hand up to silence him. "No Son, let your brother talk."

"We found a dead man!"

"Good Lord-o-mercy," chimed Mary.

"Walter Scott, what on earth is going on?"

By this time, all of the women were well into the living room with the boys. Scotty ran to be next to his mother. "That's right Mom," he said. "He's in the old root cellar down by the barn."

"A skeleton!" added Gary.

Lula Mae let go of Johnny and stood upright. "Are you boys playing a game with us?"

"No Mama," said Johnny. "We really saw a skeleton in the root cellar."

"A skeleton of a man?" asked Jesse Mae.

"Well…his head."

"Yeah; just his skull."

"His teeth were smiling at us."

"You boys are talking nonsense," said Mary. "Romey, go on back to your playhouse."

Romey disregarded Mary's orders as he stood behind the boys; completely engrossed in what they were saying. He had been rearranging things in his playhouse when he saw the boys run into the house. He had followed them in and now stood listening to their story. Gary and Scotty, tired of being upstaged with the women by Johnny, turned to him as their audience.

"Romey," said Gary. "We found a dead man."

"Yeah, a skeleton."

"Now you boys stop this nonsense!" scolded their grandmother. "There is not a dead man in that root cellar."

"Yes there is, Grandma," insisted Johnny.

"Show me." Lula Mae motioned for the boys to follow her as she started towards the door.

"No! I'm not going back down there," stated Gary, not moving from the spot where he stood.

"Me neither," Scotty backed away from the group as if he were prepared to run if they tried to make him return to the cellar.

"Johnny, come with me. Gary, you and Scotty can stay here." Lula took Johnny's hand and started to go outside.

"Good-Lord, Lula Mae, there is not a dead man in that root cellar. They probably saw a dead raccoon or something."

"No Grandma, it's a skull." Johnny led his mother through the house to the back porch, with Mary protesting all the way; intermittently telling Romey to go back to his playhouse.

"I'll go with you Lula," volunteered Jesse Mae, following behind her sister-in-law.

Louise looked at Scotty. She did not intend to trek down to the barn for what she hoped was a bunch of nonsense; for that matter, she would not even go down there if the boys' story were valid. "Scotty, you better not be lying about this. Don't you let your aunts go down there if there's nothing to be seen."

"Honest Mom, we saw it."

Lula, Johnny, and Jesse Mae began the hike down to the barn. At about the halfway point, Johnny halted.

"What's the matter?" asked Lula Mae.

"I forgot about the wasps."

"What about the wasps?"

"Well, we sort of stirred them up."

"Where?"

"At the barn."

"You mean they're swarming around the cellar?"

"Yeah. We jumped into the cellar to get away from them."

"Johnny Frank, you better not be making all of this up."

"I'm not, Mama."

The trio stood for a moment, not knowing what to do.

"I could put on Papa's bee hood and go on down by myself," said Jesse Mae.

Lula Mae thought for a moment. The idea sounded reasonable, but she felt that she should offer. "You want to do it, or would you rather I did it?"

"I'll do it," said Jesse Mae. "I've had experience with it. I've used it before to get honeycomb." They turned around and headed back to the house.

When they got back to the house, the others were waiting at the back porch. Mary had given up on trying to keep Romey uninvolved. He was too excited about the incident. "I told you they was lying," said Mary as they got closer.

"We don't know that Mama," said Jesse Mae. "There are swarming wasps down there."

"Yeah, we heard." Mary gestured toward Gary and Scotty. "These two told us about trying to blow up that wasps' nest with firecrackers. Scotty got stung and they had to hide in that nasty old cellar. But there's no dead man down there."

"Well, I'm going to put on Papa's bee hood and gloves and go back down there. I don't know if there's any skeleton down there, but somebody has to go put out that kerosene lamp they left burning in the cellar. That old barn could catch fire and burn down."

"What's the matter?" Geneva was looking through the screen door from inside the kitchen. She and Loretta had been upstairs and were unaware of what had been going on.

"We found a dead man!" Gary jumped up onto the porch; finally, maybe somebody would believe him.

The screen door opened as Loretta pushed past Geneva and onto the porch. "You didn't find a dead man," she chided.

"Yes we did," insisted Gary as he jumped off the porch and into the yard. He was too excited to keep still.

Lula Mae caught Geneva's inquisitive stare. "They say they found something in that old root cellar by the barn," she explained.

"Oh." Geneva was not impressed or convinced; she was used to her siblings' pranks.

Loretta, on the other hand was up for some excitement. "Show me," she challenged Gary.

"Aunt Jesse Mae is going to go and get it. There are swarming wasps down there."

Loretta looked at their aunt and then back to Gary, showing her skepticism, "She's going to carry a dead man up from the barn?"

"No stupid," said Johnny stepping up to lend his support to Gary. "It's a skull."

"A skull." Scotty moved toward Loretta, opening his eyes wide so as to convey the horror of it all. He knew she would believe them.

"Your papa will be back from the store with your brothers soon," Mary said to Jesse Mae. "Just you wait and let him go down there and see what's in that cellar."

"What's the matter, Mama? You act like you don't want whatever is down there to be found out."

Mary put her hands on the back of her hips and arched her back in a stance of defiance. "Good Lord-o-mercy, Jesse Mae. Go on! Go on! down there and make a fool of yourself." She turned to go back into the house; stopped and turned to face Jesse Mae again. "But I'll tell you this right now. There is not any dead man in my cellar."

By the time Jesse Mae had walked the distance to the cellar, wearing the bee hood and gloves, she was wondering why she had not let her father do the task. The temperature was pushing ninety degrees and she was soaked with sweat. The wasps were not swarming too badly, but there was no way she was about to remove her protection.

She bent over and looked into the old root cellar. Even with the daylight shining in through the open doorway and the faint light from the lantern below, the cellar was still dark inside. She could see almost nothing from her position. The netting on the bee hood obscured her vision adding to the lack of visibility. 'Oh well,' she thought; then she stepped into the hole in the ground.

The old wooden stairs were rickety as she descended into the shadows of the cellar. The burning lamp gave her a modest amount of light. As she stood on the dirt floor at the bottom of the stairs, waiting for her vision to adjust to the low light, her eyes searched the floor for anything that looked like a skull.

She looked over at the recess in the wall where the lamp was burning. Eying the broken shelving, she thought, 'What on earth were those boys up to?' She moved to the recess and peered inside. It was useless to try to see anything, wearing the bee hood.

She stepped back from the shelves. There did not seem to be any wasps in the cellar with her, so she decided to chance removing the hood. She pulled it up off of her shoulders and over her head. The cool, damp air in the cellar felt good as she shook her head and ran her fingers through her hair.

With her clearer view of the space, she returned to the hole in the wall and leaned over the shelves. The small space was lit up sufficiently for her to see what the boys were talking about. Her first reaction to the sight was to jerk back in revulsion. It was definitely a human skull. She caught her breath and leaned over again. The thing was grotesque. She forced herself to examine it closely. Then she noticed something that the boys had failed to mention; or perhaps had not noticed.

"My God," she said under her breath. Still embedded, but partially protruding from the earth just a short distance from the skull, was something that looked a lot like a tree root; but Jesse Mae was pretty sure that it was a bone.

CHAPTER SIX

"ELL LOOK-A-HERE. I WONDER WHAT HE'S DOING out this way." Frank had spotted the police car ahead of him as he pulled onto the highway.

"Is that Sheriff Files?" Guy repositioned his shoulder, which was pushing against Harold's shoulder. The cab of Frank's old truck was a close fit for three good-sized men. As children there was no problem with the boys fitting on the seat with their father, but that had been many years ago.

"Yeah," said Frank. "He has his light on; must be official business."

They followed behind the police car for a while, speculating about what the sheriff would be doing out their way. Then the car turned off the highway and down the road that led toward Frank and Mary's house. The three men fell silent as Frank turned off the highway right behind the other vehicle.

"There must be something to do with the Mainers," said Frank. "They're the only folks that live down this road except for us."

"Do you think they've done something to get into trouble with the law?" asked Harold.

"Naw, not the Mainers. They're God fearing Christians."

Guy repositioned his shoulder again. "Maybe it's a social call."

"Maybe, but why would he have...his...light...on?" Frank nearly lost his train of thought as the car in front of him passed the turnoff to the Mainers' place. He glanced briefly at Harold and Guy, and then back to the road ahead. The men were growing concerned as they followed the sheriff's car, which had just turned off the road and was now making its way up the drive to Frank and Mary's place.

As they followed behind the sheriff's car, they saw the family standing around the back porch of the house. Mary had begun to wave her hands at them; as if this were the only way anyone would see her and the others there.

Frank had begun to pick up speed when he saw the car turn onto his drive. His truck caught up with the car and the dust rose up around the two vehicles as they arrived at the house and came to a stop simultaneously.

All three men climbed out of the truck, and were quickly joined by the family as they all gathered around the sheriff's car. The door on the driver's side of the vehicle opened and a handsome, dark haired young man, who looked no more than twenty-one years old, stepped out.

"Who are you? Where's Sheriff Files?" Frank stood facing the young man.

"I'm Deputy Sheriff Tony Gavin." The deputy touched the brim of his hat and nodded his head to greet the group. "Sheriff Files is at home with his family. He's taken the Fourth off."

"Oh...well what are you doing here?" Frank looked at Mary as she and the other family members stood by.

"Well if you'd stop asking so many questions and let somebody else talk, maybe somebody would tell you what's going on," said Mary.

"We had a call that somebody had discovered a dead body," said the deputy.

"What the god-damned-hell?" Fear showed on Frank's face as he looked at the group and began counting heads.

"Now Frank just shut up for a minute," said Mary. She was experiencing a mild pleasure at keeping her husband in the dark and letting him worry. She turned to the deputy. "That's right, deputy...well sort of...I guess a skeleton isn't really a body; or is it?"

"Well, no...not really," said the deputy.

"A skeleton?" said Frank. "Who the hell found a skeleton? And where?"

"Relax Papa." Jesse Mae had just exited the house and was walking toward the group. She maneuvered her way around the others and stood next to Frank. "My name is Jesse Mae Burns. I'm the one who called you," she said to the deputy. "I was calling from the Mainers' place up the road." She looked at Frank and continued. "The boys found a skeleton in that old root cellar down by the barn."

Frank looked toward the barn in disbelief. "A skeleton of a man?"

"We don't know, Papa. It could be a woman, I guess."

The deputy slid into the sheriff's car and picked up the microphone, which was hanging from the car's dashboard. He informed the person on the radio that he was at the Austin's farm and that he was going to investigate the possible discovery of human remains by the residents. He said he would call her back when he had completed his preliminary investigation.

With the whole family now gathered around, the deputy was not sure who to address as he exited the car for the second time and closed the door. He stood next to the car looking around at the group. Since Jesse Mae was nearest to him and she had made the call, he decided to direct his attention to her. "Well ma'am, you want to show me this... uh...skeleton?"

"What about the wasps?" said Scotty.

"They should have calmed down by now," said Jesse Mae. "It's down this way." She pointed toward the barn and began walking in that direction. The other family members began to move with her.

The deputy stood where he was. "Hold on there," he said to the others. "I'm going to have to ask you all to stay up here while me and Miss Burns go down there and I examine the scene."

"The hell you say," said Frank. "This is my god-damned farm and if there's a skeleton on it, I'm going to see it."

"Mr. Austin, this is a possible crime scene. Until the time that I determine that there has been no crime committed, I'm afraid that I have to assume full jurisdiction of your place."

"What the hell does that mean?"

"Papa," said Jesse Mae, stopping and turning to Frank. "It means that he is in charge and we have to do as he says."

"Jess, I don't know what's been going on around here, but I'll be damned if I'm going to let some snot-nosed kid come on my property and tell me what to do."

"Sir, please. I don't like doing this any more than you like me doing it. I respect that this is your property; but if a crime has been committed, then I am required by law to take charge of the situation and conduct a thorough investigation. And yes, I know that I'm young, but I am a deputy sheriff and I would appreciate it very much if you would let me do my job…please."

The group stood for a moment with nobody speaking. Then; "I want to see what's down there," said Frank. "So do I." "Me too." Guy and Harold stood fast with Frank.

The deputy thought for a moment. He realized that it would be a problem if he refused to let the men see what was in the cellar. "Look; give me and Miss Burns a five minute head start and then you three men can follow us down there. But don't come into the cellar until I come out and tell you it's okay." He looked at the three men as they stood in silence. "Okay?"

"Good Lord, Frank will you let the young man get on with it so that we can all find out what's in that cellar?" said Mary.

Frank glanced at Mary without speaking, and then turned back to the deputy. "Go on then. We'll give you five minutes." He pulled his pocket watch from the pocket of his overalls and marked the time.

As Jesse Mae had speculated, the wasps had indeed calmed down. There were only a few circling the pasture and they no longer seemed to be bent on revenge for the invasion of their nest. Since the cellar was on the opposite side of the barn from the nest, Jesse Mae and Deputy Gavin were in the clear.

"It's down there." Jesse Mae stood at the open door to the root cellar and pointed into the hole.

Deputy Gavin pushed the switch forward on his flashlight, emitting a strong beam into the shadowy hole. He cautiously stepped onto the wooden stairs.

"Careful," said Jesse Mae. "Some of those stairs are pretty rotten."

"Thanks, I'm okay." The deputy descended into the damp, musty cellar. Quickly locating the recess in the wall, he leaned over the shelves and saw the skull and collarbone. He moved the flashlight around, examining the bones from different angles. There was no doubt in his mind that this was the remains of a human being. The reality of the situation hit him and he began to feel a mild sense of claustrophobia. He felt goose bumps rising up on his neck and arms and he quickly withdrew from the hole.

This was the first time he had encountered a dead person on the job. He had been a deputy sheriff for less than a year and the bulk of his professional experience consisted of breaking up fights at the local bar, intervening in a couple of domestic violence disputes, and filing papers for Sheriff Files. He was anxious about the discovery of these bones and he wanted to make sure that he followed procedures correctly.

He stood for a moment and took a deep breath, recalling instructions from his manual. He directed the flashlight beam around the cellar, looking for any signs of more remains. There was nothing out of the ordinary. He turned back toward the recess in the wall and leaned over to reexamine the bones.

He was engrossed in his examination when he heard a commotion behind him. He pulled out of the recess and turned toward the door of the cellar where he saw somebody coming down the stairs.

"Whoa...whoa...hold it," he said shining the light on the person entering.

"Hell if I will," said Frank, who was now halfway down the stairs, followed closely by Guy and Harold. Frank continued down the stairs and stood in the middle of the cellar. "Where is it?" he asked as Guy and Harold moved into the confined space and stood next to him.

Tony realized that it was useless to try and stop the men now. All he could do was try to keep them from contaminating the scene. "It's in here." Tony stepped to one side and Frank moved to the opening in the wall and looked into it.

"I'll be god-damned. Look at that." Frank stretched out his arm toward the skull.

Tony caught Frank's arm. "You mustn't touch anything! I'm going against regulations just by letting you in here. Now I have to insist; nothing is to be touched!"

"Alright, alright." Frank shook Tony's hand from his arm. He did not reach out again, but he did lean further into the opening in order to get a better look at the skull.

Guy crowded Tony away from the recess and stood next to Frank, looking over his shoulder at the skeleton. "Who do you think that is, Papa?"

Frank pulled back and stood upright, looking at Guy. "How the hell should I know? I didn't bury him here."

Harold moved between his brother and father and took a quick look at the scene; then he made his way to the stairs and out of the cellar. The stale air and heat of the day was making him a little nauseous, besides the sight of the half buried skeleton had satisfied his curiosity.

Frank turned to the deputy. "This old cellar has been down here since before my papa gave me this land. Fur traders dug it. I used to make my moonshine in here." He turned back and leaned in to look at the skeleton again. "That thing must have been down here all this time."

"I'm going to have to ask you gentlemen to leave now. We can all go back up to your house and I will call in my report."

Frank pulled back and stood upright, looking at Tony. He did not give any indication that he was ready to leave. Tony was preparing himself for a more forceful approach when Frank said, "Yeah…okay." To Tony's relief, Frank and Guy turned and climbed up the stairs and out of the cellar.

Louise was waiting on the front porch with Romey and the youngsters when Jesse Mae and the men got back to the house. Tony went to the sheriff's car to call in his report while Guy, Frank and Harold shared their thoughts on the situation with the others. Mary and Lula came out of the house with lemonade for everyone.

"Frank, what do you make of all of this? Who do you think that could have been?" Lula Mae handed Frank a glass.

"Well hell Lula, I don't know. That's what Guy asked me. Just because it's on my land, don't mean I know who it was."

"Why don't one of you kids take that young deputy a glass of lemonade," said Jesse Mae, as she filled an extra glass. "I'm sure he must be thirsty too."

"I will," said Gary. The boys were all impressed that a deputy sheriff was in their midst.

"I'll take it." Geneva picked up the glass of lemonade before Gary could get to it, and stepped off the porch.

"Well…" Gary was left dumfounded by his big sister's odd behavior. It was not like Geneva to volunteer to wait on anybody. Her unusual behavior did not escape Lula and Guy either.

"Wasn't she wearing different clothes a while ago?" asked Guy.

"What?" The question caught Geneva off guard. "Oh…I'm still in school…I'm a senior, though. I'll graduate next year. I'll be almost nineteen then."

"Do you live around here?"

"No, we live in California. We're just visiting my grandparents. How about you? Do you live in Dumas?"

"Yeah, born and raised. What's it like living in California?"

"It's great! I love the beach."

"You go to the beach with your boyfriend?"

"Oh I don't have a boyfriend." Geneva wanted to make that point clear. Then, to let Tony know that she was desirable, she added, "I date a lot, of course; but nobody steady."

"Me neither."

Static crackled over the radio; then a female voice was heard, *"Tony?"* Tony slid into the car seat, leaving one leg outside the car and lifted the microphone from its hook on the dashboard. "Yeah Janice?"

"I talked to Sheriff Files. He said you are to guard the crime scene until he arrives there tomorrow."

"What; spend the night?"

"That's what he said. Said this is the Fourth of July and he's celebrating with his family."

"Well, okay. Thanks, Janice."

"Happy Fourth, Tony. Over"

"Oh…yeah. Happy Fourth, Janice. Over and out." Tony replaced the microphone on its hook. He sat for brief moment looking through the windshield.

"So you're going to spend the night here?"

Tony looked up at Geneva. "I guess so." He brought his right leg out of the car and stood up.

"Well then I'll ask my grandma if you can have dinner with us." Geneva tried not to reveal her excitement at having Tony around all day and evening. She found the family visits here very boring and she was thrilled at the idea of having this handsome young man around to break the monotony. "I'm sure it will be okay."

"That's really nice of you, and I would love to, but I have to keep an eye on that cellar." He looked toward the cellar, which was visible from his car.

"Oh." Geneva looked towards the cellar too. Then she looked back at him. "But how are you going to keep an eye on it after it gets dark?"

Tony was deep in thought. "That's what I'm trying to figure out. I can't drive the sheriff's car through that pasture; I might bottom out and get stuck. He looked at Geneva. "Does that old barn have a back door on it?"

"No, it only has that big door on the other side, away from the cellar."

"Then I can't sleep in the barn."

"Yeah." The two were quiet for a moment as they tried to come up with a solution. They both stood looking across the pasture. Then Geneva turned to him. "Maybe my brothers and sister and I can help you put up some sort of tarp or something down there. Or you could sleep in the cellar. Doesn't it have a kerosene lamp in it? We could give you more kerosene."

"I don't think I want to sleep in that cellar, but your idea for a lean-to sounds like it might work. Are you sure it's not too much trouble?"

"No, it's no trouble." Geneva had no idea how they were going to put up a tarp, but she felt really good about being involved in helping Tony out.

The family members were still on the front porch speculating on the possibilities regarding the skeleton when Geneva returned with two empty glasses.

"Did he leave yet?" asked Frank.

"He's not leaving."

"What do you mean, he's not leaving?"

Geneva explained the situation to her grandfather and the others. "...so I was thinking that the boys could help Ton... the deputy fix up some shelter down there so he would not be out in the open all night while he keeps an eye on the cellar."

Johnny, Gary and Scotty thought this was a great idea. They were very good at building what they referred to as forts.

"Romey can help us," said Johnny, nodding his head towards Romey. "He's pretty good at building forts."

"I'm not going to put that kid up on my property. There ain't nobody going to go near that old cellar."

"Papa," said Jesse Mae. "I would guess that the deputy would like nothing more than to leave right now, but I'm also sure that he has his orders from the sheriff. He can't just leave after finding a buried skeleton."

Frank was seldom, if ever adverse to Jesse Mae's points of view. He was not crazy about the deputy wielding jurisdiction over his property, but he could always be swayed by his only daughter.

"Fine. There's an old tarpaulin down in the barn. Romey knows where the hammer and nails are. Go; go make him a...fort."

CHAPTER SEVEN

B Y SUPPERTIME THE FORT WAS FINISHED. THE boys had nailed the tarp to the side of the barn and stretched it out to meet two poles, which they had sunk into the ground; creating a simple lean-to.

Geneva and Loretta helped Tony clear the weeds and tall grass out from under the tarp. They convinced their grandmother to let them take the fold-up canvas cot out of Romey's playhouse and put it under the tarp for Tony to sleep on, so that he would not have to sleep on the ground. Johnny did not mind giving up the cot for a pallet of quilts on the floor of the cabin.

"This is great," said Tony as he sat on the cot to test its reliability. "Thank you all; thank you very much."

Romey had brought a small table down from his playhouse so that Tony could set the kerosene lamp on it. Loretta had picked a bunch of wildflowers and was arranging them in an old Mason jar, which she had found in the barn.

As a show of appreciation for their help, Tony said that they could all go into the cellar to take a look at the skeleton. Romey declined the offer, but the boys were anxious to get a second look at it; now that they were calm enough to view it in detail. The girls were thrilled to get their first look at it. They thought that Tony had a lot of guts to be willing to spend the night next to the thing.

After they had had enough of the macabre scene, Tony closed the door on the cellar and they all turned their attention to other things. Johnny, Gary, Scotty and Romey began a competition of throwing rocks at a tin can they had found in the barn; and Tony, Geneva and Loretta sat under the lean-to and talked. Tony again expressed his appreciation for their help in constructing his shelter.

"Well, we couldn't let you just sit down here on the ground," said Loretta as she rearranged her flowers.

"Well, look at this." Lula Mae stepped under the tarp, carrying a plate of food, covered with a napkin.

"Yeah, ain't it great?" Loretta abandoned the drooping flowers and spread her arms out in a gesture to present the shelter to her mother.

"Isn't it," chided Geneva from her position on the cot, as the boys and Romey joined them under the tarp.

Loretta ignored the English lesson from her older sister. "What's that?" she asked, indicating the covered plate.

"This is some supper for the deputy. You kids go on up to the house and wash your hands. Grandma and Louise have just about got the food on the table."

"Can we come back later?" asked Gary.

"You kids don't need to be bothering the deputy. Go on now." The youngsters and Romey slowly began to move out from beneath the tarp.

"Oh they're not bothering me, ma'am. I appreciate the company." The youngsters stopped where they were. Lula looked at them as they waited for her response. "Well, maybe you can come back after supper," she said. "But you'll have to be back up to the house before it gets dark. Go on up now."

Gary and Scotty jumped up and down and cheered before sprinting up towards the house, ahead of Romey, Geneva, Loretta and Johnny. Lula set the plate on the small table.

"Thank you, ma'am." Tony lifted the napkin and looked at the food on the plate.

"You're welcome." Lula Mae hesitated for a moment; then, "I was just wondering…"

Tony looked up at her.

"…do you think I could have a look at that skeleton? I've never seen anything like that before."

"Uh…" Tony replaced the napkin. He was pretty sure that Lula would hear from her children that he had allowed them to look in the cellar, so he did not feel that he had much of a choice in the matter at this point. "I don't see why not; couldn't do any harm."

"So that's what a skeleton looks like, huh?" Lula Mae felt a little squeamish with the fact that she was looking at the remains of a human being, but she could not deny the morbid attraction she felt as she observed it.

"It's my first one too," said Tony, standing next to her. "I've only been a deputy for a few months."

Lula was only half listening to him. She stared at the skull and bones. A shiver went through her body and she decided that she had had enough. "Well, thank you deputy." She turned and climbed up the stairs and out of the cellar. Tony followed her out and closed the door again.

"I'd better let you get to your dinner before it gets too cold."

"Thank you again ma'am. I appreciate all that you folks are doing for me."

"We're happy to help out." Lula turned and headed up the pasture while Tony went back to the plate of food, which he began devouring with great appreciation.

"Where the hell have you been?"

"What?" Lula was surprised to find Guy waiting by the fence as she approached it. She had been looking at the ground as she was walking; thinking about the skeleton all the time she had been making her way up the pasture. She had not noticed her husband standing and watching her.

"You been down there flirting with that son-of-a-bitch?"

"Oh for crying out loud." Guy's jealously was nothing new to Lula Mae, but he still caught her off guard from time to time. "I asked him if I could see the skeleton and he let me go into the cellar to see it."

"Yeah, I'll bet he did. Did he go in there with you?"

"What is wrong with you? He's not much more than a kid. He and Geneva like one another."

"I don't want you back down there."

"I don't have any plans of going back down there, but if I want to I will."

"The hell you will. I'll mess his face up; then see how you like him."

"Oh…" Lula stepped between the rails of the fence. "…go on in the house; supper's almost ready."

Once they got inside the house, Guy dropped the whole jealously attitude. Lula Mae went into the kitchen to help the women, and Guy had a cigarette on the front porch and waited with the rest of the family for supper to begin. Before long the meal was being served. Romey and the youngsters ate at the kitchen table while the adults ate in the dining room. With thirteen people eating at once, they were short one chair, so Scotty got to sit on the butter churn. Lula took care of serving the youngsters, while the adults served themselves.

Eventually the conversation at the adults' table got around to the imprudence of Frank and Mary during their younger days. Mary vehemently denied any responsibility for the indiscretion; claiming that Frank had manhandled her and gave her no choice but to submit to his advances.

At this point in the conversation, Lula got up from the dining table and closed the door between the kitchen and the dining room. She did not feel like explaining to her children what the term, manhandled meant.

"Oh Mama, it's always Papa's fault if something goes wrong, isn't it?" said Jesse Mae.

Mary looked from Louise to Lula. "You see what I mean?" She pitched her head towards Jesse Mae to indicate that it was Jesse Mae's last comment, which she was referring to. "They gang up against me. They always hold up for one another."

Frank understood who the word 'they' meant, but he chose not to defend himself against such foolishness and he simply ignored his wife and continued eating.

"Who, Mama; who gangs up against you?" Getting no response to her question, Jesse Mae just shook her head. Then she continued, "Why was Papa to blame for your indiscretion?"

"I don't want to talk about it." Mary took a bite of chicken and mashed potatoes and looked past her daughter at the blank wall as she chewed her food in silence. She knew that this would make Jesse Mae mad.

"Jess, let's just drop it," said Harold. He was sorry now that he had even brought up the subject of the marriage license in the first place. Now that it was all out in the open, it did not seem so important after all.

Jesse Mae however was not so willing to let her mother off the hook. "No, I don't want to drop it. She's always pretending to be so upstanding; acting like she's such a good wife and mother. And now we find out that she was a loose woman."

"Don't you talk to me like that! I told you I was manhandled. And what do you know about being a wife and a mother? What kind of wife is married to a man old enough to be her father? And as for being a mother; I guess we'll never know about that will we?"

Jesse Mae glared at her mother for a moment without speaking; then, "No Mama," she said quietly. "I guess we won't."

The room fell silent. Everybody at the table knew that Jesse Mae was unable to have children. The specific reason as to why she could not give birth had never been revealed to them, and it was rarely mentioned.

The door to the kitchen slowly opened about halfway. Loretta stuck her head through the narrow opening. It was obvious to everyone that she had heard the last part of the conversation. Lula knew that she would have to explain it all later on.

"We're finished eating," said Loretta, entering the dining room; followed by all the other youngsters and Romey. "Can we go back down to the barn?"

Lula looked at Guy. "I told them they could go back down there if they would be back up here to the house before dark."

"Fine." Guy was more concerned with eating at this point than what his children were doing.

"You be careful, Romey," said Mary. "Make sure you're back up here before dark."

"Okay Mama."

"We'll be setting the fireworks off right after dark," said Harold, trying to elevate the mood of the group. "Whoever comes back up in time can help us set off the rockets."

"I'll be back in time," said Scotty.

"Me too," said Gary. He and Scotty were still very impressed with the deputy, but there was no way they were going to miss setting off the fireworks.

Gary and Scotty noticed that Johnny and Romey were already out of the house so they ran to catch up with them; leaving Geneva and Loretta behind. Geneva looked at her mother as if she wanted to say something.

"What is it, Geneva?"

"Can Loretta and I watch the fireworks with Tony?"

"Who's Tony?" asked Guy, knowing perfectly well who Tony was.

"The deputy," said Loretta.

"It'll be dark when we set off those fireworks. I'm not having my daughters alone with some strange man after dark."

"Daddy, he's a deputy sheriff." Geneva looked from Guy to Lula.

"Why don't you let them stay down there for a while? It won't hurt nothing. They can each carry a lantern and I'll go down and walk them back up."

Guy looked at Lula. "I'll go down and get them when the fireworks are finished."

Geneva beamed with happiness. "Can we take him a piece of cake?"

"Why sure you can," said Mary. "And you can take him some hot coffee too." She looked at Jesse Mae as if to say, 'See what a good grandma I am.'

Half an hour before nightfall, the boys and Romey were ready to head up to the house to help Guy and Harold set off the fireworks. They each carried an armful of sticks, and they dropped them in the middle of a cleared space that they had all worked on earlier so that Tony and the girls could build a campfire next to the lean-to.

Geneva sat on one of several apple crates that she and Loretta had placed around the space, and Loretta was arranging the sticks for the fire.

"Come on Romey," said Johnny, grabbing Romey's hand and pulling him behind him as he made a break for the house. Scotty and Gary immediately followed, in an attempt to overtake them and win the race.

"Tell Mama and Daddy that we're going to build a fire, so they won't be worried when they see it," called Geneva to her departing brothers. She got no response from them, as they raced up the pasture, but she assumed that they had heard her and would do as she asked.

Tony, who had excused himself for a moment came around a corner of the barn carrying an armful of miscellaneous pieces of lumber to add to the pile that the boys had started. "Are you sure that it's okay with your grandpa if we burn this wood?"

"Yeah, he won't care," said Loretta, not knowing at all what her grandfather would think about them burning the wood from a pile of scrap lumber that they had found inside the barn.

Tony arranged a few sticks over the pile of kindling and dry grass that Loretta had prepared. Loretta had the book of matches, which Johnny had snitched earlier. She struck a match and lit the fire. In a moment the sticks ignited and Tony added some larger pieces.

Soon the fire was burning nicely and the three of them sat around it watching the flames. After a while, the conversation reached a lull and each one of them sat quietly waiting for someone to speak. "Have you ever killed anybody," asked Loretta, proud of herself for thinking of something to say.

"No," said Tony.

There was another brief moment of silence. Loretta abruptly stood up and said, "I'm going up to help with the fireworks." She began walking away.

"No," said Geneva. "You can't go back up; Daddy will make me come up if you do."

Loretta stopped and looked back at the others. She shrugged her shoulders. "Oh well." Then she turned and walked toward the house.

Geneva and Tony glanced quickly at one another and then Geneva turned back and watched Loretta walking away. "Now Daddy will make me come up to the house too."

"Maybe not," said Tony. "I'm glad she left." Geneva looked back at him. "It's not that I don't like her or anything," he said. "It's just that I like being alone with you."

"Oh." Geneva could not hold back her smile. "I like it too."

"What are you doing up here?" Guy stopped pounding the stem of the rocket into the ground when he saw Loretta approaching. "Where's Geneva?"

"She's still down there with Tony." Loretta rolled her eyes from one side to the other to indicate a sense of monotony. "I got bored. I want to help with the fireworks."

"No you don't. You go down there and get your sister. Tell her that I said she has to come up now."

"Oh Daddy, I don't want to. I want to help with the fireworks."

"We're not ready to set them off yet. Go on, do what I tell you."

"Cripes!" Loretta stomped her feet and turned to go back to the barn.

Lula was sitting on the front porch with the other women. She had heard the conversation between Loretta and Guy. She called out as Loretta walked past her. "Loretta." Loretta stopped and looked at her mother. Lula continued, "Never mind; leave Geneva alone."

Guy gave the rocket stem one last pound into the ground and stood looking toward the porch.

"Fine," said Loretta and sat down on the steps of the porch.

Guy walked over to Lula. "I said for her to go get her sister."

"And I said never mind. Geneva is just fine right where she is."

"I'll be god-damned." Guy turned away from Lula and then turned back to face her. "She is not going to sit down there with that man where we can't see what's going on."

"If you'll look, you can see them. They're sitting by a fire they made."

The group all looked toward the barn. They could see the fire clearly, but Geneva and Tony were just indistinct forms of muted colors.

"I can't see what they're doing."

"You're not supposed to see what they're doing. Geneva is a good girl. She's not going to do anything she's not supposed to do." As the last words were coming out of her mouth, Lula Mae realized that her statement would seem like a judgement directed at Mary. She glanced apologetically at her.

"Don't look at me that way," said Mary. "I was a good girl too. Nasty men don't care if a girl says no."

Lula looked back at Guy. "She's fine. Let her be. Why don't..." She was interrupted by a rapidly escalating series of pops, whizzes and whistles. Harold had set off a few of the fireworks that did not need darkness to be enjoyed. The youngsters were cheering. Guy immediately turned and hurried back to join them; conceding to Lula's wishes. Right now, he had more important things to think about.

As soon as the sky turned dark, Guy and Harold set off the rest of the fireworks; allowing the youngsters to ignite a few under their supervision. The effect was spectacular. Everyone enjoyed it. Then they all went into the house to have some homemade ice cream.

Everyone had had their fill of ice cream. Romey and the children were in the living room playing checkers. The adults were at the dining room table. Guy set his empty ice cream bowl down on the table and looked at Lula Mae. "Well?"

"Yes, Honey, it's time for her to come up now. Go on down after her."

Geneva slapped a mosquito on her neck. She was glad that she had taken her mother's advice and changed into Levis and a long sleeved shirt. The fireworks had been over for at least half an hour. She was expecting her father to be walking down the pasture at any minute.

Her visit with Tony had been wonderful. It was almost like being on a date. Contrary to what she had told Tony, dating was something she had very little experience at. She had been to a few school dances, but being in a crowd was not the same as being alone with a boy. Her father always insisted that she come straight home after the dances. She did not have a boyfriend, so on Saturday nights she usually wound up going to the movies with her girlfriends.

"If you let your hair down, it might help keep the mosquitoes off your neck." Tony got up and placed another board on the fire and then moved back to his apple crate next to Geneva.

"Yeah, I guess you're right." Geneva took hold of the rubber band, which held her hair in a pony tail. "It's too hot to wear it down in the daytime." She began struggling to loosen her hair. "Darn! My hair is tangled in the rubber band."

"Can I help?"

Geneva felt her pulse quicken, and a surge of adrenalin through her body at the thought of Tony's hands in her hair. "Uh...sure."

They had been sitting side by side so that they could each watch the fire. Tony now turned to face her. Her heart beat even faster when he pulled his apple crate close and she felt his legs; one against her hip and one against her knee. She turned her face away from him to make it easier for him to reach her pony tail. She could feel the gentle tugging on her scalp as he worked with it.

The task proved to be a little more difficult than Tony had imagined. He edged toward her and rested one arm against the top of her shoulders. She felt herself leaning towards him. She could feel his breath on the back of her neck as he brought his face nearer, in an effort to see the rubber band more clearly.

Finally she felt her hair spring free and tumble down. Tony's hand rested on her shoulder as she turned her face toward him. She had seen this scene in movies many times, and she could not believe that she was actually living it. Tony leaned in and she closed her eyes just as their lips touched.

"Aghh! What are you doing?" Geneva pushed Tony away from her and wiped her shirt sleeve across her mouth.

"What's the matter?" said a bewildered Tony.

"You put your tongue on my mouth."

Tony was confused. "I was kissing you."

Geneva suddenly realized that she had overreacted to a simple act of affection. She had never been *French kissed* before, and Tony had taken her off guard. "Oh," she said quietly.

"You've never been kissed before have you?"

"Yes I have...well...not like that."

"If I don't use my tongue, can I kiss you again?"

A wave of relief flowed over Geneva. She had feared that she had spoiled the mood. She was happy to get another chance. "Uh...yeah, okay."

Tony leaned toward her again and pressed his lips gently against hers; this time she offered no resistance. It was a brief innocent kiss. He drew back and looked into her eyes.

Geneva took a deep breath and mustered her courage. "Would you like to kiss me that other way?"

Tony put his hands on Geneva's knees. "Turn around this way," he said, pulling gently. Geneva brought her knees around and faced him. Tony inched forward, hugging her legs with his own. He held her hands in his and pulled them to his chest. He leaned toward her. "Just let your lips relax," he whispered. "And they'll part a little."

Their lips met again and Tony very slowly slid his tongue between Geneva's lips. It felt strangely wonderful to Geneva and it was over much too quickly. They sat looking at one another in the dim light cast by the fire and lantern.

After a moment, Geneva leaned toward Tony and he kissed her again. She reciprocated this time and found herself totally caught up in the moment. The kiss ended and they sat holding each other's hands.

"I like you very much," said Tony.

"I like you too." They looked at one another for a moment and then Geneva looked toward the house. Her body suddenly grew rigid and her grip tightened on Tony's hands. Her jaw dropped and she drew in a deep breath.

"What?" Tony looked to see what had startled her.

Geneva let go of Tony's hands and moved her apple crate away from his. Halfway down the pasture walked a pair of shadowy figures carrying a lantern.

"I hope he didn't see us."

"That's not your dad."

Geneva's panicked response to the thought of being caught kissing Tony by her father had clouded her judgement. She looked more closely now. Then she heard the faint sing-song taunt from her kid sister, "...k-i-s-s-i-n-g."

A moment later Loretta and Johnny approached within a clear hearing distance of the couple. "You better be glad that Daddy didn't want to come and get you," said Loretta. "We could see what you guys were doing."

"Hi you guys," said Tony; downplaying the fact that the two youngsters had seen Geneva and him kissing. "Those were some fireworks, huh?"

"Yeah," said Johnny, forgetting about the gibe.

"So what have you two love bugs been doing all this time?" Loretta was not going to let them off the hook so easily.

"Loretta, don't tell Mama and Daddy," said Geneva. "You neither, Johnny."

Johnny shrugged his shoulders. "Why would I tell? You weren't doing anything wrong."

"Loretta?"

"What do I get if I don't tell?"

"What do you want?"

Loretta pulled an apple crate closer to the fire and sat down. She rested her elbows on her knees and her jaw in her hands. "Hmmm."

Geneva exchanged a glance with Tony, hoping that Loretta would agree to remain mum. Tony looked at Loretta.

"Geneva tells me that you guys like ghost stories; is that right?"

Loretta's head remained resting in her palms as her eyes turned up to meet Tony's. "Yeah."

"How would you like to see a real ghost?"

Loretta dropped her hands and sat upright. "What do you mean?"

Johnny pulled up an apple crate and sat down.

"If you and Johnny promise not to tell on your sister, I'll take you to see a real ghost some night…that is if your mama and daddy will let me."

"What kind of ghost? Where?" Loretta looked at Johnny and Geneva.

"There's no such thing," said Johnny.

"I swear it's true." Tony raised his right hand as if in a courtroom. "She's in an old house just off the road to town. If I take you guys there, you will either hear her or see her."

Johnny and Loretta looked at one another and came to a silent agreement. "Okay," said Loretta. She stood up. "We better get back up to the house before Daddy comes down here after us." Johnny stood up and he and Loretta began walking away.

Tony put his hand up and gave a small wave to them. "Good-night you guys. I'll see you in the morning."

Geneva grabbed Tony's hands. She leaned over and gave him a quick kiss and then stood up. "Good-night." She picked up her lantern and ran to catch up to her siblings.

CHAPTER EIGHT

GARY AWOKE AT THE SOUND OF A car door closing. He slowly opened his eyes and gazed sleepily at the inside wall of Romey's playhouse. The night before had been very warm, so instead of crawling into his sleeping bag, he had gone to sleep on top of it. He remembered dreams of being chased by skeletons during the night. Now he found himself lying on the bare floor next to the pile of fabric, which was his sleeping bag. He heard voices coming from somewhere outside the playhouse. He rolled over to see Johnny's pallet and Scotty's sleeping bag were both empty.

The familiar smell of frying bacon and sausage permeated the morning air. Gary got up from the floor and slipped on his Levis. Looking through the screen door, he saw most of the family on and around the back porch. He exited the playhouse and walked up to his mother, who was standing in the yard. Without speaking, Lula Mae put one arm around him and immediately returned her attention to the deputy, who was standing next to an older policeman who had apparently just arrived.

The two policemen were talking to each other. They stopped talking and both turned and walked toward the family. The older man addressed the family. "Morning folks." He touched the brim of his hat and nodded to them.

"Hey Karl," said Frank. Mary came out of the kitchen and stood on the back porch.

The sheriff turned back to the deputy. "So where's this corpse?"

"It's down by the barn." Tony pointed toward the old cellar.

"Nobody's disturbed anything?"

"No sir. I slept down there all night. I've kept the area in view since I arrived yesterday...uh, except for the few minutes when I went to the outhouse."

"Unh-huh. Well, let's get down there. I want to see this."

"Would you like some coffee, Sheriff Files?" asked Mary with a welcoming smile. Sheriff Files had held his office for many years. Most of the farmers and townspeople were acquainted with him.

"Maybe later, Mary. Thanks."

The two police officers walked across the yard towards the barn. The sheriff stopped abruptly and turned around. Frank, Guy, Harold, Johnny, Loretta, Gary and Scotty were all right behind him. "Are you all planning on going down there?"

"Guy and Harold and me will go," said Frank. He pointed his finger toward the house. "You kids stay here. Get on back to the house."

The youngsters stood where they were and gave no indication that they were about to follow their grandfather's orders. "God-damn-it," said Frank. "You kids can't all go traipsing down there. This is official business." He looked at Guy and Harold as if to say, 'Do something.'

"Daddy, I want to go," said Loretta.

"No," said Guy. "You kids go on back and finish your breakfast."

All of the boys turned to go, but Loretta stood fast.

"Honey," called Guy to Lula Mae.

The women had returned to the kitchen. Lula could see what was going on from the kitchen window. She called out, "Loretta, Johnny and Gary; get up here!"

The youngsters knew that the tone in their mother's voice meant there would be no negotiations on the matter. With a sullen expression on her face, Loretta turned and slumped behind her brothers and cousin as they all walked back towards the house.

The sheriff was larger than the average man. He stood six feet tall and weighed about two-hundred-fifty pounds. He was not too enthused about crawling down into a dark hole in the ground. With more than a little effort, he made his way down the steps. Once inside the cellar, he stood for a moment, looking about.

"It's over here," said Tony, pointing toward the recess.

The sheriff stepped to the opening in the wall and leaned over the shelves; examining the scene inside. He shined his light around inside the recess and brought it back to the skull. "Yep, that's a human skull alright."

A little over five minutes passed and the two men emerged from the cellar. "Frank," said the sheriff. "I'm going to have to ask you to let me open up this cellar."

"What do you mean? …It is open."

"What I mean is take the top off. It's too damn dark down there to see anything properly."

"Oh," said Frank with a look of indecisiveness. "I don't know…"

"Frank, you've never used this old trappers' cellar for anything but your moonshine, years ago. You have your other cellar up by your house. This is just a place where kids can get into trouble. I'll send someone out to fill it up after we're through here if you want; maybe even pay you a little something for your inconvenience. "

"Oh…well okay; tear it off."

Sheriff Files turned to his deputy. "Tony, see if you can round up some tools from Frank here, and then I want you to tear the top off of this old cellar. I'll go back up to my car and fill out the necessary forms on my preliminary findings. After the cellar is open, I'll inspect the site in detail."

"Yes sir," said Tony, looking to Frank.

"There are a couple of shovels in the barn," said Frank. "That'll get you started with the dirt on top. I'll have one of the kids bring down a crowbar and a hammer."

Tony nodded his head to Frank. "Thanks." Then he proceeded to the barn.

"Make damn sure you don't disturb anything below," said the sheriff.

"I won't sir."

The four older men began making their way back up to the house and Tony went into the barn. The big door creaked on its rusted hinges as he pulled it open, allowing the morning light inside. Against the far wall, he spotted two shovels. As he walked toward the shovels, he thought that he heard a strange sound. He stopped and looked around. The barn was quiet; then he heard it again. He could not quite identify the sound. He turned to his left, and then to his right. He fixed his eyes on the dark corner, which the daylight had not reached. "Is somebody there?"

Silence was the only response to his inquiry. He stood for a moment, listening. Deciding that it was nothing, he turned back in the direction of the shovels. The sound again! He spun around with his hand on his holstered pistol. He halted abruptly when he saw a mother hen with her chicks meandering through the open door of the barn. He relaxed his stance and turned back toward the shovels; thankful that nobody had been there to see him as he almost took out a mother hen.

He took a step toward the tools, but halted once more. There was no doubt now, he had heard the noise again. This time he knew it had come from the dark corner of the barn. Suddenly snickering rose out of the darkness, as he saw two heads of red hair emerging into the light.

"What are you two doing in here?"

"Shhh." Loretta waved her hand at Tony. "Don't let Daddy know we're in here."

Johnny ran to the open door and peeked around the corner. "They're gone. They're headed back up to the house."

"Well, let's get digging." Loretta walked to where the shovels stood against the wall and took hold of one.

Frank, his two sons and the sheriff climbed the steps of the front porch. "Have a seat Karl," said Frank, gesturing toward several chairs on the porch as he eased himself into his rocking chair.

Lula Mae pushed the screen door open and came out and stood on the porch, holding the door open while Geneva; carrying a tray, maneuvered through the doorway. The tray held four cups of hot coffee, a small pitcher of cream, and a bowl of sugar with a spoon in it. Geneva set the tray on a small table so that the men could help themselves, and then she went back into the house.

The women joined the men on the front porch to hear what the sheriff had to say. Romey came out of the house and stood quietly next to Frank. Geneva, Gary and Scotty sat on the sofa inside the living room peering over its back at the adults through the large open screened window.

"The sheriff's having his deputy pull the top off of that old cellar so that he can examine those bones," said Frank.

"What do you think happened down there Sheriff?" Jesse Mae sat in the porch swing with Louise.

"I don't know, Jesse Mae; I couldn't tell much in that dark cellar."

"That's probably an Indian," said Louise. "I've read about other bones being dug up around these parts; along with pottery, arrowheads and things like that. Experts estimated the things had been buried more than a hundred years."

The sheriff took a long slow sip from his coffee cup then set it on the small table next to his chair. "Well, I don't want to go jumping to any conclusions; not before I do a thorough investigation."

"I'll head up to the house and bring back a hammer and a crowbar," said Johnny as he was walking away from Tony and Loretta.

"Don't tell Daddy that I'm down here." Loretta added a little skip to her step as she walked across the dirt floor of the barn; eager to get started on the cellar.

Fifteen minutes later, she and Tony had made notable progress in their effort to remove the soil, which had covered the rafters and planks that formed the roof of the old root cellar. They stopped their work when Johnny, Gary and Scotty joined them, huffing and puffing from their race down the pasture. The boys dropped the tools, which they had carried with them and took a moment to catch their breath.

Halfway between the house and the barn, walked Geneva and Romey. Geneva was carrying a bucket, which Tony hoped was filled with water. It was only a little past nine a.m. but the temperature had climbed rapidly after the summer sun had risen above the forest trees.

"Here, you dig for a while." Loretta thrust her shovel at Johnny.

"I'll dig," said Gary.

"Me too." Scotty ran to Tony, anxious to have the shovel passed on to him.

Tony released his grip on the shovel as Scotty pulled on it. "Have you kids ever read Tom Sawyer?"

"Who's Tom Sawyer?" asked Johnny.

"He's that kid that got those other kids to paint the fence for him." Loretta plopped down on an apple crate.

"Oh yeah," said Johnny. "Like Alfalfa, in *The Little Rascals*." He pulled up an apple crate for himself and sat down next to Loretta. He and Loretta giggled as they watched Gary and Scotty struggling with the shovels.

"Hi," said Tony as he walked to meet Geneva and Romey. He reached for the bucket. "Let me help you with that."

Geneva loosened her grip on the bucket handle and allowed Tony to take it. "It's cool well-water. I thought you might be getting thirsty."

"You were right. Thanks." Tony stopped walking and dipped the dipper into the water and lifted it to his lips, taking several swallows.

Just before Geneva and Romey had started towards the barn, Mary had reminded Romey that he was not to do any running. Romey, however, was excited and anxious to join the youngsters in what looked like fun to him, so when Geneva and Tony stopped and left him on his own, he forgot his mother's instructions and continued on; hurrying to the others with an awkward, somewhat clumsy gate; half walking and half running.

Geneva made no effort to prevent Romey from disobeying Mary's orders as she watched him gain distance from Tony and her. After Tony had had his fill of water, he and Geneva continued on; walking slowly.

"I had a good time last night." Geneva looked at the ground and kicked a dirt clod, avoiding Tony's eyes.

"Me too. You didn't tell anyone about the kissing did you?"

"Oh gosh no!" Geneva looked up at Tony. "I wouldn't want my daddy to know."

"Good; cause I don't want him to know either."

Geneva smiled, and then turned her attention to the others just ahead of them. "So who do you think that is in the cellar?"

"I don't know. It looks like it's been down there for years."

It took almost an hour for them to remove the remaining soil from over the cellar. The late morning sun had already begun to dry the clods of dirt that were tossed aside. Tony, in concern for the youngsters' safety, told everyone to stand back and allow him, alone to remove the roof of the cellar, consisting of several heavy beams and planks.

Leaving it practically intact, he dragged the roof away from the hole and allowed the others to move closer to get a new look at the inside.

They all stood around the open pit, looking, with renewed interest, at the now more visible details of the site.

The faint sound of a high pitched whistling noise made the group look toward the house where the sound had originated. Guy stood at the fence waving to them. "Dinner," he called; barley audible to them.

"This is mighty nice of you folks to feed me and my deputy this way," said the sheriff as he dipped what was left of his biscuit into the chicken gravy on his plate.

In many of the farming households, the noon meal had long been the main meal of the day. The tradition had carried over from the times when the men and boys had toiled in the fields, tending crops; and a hearty meal was needed to give them energy to finish out their day. Supper; the evening meal, usually consisted of leftovers from this meal. Though none of the family members worked the fields any longer, this tradition had continued in Mary and Frank's household.

"It's our pleasure, sheriff," said Mary as she offered the platter half full of fried chicken to him. "Please have another piece of chicken."

"Thank you ma'am." The sheriff took another thigh. "I reckon it would be alright if the lot of you wants to come down to the cellar and take a look when my deputy and me go back down there."

"I'd like to get a better look at it," said Jesse Mae.

"Well you won't catch me hiking down that pasture," said Louise. "You all will just have to tell me about it."

"I've already seen it, so I'll stay up here with you," said Lula.

"Now Lula Mae, you know you want to go back down there," said Mary. "I'm not going to traipse down that pasture. These old bones of mine would be hurting all night. Louise and me will stay here; the rest of you can go on down there and look."

"Well, okay." Lula Mae was pleased by her mother-in-law's willingness to stay with Louise. She had only volunteered to stay, out of consideration for Louise. She really wanted to get a better look at the skeleton.

While the adults sat around the dining room table, the younger children and Romey sat at the kitchen table. Johnny and Loretta had begun to lose interest in the skeleton and were busy speculating about how they were going to manage visiting the haunted house that Tony had told them about.

Sheriff Files had instructed Tony to stay outside and keep an eye on the cellar, so Geneva had joined him outdoors to eat with him. Romey had planted a small cluster of pine trees next to the house, amongst which Frank had built him a table with a couple of benches. It was relatively cool in the shade of the trees and that is where the couple had decided to sit.

"What will the sheriff do with those bones?" Geneva poured herself more iced tea.

"Well, I'm not sure," said Tony. "I imagine we'll box them up and take them into town."

"And then what?"

"Uh…we'll try to determine how long they've been buried; check our missing person's files…stuff like that."

"My grandpa isn't in any trouble over this is he?"

Tony was caught off guard by Geneva's question. He had not really considered that Mr. Austin might be under suspicion for any wrongdoing. "What? No…no of course not. Like I said; those bones have been down there a long time."

By two p.m. the meal was over, the dishes washed and put away and everyone had rested a bit. The hottest part of the day was ending and Mary had allowed Romey to get up from his mid-day nap.

The men of the family sat on the front porch talking with the sheriff, all of them waiting for the heat of the day to subside before heading down to the old cellar. Mary opened the screen door onto the porch. "Guy, you and Harold watch Romey, and don't let him overtire his self. It's still pretty hot." Romey passed through the doorway and onto the porch.

"We'll take care of him, Mama," said Guy as Romey walked toward him.

The sheriff stood up from his chair. "I don't reckon it's going to get much cooler. Let's go see what we got down there."

The group stood around the open pit that had been the root cellar. The sheriff and his deputy were the only ones in the hole. They had removed the remaining shelving from the side of the cellar and the sheriff was working with a small garden spade, which he had borrowed from Mary. He was carefully digging around the bones; gradually revealing the skeleton.

As he continued to dig, he discovered in the clay surrounding the skeleton; what appeared to be a hunting knife made out of bone, a couple of objects that were obviously the remnants of leather moccasins, and what he was pretty sure was a braid of black hair. Tony was photographing the items with a flash camera, which Sheriff Files had brought with him for this purpose.

As the digging got nearer to the bones and skull, the sheriff put down the spade and continued scraping away the damp earth with a pocketknife. As he cleared the earth from beneath the skull, his knife came across something hard. "Hmmm…what's this? Looks like…some kind of…" He dug a little more and then picked something out of the soil with his fingers. He held the object up for a better look. "It's an arrowhead; an Indian arrowhead." He turned toward Tony and held the item in front of him. "Tony, take a picture of this."

Tony snapped the picture and the sheriff placed the v-shaped stone aside and continued to dig with his pocketknife. In just a few minutes he had dug up seven arrowheads; all of which had been buried beneath the neck and collarbone of the skeleton. He placed the stones in a semicircular pattern on the ground next to him. "Hmmm…must have been some kind of necklace." He looked up. "Well Frank, looks like you have yourself an archeological specimen here."

"What the hell does that mean?" said Frank.

"That means that this is not a crime scene." The sheriff looked at Harold. "Your missus was right, Harold. She said that this was probably an old Injun. The thing has probably been under this ground a hundred years."

"That's a Indian skeleton?"

"Must be. All this stuff looks like authentic Indian relics to me. If you don't mind, I'll take them with these bones and give everything to the college in Little Rock. They have ways of determining how old things are. The relics are technically your property. If you want, I'll return them to you but I'm sure the college would like to have them to study."

"Aw hell," said Frank with a wave of his hand. "Take the whole lot. I don't want that stuff." He looked at Romey and then back to the sheriff. "But I want Romey to have one of them arrowheads. He collects them."

"Sure; no problem with that." The sheriff offered Frank an arrowhead.

"No Papa!" Romey looked at the item still in the sheriff's hand with fear in his eyes. "I don't want one."

"Oh my Lord." Jesse Mae put her arm over Romey's shoulders and pulled him to her. "Romey, don't be scared. That's not a real Indian down there. That's just some old dog's bones. Come on I'll take you back to the house." Jesse Mae began walking away with Romey.

"I'll go with you," said Lula Mae. Her curiosity had been satisfied, and she no longer found the skeleton of interest. "Geneva, you and Loretta come with me. I want you to help me with some laundry."

The girls had also lost their interest in the old cellar. They followed their mother without protest, making their way up the pasture.

Johnny picked up a small rock and threw it at the tin can that he and the others had been using as a target earlier. The sound of the can being hit with the rock inspired Gary and Scotty to join him and they wandered away from the edge of the cellar to enjoy their target practice.

After concluding that this was not a crime scene, the mood of the men had lifted and they began to banter with one another. Frank, Harold, and Guy pulled up apple crates and sat on the edge of the hole watching the other two men as they finished extricating the complete skeleton from the clay and documenting it with photographs and notes.

Mary did not like the look in Romey's eyes as he and Jesse Mae walked up the steps to the front porch where she and Louise sat. She looked at Jesse Mae. "What's wrong?" she said in an accusatory tone.

Jesse Mae still had one arm around Romey's shoulder. "He's alright." She pulled Romey closer to her. "Aren't you, Son?"

"Don't call him Son!" Mary was on her feet now.

"Oh Mama, for Christ's sake!"

"And don't you take the Lord's name in vain while you're under my roof." Mary reached out and pulled Romey away from Jesse Mae's grasp and drew him close to herself. "Now, what's the matter with him?"

"It's those god-damned bones. He's scared of them."

Mary pressed her lips together tightly and glared at her daughter for defying her edict on language.

"Oh good Lord." Jesse Mae let her shoulders drop and shook her head as she walked inside the house.

Mary walked with Romey to the porch swing with her arm around his shoulders and sat him down there. She said to him, as she sat next to him, "You just never mind about those old bones, Son."

"What does the sheriff think about them?" Louise asked as Lula Mae climbed the steps.

"He thinks they belonged to an Indian; like you said. He said they might have been buried down there for more than a hundred years."

"Well, that's a relief." Louise looked at her mother-in-law. "I was afraid he might have suspected some foul play from some of us."

"Humph," snorted Mary. "Any foul play going on around here...we all know whose bones they'll find."

"Romey, did you like those fireworks last night?" said Lula Mae in an attempt to redirect the conversation.

Tony used the time spent at the root cellar to work on winning Guy over. He made an effort to be friendly and impress Guy with his maturity and good manners. He really liked Geneva and he knew that if he was going to have a chance of seeing her after he and Sheriff Files left the farm today, he would have to get on the good side of her father. His plan worked. In spite of himself, Guy could not help but like the young man. He was very polite and well mannered and showed a lot of good sense.

The afternoon sun was beating down on the two lawmen, and Sheriff Files was hot and tired; so it was not long before he decided that they had dug up all of the bones and artifacts that they were going to find. He and Tony placed the items in gunny sacks that Frank had given them, and carried them up the pasture to the house, where they loaded the sacks into the sheriff's car trunk.

As a matter of routine, when the sheriff took time off and left Tony on duty, he left the police station's only official automobile with the deputy and took the deputy's personal car for his own use. He had driven to the farm in Tony's car, so the two men proceeded to switch their personal items from the other's vehicle to his own. The sheriff then said his good-byes to the family and got into the police car and drove away, leaving the family standing around the deputy's car, waiting to say good-bye to him.

Tony stood next to his car with the driver's door open. He looked at Geneva, who was nodding her head slowly; silently encouraging him to follow the plan that she and he had discussed earlier.

"Mr. Austin," said Tony.

The three older men in the family all responded to him.

"Uh...I mean Guy."

"Yeah Tony; what is it?" Guy had begun calling Tony by his first name while they were down at the cellar.

"I was just wondering if you and Mrs. Aust...I mean Lula Mae; would mind if I took Geneva to the movies tonight."

"I want to go to the show," piped Gary.

"Me too," said Scotty, pulling at his mother's dress sleeve.

Immediately, Tony realized that if he invited the younger children, it would increase his chances of getting a date with Geneva. "Sure; I have room in my car for all the kids."

"I don't know," said Guy.

"Why don't we all go?" Lula looked around at the others. "Louise, you and Harold like to go to the picture show don't you?"

"Yeah, sure," said Harold.

"Walter Scott!" Louise pulled Scotty's hand away from her sleeve, terminating his mute plea to go to the movies. She turned back to Lula Mae. "I think it might be fun." She looked at Mary. "Who else wants to go?"

"You're not getting me to go to one of those vulgar moving picture shows," said Mary. "And Romey don't want to go either."

"Aw Mama." Romey was disappointed, but he knew that it was of no use to argue about it.

"Jesse Mae?" said Louise.

"I think I'll stay here with Mama and Papa and Romey." Jesse Mae looked at her father. "You don't want to go do you, Papa?"

"Aw hell no." Frank turned and walked back towards the house. "A god-damned waste of money."

Lula Mae and Louise walked behind Frank as they began to plan the evening. "You and Harold can ride with me and Guy," said Lula. "And the kids can ride with Tony. She turned back to Tony. "We'll see you later Tony."

"Bye," added Louise, offhandedly; quickly returning her attention to Lula Mae.

CHAPTER NINE

A T AROUND FIVE P.M. TONY'S CAR PULLED onto the property and headed up the drive to the Austin's residence. Tony had had just enough time to go home, take a quick bath, shave and return to the farm.

Frank was sitting on the back porch, watching as Tony approached. "Here he comes," he called out. He knew that the children had been waiting for Tony to arrive.

Within fifteen seconds the screen door burst open as Gary and Scotty flew through it; barely touching the back porch as they jumped over the wooden steps and onto the bare dirt of the back yard. They were full of energy and very excited about going to the movie theater with a deputy sheriff. They danced around in the yard like marionettes while Johnny stood next to his grandfather shaking his head with embarrassment for them.

All three boys wore Levis, short sleeved cotton shirts, and shoes. Their hair was slicked back with Vitalis. Loretta stepped onto the porch wearing a black straight skirt, black low heeled pumps and a white sleeveless blouse with a high turned up collar. It was unusual to see them all looking so neat and clean while they were on vacation. Part of what they liked about visiting the farm was the fact that they did not have to pay any attention to how they dressed. Of course they had no objections to dressing up if it meant getting to go to the movies.

Loretta's clothes and her French curl hairstyle made her look older than she was; but the illusion quickly faded when she slapped Johnny on the back of his head and then jumped off of the porch and ran; immediately pursued by her adversary.

Tony's car came to a halt a short distance from the back porch and he opened the door and stepped out. He had traded his uniform for a pair of Levis and a white T-shirt. Frank looked at him, thinking that he now appeared even younger than he had when he was in uniform; and nothing like a law enforcement officer should look.

"Hi Mr. Austin," said Tony as he approached the porch.

Frank nodded to him. "Deputy."

"Sheriff Files called the college. They're going to send someone down to pick up the skeleton and artifacts as soon as they can. You should be getting a letter from the school, thanking you for your donation."

"That's good," said Frank without a hint of enthusiasm.

Guy stepped through the doorway and onto the porch.

"Hi Guy." Tony stood with his hands in his front pockets.

Guy gave a quick glance at Tony. "Hi Tony." He then turned toward the frolicking children. "Kids!" The youngsters stopped their horseplay and made their way towards him. "I'm going to give you each a quarter." The youngsters surrounded him with outstretched palms. "That's enough to get you into the show and buy some popcorn. Don't loose it."

At that moment Geneva walked onto the porch. Her hair was down and she had on a full, pink colored skirt, which had on one side, an embroidered black silhouette of a Poodle on a leash. Her three starched petticoats made the skirt stand out in a bell shape. She too, wore a white sleeveless blouse with the collar turned up.

"Hi", said Tony, trying not to look too enthusiastic in front of his date's father.

"Hi," Geneva also made an effort to suppress her enthusiasm. She had appreciated Tony's handsome face from the first time they met, but she had no idea that underneath his deputy sheriff's uniform was also this very attractive physique. She glanced around at the others in order not to stare at him. Her self esteem kicked up a notch or two at the thought that he was pursuing her.

Guy turned to Tony. "You kids can go on ahead. We'll be here about fifteen minutes more. Their mothers are still fixing their hair." He turned and went back inside.

Geneva looked back at Frank as she walked toward Tony's car. "Bye Grandpa." They all climbed into the car; Geneva and Loretta in the front seat with Tony; Johnny, Gary and Scotty in the back seat.

Halfway into town, Tony lowered the volume on the radio, which had been playing rock-and-roll music. He slowed the car down to a crawl and looked to the opposite side of the road, drawing the attention of the others in that direction. "There's the house."

Everyone strained to get into a position where they could see the old house, which was set back off the road in a low lying marshy, bayou; partially hidden by trees growing out of the water.

"Why is it in the water?" asked Gary.

"It wasn't always," said Tony. "When they built the dam about twenty years ago, the whole area on that side of the road filled up with a couple feet of water. My pa said it was always a flood area. He said they never should have built houses down there.

"When we come back by here it will be dark and I'll stop and show you guys the ghost lights in there."

Silence prevailed as the car slowly passed the house. Then, with the house behind them, Tony turned the music back up and picked up speed. The sing-alongs began and the house was temporarily forgotten.

Parking spaces were abundant in the small town and Tony found one about a half block from the theater. He backed into the space as Geneva began to give instructions to her younger siblings and cousin before they would be jumping out of the car and running ahead. Scotty was not accustomed to their usual routine at the movies, so she reminded them all of the procedure. "You guys wait for us in the lobby or right outside the front doors after the movie."

"Yeah, yeah," was the reply from her oldest brother.

"I mean it Johnny. If you're not there when we come out, I'll tell Daddy."

"I'll make sure they're there," said Loretta as she opened the front passenger door and exited the car. Geneva and Loretta had discussed the strategies of the evening beforehand. Loretta had agreed to sit with the boys so that Geneva and Tony could have their show-date. The car doors slammed shut leaving Geneva and Tony alone.

Tony took Geneva's hand in his. "You look beautiful tonight." Immediately fearing that his compliment might be misconstrued, he added, "I mean, you looked beautiful before, but…I like that skirt."

"Thanks." Geneva looked up at him. Slowly, Tony lowered his head so that his lips touched Geneva's lips. Geneva closed her eyes and let him kiss her.

"Hey Tony!" The brief kiss was interrupted by one of Tony's friends who was walking by with his girlfriend. Tony waved hello as the other couple passed.

"We'd better get into the theater before the show starts," said Geneva.

They found their seats in the balcony, where several other couples sat together. A few boys sat in the front row of the balcony and looked over the edge in order to heckle their friends below. Geneva and Tony sat in the middle seats so that they could hold hands and share an occasional kiss while the movie played.

During the intermission, before the second feature began, Lula Mae found them. She made her way down the row of seats behind them and leaned over to talk to Geneva. "You kids go straight home after the picture. Your daddy and me and Harold and Louise came in late, so we'll probably stay to see the part we missed. We'll be home a little after you kids."

"Okay," said Geneva hoping that her mother would make her visit short; which she did.

All the youngsters had a good time and they all met out front just as planned. They had enjoyed the double feature and now they were anxious to see the haunted house.

Tony began slowing down the car as the old house became visible in the pale moonlight. "There it is." He looked towards the house and the others craned their necks and vied for better positions so that they would each have a clearer view. He shifted into a lower gear, pulled the car to the side of the road and stopped. Silence surrounded them as they stared through the night at the dark image of the old wood framed house that they had seen earlier when it was still daylight.

There was enough moonlight to give the old house and the surrounding area a soft glow. A slight breeze moved the surface of the water, reflecting small points of moonlight amongst the reeds and shrubs. Bullfrog calls and cricket chirps were the only sounds as the six pairs of eyes peered from the parked car.

After a moment; Loretta, who had been staring intently out of the open passenger's side window, turned to Tony. "I don't see any lights."

"There!" Johnny opened the rear door and jumped out of the car. "I saw it! I saw a light right there." He pointed a finger toward the house as he moved along the water's edge.

Loretta bound from the front seat, and hurried to the grassy area in front of the car where Johnny now stood. "Where? I don't see any light."

"It was on the porch," said Johnny.

Tony called out to Loretta, "The light comes and goes; it's not always there. You have to watch close to see it when it happens." He leaned across Geneva and quietly pulled the passenger's door closed. He turned to Gary and Scotty who were still in the rear seat of the car. "If you guys get out of the car you can see better."

Gary and Scotty, who had been staring at the house, turned and looked at Tony. They were silent for a moment. They glanced at one another and back to Tony. "No, that's okay," said Gary. "We can see okay from here."

Geneva turned around and looked at her little brother and cousin. "Gary, you can't see anything from in here. You and Scotty get out of the car and look for the lights. Johnny and Loretta are right there and Tony and I will be right here. There's nothing to be afraid of."

"I'm not afraid," said Scotty, defiantly. He climbed boldly from the car, but once out, he immediately looked around and took on an air of caution as he hurried to stand next to Johnny and Loretta. Geneva and Tony continued to look at Gary without speaking. After a moment Gary yielded to their intimidating glares and he slowly exited the car and scurried to stand behind the others, as they waited for the lights to appear again.

As soon as they were alone, Tony put his arm around Geneva and pulled her to him. They had perfected their kissing technique while in the movie theater, and it had been very enjoyable for Geneva; however, in her naïveté, she was not expecting what came next. The touch of Tony's hand upon her breast shocked her and she pulled away instinctively.

"What's the matter? They can't see us; they're too interested in that house." Tony's hand reached out again.

"I don't do that!" Geneva pushed his hand away. Part of her longed to let him touch her, but she was afraid. She had never been touched like that. She and her girlfriends often talked about being felt up. Most of them had experienced it and she had looked forward to it happening to her, but now that her opportunity had presented itself, she could not go through with it.

Tony pulled back and looked at her. Employing his best wounded look, he said, "I thought you liked me."

"I do like you." Geneva began scooting across the car seat towards the door. "But I don't do stuff like that."

The other youngsters paid no attention to Geneva when she came and stood a few feet behind them, joining them in their surveillance of the eerie scene. Tony quickly made his way out of the driver's side of the car and came around and stood next to Geneva. "I'm sorry," he whispered into her ear.

"That's okay." Geneva, standing with her arms crossed over her chest, butted Tony's shoulder affectionately with her shoulder. She smiled up at him and then directed her attention back to the house. "Is this place really supposed to be haunted?"

Gingerly, Tony put his arm on Geneva's shoulders and moved a little closer to her. When she did not pull away, he said, "Well, there are a lot of stories about it. I don't really believe in ghosts, myself."

Loretta turned abruptly and walked back to Geneva and Tony. She stood in front of them with her hands on her hips with an attitude of defiance. "There aren't any lights out there."

Embarrassed by her close proximity to them, Tony removed his arm from Geneva's shoulder. "Well, you have to keep looking." He motioned toward the house with one hand. "The lights only appear once in a while. If you don't keep watching, you'll miss them."

Loretta stood her ground. "Yeah righ…"

Just then, the boys began shouting, "Oh!"…"Cool!"…"I saw it! I saw it!"

Loretta quickly turned to see what the boys were yelling about. She stepped back to the edge of the water where they were standing. She stamped her foot in frustration. "Liars! There isn't anything..." She let her sentence run out as she stood with her jaw hanging down.

For a brief moment a small greenish light flickered just in front of the porch of the old house and then it disappeared. The whole group had seen it and they all stood in silence as if spellbound.

"What was that?" Geneva moved closer to Tony.

"Uhhh..." Tony put his arm around Geneva's shoulders again.

The little immobilized crowd looked on as a second light appeared out of the darkness; this time halfway between them and the house.

"It's coming this way," said Loretta.

"That's that thing!" Gary began backing away from the water's edge and closer to Geneva and Tony.

"What thing?" said Johnny with as much sarcasm as he could manage to express with just two words. He did not want to appear frightened.

"That thing that tried to get me night-before-last."

"Oh you little baby, that's..." Johnny stopped talking when two more lights flickered and seemed to be moving towards the group. He looked around at the others to see how they were going to react.

"Uh..." Scotty was walking sideways towards the car; his eyes searching for the advancing lights.

."Aghhh!" Loretta, having seen another light, broke from her stance and bolted toward the car. The others did the same. The car doors slammed shut, the locks went down and the windows were all immediately rolled up.

"Let's get out of here." Geneva's fingers were digging into Tony's arm.

"No," cried Johnny. "It can't get us in here. I want to see what it is."

Gary and Scotty began yelling their protests at the top of their lungs. They wanted to go now!

Tony pushed in the clutch and started the car. The radio came on; blaring rock-and-roll music, adding to the noise of the screams. He put the car into gear and pushed down on the accelerator. Instead of moving forward, the car began to slowly slide down the slope toward the water. He immediately let up off the gas and hit the brakes, but the car continued to slide. He stepped on the accelerator again, but the only result was that the rear wheels, which were now sinking deeper into the mud, spun without gaining any traction; the car was stuck.

"Come on, get us out of here," urged Loretta.

Tony gave the car more gas, but it did not move. The others were now urging him to get away from the place as they watched for more lights. "Shut up, you guys," said Geneva, turning off the radio. She held onto Tony's arm and they all sat in silence as he tried again to get the car out of the mud.

Suddenly a brilliant white light filled the car. The girls screamed as they all turned, searching for the source of the light.

"Geneva?"

"Mama!"

Lula Mae was getting out of Guy's car, which had just pulled off of the road, and stopped behind Tony's car. She walked quickly down the slope and approached the driver's side of the car. "What are you kids doing?"

Tony put the car in neutral and pulled on the emergency brake. He rolled down his window on the driver's side of the car. "Hi Lula Mae. I think we're stuck."

Lula Mae stood next to the car, looking down to see if she could see which wheels were buried in the mud. By now Guy and Harold had joined her, and Louise was at the edge of the road.

"They're stuck," said Lula Mae. The men walked around the car, examining the situation by the light cast from the headlights of Guy's car.

"You boys get out of the back seat," said Guy, when he saw that the rear wheels were indeed imbedded in the mud. Harold tried to open the rear door of the car on the side nearest the road. "Scotty, unlock this door," he said.

Scotty opened the door and he and Gary hastened out and moved quickly to stand next to their mothers. Johnny climbed out with his usual nonchalant attitude.

Guy moved to the driver's side of the car and addressed Tony. "What the hell were you trying to do? Why are you stopped here?"

Tony was embarrassed that he had allowed himself to get stuck in the mud. "Well…" he said, killing the engine and getting out of the car. "I pulled off the road to show everyone that old house over there." He pointed to the house.

"That thing was in there. It came out of that house and was after us!" Gary could not confine his excitement any longer.

"What thing?" said Guy.

"Oh Daddy," said Geneva, as she and Loretta climbed out of the car from the driver's side. "We were just teasing everyone; telling them that that old house is haunted." She downplayed the fact that she had also been frightened.

"I told them that I would show them a haunted house," said Tony with a sheepish grin.

"There it is!" Loretta was pointing to the glowing vapor, which was again at the edge of the porch of the house.

"Oh Loretta, that's nothing but swamp gas," said Lula Mae.

Loretta looked at her mother. "Swamp gas? What's that?"

"It's gas that comes up out of the swamp and glows in the dark when it burns."

"What?" Johnny did not want to give up on the idea of a ghost that easily.

"Guy," said Tony, embarrassed. "Can you give me a hand getting my car back up onto the road?"

"I should just leave you here. That was a damn fool thing to do." The two men stood for a brief moment. Then Guy said, "Do you have any rope in your trunk?"

Most of the residents around the region carried rope with their vehicles as a matter of habit. It was not unusual to need a tow now and then.

"Yeah, I do. Thanks Guy." Tony got the rope out of his trunk and tied it to his front bumper. Guy took the other end of the rope and tied it to the trailer hitch on his rear bumper. In a few moments Tony's car was back on the road and all of the youngsters began climbing back in.

Guy got out of his car and walked back to Tony as Tony was replacing the rope in his trunk. "We'll follow you to the house. No detours."

"No sir," said Tony.

Guy got back into his car and waited for the other car to pull around him and they all drove back to the farm.

Frank was sitting in his usual spot on the back porch when the two cars pulled up to the house. He waited as everybody but Geneva and Tony exited the cars and made their way toward him. The light from the kitchen spilled out into the back yard, lighting their way. "It's late," he said.

"Yeah, well, we had to pull Tony's car out of the bayou," said Guy.

Johnny, Loretta, Gary and Scotty positioned themselves on the edges of the porch around their grandfather, while the adults remained standing.

"The bayou?" said Frank.

"Grandpa?" Johnny turned toward Frank. "Have you ever heard of swamp gas?"

"What?" Frank tried to divide his attention between his son and grandson.

"Yeah," said Guy, disregarding Johnny's question. "Tony stopped by that old house in the bayou to try and scare the kids and he damn near slid into it. I had to tow his car back up to the road."

"You mean that old house where Jesse Mae stayed when she had that sickness?"

"Oh yeah, that was the house wasn't it? There was no water around it then. There was an Indian woman living there. What was her name?"

"Rena Two Eagles…a mighty fine young woman, that one…strong too. Jesse Mae stayed there all that time and Rena never came down with the sickness."

"Mama was there every day too, remember? She never caught it either."

"Well that was because she was too damn ornery to catch anything."

"How long was Jesse Mae there, anyway?"

"Oh…I don't remember; a couple of months I guess."

"Grandpa!"

"What Johnny?" Frank tapped his smoking pipe on the edge of the porch to loosen the ashes in it.

"Do you know what swamp gas is?"

"Of course I know what swamp gas is. It's…"

Johnny looked up and saw Romey who was standing in the kitchen just behind the screen door. He did not like the answer he was getting from his grandfather, so he disregarded it and turned his attention to Romey. "Romey! We saw a ghost!"

Johnny, Loretta, Gary and Scotty scurried into the kitchen and ushered Romey through the living room and onto the front porch where they proceeded to embellish the story of their close encounter with the supernatural.

Harold, Louise, Lula Mae and Guy all went into the house, leaving Frank alone to enjoy his solitude. Mary was sitting in the living room next to the console radio. Her favorite preacher of the airwaves was just finishing up his program; telling all of his devoted followers the address to send their donations. She did not respond to the returning movie-goers as they congregated in the kitchen. Everybody knew that Mary loved her radio church programs and they knew better than to interrupt her when she was listening to them.

As always; there was a pot of coffee on the kitchen stove. Lula Mae turned on the gas burner underneath the pot to heat up the coffee.

Louise began taking saucers from the cupboard and placing them on the table. "Lula Mae do you want a piece of pie? I know Guy and Harold do."

"Yeah, I think I will have a piece." Lula Mae pulled the chair out from the table and joined the others who were already seated.

"How were the movies?" Jesse Mae had just left her mother's bedroom and entered the kitchen through Romey's bedroom. She was already dressed in her nightgown. She was less than enthusiastic about sharing her mother's bedroom with her, but the crowded conditions made it necessary, and sharing a bed with a relative or friend was a common practice in this farming community.

"One was pretty good. It had Rita Hayworth," said Louise.

"That was a good picture," offered Lula Mae. "What was the name of it?"

"Miss Sadie Thompson." Louise was cutting pieces of apple pie and placing them on the saucers. "You want a piece of pie, Jess?"

"No thanks, I had a piece not long ago. So what was the movie about?"

Louise passed around forks for everybody. "Some poor woman who got herself into trouble with men."

"She was a tramp," said Guy.

"Will you shut up? The kids might hear you. I don't want them to hear that." Lula Mae got up to pour the coffee, which was now heated.

Guy gave his wife a perplexed look. "They saw the movie."

"I know they did, but they didn't understand what was going on. And they never called her that in the movie."

"Never mind not letting the kids hear it." Jesse Mae pulled out a chair and sat down. "Don't let Mama hear it."

"Don't let Mama hear what?" Mary walked into the kitchen. Her program had finished.

"Oh Guy and Lula were just talking about one of the movies they saw."

"I'll bet it was nasty. All the picture shows are nasty these days."

"It was a very good movie," said Louise, reaching for another saucer. "You want a piece of pie?" She looked at her mother-in-law.

"Yeah." Mary grabbed a chair from against the wall and pulled it up to the table. She sat down as Lula Mae placed a full cup of coffee in front of her. Without the least acknowledgement to either Lula or Louise for waiting on her, she took a bite of pie and said, "So was anything decent playing?"

"Hop-a-long Cassidy," said Harold. "Romey would have liked it."

"Yeah and what would he have thought about that other one; the one I shouldn't hear about? I'll bet it was about some nasty woman."

"Sadie Thompson," offered Louise. "And yes, you could say she was."

"I knew it. They shouldn't be showing pictures like that to decent folks."

"Mama, you don't know anything about that movie, so how can you make a judgement?" said Jesse Mae.

"Oh here we go; Miss Highfalutin."

Jesse Mae opened her mouth to respond and then changed her mind. She saw no sense in arguing with her mother. As she stood up she said, "Oh never mind, I'm going to bed. Good-night all."

"Wait," said Harold. "Guess who Guy and I ran into when we were getting popcorn."

Jesse Mae paused and stood looking at Harold. She put out her hands and shrugged her shoulders with a show of frustration. "Who?"

A cranky attitude was nothing unusual for her; especially when her mother was in the room.

"Do you remember a boy named Roger Crawford? His mama had a general store in town."

"I used to sell eggs to her," said Mary.

"Remember, he was the only kid around with his own pickup truck? He used to give us rides home from the river."

"She died about a year ago." Mary cut into her pie with her fork. She brought the fork up to her mouth and hesitated. "All that money and she died a young woman. I guess money can't buy you good health." She put the pie in her mouth and chewed.

Jesse Mae sat back down in her chair. "What about him?"

"Guy and me ran into him at the picture show. We had a good visit with him during intermission. He's not doing too good."

Guy reached over and took the last piece of apple pie. "He's got some kind of disease, cancer I think he said."

Harold scraped the last of the crumbs from the pie tin. "He looked really bad. I was surprised that he was even at the picture show. He said that the show was his only entertainment these days."

"Poor man," said Mary. "He's all alone. His wife just up and left him a few years back. They never had any kids. I don't think she was able; you know?" With this statement, Mary deliberately avoided eye contact with Jesse Mae. It was her way of twisting the knife in Jesse Mae's psychological wounds, and pretending to be unaware that she was saying anything hurtful.

Louise and Lula Mae glanced at Jesse Mae and then at one another. They were dismayed at the way Mary would take any opportunity to make her only daughter feel inadequate as a woman because she could not have children.

Jesse Mae seemed oblivious to her mother's attempt to goad her. "Yeah I remember him. Didn't he go away somewhere before he finished high school?"

"He went to prep school first and then to college," said Harold. "He became what they call an investment broker. He was always rich, but I imagine he's really rich now. Those people don't do anything but make more money."

Mary looked at Jesse Mae. "Too bad he's on his death bed; maybe you could have snagged him."

"Now Mama, why would I want to do that?"

"Well, you buried one husband and made a bundle. Why not another?"

Jesse Mae rose from her chair again. "Good-night all." She went into Mary's bedroom and closed the door.

Guy looked at Lula and pitched his head in the direction of the cars parked outside. "Honey."

It was understood by Lula Mae that he was telling her that he wanted Geneva to come in and for Tony to leave, but Lula Mae felt otherwise. "In a minute. It's not going to hurt nothing for her to sit out there and talk."

"They've been talking all night. Go tell her to come in."

"I'll tell her in a few minutes." Lula found her husband's attitude toward Geneva and Tony irritating. She felt that this was a good opportunity for Geneva to get some experience with boys while being in a safe environment. "They're not hurting a thing sitting out there."

"Guy," said Mary, ignoring Lula Mae's authority. "That's a grown man out there with your young daughter. That's the way girls get into trouble."

Lula Mae turned to Mary. "Well god-damn-it, I said they're not hurting nothing." There were certain areas where Lula Mae would not allow anyone to dictate what she should or should not do. One of those areas was the method of raising her children. She especially resented her mother-in-law's interference. "I'll go out there and tell Geneva to come in when I think it's time." She was tempted to make a reference to Mary's past, but she refrained from it.

Guy glared at her as if to challenge her decision to go against his wishes, but he had learned over the years, when to drop a subject and to quietly defer to his wife's decisions. He said nothing.

"I wish you wouldn't take the Lord's name in vain in my house." Mary directed her dogma toward Lula Mae, but she looked at Guy in an attempt to encourage him to support her against his wife. Guy shook his head with resignation and sipped his coffee.

"I'm sorry," said Lula Mae to Mary. "But you need to leave my kids' upbringing to me. I think I've done a pretty good job so far."

"I agree," offered Louise. "Geneva is a fine young lady. Nobody has to worry about her getting into trouble." Louise had no problem with reminding Mary that she had no right to criticize others for something that she had done herself. She smiled a condescending smile at Mary and then turned toward Harold. "More coffee, Harold?"

Geneva was indeed very level headed and sensible, but she was also a teenage girl. She, of course had no intentions of letting Tony go too far with her. The fact that the inside of the car was dark and private was in Tony's favor, but Geneva felt secure with the fact that her whole family was within fifty feet of her. This gave her the courage to try things that she would not ordinarily try if she were in a more vulnerable situation.

Tony was enjoying himself immensely and was willing to go along with whatever Geneva wanted to do.

Geneva had quickly mastered the art of French kissing and as she and Tony held each other and engaged in the activity, a new sensation came over her. She was no longer letting Tony direct all the moves. She found herself putting her hand against his chest and matching his fervor in his kiss. She suddenly realized that this was the feeling that could get a girl in trouble and she was thankful that they were outside her grandparents' house.

"Mama said it's time to come in!" Loretta's head was thrust through the open car window.

The two lovers quickly broke from their embrace.

"Loretta Fay; I'm going to clobber you!" Geneva swiped her hand in the direction of Loretta's head, but Loretta was too quick. She pulled her head back out of range of her angry sister.

"You better come in or Daddy's going to come out here and get you." Loretta walked briskly back to the house as she spoke.

"I better go in." Geneva reached for the door handle.

"Can I see you tomorrow?"

Geneva turned back to him. "I don't know. We're all going down to the river tomorrow."

"Oh." Tony hesitated; he did not want to seem too pushy.

"Why don't you just show up at the river? They'll surely invite you to eat with us."

Tony felt a surge of encouragement. "Sure, I can do that."

"We'll be there around ten, I imagine."

"Well then, I'll see you there."

Geneva hesitated. "Well, good-night."

Tony leaned over and put his lips to hers. They kissed briefly. Geneva opened the passenger door and slipped out of the car. She stood and watched as Tony's car pulled down the drive and turned onto the road and disappeared. Then she made her way to the back porch.

"Looks like you got yourself a beau." Frank held his pipe in his hands, packing tobacco into its bowl.

Geneva walked slowly up the steps of the porch. "He's really nice, Grandpa. Don't you think so?"

"He seems like a nice enough fella."

Geneva opened the screen door leading to the kitchen. "Good-night Grandpa." She felt the embarrassment of having all eyes on her as she entered the kitchen. Her sense of euphoria had suddenly left her as she tried unsuccessfully to walk past the adults at the kitchen table without incurring comments.

Loretta was standing next to the table with her arm on her mother's shoulder. When Geneva looked at Loretta, she covertly mouthed at Geneva the last word of the sing-song taunt, which she so often repeated; "k-i-s-s-i-n-g."

Geneva gave Loretta a defiant look and Loretta turned away from her with a big smile on her face.

"Did Tony leave?" asked Lula Mae.

"Unh-huh."

Lula Mae gave Loretta a quick hug and then gently pushed her away from her. "You girls go on and get ready for bed now. Tell the boys to tell Romey good-night and to get ready for bed."

Geneva and Loretta told everybody at the table good-night, kissed their mother and father and headed upstairs through the dining room. When the two of them were in the living room, the group at the table heard Loretta call out loudly, "Johnny, Gary and Scotty! Go to bed!"

After a short while, the boys had said their good-nights and gone out to Romey's playhouse and Romey had gone to his room. Guy stood up from the table. "I'm going to bed." He looked at Lula Mae. "You coming?"

"In a while," said Lula.

"Well, good-night all." Guy kissed Mary on her cheek.

Harold stood up. "I'm ready too." He also kissed his mother on her cheek.

"I'll be up soon," said Louise.

The three women were left alone and there was silence in the house. Then the faint sound of music was heard from upstairs. Mary looked at Lula Mae as if to say, "Do something about that."

Lula Mae stood up. "I'll be back down in a minute." She and Louise were accustomed to sitting up after all the others had gone to bed.

Lula Mae entered the girls' bedroom. "You girls turn that music off."

Loretta lifted the needle off the vinyl record. "We had it low."

"I know you did, but it can still be heard in the rest of the house. You can play it tomorrow."

Lula Mae sat on the edge of the bed where Geneva sat reading a magazine. "Geneva, I want you to be careful with Tony."

Geneva put down her magazine. "What do you mean?"

"I mean I don't want you getting serious about him. We're only here for a couple of weeks, and you will probably never see him again after that."

Geneva dropped her head. "I know."

"She's already serious." Loretta sat on the other side of the bed and leaned against the headboard.

"It's fine to go to the show with him and sit in the car with him, but it's not going to be anything more than that."

"I really like him, Mama."

"I know you do, but if you get serious about him, you're just going to get hurt. He's not going to wait for you to come back to visit in two years and he's not going to pick up and move to California.

"You'll be back in school pretty soon and you'll be meeting boys and going out with them. So just keep in mind that this is just a casual flirtation and don't do anything foolish."

"I won't Mama. You're right."

Lula Mae hugged Geneva. She hoped that she had taken her advice seriously. Geneva had always been level headed and responsible, unlike her younger sister, sitting on the other side of the bed. Lula Mae leaned over and hugged Loretta and told them both good-night, and went back downstairs to the kitchen.

"Louise thinks we might get some money for those old Indian bones," said Mary as Lula Mae rejoined the other women.

"Really? Who from?" Lula Mae resumed her place at the kitchen table.

"Well, not for the bones," said Louise. "But there might be more artifacts like those arrowheads and things. Collectors will pay good money for some of that stuff. The museums won't want to pay for anything, but collectors will."

"Well, what will happen to the bones?" Lula Mae poured more hot coffee into her cup to warm it up.

"I don't think they can sell human remains. Those probably are already property of the state. They will probably go to some college or a museum."

"I don't care about those old bones," said Mary. "But if we can find treasures, I'll sell them. I should send Guy and Harold down there first thing in the morning; before those people from the college start digging around. That might be a graveyard down there."

"Mary," said Lula Mae. "Those bones were found by mistake and the sheriff had to investigate them. You wouldn't want to deliberately dig up people's graves would you?"

Mary felt a twinge of guilt. She really did consider herself a highly moral person, and a grave was indisputably hallowed ground. But she hated to give up what she considered rightfully hers. She felt entitled to anything of value found on her property. "Well, it's not like they was Christians. They probably never even had a decent burial. They was probably just thrown in a hole and covered with dirt. If we find any more bones, we could bury them again and give them a proper Christian funeral. That's the only way they're going to go to meet their maker."

Mary's argument for her case was not convincing the other two women. Louise looked at Lula Mae and then back to Mary. "Maybe Lula is right. It does sort of seem like grave robbing."

"I don't think anyone should go digging down there anymore," said Lula Mae.

"Well, good Lord-o-mercy." Mary looked at Louise and then at Lula Mae. She knew that she did not have a convincing argument against them.

The three of them sat in silence for a moment. Then Mary said to Lula Mae, "Are you going to start that bread?"

Lula nodded her head. "Yes, I'll start it in a few minutes."

"Well, I'm going to bed." Mary rose from her chair and walked toward her bedroom. "Good-night."

Louise and Lula said good-night to Mary, and sat in silence for a moment.

"I'm not at all sleepy," said Louise. "I think I'll make those pies tonight, instead of in the morning."

The two sisters-in-law began their culinary tasks and enjoyed their time alone together as they chatted away into the night.

CHAPTER TEN

BY EIGHT A.M. BREAKFAST WAS OVER AND the women began frying chicken and making potato salad for the picnic. The apple pies were finished and the bread rolls were baking.

Loretta came from upstairs, where she and Geneva had been listening to their record player. She walked quietly into the kitchen and went directly to her mother, who was standing at the sink washing a large mixing bowl. She whispered into Lula Mae's ear.

"Why; what does she want?" said Lula Mae as she put the bowl on the counter to drip-dry and began washing a pot.

Loretta looked around at the other women who were paying no attention to her. She turned back to Lula Mae. "She wants to talk to you." Loretta was uncharacteristically soft spoken.

"Well, tell her I'm busy. She can come down here if she wants to talk."

Loretta let her shoulders drop in an expression of exasperation and raised her voice to a normal speaking volume. "She can't! That's why she told me to come and tell you to come up."

"What's the matter?" asked Mary.

"What do you mean; she can't? What's the matter?" Lula Mae was suddenly concerned. She picked up the dish towel and began drying her hands in preparation for going upstairs.

Loretta gave her mother a wide eyed look as if to indicate that it was something confidential.

"What's wrong?" asked Jesse Mae.

"Is something wrong?" added Louise.

"What's the matter?" insisted Mary as she followed Lula Mae out of the kitchen with Louise and Jesse Mae right behind her. Loretta, having done her duty for her sister went out the back door, letting the screen door slam shut.

Geneva's face registered a slight level of horror at the sight of her aunts and her grandmother traipsing behind her mother as they all entered the bedroom. She was sitting on the vanity bench with her knees held tightly together.

"What's wrong?" Lula Mae walked quickly towards her.

Geneva's mouth dropped open slightly and she looked at the other women behind her mother. "Uh…"

"What is it?"

Geneva motioned with her hand for her mother to come closer, so that she could whisper to her.

Lula Mae leaned in to listen to what she had to say, and then she stood upright. "Well, good grief, Geneva; you scared me."

"What's wrong?" Mary advanced into the room.

"Oh, she's just started her period."

"Well, good-Lord-o-mercy." Mary's hands went to the back of her hips as she assumed her usual stance. "We thought something was wrong, Geneva."

Geneva averted her eyes from the others. She found the whole situation extremely embarrassing.

"You're not due until next week," said Lula Mae. "We don't have any Kotex. Mary can I get some rags from you?"

"Rags?" blurted Jesse Mae.

Lula Mae looked at her sister-in-law. She resented the ability that Jesse Mae had to make her feel humiliated with a single word. "Yes, rags."

"I have some Kotex in my car. I never go anywhere without them." Jesse Mae looked at Geneva. "You just stay where you are, Hon. I'll be right back."

"Thanks, Aunt Jesse Mae." Geneva, being a city girl was abhorred at the idea of wearing rags between her legs. She was already upset because she would not get to go swimming with Tony today. "Why did this have to happen now?" she lamented.

Louise and Mary quietly made their way back downstairs. Menstruation was something that all of the women understood and they showed a high degree of consideration for anyone dealing with it. Lula Mae put her hand on Geneva's shoulder. "Oh, now, it's not that bad. Since Aunt Jesse Mae has some Kotex, you can still wear your swimsuit; you just can't go swimming, that's all."

"But Tony will be there and he will want me to go swimming with him. What can I tell him?"

Lula Mae was not surprised at the fact that Tony knew they would be at the river and had made plans to join them. "Oh..." she thought for a moment. "...tell him you have an ear infection and you don't want to get water in your ear."

Geneva was beginning to feel more relaxed as she realized that the situation was not as dire as she had perceived it to be. "Yeah, I guess I can do that."

"Here you go." Jesse Mae re-entered the bedroom with a brown paper bag, containing a box of sanitary napkins. "I'm sorry it's not a full box, but these should hold you for a while." She handed the bag to Geneva. "Look at it this way Hon, now you can fix your hair up nice and wear some make-up to the picnic."

"Oh...yeah." Geneva smiled broadly, her mood much improved.

"I can help you fix your hair." Jesse Mae lifted Geneva's hair up and held it atop her head.

"Okay," said Geneva, with growing enthusiasm for the alternatives, which her predicament had provided.

Lula Mae eyed her oldest daughter as she interacted with Jesse Mae, *the sophisticated aunt*. She felt a sense of jealousy that she tried to ignore. On one hand, she wanted Geneva to turn the situation around and to be self assured and confident, but on the other hand, she felt that it was her place to help her daughter and not Jesse Mae's. "Well, I'm going to get back to the kitchen." Lula Mae stood where she was and waited for a response, but her words were unheeded as Jesse Mae and Geneva fussed with Geneva's hair.

"Why don't we put it up?" said Jesse Mae. "I'll run downstairs and get some hair pins and hairspray while you put the pad on." She then skipped down the stairs as if she were a sixteen year old girl.

"Do you want me to help you with your hair?" asked Lula Mae.

"No, that's okay; Aunt Jesse Mae and I can do it." Geneva sat holding the brown paper bag with the sanitary napkins in it. She was anxious for her mother to leave the room, so that she could go about her business. She had no idea that her relationship with her aunt was making her mother feel insecure.

"Okay." Lula Mae walked out of the bedroom as Geneva took the sanitary napkins out of the bag. When she got back to the kitchen, Mary and Louise were busy with the food for the picnic.

Mary turned to Lula Mae. "You see how that woman is? Miss Highfalutin. She wasn't too good for rags when she was growing up. After she went away to college and married herself a lawyer, she thought she was better than everyone else."

"Oh well," said Lula Mae. "To be honest I'm glad she had the Kotex. I don't want Geneva to be embarrassed."

"You watch out for that woman. She'll turn your kids against you."

"Oh Mary," said Louise. "All she did was provide an easy solution to a problem. She did Geneva a favor."

"Yeah, okay." Mary looked at Lula Mae. "Just remember; I told you so." She went back to preparing the potato salad.

A moment later the screen door flew open and Loretta ran into the kitchen, followed closely by Johnny. "Johnny found a necklace."

Lula Mae was washing a skillet. She stopped and looked at her two children. "Found a necklace? Where?"

"In that old root cellar where the bones were found." Loretta moved around the edge of the table, keeping it between her and Johnny; creating a barrier to prevent him from hitting her for telling on him. "He's been digging down there."

Lula Mae dried her hands on the towel hanging at the end of the counter. "Johnny Frank, you know you kids are not supposed to be down there." She looked at the necklace in Johnny's hand. "Let me see that." She took the necklace from Johnny.

Mary and Louise stopped their work and moved closer to Lula Mae, so as to get a better look at the necklace. It was dirty and tarnished, but it was apparent that it was made of silver and turquoise. Johnny had cleaned it up a bit before his sister had discovered him at the task, and its physical properties were now quite obvious.

"Good-Lord-o-mercy! Let me see that." Mary took the necklace out of Lula Mae's grasp. She turned it from side to side and then held it up next to the window in order to get a better look. "I knew there was treasure down there." She turned to her grandson. "What else did you find?"

"Nothing yet." Johnny was pleased that he was being validated for his efforts instead of scolded.

"Well you go back down there and see what else you can find." Mary took the necklace to the sink and began pumping water over it.

"Hah!" Johnny exclaimed to Loretta; sneering at her attempt to get him into trouble.

"Mary I don't think that's a good idea. He could destroy valuable artifacts that might be buried down there." Louise resumed packing the picnic basket. "And Frank did tell the sheriff that he would leave the area alone until someone from the college could dig through it."

"You think they're going to tell anyone if they find more jewelry down there? I don't know why Frank agreed to that anyway." Mary turned to her grandson. "You go on back down there, Johnny. See what else you can find."

Johnny was elated with his grandmother's approval. "Okay." He turned and started toward the screen door.

"I'll go with you," said Loretta, following behind him.

"Just hold on there," said Lula Mae.

The youngsters turned and looked at their mother.

"Your grandpa said he didn't want anybody digging around down there. Besides, I want you kids to stay around the house. We're almost ready to go to the river."

"It don't matter what that old man says," said Mary as she dried the necklace. "I said they can dig down there."

"Well, we'll see when we get back" Lula Mae helped Louise fill the basket. "You kids go get your swimsuits on, and tell Gary to get his on."

"And tell Scotty to get his on; will you?" said Louise.

Mary hooked the necklace around her neck. "How does it look?"

Louise closed the lid on the picnic basket. "It's very pretty."

"It looks expensive," said Lula Mae.

Mary went into her bedroom to check out the necklace in her dresser mirror while the rest of the family readied themselves for an outing at the river.

Romey sat on the back porch and watched the others load the cars with towels and quilts for the picnic. He would have enjoyed going with them, but Mary did not want to go and she would not allow Romey to go without her. He was disappointed, but not upset; he was used to staying behind with Mary.

Frank was not going to the river either. He had no interest in swimming, and he had business to attend to. He had plans to go and collect his rent from his sharecroppers, and negotiate a new contract with them.

Within a short while, the visiting relatives were climbing into their three cars. Geneva, Loretta and Johnny would ride with Jesse Mae. Gary and Scotty would ride with Guy and Lula, and Harold and Louise would ride in their own car with all the inner tubes, quilts, towels and food.

Mary, Frank and Romey stood next to the cars wishing everyone a good time as they all climbed in. "Here's Bobby Dean," said Mary, when she noticed the postman's truck driving up toward the house.

The mail truck pulled up next to the group and stopped. The driver, Bobby Dean had been carrying mail in the area for more than forty years. All of the residents knew him by his first name. "Howdy folks," he said to Frank, Mary and Romey through the open window of his truck.

"Bobby Dean," said Frank with a nod of his head.

The mailman turned in his seat to reach something in the back of his truck. "Got the Sears Catalog here. It's too big to go in the mailbox." He turned back and handed the catalog out of the window to Frank. He looked over at Mary and hesitated a moment without speaking. She suspected that he had some good gossip for her and did not want to discuss it in front of Frank and Romey.

The residents in this area enjoyed hearing the latest goings on, which he often delivered with their mail. Frank, however, was one of the few exceptions to this rule; he had no appreciation for Bobby Dean's *stories*. Mary figured that she would just have to wait for the news until he came back another day.

Bobby Dean looked around at the group. "Looks like you folks are going to the river."

The others confirmed that yes they were going for a picnic down at the river.

Bobby Dean looked at Frank. "Any more bones been dug up around here?"

Frank frowned at the gossipy postman. "There's nothing of any interest going on here."

Bobby Dean took the hint. He said good-bye to the group and turned his truck around and drove away.

Frank shook his head slowly as he watched the truck pull down the drive. He turned to Romey with a smile. "Look-a-here, Son; the Sears Catalog."

Romey always enjoyed looking through The Sears Catalogs. The family members were happy that he would now have something to entertain himself with while they were all at the river. Mary walked back inside the house with Romey while Frank got in his truck and drove off to go see his sharecroppers; and the others headed off for a day of picnicking and fun.

Romey walked enthusiastically to the front porch to sit in the porch swing and look through the catalog while Mary went back into her bedroom to appreciate the beautiful necklace around her neck. In a few moments, Mary walked onto the front porch. Romey looked up from his catalog.

"Son, I want you to sit right here and don't go off the porch. Mama's going to go down to the barn for a little while."

"No Mama. Don't go down there."

"Oh now don't worry. There's nothing bad down there. Mama's just going to do a little digging. Maybe I'll bring you back another arrowhead."

"I don't want one, Mama."

"Now Romey, you do as I say. I won't be long. You stay right here and look at your catalog till I get back. You understand?"

"Okay, Mama." Romey sat in the porch swing and watched as Mary crawled between the boards of the fence with much difficulty and began her decent down across the pasture toward the barn; then he went back to his catalog.

The large oak tree grew on the bank of the river at an area where a backwash created an ideal spot for swimming. The branches of the tree spread out over the water. There was a heavy rope tied to one of the branches, creating a *Tarzan* swing. Johnny, Loretta, Gary and Scotty were taking turns swinging on the rope, which would carry them from the shore to a point in the river where they would drop into the water.

The *Tarzan* call echoed off of the damp clay banks of the cove as Loretta's legs flailed through the air. Her red hair lifted above her head as she dropped from the rope and into the water a short distance below her. She was a poor swimmer and a little afraid of the water, but she was not going to let her younger brothers and cousin show her up; besides, the water was just a little over four feet deep here; she could stand touching the bottom and her head would still be above the water's surface.

She did not like being under the water so she struggled to gain her footing as quickly as possible after plunging through the surface and lightly touching the muddy bottom below. Facing away from shore and gasping for air; she raised her head out of the water and heard the feeble attempt of her constant competitor in life; Johnny, as he screeched out his discordant version of the famous call.

Splash!!! Loretta felt something hit her from behind and she lost her balance and fell forward into the murky water. She saw the river closing around her face as she gasped for air, but instead of air, it was the river water that entered her throat and lungs. Choking and trying to expel the fluid from her lungs, she floundered desperately; arms flailing about, trying to find anything with which to steady herself. Her feet were touching the bottom of the river, but her hysteria kept her from gaining her balance in the slippery mud. She was overcome with panic. She tried to scream, but she could not find the air to do so.

A short distance from the water, Tony was sitting with Geneva on a quilt spread out on the ground. Geneva's small battery operated radio was playing Country music while they basked in the sun, getting a tan. Geneva saw the concern register on Tony's face as he stood up and looked toward the river. She turned to see what he was looking at. There was Loretta, flailing about, and Johnny, totally unaware of his sister's distress as he dog paddled to shore.

In an instant, Tony was in the water, swimming rapidly towards Loretta, who was about thirty feet away. He reached her in a matter of seconds and lifted her out of the water as she continued to flap her arms, and gasp for air while desperately attempting to gain control of her equilibrium.

"You're okay! Relax! I've got you." Tony stood in the water, which came up to just below his chest. He held Loretta; her back toward him, with his arms around her waist. Realizing that she was safe, Loretta coughed and spat water as she caught her breath. In a moment she had calmed down and allowed Tony to take her back to the shore.

The three boys stood on the shore, watching in silence as the scene unfolded. None of them had realized that Loretta was in trouble. Johnny was aware that he had knocked Loretta off balance when he bumped her, but he had no idea that there was a problem. After offering his obligatory "Sorry", he had then concentrated on making his way back to shore. None of the children were strong swimmers; that is why they were restricted by their parents to the shallow areas of the river.

"What happened?" Geneva walked to meet Tony and Loretta as they waded out of the water by the tree where the boys stood.

Loretta hit Johnny's shoulder with her open hand. "You landed on me!"

"I said I was sorry." Johnny showed little reaction to the slap against his arm.

"You almost drowned me!"

"He didn't mean to, Loretta. It was an accident." Geneva did not want to draw the attention of the adults who were just a short distance away. If their mother realized that Loretta could have drowned, she would make them all stay out of the water. Geneva liked the idea that her siblings were preoccupied with swimming, instead of hanging around with Tony and her. "You guys better behave or Mama will make you stay out of the water."

The others knew that she was right, and none of them wanted to be kept from playing in the river. Loretta pushed Johnny as a final act of retaliation, and they all resumed their fun as if nothing out of the ordinary had happened.

Geneva and Tony walked back to their quilt. "That was...heroic of you," said Geneva. The term sounded a little corny, but she could not think of any other term to express how impressed she was by Tony's actions.

"Well, not really. The water isn't very deep."

"Maybe not, but she could have drowned."

Tony shrugged his shoulders. "Yeah, I guess she could have." He was enjoying Geneva's admiration of his physical prowess.

"You know, I think you should go for a swim. I'll go help with lunch and I'll meet you back at our quilt in a little while."

The idea of going for a swim was very appealing to Tony, but he did not want to seem selfish; he wanted Geneva to know that he was willing to stay with her. "Oh, that's okay; I don't have to go swimming," he said.

"Oh don't be silly. You've got your swimsuit on and you're already wet. Go on, I don't mind."

"Are you sure you don't want to just wade out a little? The water's great."

"No, I don't want to make my ear infection worse. I don't mind not swimming. It's just nice being out here."

"Okay." Tony splashed into the water and swam to the deeper area where people were diving off the high bank.

Lula Mae, Louise and Jesse Mae were sitting together on their quilt, which was spread out on a grassy area under the shade of a tree adjacent to the parked cars. Lula Mae wore a pair of shorts and a halter top. Louise wore a lightweight gingham dress, she had no interest in swimming and she was rarely seen in anything other than a dress. Jesse Mae wore a risqué two-piece swimsuit. They each had a metal cup filled with iced coffee, and Jesse Mae was smoking a cigarette.

"Hi," said Geneva as she approached her mother and aunts.

Lula Mae put her arm around Geneva's shoulders when Geneva sat next to her on the quilt. "Are the other kids doing okay?"

Geneva's quilt and the tree where the other youngsters were playing were on the opposite side of an embankment, and out of view from the women.

"Yeah, they're fine," said Geneva. She turned to Jesse Mae. "Aunt Jesse Mae, I'm on my last Kotex. Do you have any more?"

"No I'm sorry, Geneva; I didn't bring any more with me."

Geneva turned to her mother. "Mama, can we go into town and get some?"

Lula Mae had never learned to drive, and Geneva did not have her license yet. "You know your daddy won't drive us into town right now."

"But what am I going to do?"

"Well, just make them last as long as you can."

"Oh Mama!" Geneva was very fastidious about her personal hygiene. She hated the idea of leaving a sanitary pad on for too long.

"Now there's no use arguing about it. You'll just have to make do."

"I'll go get you some." Jesse Mae reached for her dress; a lightweight, cotton frock, the same red color as her swimsuit; sporting buttons on the front from top to bottom.

"You don't need to do that. She can make do." Lula Mae felt compelled to object; although she had little doubt that her objections would sway Jesse Mae's decision on what to do.

"Oh Aunt Jesse Mae, I can't ask you to…"

"My Lord, what's the matter?" The others were startled by the look of concern on Louise's face as she looked past them, struggling to get to her feet. They turned to see what she was looking at.

Walking towards them were Guy, Harold, and Tony. Harold had his hand on Guy's shoulder as if giving him support. Guy was holding his left elbow with his right hand.

Lula Mae was on her feet in an instant. "What's the matter?" She rushed to her husband.

"He slipped and hit his elbow on a rock," said Harold. "I think he may have broken it. I'm going to take him to the doctor's office."

"It's not broken," protested Guy.

Lula Mae took Guy's left hand and lightly touched his elbow. "Let me see."

"Ow!" Guy pulled his arm away from Lula Mae. "God-damn!"

"I'm sorry." Lula Mae went to the quilt and slipped on a blouse and picked up her purse. "I'll bet it's broken. Come on Harold; we better get him to a doctor."

"The doctor won't be in his office today," said Louise. "You'll have to take him to the hospital."

"Why don't I take him?" Jesse Mae had her dress on and buttoned. She was slipping on her sandals. "I need to go into town anyway." She glanced at Geneva.

"I don't care who takes me." The pain in Guys arm was convincing him that medical attention was probably the best course of action to take. "Let's just go."

Guy, Lula and Jesse Mae quickly got into Jesse Mae's car, which was sitting in the shade of the trees with its top down. Jesse Mae started the car engine and slowly drove towards the road.

Lula Mae turned her head and yelled, "Watch the other kids, Geneva."

Jesse Mae turned to Guy as she pulled onto the road. "That's what you get for showing off," she said with a sly grin.

Guy shot a quick look at Lula Mae who was sitting between him and Jesse Mae in the front seat of the convertible. He then leaned forward to look past Lula at his sister. "I wasn't showing off. I was just having a good time."

"I saw those Carlson girls watching all of you men. And you know that you wouldn't let Harold or Tony show you up in front of anyone; especially pretty girls."

"Why Jesse Mae, those girls aren't much older than Loretta. Why on earth would a man Guy's age want to show off in front of them?" Lula Mae looked at her husband with a look on her face that showed a little less concern for his pain. Her denial of Guy's intentions was half hearted; she knew him to be a flirt. She just did not want her sister-in-law rubbing it in her face.

"Aw, don't look at me like that," said Guy to his wife. He looked forward at the road ahead of him. "You have to get something started, don't you Jess?"

Jesse Mae nudged Lula. "Lula Mae I'm just teasing with you. Don't you think he knows better than to flirt with someone right in front of you?"

Lula Mae felt a little foolish for letting Jesse Mae bait her like that. "Well," she also looked at the road ahead. "…those girls were watching him; I saw them."

"Oh pooh," said Jesse Mae. "They weren't watching him; they were watching Tony. Guy was just trying to show Tony up." She smiled broadly at Guy while he looked back at her with a frown on his face.

Lula Mae decided to drop the subject. She did not want Guy to get started on his jealously over her and Tony.

They had reached the highway now and Jesse Mae accelerated. It was difficult to carry on a conversation with the wind whipping around them. Jesse Mae turned on the radio and the three of them listened without speaking while Johnny Cash sang about walking the line.

Within twenty minutes they pulled into the parking space in the hospital parking lot. Jesse Mae pointed to the emergency room entrance. "We have to go over there." They got out of the car and walked through the crowded parking lot.

"There sure are a lot of sick people today," said Guy. "I hope this doesn't take too long."

"Well, however long it takes, you have to get this looked at." Lula Mae was genuinely concerned for him.

As they had anticipated, the emergency room waiting area was quite crowded. They were told by the nurse at the admitting desk that, due to the holiday there was only one doctor on duty. She said that they might have to wait up to an hour. Lula and Guy sat down and Jesse Mae went to the cafeteria to get them some coffee.

Jesse Mae walked out of the cafeteria with three cups of coffee on a tray. She stopped short; almost running into a tall thin man in his early forties. "Roger."

"What are you doing here?" the man asked. He was Roger Crawford, the childhood acquaintance who Harold and Guy had mentioned seeing at the movie theater.

"I…uh…Guy…my brother…well you know Guy. He might have a broken arm. He and his wife are in the waiting room. They're waiting to see a doctor. I had to drive him here. Why are you here?"

Roger sighed deeply as he looked intently into Jesse Mae's eyes. "My doctor called me in. He said he had to discuss something with me, right away."

Jesse Mae stood for a moment, waiting for Roger to continue. When he did not, she said, "And?"

"I'm glad I ran into you. Can you and I talk somewhere?"

Jesse Mae suspected that this was important. "Yeah," she said, trying to decide what to do with the coffee. "Why don't I take this coffee to Guy and his wife and then meet you back here in the cafeteria?"

"Sure, I'll wait for you inside." Roger went into the cafeteria and Jesse Mae headed for the emergency room.

Lula Mae had a wet cloth holding it around Guy's elbow when Jesse Mae got to them.

"Does it still hurt?" Jesse Mae held the tray where they could take their coffee.

"Hell yes it still hurts."

Jesse Mae and Lula both looked around the room in embarrassment. The room was full of people, including children.

"Honey…" said Lula, trying to impress upon him that he should not swear in public.

Ignoring his wife and sister's show of disapproval, Guy reached for a cup with his free hand.

"How long did she say it would be?" asked Jesse Mae; referring to the admitting nurse.

"She said it would be about an hour." Lula Mae took her coffee from the tray.

"Well, you know what; I have some shopping that I need to do. You know those things for Geneva. I think I'll go do that now. I won't be too long."

"Okay," said Lula Mae.

Jesse Mae went back to the cafeteria where she found Roger sitting at a table holding a cup of coffee. She took her cup from the tray and placed the tray on the table next to him and took a seat. "So what's up?"

"The cancer has metastasized."

"How bad is it?"

"The doctor just told me that I might have a month to live; if I'm lucky."

Jesse Mae reached across the table and took Roger's hand in hers. "Oh Roger."

"Which means that if I'm going to ever see my only child it will have to be very soon. I can't wait for our plan to fall into place."

"But…how…?"

"The doctor gave me a month at most. I could die at any time. I need to see him as soon as possible."

Jesse Mae pulled her hand back from Roger's. "You've had twenty-five years to see him, Roger. I would never have kept him from you if I thought you wanted to see him."

"Jess, I told you…I didn't know you were pregnant when I left. I was just a dumb kid. When my mom saw me with you in my truck, she had a fit. She told my dad that if they didn't send me away that you would wind up pregnant and I would have to marry you. I told them that I wanted to marry you. But of course they said that would never happen."

"Of course," said Jesse Mae, sarcastically. "Your mother always looked down on me and my family. I could feel her watching me when Brenda Glass and I would go into her store for a Coke after school; she was always so condescending with her phony politeness. She would ask Brenda and me how our families were; as if she really cared. She barely knew my family.

"A couple of months after you were gone she asked me if I was gaining weight. It scared me when she asked me that. I didn't realize that anyone else had noticed my weight gain. I didn't know what to say. I knew very little about being pregnant or what the signs were, but I had my suspicions. I knew something was wrong; something was changing in my body, and I had always heard that if you kiss a boy a certain way, you could wind up having a baby. I lied to her; I told her that I hadn't noticed any increase in my weight.

"Then she started acting genuinely friendly with Brenda and me. I thought she liked me. One day Brenda was sick and didn't go to school, so after I got out of school that day I went into her store by myself. She gave me a free Coke and sat down and talked to me. She started talking about you. She asked me if I liked you and I told her yes. Of course I didn't tell her how much I liked you, or that you and I had spent time alone together.

"Then she asked me if I had begun menstruating. She had to explain to me what she meant; I had never heard that word. I told her that I had started when I was twelve years old, but that I hadn't bled for a few months. I asked her if that was normal; for it to just stop like that. I told her that my mama never talked to me about it.

149

"She looked away from me and was quiet for a moment. It made me very nervous, the way she acted. When she looked back at me her expression had changed. She wasn't friendly anymore. She told me that she was very busy and that I should probably be getting home. That was the last time she said anything more than a cold 'hello' to me.

"Not long after that my mama realized that I was pregnant and she made me pretend to have tuberculosis and go live with Rena. I never went back to your mother's store. I never spoke to her again."

Jesse Mae wrapped her hands around her coffee cup and stared at the coffee inside. A sad smile came across her face and she shook her head slowly. "I was so in love with you Roger." She raised her eyes to meet his. "I lived in that dumpy little house almost four months with that Indian woman; Rena Two Eagles.

"Mama paid her for letting me stay there and not tell anybody that I was pregnant. She had been deserted by her husband and she needed the help. I pretended to have tuberculosis so that nobody would visit me and discover my condition. My mama hounded me all that time to tell her who the baby's father was, but I wouldn't tell her. And then I had to pretend that my only child…the only child that I would ever have…was my brother."

CHAPTER ELEVEN

"BY THE TIME I WAS OLD ENOUGH to see how wrong the whole charade was, it was too late. Romey had bonded with Mama. Taking him from her would have broken his heart."

"That's why I want to make it right with you Jess. As executor of Romey's estate you will have access to almost a million dollars. You can do with it as you please."

Jesse Mae remained silent. She avoided eye contact with Roger while she sipped her coffee.

"My mother was so sorry for what she had done. She bore the guilt her whole life. She regretted hurting you, but she really regretted never getting to know her only grandchild. She always thought that I would have other children.

"When she told me about Romey a couple of years ago, I was angry with her. She cried and begged me to forgive her. That's when she told me about the trust fund she wanted to set up for him. I think she knew she was close to death.

"Anyway, she told me that it was my decision whether to contact you or not. She said that she was through trying to control other people's lives.

"I don't know why I waited so long to get in touch with you." Roger took a sip of his coffee and set the cup back down on the table; he stared at the cup for a moment, his fingers turning it slowly one way then the other. He raised his eyes to meet Jesse Mae's eyes, which were now looking at him. "Yes I do. I was ashamed. I was so full of myself.

What would people think if they knew that I had an illegitimate son…a retarded, illegitimate son?"

Roger looked at his coffee cup again. "It's funny how all of the things that we've thought to be so important in our lives, become so meaningless when we know that our life is at its end."

"I'm truly sorry for your misfortune, Roger." Jesse Mae took Roger's hand in hers. "You have to understand that Romey's welfare is my main priority. If I let you meet him, you can't let on to him in any way that you are his father. Not to Romey; not to anybody." Jesse Mae sighed deeply as she considered her next move.

"I can take you to meet him right now if you like. He and Mama are alone at the house. Papa might be there, but that's okay. I'll just tell them that you're a friend of mine and that I ran into you here and that you're going to the river with me. I'll tell them that I had to pick something up at the house. You can meet Romey then. But remember, Romey knows and loves his grandma as his mama. In fact, nobody but me, Mama, Rena, and you know that Romey is my son. And nobody but you and I know that you are his father."

"You don't have to worry, Jess. I've caused enough pain in your life. I'll go to my grave with our secret. I just want to meet my son; to see him, to talk to him before I die."

Jesse Mae saw Romey sitting alone on the front porch as she pulled into the drive leading up to the house. "I don't see Papa's truck. I guess he's not back yet."

"Is that Romey?" Roger looked toward Romey, who was now standing on the front porch, watching as the car approached the house.

"Yes." Jesse Mae looked at Roger in an effort to read on his face what he was feeling at that moment. She had always been very protective of Romey. If she sensed that Roger was feeling ashamed or disappointed by his son, she would turn the car around and refuse to let him meet him.

Roger turned and looked at her. He had a half smile on his face and tears were forming in his eyes.

"Now don't go getting mushy about this." Jesse Mae looked at Romey on the porch. "He won't understand and you might upset him."

"Right." Roger wiped his eyes as he turned his attention back to his son.

A feeling of tenderness came over Jesse Mae as she looked at Roger again. For the first time since they had reconnected, she saw the boy that she had been so in love with when she was just thirteen years old. She remembered how it was between them; how he had been tender and loving towards her. He was basically a good person, and she had been right in loving him.

A low cloud of dust swirled around the tires of the car when Jesse Mae brought it to a stop near the back of the house. Romey remained on the front porch. He was now standing at the edge of the porch peering at the strange man with the woman he thought was his sister.

Jesse Mae and Roger got out of the car and walked the length of the house to where he was. "Hi Romey, what-cha-doin'?" said Jesse Mae as she and Roger looked up at him.

"Hi Jesse Mae. I'm just waiting for Mama. She went down to the barn."

"What?" The two on the ground walked to the steps at the front of the porch and began to climb. "Why did she go down to the barn?"

"She's digging for treasure."

"Oh for crying out loud." Jesse Mae looked toward the barn. She had a clear view of the barn but she did not see her mother. "She's down in that hole, digging." Jesse Mae returned her attention to Romey and Roger. "Oh well, it's just as well.

"Romey this is an old friend of mine. His name is Roger."

Romey looked at Roger with interest. He always liked meeting new people.

"Hi Romey." Roger extended his hand.

"Hi Roger." Romey shook his father's hand.

"How long has Mama been down there, Romey?" asked Jesse Mae.

"Oh, not too long." Romey seldom bothered to look at a clock. He knew how to tell time, but it never seemed important to him.

"Well I hope she's careful." Jesse Mae motioned toward the porch swing. "Have a seat Roger."

Roger sat down as Jesse Mae picked up the Sears Catalog, which Romey had left on the swing. She handed it to Romey. "Romey why don't you sit down here with Roger and show him the Sears Catalog? I'm going to go into the kitchen and get us some iced tea. I'll be right back."

Romey sat next to Roger and began pointing out the various items in the catalog, which intrigued him the most.

Jesse Mae opened the screen door to the living room, and hesitated for a moment to see how the two men would get along. With his back toward her, Romey was unaware that she had not already left them. She watched Roger's eyes as he exclaimed to Romey that he too liked browsing through the catalog; he was obviously pleased to discover this common interest. He looked up at Jesse Mae while Romey turned the pages. He mouthed the words, "Thank You" to her before she quietly let the screen door close and went to the kitchen for the iced tea.

The tea was already brewed and chilled in the refrigerator, but she took her time in preparing it. She wanted to give Roger and Romey a moment alone together. She wondered what Roger was thinking about Romey as she filled Romey's favorite Hop-a-long Cassidy glass. She filled the other two glasses for herself and Roger and placed them all on a tray, which was resting on the counter top.

She left the tea on the counter and walked to a window that had a clear view of the barn and the pile of dirt next to it, which had covered the roof of the old root cellar. She stood for a moment, looking across the pasture; wondering what her mother was doing down there. Being here with Roger had stirred up old resentments in her. She had never really forgiven her mother for forcing her to conceal her pregnancy and pretend to be quarantined in that old house with Rena for all that time.

Her mother's threat that she would force her to give her baby up for adoption if she did not do as she demanded echoed in her memory. What would her life had been like, had she and Roger been allowed to marry? Would Romey have been different if she had been allowed to give birth to him in a normal manner? Would she have been able to have other children, had she not contracted that infection from unsanitary conditions at his birth?

Jesse Mae turned from the window and picked up the tray of tea. It had been a long time since she had dwelled on these questions. She had accepted the situation and gotten on with her life. She had had a good life. There were even times when she felt that her mother had been right in doing what she did. But now as she walked to the porch, hearing the two men laughing with one another and getting along so well, she seriously questioned those past decisions.

She opened the screen door to find Romey standing in front of Roger, who was still sitting in the swing. They were both laughing. Romey took his seat again next to his father.

"What are you two laughing about?" Jesse Mae put the tray of filled glasses on a small table and pulled the rocking chair in front of the swing where she sat down and reached for the glasses, one at a time. She handed the glasses to the men and took one for herself.

"Romey was telling me about his nephews having a run-in with some wasps that they were pestering. He was showing me how the boys said they were running and swatting at the wasps with their hands." Roger smiled broadly at Romey while Romey smiled sheepishly then sipped his tea.

The three sat and talked for a few minutes more. Roger noticed Jesse Mae looking at her watch. "Are we running out of time?" he asked.

Jesse Mae looked a Roger and then at Romey. She could see how Romey had taken to Roger and vice-a-versa. This would probably be the only time they would ever spend together.

She thought about the trust fund. She knew that her mother would know that Roger was Romey's father when she learned about it. She considered going down to the cellar where Mary was digging and telling her about him; or she could just stay here on the porch with Romey and Roger until she came back up, and then tell her. What difference would it make at this point if she knew who Romey's father was?

Then Jesse Mae imagined the scene it would cause if she followed through with either of those plans; it would be sheer disaster. No; it would be better to leave now and tell her later, when Roger was not around. Leaving before she came back up would be the best course of action. It had just been a stroke of luck that she had been down at that old cellar when they arrived. It had bought them this precious time together.

Jesse Mae was ready to tell Roger that it was time to go; but as she looked at the father and son, she decided to take a chance and give them a little more time together. She formulated a plan in her mind. 'If she comes back up while we're still here; I'll just tell her that Roger is an old friend. I'll give her a phony last name. If I tell her his real name, she'll put two and two together and she'll suspect the truth. I want this to be a pleasant, easy visit. I'll tell her the truth later.'

"No," said Jesse Mae. "We have a little more time. Romey, why don't you take Roger out to your playhouse and show him around?"

Roger looked surprised. Jesse Mae had told him that it would have to be a very short visit. He was delighted at this suggestion.

"Mama said I have to stay on the front porch," said Romey.

"It's okay." Jesse Mae put her hand on Romey's shoulder and gave him an affectionate pat. "I'll tell Mama that I said you could. She won't be angry with you."

A smile came across Romey's face. Seeing the two men smiling; Jesse Mae could see the resemblance between them. She hoped that her mother would not return while Roger was still here. If she were to recognize the resemblance she would surely cause a row.

Romey took Roger by the hand and led him down the steps of the porch and around the side of the house towards the playhouse in the back yard.

Jesse Mae sat in the porch swing, gently pushing one foot against the wooden planks of the porch; moving the swing back and forth. She sipped her iced tea in silence. She was a very tenacious woman when she set her mind on something. This was a unique opportunity for her and Romey. Not only would the trust fund take care of her in style for the rest of her life; it would also open up a whole new world for Romey. She would not let her mother stand in the way. She had made one huge mistake in judgement when she allowed her mother to take over Romey's life. This time it would be different. This time Jesse Mae would decide what was best.

Mary sat on the apple crate at the bottom of the old cellar wishing that she had brought water with her. It was almost noon and the hot sun was directly overhead. The oppressive heat and the exertion of digging had gotten to her.

So far, she had found nothing. She wiped her brow and looked at the recess in the earth where she had been searching. She rested for a moment more, and then picked up her spade and resumed her task.

Presently she felt the garden spade hit something solid, and a surge of excitement shot through her. 'Finally!' she thought as she dug faster. After several minutes of frantically scraping away at the dirt, which was covering the object, she took hold of it and pulled a suitcase out into the sunlight.

She was elated; she had found her treasure. She opened the suitcase and began going through its contents. As she looked through the items, a realization came over her; these things were familiar to her. With the recognition of the objects, another memory surfaced. She touched her neck where the necklace had been and pictured it as she had seen it many years ago.

Her reverie was interrupted by a noise. She turned to see a small amount of dirt cascading over the edge of the cellar wall. She looked up and searched the perimeter of the pit to see what had caused the dirt to fall. The sun flashed in her eyes as she looked up; causing her to look away for an instant. She shaded her eyes with one hand and looked up again. A shadowed figure appeared above. With the brightness of the sun behind the figure, she was unable to make out any features… "Romey?"

Jesse Mae stood looking through the screen door of Romey's playhouse. She watched the father and son sitting on the small chairs with the checkerboard on top of the old trunk between them.

"Oh no!" Roger slapped his forehead in a mock show of exasperation. "You beat me again."

Romey smiled with pride as he replaced the checkers on the playing board, readying them for another game.

"Hey you two." Jesse Mae pushed the screen door open and stepped into the playhouse. She stood just inside, holding the door open. Romey and Roger looked up from their game.

"I won three games," said Romey.

"He's good at this." Roger was obviously enjoying himself.

Jesse Mae smiled sadly at Roger. "We better go."

Roger looked back at Romey; the joy gone from his face. He glanced at the checkerboard then at Jesse Mae and back to Romey. He sighed and swallowed, trying to dislodge the lump in his throat. "Well…good-bye Romey. It's been nice getting to know you." He extended his hand to Romey and they shook hands.

"Bye Roger." Romey did not pick up on the sadness felt by both Roger and Jesse Mae. To him this was just the end of a friendly visit with a nice man.

"You go on back to the front porch and wait for Mama, Romey." Jesse Mae stretched out one arm towards Romey, signaling for him to get up and move past her and through the doorway. She momentarily laid her hand on Romey's back as he walked past her. She remained holding the door open for Roger as he followed behind Romey.

The three of them walked together until they reached Jesse Mae's car. Jesse Mae put her arm around Romey's shoulder and kissed him on the cheek. "Bye Son."

"Bye Jesse Mae." Romey looked back at Roger as he continued along the side of the house to the front porch. "Bye Roger." He waived and then rounded the corner of the porch and disappeared.

"He liked you a lot," said Jesse Mae as she drove the car out onto the road.

"I was a fool, Jess," said Roger. "That innocent, loving man...I've had all this time to get to know him..."

The former lovers looked at each other without speaking. They had both made mistakes in their lives. Being together now gave them each a small bit of comfort.

Jesse Mae pulled her car into the parking place in front of the department store and killed the engine. She turned to Roger. "Just buy the first blouse you can find in size eight. Ask the sales lady to help you. I'm going to run across the street to the drugstore. I'll either meet you back here at the car or I'll come into the store; and please hurry. I'm sure Guy and Lula are waiting for me." She got out of her car and ran across the street, dodging traffic; while Roger headed in the opposite direction.

In less than five minutes Jesse Mae was out of the drugstore with the box of sanitary napkins in a bag. As she hurried back across the street she was happy to see Roger coming out of the department store. They both climbed back into her car at the same time. "Let me see what I bought."

Roger took two silk blouses out of the bag he was holding and held them up for Jesse Mae to see. Jesse Mae paused for a moment and gave Roger a look of approval. One at a time, she took the blouses from him and held them up in front of her. "These are nice." She lowered the garments and looked at Roger. She liked the style and the colors. "You did real good. And buying two was a good idea; it took me longer to make up my mind, so I finally bought both of them." She started the car and pulled into the street.

The hospital was only a few blocks away from where they were. Roger directed Jesse Mae to his car, which was parked in the hospital parking lot.

"Oh shit! They're waiting outside for me." From her car, Jesse Mae could see Guy and Lula standing outside the emergency room entrance, smoking cigarettes. "Quick; get out; I don't want them to see you with me."

"Call me when you get home," said Roger as he hurriedly got out of the car. Stooping low so as not to be seen by Lula and Guy, he moved toward his own car. When he got there he stood upright and turned back to Jesse Mae. He opened his car door, but did not get in. He stood facing her as she drove past him.

Their eyes met as Jesse Mae moved past him. She tried to smile, but it just would not happen. "Bye Roger," she said softly, and went on.

"I'm sorry. I'm sorry," said Jesse Mae, as she pulled her car up next to Guy and Lula. "I got to shopping and couldn't decide on which blouse to buy." She held up the blouses. "So I bought them both." She tossed the blouses and the bag from the drugstore into the back seat. "I just lost track of time. Have you been waiting long?"

"Long enough," said Guy, holding the car door open so that Lula Mae could get in before him.

"About twenty minutes," said Lula Mae, sliding across the car seat to the center of the car.

Guy got in and closed the door a little harder than was necessary. He was wearing a sling around his neck with his arm resting in it at a ninety degree angle. "That god-damned doctor kept us waiting over an hour."

"Well, there were people ahead of us. What did you want him to do?" Lula Mae was tired of listening to her husband complain.

Jesse Mae pulled away from the curb. "So, what did the doctor say? Is it broken?"

"It's just a bad bruise," said Lula Mae. "He said for him to keep from moving it as much as possible for a while. It should be okay in a couple of days."

Guy held up his arm to show Jesse Mae. "He said I should take some aspirin and keep it in this sling until it feels better."

"Thank God it wasn't broken." Jesse Mae pulled out of the parking lot and onto the street. She was relieved that they were focused on Guy's arm and not making an issue out of her being gone so long.

Frank left his truck under the shade of the large oak tree at the base of the drive to the house. The afternoon sun was bright and hot and there were no breezes stirring. He wiped his forehead with his bandanna as he walked up to the house. He went into the kitchen and; instead of drinking from the pail of water sitting on the countertop; he pumped a glass of the much cooler water, which came straight from the well and drank that.

The house was quiet. He could hear the fan oscillating in Romey's bedroom. The others would be gone for a couple more hours. He finished his water and walked toward the front porch to sit. As he passed Mary's bedroom, he expected to see her lying on her bed, resting. She was not there. Her fan was not running and her bed was neatly made.

He walked through her bedroom and into Romey's adjacent bedroom. Romey was asleep on his bed, wearing just his boxer shorts and an undershirt. The fan was turning back and fourth, cooling him with a soft breeze.

Frank walked back through Mary's bedroom and into the living room. He climbed the stairs and looked for Mary in the upstairs rooms. She was not in the house.

"Mama?"

Frank heard Romey calling for his mother. The creaking of the upstairs floorboards had awakened him. Frank went back downstairs and into Romey's bedroom. Romey was sitting on the edge of his bed. "Where's your mama, Son?"

Romey looked about the room as if looking for Mary. He was still a little groggy form his nap. Then he remembered. "She's down at that old root cellar, looking for treasure."

"What?" Frank walked briskly back to the front porch with Romey close behind him. He stood on one end of the porch looking down the pasture to the root cellar. "How long has she been down there?"

"A long time."

"God-damned fool woman," muttered Frank as he stomped down the steps of the porch and headed across the front yard in the direction of the cellar.

"Go get her, Papa." Romey was glad that Frank was going after Mary. He felt that she had been down there long enough and he wanted her back at the house with him.

Frank began to sweat profusely as he traipsed through the high grass on his way down to the cellar. He wiped his forehead again and cursed under his breath. He had very little patience with his bull-headed wife, but at the same time, he was concerned for her. She did not do well in the summer heat, and overexerting herself in the midday sun could very easily make her sick.

"Mary!" He called as he approached the hole in the ground. There was no answer. "Mary!" he said again with more force. Still no answer. He reached the edge of the hole and looked into it. It was empty; nothing but a few digging tools at the bottom of it.

He turned and looked toward the house. "God-damn." He felt that the long trek in the hot sun had been unnecessary. He pulled out his bandana and once again wiped the sweat from his forehead and eyes.

"Mary!" Perhaps she was in the barn. He went into the barn to see if she was there. Nothing but farm tools and a few chickens milling about. The shade inside the barn did little to cool him. The air inside was unmoving and thick feeling.

Romey sat in the porch swing watching as Frank crawled through the fence. He stood and went to the railing as Frank approached. "Where's Mama?"

"Hell, Romey, I don't know. You said she was down there at that cellar."

Romey stood with a look of confusion on his face. He obviously had no idea where Mary was. This was highly unusual. Mary and Romey were always together, and she kept a very close watch on him. Frank thought about the outhouse, but that could not be where she was. She would not use the outhouse. In all the years that Frank had known her, she would only use an outhouse when she was at somebody else's home. Here, she used her chamber pot.

"Now Romey, don't you worry about your mama." Frank could see that Romey was becoming distressed over Mary's absence. Concern was also growing in Frank's mind. "She's probably down at the henhouse," he said in an effort to calm Romey.

"But she already got the eggs this morning."

"Well, maybe she's just checking on the chickens." It occurred to Frank that he must be right. She had to be around somewhere. She would be down in the henhouse doing something. "You sit down and relax, Son. I'll go down to the henhouse and get your mama."

Romey obediently resumed his seat in the porch swing and Frank walked through the house towards the back yard looking for his wife or anything out of the ordinary as he passed through.

The screen door slammed behind him as he walked onto the back porch. "Mary." He called out. There was no answer; just the soft clucking of a few chickens and an occasional snort from the pigpen.

He looked through the screen door of Romey's playhouse as he passed it and also opened the door and looked inside the smokehouse. Both structures were empty.

"Mary," he called out again. It was too late in the day to be milking the cows or gathering eggs. He continued on toward the henhouse. A loud squeal came from the pigsty as he walked past it. He glanced in that direction and noticed something unusual. Between the planks of the fence; the slop trough, which held the pig's food, was partially visible. Frank stopped walking and focused on the trough. He stood for a moment, transfixed by the incredulity of what he thought he was seeing.

Two pigs were at the slop trough, which was about eighteen inches deep; their heads thrusting about within it. There was nothing unusual about this in itself; but the thing that held Frank paralyzed in his tracks was a piece of fabric hanging over the edge of the trough. The fabric was blue and white plaid...It looked like Mary's dress.

Frank began walking towards the pigsty, telling himself that there was some reasonable explanation for that fabric to be in that trough; some explanation other than the one, which was forming in his mind.

Despite his attempt at rationalization, a terror began to seize him as he approached the snorting animals. He could not deny that there was something terribly wrong here.

Suddenly; with all his doubts dispelled, he bolted toward the pigsty, bringing into focus the horrible image of what was in the trough. "Mary!" he screamed as he thrust his body up and over the fence catching a clear view of his wife's flesh being lacerated by these ravaging beasts. He landed hard on top of a large sow.

Frenzied squealing erupted as Frank tumbled over the first pig and landed on his back on the ground. He kicked the second pig, sending them both into a hysterical attempt to escape. They ran helter-skelter; bumping into, and climbing over the other pigs in the pen, which had been lying about. All the animals were on their feet now, running around the pen, squealing and screeching wildly.

Frank's mind was his enemy at this moment. The image of Mary falling into this dirty wooden feeding box, and fighting against these filthy swine as they savagely attacked her, flashed in front of him. He struggled to gather his thoughts as he pulled her blood covered body out of the trough.

There was a loud roaring noise in his head, competing with the sounds of his own screams, which seemed to be coming from somewhere outside himself. He could not be sure, but it looked like Mary's nose was gone as he wiped away at the blood on her face and shook her in an effort to make her show some sign of life.

With great effort, he picked up her limp body and carried her out of the pigsty and toward the house. He strained to keep his balance, but within a few steps; fell to his knees. Mary's body dropped to the ground and rolled away from him. He crawled to her and once again pulled her to his chest and held her in his arms.

"Oh God!...Oh God!" he cried as he rocked her back and forth and stared into the eyes of Romey, who was now standing in the backyard watching the scene in stupefied silence.

CHAPTER TWELVE

JOHNNY JUMPED FROM THE BACK SEAT, OVER the edge of Jesse Mae's Cadillac convertible just before it came to a complete stop in the parking area next to the house. He had seen this done in a movie and he had wanted to imitate the action for a long time. Scotty and Gary had seen the same movie and they thought this was really cool. They both jumped from Guy's car; exiting both sides at the same time, as he pulled up next to Jesse Mae. Harold and Louise, who were following in their own car right behind them, both yelled unheeded reprimands at Scotty.

The three boys, totally disregarding their parents' ineffectual attempts to restrain them, ran to Romey's playhouse. Sunburned and wearing damp swimsuits; they were still full of energy and eager to find some new amusement. Loretta, who had waited for Jesse Mae's car to come to a complete stop before she opened the door and jumped out, quickly ran to catch up with them.

Guy, Lula, Harold, and Louise began collecting towels and picnic supplies while Jesse Mae and Geneva headed for the back door of the house.

"Guy...Harold..." Jesse Mae's voice was peculiar; with a sort of forced calm. Harold did not hear her; he was busy talking to Louise about unloading the car; but Guy looked toward her as she and Geneva stood motionless, focusing their attention on the porch.

"What's the matter?" asked Guy.

Without a word, Jesse Mae and Geneva turned and looked at Guy. The look of fear in their eyes alarmed him.

Gary R. Austin

The phrase, 'What's the matter?' had caught the attention of Harold, Lula, and Louise. They all stopped what they were doing and looked toward the others, picking up on the sense that something was wrong.

"What is it?" Guy was now walking toward his sister and daughter. As he approached them, they turned and looked at the porch, directing his attention to it. Spread across the surface of the steps and porch; leading into the house through the kitchen door was an almost uninterrupted trail of blood.

"Mama!...Papa!" Guy bolted onto the porch and through the back door, followed closely by the others. He ran into Romey's bedroom and was momentarily relieved by the typical scene presented there. Romey was lying on his bed with the fan circulating air around him.

Jesse Mae rushed past Guy and sat on the bed next to Romey. She grasped his shoulders and asked him if he was okay. Romey had locked eyes with Guy, and without speaking or acknowledging Jesse Mae, continued to stare blankly at him. At the same instant Harold was pushing past Guy, following the trail of blood, which led through Romey's bedroom and into Mary's bedroom.

"Oh my God!!!"

The commotion coming from inside the house alarmed Loretta and the boys who were still roughhousing outside. They stopped playing and ran to the house; halting briefly when they noticed the blood on the porch. Avoiding the blood stains, they rushed inside and crowded into Romey's bedroom. They tried to continue on into Mary's room, but they were blocked from entering by Louise, who stood in the doorway preventing them from witnessing the horrendous scene, which was unfolding in front of her. The frightened children struggled to see around their aunt and mother, but Louise stood fast.

Inside Mary's bedroom, Guy and Harold were on the bed with their blood covered mother, calling to her through their tears; checking for signs of life. Jesse Mae was at her father's side, who was sitting in a chair next to the bed; his hands, clothing, and face, all smeared with blood. He sat, unspeaking, looking at his hands, which were resting, palms up on his thighs. Lula Mae stood to one side of the room, holding Geneva in her arms, trying to calm her as she cried hysterically.

The pandemonium was terrifying to the other children, as they stood behind Louise, trying to see what was going on in the next room.

"No!...No!" cried Guy as he accepted the fact that there were no signs of life in his mother's body; and he pulled her close and began to rock back and forth with her.

Harold had pulled back form his mother's body and was struggling to catch his breath between sobs as he looked at Guy.

"Papa?" Jesse Mae squatted in front of Frank, holding his face in her hands, trying to force him to make eye contact with her. "What happened?"

Frank blinked and he stirred from his stupor. He looked about the room and then he looked at Jesse Mae. An expression of fear and confusion was in his eyes. "The pigs got her...the god-damned pigs got her."

"Mama!" cried Loretta, still struggling to get past her aunt Louise.

"Go back Loretta. Take the boys and go upstairs." Lula Mae peeled Geneva's arms from around her neck and held her wrists, preventing her from grabbing her again. She looked intently into Geneva's eyes. "Go upstairs Geneva. Take the other kids and go upstairs."

"No Mama!" Geneva held her mother's stare. She was horrified and she did not want to leave her.

"I need you to go upstairs, Geneva; and take care of the other kids. I'll be up in a little while. Now go!" Lula Mae let go of Geneva's wrists and motioned for her to leave the room.

Hesitantly, Geneva turned and walked toward Louise and the other youngsters who were behind her. Louise did an about face toward the children as she stepped aside to make way for Geneva. She put her hand on Scotty's shoulder. "Scott, go upstairs with the other kids. Mama will be up shortly." Scotty looked at his mother and stood fast as Geneva herded Johnny, Loretta and Gary away from the scene. "Go on now," said Louise, and gave Scotty a gentle push towards Geneva, who put her hand on his back and guided him out of the room. With the children gone, Louise and Lula turned their attention back to the adults.

"Papa, that's crazy," Jesse Mae was saying. "Pigs don't attack people."

Frank turned and looked at Mary's body as she lay on the bed where he had positioned her after dragging her into the house. "I shot 'em; every last one of 'em."

Lula Mae turned from the tragedy before her and walked back into Romey's bedroom. Romey was lying on his bed in the fetal position. He looked up at Lula Mae with uncertainty in his eyes and said nothing. Lula Mae sat on the edge of the bed. She leaned over Romey and hugged him. He did not respond to her touch. She pulled back and looked at him again. "Romey?" She put her hand on his forehead to see if he was running a fever. "Are you okay, Son?" She read nothing but confusion in his eyes; as if she were looking into the eyes of an infant. "Oh Romey," she sobbed as she embraced him again. It was obvious to her that he was severely traumatized. She held him and looked back into Mary's bedroom through the open doorway.

"How Papa? How did the pigs get her?" Guy's voice was almost unrecognizable to Lula Mae. He was crying and talking at the same time. His words sounded almost accusatory. Lula Mae rose from Romey's bed and went back into Mary's bedroom.

Louise was standing next to Harold with her hands on his shoulders, coaxing him away from his mother's bed. Breaking into uncontrollable sobbing, he stood and walked with her out of the bedroom, through the living room and onto the front porch.

Guy remained on the bed, cradling his mother's dead body in his arms. Lula Mae moved next to him on the bed and put her arm around him.

Jesse Mae stood next to Frank, with one arm resting on his shoulders. She pulled him closer while he remained in the chair, sobbing quietly. Tears filled her eyes as she finally allowed herself to turn her attention to her mother lying on the bed.

Nothing more was said for the next few minutes. All that was heard throughout the house were the sounds of sobbing.

Presently, Louise reentered the bedroom. "I'm going to drive up the road to the neighbor's house and call the sheriff. He'll call the coroner for us. I'm going to take Harold with me. We'll be back in a few minutes."

The sobbing had subsided, but nobody responded verbally to Louise's statement. Lula Mae looked at her and nodded her head in agreement.

It took the sheriff and the coroner a little more than an hour to get to the house. In the meantime, Jesse Mae had convinced Frank to move onto the front porch with her, and Louise had taken Harold upstairs to try and get him to lie down for a while. With the coroner's arrival, Guy had reluctantly left his mother's body and joined Frank and Jesse Mae on the porch. Lula Mae had sent the children out to Romey's playhouse with iced tea and then made a fresh pot of coffee for the adults.

Repeatedly, Lula Mae had checked on Romey, but she had failed to get any response from him other than the silent look he gave her as his eyes followed her when she would enter his bedroom. She decided that keeping still on his bed was the best thing for him right now, so she did not encourage him to get up. She did take him a glass of cool water, but he had refused to drink; merely continuing his silent stare.

At around four-thirty p.m., the coroner left with Mary's body. It would be held at the morgue overnight and sent to the funeral home the following morning where the family could go and make arrangements.

Lula Mae and Louise helped their husbands get out of their clothes and wash the blood off themselves. Jesse Mae looked after Frank. The doors to Mary's bedroom were closed. The women would clean the bedroom the following day. Earlier, Louise had built a fire under the cauldron in the back yard so that there would be plenty of hot water for bathing and cleaning. The three women did their best to clean the stains from the floor. The dry wood on the porch; and the carpet in Romey's bedroom had absorbed the blood and it was impossible to remove it all in one cleaning, but they at least managed to get the greater part of it up. The linoleum, which covered the kitchen floor, was now free from any signs of what had taken place.

Louise was in the kitchen fixing supper. Her eyes were red and swollen from crying, but they were dry. She was a very pragmatic woman. When there were duties to perform, she knew how to put her emotions on hold and do what was necessary.

Jesse Mae had convinced her father to lie down in his bedroom; where he continued to go in and out of states of fitful sleep. Guy and

Harold sat on the front porch in silence. Their emotions had been spent and they were exhausted.

Jesse Mae sat on the edge of Romey's bed. A wash basin filled with cool water rested on the nightstand next to her. She lifted a washcloth from the cool water and wrung it out. She folded it and gently placed it on Romey's forehead. Romey had not left the bed since they had returned from the river and found him there.

Lula Mae stood in the doorway, looking into Romey's bedroom. She had taken a short break from helping Louise in the kitchen to see how Romey and Jesse Mae were getting on. "How is he?" she asked.

Jesse Mae looked up a Lula. "The same." She was growing more and more concerned with Romey's emotional state. "I can't get him to talk to me. He just keeps staring at me." She turned back to Romey and brushed his cheek with the back of her hand.

"Do you think he saw what happened?"

Jesse Mae looked back at Lula Mae. "Oh…I don't think he did. Papa said that he was here on the bed when he came home. He told Papa that Mama was down at that old root cellar. He did see Papa carrying her out of the pigsty though.

"Papa said that he didn't remember much after he saw Mama in that slop trough. He only remembered screaming and crying a lot; said that must have been what caused Romey to come outside. He said that he was holding Mama and then he looked up and Romey was standing there staring at them." A lump formed in Jesse Mae's throat and tears filled her eyes. She turned back to Romey and took the wash cloth off of his forehead and dipped it in the cool water again.

Lula Mae remained in the doorway for a moment and then turned and went back into the kitchen. She walked to the stove and checked on the pot of boiling potatoes.

Louise was standing at the sink, looking out of the window. "The sheriff and his deputy are still out there. I wonder what they're looking for."

The five children sat on a varying collection of chairs and boxes outside of Romey's playhouse. They too watched the sheriff and Tony with growing curiosity.

The carcasses of the dead pigs were still lying in the pigsty where they had fallen when Frank shot them. Flies were swarming around them and they were beginning to smell.

"They're going to cut those pigs open to see what's in their bellies."

"Oh, Johnny shut up!" Geneva was in no mood to hear her brother spew any wisecracks about their grandmother and those pigs. She had recovered somewhat from the initial shock of the whole incident, and although she and the others had never developed a very close relationship with their grandparents, they all shared a detached fondness for them, and the situation was certainly very upsetting for them.

In truth, the incident had affected them all deeply; including Johnny. Aside from the fact that it was their grandmother who was now deceased, none of them had ever had any experience with a human death before.

"What?" said Johnny. He was truly at a loss as to why Geneva had snapped at him. He was innocent of any intention to make light of the situation. His observation was purely analytical in its origin. "They are. They have to see if…"

"Never mind," said Geneva resignedly, feeling that she had overreacted to his comments. She understood that they were all upset. "Just…lets wait and see what they do, okay?"

Johnny shrugged his shoulders in a gesture of agreement.

The sheriff and Tony were walking slowly towards the house, looking at the ground where Mary's body had been dragged. Tony was making notes on a small pad of paper. They stopped before they got to the porch and the sheriff pointed to the ground. They walked towards the area where the cars were parked. They reached the vehicles and stopped. They turned around and took a few steps toward the pigsty. The sheriff bent over and examined the ground closely. Tony squatted next to him and also studied the dirt. The sheriff made a sweeping motion with his hand, first pointing at the cars and then toward the pigsty. Tony nodded his head and made more notes on his pad. They both stood up and the sheriff walked toward the house.

"Excuse me ladies." The sheriff peered through the screen door, leading into the kitchen.

"Come in Sheriff Files," said Louise, walking toward the door.

Lula Mae followed behind her and they stood near the door looking at the sheriff as he stepped into the kitchen.

"I'm sorry to have to ask this, but I really need to talk to Frank for a minute."

Louise and Lula looked at each other, each seeking a response from the other as to what to do. Then they looked back to the sheriff. "Well… he's sleeping," said Louise.

"I'm sorry, but this is important. It will only take a minute."

"What is it, Sheriff?" asked Louise.

"Maybe nothing. Would you wake him please; and ask him to come down?"

"Why don't we take you up to his room, and you can talk to him there?" said Lula.

"That would be fine."

The two women quickly checked their meal, turning down burners so that the food would not burn. Then they led the sheriff up to Frank's room. They could have just directed him up, but they were both curious as to what the sheriff had to say.

The door to the bedroom was open and Frank lay on his bed, staring at the ceiling. An oscillating fan, circulating air throughout the room, stood on the night stand next to the bed.

"Frank," said Louise as she entered the room followed by Lula Mae and the sheriff. "Sheriff Files wants to talk to you about something."

Frank turned his head to the group. He raised himself up on his elbows. "What is it Karl?"

Louise and Lula Mae stood just inside the door as the sheriff walked to the foot of the bed and looked down at Frank. "I'm sorry to bother you Frank, but I need you to tell me again, how you came to find Mary in the pigsty."

"What do you mean? I told you all that already."

"I know, Frank; I know you did, but I have to be completely clear about what happened. I want to make sure that I haven't forgotten anything."

"Well that god-damned deputy wrote everything down, didn't he?" Frank immediately regretted belittling Tony, but he was frustrated and angry from feeling so helpless and his first instinct was to lash out.

"Frank will you just indulge me here? Something has come up that I need to be clear about."

"The pigs got her!" Frank sat up and swung his legs over the edge of the bed. "How much clearer can I be?"

"I know this is a difficult time for you Frank. I wouldn't bother you if it wasn't important."

Frank sat for a moment looking at the sheriff, and then he said, "Fine. What do you want to know?"

"Just tell me where Mary was when you first found...her body." Sheriff Files hated to refer to Mary as a body. He had known her for many years.

"She was in the god-damned slop trough, Karl. The fucking pigs were eating her!"

Lula Mae turned and left the room. She could not bear to imagine the scene, which was being described. Louise, with her stronger constitution; stayed to listen and also to lend moral support to Frank.

The sheriff took a moment to let Frank calm down, and then he said, "And what did you do when you found her?"

Frank looked at the sheriff in disbelief. Why was he asking him these questions? He had already told him what happened. The sheriff just stood there looking at him. Frank turned away from the sheriff and let out a sigh of exasperation. He remained silent for a moment, as he struggled to recall what had taken place. Then he spoke. "I climbed over the fence and jumped into the trough...I pushed the pigs off of her and dragged her out of the pen. I don't remember much after that. Everything is all still a little fuzzy."

"Just take your time. Give it some thought."

Frank glanced at Louise. He looked like he was about to cry again. He dropped his head and looked at the floor. Louise went over and sat down beside him on the bed. She took his hand and sat in silence. After a moment, Frank continued. "I...I carried her out of the pen. She was heavy; I stumbled and dropped her, then I had to drag her on into the house. Romey was standing there; outside the house. I think I told him to go back inside...I meant to tell him...anyway, I put her on her bed. She was heavy, it took me a while. Then I saw Romey standing in the doorway. He never said nothing. He just stood there, watching me. I told him to lay down on his bed, and I got my shotgun and I killed those god-damned pigs."

"Were they all still in the pen?"

Frank looked up at the sheriff. "The pigs? Yeah, why?"

"And you carried her out of the pigsty, dropped her and then dragged her into the house; in a straight line?"

"Well god-damn-it Karl, what do you think I did; drag her around in circles?"

The sheriff took a deep breath and continued. "Something heavy was dragged either from the parking area, into the pigsty or from the pigsty to the parking area."

"What?" said Frank exchanging glances with Louise.

"Tony and I have been examining the scene. There are two trails that are very similar; as if both trails were the result of Mary's body being dragged on the ground. One of the trails goes from where you stumbled just outside the pigsty, to the house. The other looks like it goes from the parking area straight into the pigsty."

Louise and Frank looked at one another. This made no sense to them. Frank turned to the sheriff. "Mary was in the pigsty."

"Are you saying that Mary was dragged into the pigsty?" asked Louise.

"It looks that way."

"Somebody put her in there?" Frank's pulse was racing again. He was trying to remain calm, but the thought of his wife being deliberately put into that slop trough was overpowering. He began to hyperventilate.

Louise put her arm around Frank's shoulders and pulled him close to her. "Sheriff," she said. "Are you saying that somebody killed Mary?"

"I don't know that," said the sheriff. "I'm just trying to put the pieces of the puzzle together."

"You think I killed her?" Frank stood up from the bed. "Is that what this is all about?"

"No Frank! I don't think you killed Mary. But it's just possible that somebody did."

Louise stood up. "Why?"

"Well now, that's something I'll have to figure out. This might all amount to nothing."

"What's going on?" said Guy as he, Harold and Lula Mae entered the room. Lula Mae had told them that the sheriff was asking Frank questions.

Frank turned toward Guy. "Karl here thinks that somebody killed your mama and put her in that slop trough."

"What?!" said Guy; echoed by Harold and Lula.

The sheriff held up one hand in an attempt to calm everyone down before they got too worked-up. "Now folks, let's don't get ahead of ourselves. I haven't reached any conclusions yet. I need to do some investigating."

"Why would anybody want to kill Mama?" asked Guy.

The sheriff dropped his hand and looked at Frank. "I don't know if anybody did. I want the coroner to perform an autopsy."

"No." Jesse Mae stood in the doorway. She had heard the voices and come upstairs to see what was going on. "They're not going to cut her up." She looked around the room. "When was I going to be told about this? Who says that Mama was murdered?"

The group was quiet for a moment. The word 'murder' had not been mentioned before now. Everyone had been avoiding the term, hoping that it would not apply.

Quietly, Sheriff Files responded, "Nobody is saying that. This is all just preliminary investigating. I have to examine all possibilities. Could be that it was all an unfortunate accident."

"The sheriff found two trails where your mama had been dragged." Louise directed her words to Harold. "He thinks that she might have been *put* into the pigsty instead of accidentally falling in."

Harold was at a loss for words as he looked around at the others, hoping for some input from them. This new information was hard for all of them to accept and they remained silent for a moment.

"Why?" Jesse Mae looked at the sheriff defiantly.

"Why what?" he responded.

"Why would anybody do that to Mama? That's crazy."

Sheriff Files was aware that everyone was in a highly emotional state and he did not want to upset them anymore than they already were. "That's merely a possibility. Like I said, I have to consider every angle. So, why don't we just wait for the coroner's report? I'm going back to my office and when I get the results, I'll come out here and let you all know what they say."

The group was silent.

"In the meantime…" The sheriff hesitated. He was trying to think of a tactful way to say his next words. "I want everybody to stay clear of the pigsty and the area where the drag marks are. Tony is marking it off now." He looked around at the group for any resistance to the idea. Nobody spoke, so he continued. "I'm having Tony spend the night here in order to insure that the scene is not disturbed."

"You can't be serious. He's going to keep an eye on us?"

"Now Jesse Mae, I don't like doing that, but that's what needs to be done. Chances are that nothing will come of any of this, but the possibility exists that there might have been a murder committed. Now I have to do what I have to do. Besides, if there is a killer on the loose, I want you all protected."

"I don't need no god-damned kid here to protect me and my family," said Frank.

"Frank," said Sheriff Files. "I don't mean to be insensitive…but your wife's body is in the morgue. Need I say more?"

Frank pulled his shoulders back and stood tall as if to challenge the sheriff and everybody stood in silence as the two men looked at each other. After a brief moment, Frank's posture relaxed and he turned away and sat on the edge of the bed with his head lowered.

Jesse Mae took up the challenge. "You think one of us did it."

"Now Jesse Mae, that's just not true. I know you're all good, decent folks. Why, I've known this family for more than twenty years, but I have a job to do. There's suspicion of foul play here and I intend to investigate. I would appreciate all of you cooperating with me and maybe together we can get to the bottom of all this." The sheriff paused and looked around to gauge the family's reaction. "I should think that all of you would want to find out if this was an accident or not."

Frank looked up at the sheriff. "You're right, Karl. We'll do whatever you want."

"Thank you Frank. Now I'm going back to my office and call the coroner. I would like your approval on that autopsy."

"If you have reasonable doubt as to the cause of death, you don't need his approval," said Jesse Mae.

"That's right, I don't, but as I said, I would like you all to cooperate with me. I'm not the bad guy here, Jesse Mae. Mary was a friend of mine. If somebody other than those pigs is responsible for her death, I intend to find out who it is."

"Do what you need to do, Karl," said Frank. "We'll help you any way we can."

"Good. For starters I'd appreciate it if you would see to it that Tony gets some supper. He'll be as little trouble to you as possible. He can sleep in the car, but he doesn't have anything to eat."

"Of course we'll see to it that he gets supper," said Lula Mae. "And breakfast too. He can eat with us. And we'll put him up for the night. He don't need to sleep in his car."

"Thank you ma'am." The sheriff walked toward the bedroom door. "I'll be back around eight o'clock tomorrow morning."

"You can have breakfast with us too, Sheriff," said Louise.

"Thank you all." The sheriff nodded to the others and left the room.

Jesse Mae followed right behind the sheriff, saying to him, "I want to see that trail you're talking about."

Louise saw the tears welling up in Harold's eyes. She put her arm over his shoulder. "Come on Harold, why don't you go back to the porch and I'll get you a glass of tea," she said as they too left the room.

"I'd better check on supper," said Lula Mae. She turned to leave. "I'll call you all when it's ready."

"I don't want no supper," said Frank.

"I don't either." Guy sat on the chair next to Frank's bed.

Lula Mae hesitated for a moment, unsure of how to respond. She wanted to do something to help them feel better, but she was at a loss as to what, if anything, she could do. "Well," she said. "there'll be food later on if you get hungry." Then she left the room and returned to preparing supper. She knew that the children would be hungry, and somebody had to take care of the basics.

Guy and Frank sat in silence for a moment. There had never been much intimacy between them, but they cared a lot for one another. Aside from a few altercations between them during Guy's rebellious teenage years, they had always gotten along well and showed one another respect. But at some point, within the past several years, their

177

relationship had become somewhat superficial. Hunting, politics, or business, were always the prominent topics they would discuss when they got together.

Now, with the two of them sitting alone together, sharing their grief, Guy had an almost overwhelming desire to hug his father and cry on his shoulder...but he could not. He had never allowed himself to show his emotional vulnerability to his father, and even at this most tragic moment, he felt that he could not open up to him...then...

"She was a good woman." Frank looked at his son as the tears flowed from his eyes.

Guy struggled with his emotions, as his breathing became deep and irregular and he felt the sobs rising from his heart and spilling out into the room. He moved to the bed and sat next to Frank. He put his arm around his father's shoulders and allowed the tears to flow. "I know Papa. I know."

"Show me this trail." Jesse Mae was following the sheriff as he stepped down from the back porch. They walked to the area where the cars were parked. The dirt was softer here than in the rest of the yard, due to the erosion caused by the constant weight and movement of the tires.

"You see those marks?" Sheriff Files pointed to a couple of parallel indentations in the sandy soil.

"I see some lines in the dirt. Is that what you're talking about?"

"Those are tracks from your mama's shoes." He then pointed to an area on the ground, which was darker than that around it. "That's blood. Your mama didn't end up here, so she must have been dragged *from* here. My guess is from a vehicle."

Jesse Mae followed as he moved away from the parking area and began walking toward the pigsty. "You can see that the dirt is harder here, but every so often there are these drag marks." He looked at Jesse Mae. "Your mama's shoes."

The sheriff followed one of two lines of rocks, which Tony had laid out on the ground. Jesse Mae noticed the blood soaked dirt along the lines. The line the sheriff followed ran directly to the pigsty. "Notice that there are two sets of drag marks and blood stains between the house and the pigsty." He pointed to another line of rocks that followed a direct path to the back porch. "One set starts just outside the pigsty. The other set goes into the pigsty." He stopped and turned to Jesse Mae. "Your mama was dragged *into* that pigsty before your papa carried her *out*."

Jesse Mae looked down at the marks in the dirt and then brought her eyes up to meet the sheriff's. "Why would anyone want to kill Mama?"

"I don't know, Jesse Mae, but it's my job to find out."

"Who do you suspect?"

"I don't have any suspects. I don't have any motive. All I have right now are these tracks and blood stains. So will you help me keep everyone away from them so that Tony and I can see if we can come up with anything more tomorrow?"

"Of course; we'll all keep clear of them." Jesse Mae looked at the slaughtered pigs in the pigsty and then turned back to the sheriff. "Do you think Papa did it?"

The sheriff was quiet for a moment as he looked Jesse Mae in the eye. He gave her question serious consideration. "No. Like I said; I don't have any suspects."

"Good; cause I know Papa would never do such a thing. I don't mean 'good' that you don't have any suspects; I mean 'good' that you don't think Papa did it."

"I know what you mean." The sheriff looked over at Tony, who was standing with Geneva and the other youngsters next to Romey's playhouse. "Tony."

"Yeah Karl?"

"Let these youngsters get a good look at these here marks in the dirt so that their curiosity will be satisfied and then make sure that everyone keeps away from them. I'm going home. We'll go over this area with a fine tooth comb tomorrow morning when I get back out here."

It was nearly six-thirty when Sheriff Files got back to his office. There was nobody being held in the jail cell in the rear of the building, so his secretary, Janice had already locked up and left for the day.

He sat down at his desk and reached for the telephone. He was hoping that the coroner had not quit for the day. He dialed the number and waited as the phone on the other end of the line began to ring. He let the phone ring several times and finally gave up. He took the telephone receiver away from his ear and was about to replace it in its cradle when he heard somebody on the other end saying, "Hello... hello..." He quickly returned the receiver to his ear. "Jimmy, is that you? Karl here. I thought I had missed you."

When the sheriff told the coroner that he wanted him to perform an autopsy on Mary's body, the coroner replied that it might not be necessary. He said that he was still working on Mrs. Austin's body, and that he had already found incriminating evidence. He continued to say that he had discovered that the body had four deep puncture wounds in the abdomen, and that the shape of the perforations and their pattern indicated that the probable instrument used was a pitchfork. His opinion was that Mary had been murdered.

The sheriff told him that he would still like an autopsy. He wanted to know if the cause of death was from the pitchfork or the pigs. He thanked the coroner for his help and hung up the receiver.

Looking to one side of his desk, he noticed a note; it was from Janice. The note said that a teacher from the college had called and wanted the sheriff to call him back the following day. It seemed that the skeleton, which was found in the old root cellar, was not as old as they had all assumed. The teacher had cleaned the clay out of the mouth and off of the hands and found that one of the upper molars had a metal filling in it. They had also found a wedding band on the ring finger of the left hand.

CHAPTER THIRTEEN

TONY SHOWED THE YOUNGSTERS THE MARKS LEFT on the ground from Mary's shoes. He told them that he and Sheriff Files had to do a report on what had happened, and that the marks were part of the evidence, which they had to document. He asked them to please stay away from the marks, but made no reference to killing or murder; so as not to add to the trauma that they had already felt, and also to avoid alarming them with the idea that they might also be in danger. They were all very agreeable to Tony's requests and promised to stay away from the area.

About an hour later, with the house quiet and still, Lula Mae closed the screen door gently and stepped onto the back porch. She eyed the stains in the aged wood of the porch as she stepped over them and down into the yard; wishing that she could get them out. She walked to where Tony and the children were taking turns throwing darts at a bull's eye target made of cork, which they had taken out of Romey's playhouse and hung on the outside wall. She stood between Gary and Scotty with an arm on each one's shoulders as they watched Loretta taking her turn with the darts. "You kids come on in and get ready for supper." She looked at the deputy. "You too, Tony."

Loretta threw her last dart and they all began making their way toward the house. Nobody was speaking as they walked next to the marks in the dirt where Mary's body had been dragged. Then Gary looked up at his mother. "Did somebody murder Grandma?"

Lula Mae glanced down at Gary. "I don't know Son." She knew it would do no good to try and avoid talking about it, but she was

181

not ready yet. "Try not to think about it. Just come in and have some supper."

They all entered the house in silence. Since none of the adults wanted to eat at this time, Lula Mae sat the youngsters in the dining room. Very little was said during the meal. The only dialogue was that, which had to do with serving and sharing the food.

On the front porch, Harold and Guy sat talking quietly. Frank had not left his room; and Louise, after comforting Harold had returned to the kitchen to help Lula Mae with the meal. Taking a short break from cooking, the two women each took a cup of coffee and joined Tony and the youngsters at the dining table. Jesse Mae had finally gotten Romey to have some buttermilk with cornbread crumbled into it. She now sat with him in his room as he ate. He still had not spoken since they had returned from the river.

Harold leaned back in the porch swing. "Should we do something?"

Guy was sitting on the steps of the porch. He responded to Harold without turning to look at him. "What do you mean?"

"Well...I don't know. It just seems like we should do something."

Guy stared out over the grass leading down to the road. An old farmer was passing by, sitting high on the seat of his wagon, which was being pulled slowly along by a single mule. Guy thought back to his childhood years when his father would drive a wagon very much like the one he was watching now. He remembered his mother as a young trim woman sitting proudly on the seat next to her husband as the family made their way into town to sell her peach and plumb preserves, which she had prepared at home and sealed in Mason jars. He remembered her smile and the church hymns that she liked to sing as they rode along.

He broke his reverie and turned to Harold, who was now leaning forward in the swing with his elbows on his knees, and his head down. "There's nothing to do," he said. "Not now anyway. In the morning, you, Jesse Mae and me will go into town and make funeral arrangements."

"What about Papa?"

"He told me he didn't want to go with us. He said for us to arrange everything."

Harold continued looking down. "Do you think Papa...do you think...?"

"What?"

Harold raised his head and looked at Guy. "Do you think he did it?"

Guy looked away from Harold. He felt as if his innermost thoughts had been found out. He had struggled to keep from even considering the possibility of what Harold was asking him. This was crazy, but here it was; put to him by his older brother. He turned back to Harold. "I don't know. What do you think?"

"I think you've both lost your minds." Jesse Mae stepped through the doorway and onto the front porch, quietly closing the screen door behind her.

The two men looked at their sister.

"How could you even consider such a thing? That's your father lying up there in his bedroom crying his heart out, for God's sake!"

Harold and Guy squirmed with guilt as they looked at each other. Neither one of them knew how to respond to Jesse Mae's remarks. She sat down in the swing next to Harold and flipped open the lid of her gold cigarette case. Using her long fingernails, she delicately removed a cigarette from inside.

Harold leaned back in the swing, causing it to begin a back-and-forth motion. Jesse Mae, with her usual controlling attitude, immediately planted her feet on the floor of the porch to stop the movement of the swing.

Although Harold was the oldest of the siblings, he had never been the most assertive one of the bunch. He leaned forward in the swing again and said, "I was just asking."

Jesse Mae flipped the top closed on her cigarette case, making a snapping sound. She leaned forward and picked up a book of matches from the porch railing and placed the cigarette case there. She lit her cigarette and inhaled deeply. She shook the match until the flame was extinguished and then flipped it over the railing and into the grass below. Without speaking, Guy reached for the book of matches in her hand. He took the matches and helped himself to one of her cigarettes, and lit it.

Harold had never smoked, and he did not particularly like being around burning cigarettes. He stood up and moved to the end of the porch. He leaned against the rail, facing the other two. "I think the sheriff is suspicious."

Jesse Mae let a stream of smoke escape from between her lips. "I know. I think he is too. Although I asked him if he thought Papa did it; and he said no."

"But Papa and Romey were the only ones here," said Guy. "Does he think that Romey did it?"

"He said that he didn't have any suspects. He's not even sure if it was a murder or not."

"Why would Mama be where the cars are parked?" asked Harold.

"Yeah," said Guy. "Romey told Papa that she was down at that old cellar."

"Maybe she was coming back to the house by way of the road," said Jesse Mae. "It's easier walking on the road than up that pasture. Anyone could have driven by and given her a ride up to the house here."

"She wouldn't get in the car with just anybody." Guy flipped his half smoked cigarette into the green grass. "And why would anybody want to hurt her?"

"Don't waste those." Jesse Mae was referring to the cigarette. "I don't want to have to go into town for more."

Guy got up from the porch steps and retrieved the still burning cigarette from the yard. He knocked the fire off of the end of it and placed the remainder behind his ear.

"Maybe she wasn't in a car," continued Jesse Mae. "Maybe somebody drove up and she went to the car to talk to them."

"But why?" said Guy.

"Aw hell, Guy; I don't know." Near tears; Jesse Mae leaned back in the swing and fell silent.

Guy sat back down on the steps of the porch with his elbows on his knees and stared across the yard. They all remained silent for a while. Then Jesse Mae threw her lit cigarette into the grass and covered her face with her hands as she began to weep.

Emotional intimacy was not a common practice in the Austin household, and Jesse Mae's obvious need to be comforted added to her brothers' distress. Guy and Harold looked at one another, neither of them knowing exactly what he should do. Then, instinctively Harold moved back to the swing and sat next to Jesse Mae. He put his arm around her and she leaned her head against him and cried harder; welcoming her big brother's compassion.

After a moment Jesse Mae's weeping subsided. She pulled away from Harold, wiped her eyes and lit another cigarette. Quietly, the three siblings continued to sit together in a rare show of appreciation for one another's company.

Lula Mae and Louise sat at the dining table with a clear view of the brothers and sister. They were glad that they were commiserating with one another, and it gave the sisters-in-law an opportunity to take their focus off of their spouses and concentrate their attention on their children and Romey. It seemed to them both that the youngsters were adjusting okay, but they were still concerned for Romey.

Lula Mae had tried to persuade Romey to join them, but she had been unsuccessful in getting him to leave his bed. She told him that if he changed his mind, they would be in the dining room. Occasionally, when she would go into the kitchen for something, she would look in on him. Invariably, she found him, still lying on his side, looking at the door, which led to Mary's bedroom.

"Who's going to take care of Romey now?" Loretta asked, as Lula Mae returned to the dining room after checking on Romey.

"I don't know," said Lula Mae, reclaiming her seat at the table. "Maybe your Aunt Jesse Mae will go ahead and put him in that school."

"But Grandma didn't want him to go to that school," said Geneva.

"I know that, Geneva, but who's going to take care of him? He can't stay here alone with Grandpa."

"Why can't he come home with us?" Loretta reached for more fried chicken.

"Romey can't stay by his self," said Lula Mae, gently slapping Loretta's hand and picking a piece of chicken for her from the platter using the serving fork. "You kids go to school all day and me and your daddy have to go to work."

Louise poured more iced tea for Scotty and Gary. "Jesse Mae was determined to put Romey in that school, before. I don't think there's anything going to stop her now."

185

After supper, Louise and Lula Mae decided that the adults needed to spend some more time together without the children around, so they suggested that the youngsters and Tony go out to Romey's playhouse and play a game of Monopoly. They all thought this was a good idea. It had been decided during supper that Tony would sleep in the playhouse on the cot; Johnny and Gary would sleep on a pallet on the floor in Geneva and Loretta's room, and Scotty would sleep with Harold and Louise.

At around eight p.m. Louise went up to Frank's room and talked him into coming downstairs for a while. Very little food was consumed, but the coffee flowed freely as they all sat around the dining table reminiscing and discussing the current situation and the varying options for the future.

Jesse Mae split her time between the dining room and Romey's room. She made herself a pallet on the floor next to Romey's bed. Sleeping in Mary's bed was of course not an option, and she did not want to sleep on the sofa because she wanted to be close to Romey. While preparing the pallet, she convinced Romey to come to the dining table and have a piece of apple pie. Soon after he finished the pie, he went back to his bed. Jesse Mae sat with him until he fell asleep around nine-thirty and then she rejoined the others at the table.

Just before eleven o'clock, the children were sent to bed, and by twelve-thirty the adults; exhausted, physically and emotionally, had also gone to bed.

Sometime during the night, Gary found himself lying awake on his pallet dealing with a dilemma; he had to pee. He lay in the darkness, thankful that he had not wet himself, but also at odds with what to do. There was a chamber pot in this room, but he was much too modest to turn on the flashlight and use the pot, for fear that his sisters might awaken and see him.

The only other option was to go downstairs and pee off the back porch. Johnny lay next to him, sound asleep. Gary knew that it would do no good to wake his brother and ask him to go to the back porch with him. Johnny was reluctant to indulge Gary's paranoia even when he was wide awake; waking him from his cherished slumber would most likely get Gary a hard blow from Johnny's fist and nothing else.

After a while, Gary's bladder helped him with his difficult decision. He had no other choice. He could not hold it until morning. The flashlight was on the floor, on the other side of Johnny. Gary was careful not to nudge Johnny as he reached over him and fumbled around in the darkness, trying to find the light. His fingers finally found the light and wrapped around it. With the push of the button, the light filled the room. Johnny and the girls remained motionless, they were all sound sleepers.

With the beam from the flashlight breaking through the darkness ahead of him, Gary made his way out of the bedroom and down the stairs. He considered going onto the front porch to pee. It was closer to where he now stood at the bottom of the stairs and it was also much higher off the ground than the back porch; providing a safe distance between a person standing on the porch and whatever might be lurking in the yard, waiting to snatch that person off.

He would feel safer on the front porch, but his grandmother had warned all of the boys and men in the house that they had better not pee on her flowers, which bordered the front porch. His conditioning to his grandmother's edicts, even though she was gone, urged him on into the uncertainty of the low standing back porch.

The night was warm and the windows and shades were open, allowing the faint moonlight to cast unfamiliar shadows, which were now surrounding him as he made his way through the living room in his elevated state of anxiety.

Constantly turning from side to side in an effort to observe his surroundings, Gary made his way through the living room, dining room, and across the kitchen to the back door. Standing just inside the kitchen, he raised the flashlight and let its beam shoot through the screen door and around the back yard, searching for any movement or unusual shapes while he remained within the safety of the house.

When he was fairly confident that there was nothing roaming around out there, he lifted the hook from the eyebolt on the door. He stepped out onto the porch and placed the flashlight on the boards beside his feet, allowing the beam of light to shine into the darkness. Standing on the edge of the porch, he quickly emptied his bladder, grabbed the flashlight and hurried back inside the house.

With the hook replaced through the eyebolt and his mission accomplished, Gary walked back through the house. The shadows did not look nearly as foreboding as before. He felt good about his bravery in the face of danger. He felt proud.

As he walked through the living room, being careful not to make noise and wake the others, he glanced out of the window in the direction of the barn and the old root cellar. What he saw stopped him in his tracks. He blinked his eyes in an effort to clear his vision. A chill gripped him and he felt goose bumps rise on his arms and back. As he moved closer to the window to get a better look, the image was unmistakable. There was a ghostly glow coming from the hole in the ground that used to be the root cellar.

He stood for a moment, straining his eyes in order to see more clearly. Everyone was always telling him how he imagined things; he wanted to make sure that he was seeing what he thought he was seeing. There was no mistake in his mind; there was light coming up from the hole.

Finally sure of himself, Gary made his way back upstairs. He hurried to Johnny and began shaking him awake. Johnny's arm struck Gary across the chest and pushed him backward. "Knock it off!" the drowsy brother mumbled.

"You gotta see this! There's a ghost in the old root cellar."

Immediately, Johnny was awake, but still skeptical. "What?"

Gary jumped up and ran to the window. "Look, there's a light coming up from the hole!"

By this time, the girls were awake. "What's going on?" asked Geneva, remaining in bed. Loretta covered her head with the sheet and turned away from the others, she had not heard any of the details as to what was going on and she did not want to.

The boys neglected to answer their sister as Johnny joined Gary at the window. Gary turned the flashlight off and laid it on the window sill. They both focused their full attention on the area next to the barn. Staring intently, Johnny said, "I don't see anything."

Gary's heart sank. There was no longer a glow. The area was dark except for the faint light cast by the moon. "Ow!" he said, reacting to the blow from Johnny's fist against his shoulder.

"You little baby! There's nothing down there." Johnny returned to the pallet and pulled the sheet over him.

"Go back to bed Gary," said Geneva, turning away from the window and her little brother.

Gary stood at the window rubbing his shoulder and looking towards the barn. He was certain that he had seen a light in the hole. Then he saw something that raised those goose bumps again. He leaned closer to the window screen to get a better view. Was he imagining this, or was he really seeing a dark shape emerging from the ground where the hole was? He turned and ran to the pallet, jumped under the sheet and closed his eyes. He did not want to see anything else until he saw sunlight coming through that window.

The next morning, Gary and Scotty were the last of the children remaining at the dining table. Louise and Lula Mae had decided to let the youngsters eat breakfast in the dining room because the adults had been congregating in the kitchen since dawn and they saw no reason to disrupt them.

Tony, Geneva, Loretta and Johnny had finished their breakfast and gone outside. Tony was examining the area around the pigsty, while the others sat outside Romey's playhouse, watching him and speculating on various possible scenarios that he might come up with.

Jesse Mae and Romey were at the table with Gary and Scotty. Jesse Mae had been successful in convincing Romey to get dressed and come have breakfast with her. Romey was still very quiet, but at least he had said a few words this morning and he had eaten some eggs and toast.

Gary and Scotty were also uncharacteristically quiet, due to their concern for Romey's welfare. They understood the gravity of what he had witnessed. In an effort to encourage Romey to eat, Gary held a table knife over the jar of plumb jam and said, "You want me to put some plumb jelly on some toast for you, Romey?"

They all felt encouraged when Romey nodded his head at Gary. Jesse Mae reached for the jar and placed it within Romey's reach. "Thank you Gary," she said. "That's very sweet of you; but I think it would be a good idea if Romey spread the jam on his toast himself." Jesse Mae believed that Romey needed to resume his normal pattern of activity as a step in hastening his recovery from the emotional shock, which he had suffered.

Romey slowly picked up his knife and the piece of toast from his plate and proceeded to spread the jam on it.

Carrying a pot of hot coffee, Lula Mae entered the dining room through the kitchen door. "You want some more coffee, Sis?"

Ordinarily, Lula Mae did not address Jesse Mae with the nickname, which she endearingly used towards her other sisters-in-law and her own sister. Her relationship with Jesse Mae had never been on a very intimate level; but after what had happened, and with the fact that they all shared a common grief; she felt such compassion for her, that she was now inclined to do so.

She felt very sorry for Jesse Mae. She knew that Jesse Mae's grief was much greater than her own. She could not imagine how she would feel if she had lost her own mother like that. Despite the animosities, which Jesse Mae and Mary had expressed toward one another, Lula Mae believed that underneath it all they did love one another.

Lula Mae's relationship with Mary had also been difficult; and quite often strained to the breaking point; but over the years they had developed a bond, and they had shared a fondness for one another. It was an effort now, for her to hold back her own tears in order to be supportive of Frank and his children, but she could not allow herself to be so selfish as to put her own feelings before theirs. She felt that she could not begin to comprehend the pain that they all must be suffering, and this concern for their well-being mollified her own grief.

"Thanks, Lula Mae." Jesse Mae lifted her cup as Lula poured the coffee into it.

After filling Jesse Mae's cup Lula put her hand on Romey's shoulder. "Do you want some more coffee, Romey?"

Romey looked up into Lula Mae's eyes. He and Lula shared a very tender love for one another. He nodded his head and said, "Un-huh."

She poured Romey's coffee and then turned to Gary. "Gary, if you and Scotty are finished, why don't you go on outside…but stay away from that pigsty."

"Okay." Gary and Scotty left the table and went to the front porch.

Lula Mae set the coffeepot on a folded kitchen towel that was on the table. She pulled a chair into place and sat down. She looked at Jesse Mae. "So, how are you doing?"

Jesse Mae looked at her sister-in-law. She shrugged her shoulders. She was touched by the tenderness that Lula Mae had been showing her. Ordinarily the two of them were rather superficial and curt to one another. Lula's concern for her welfare now made Jesse Mae sorry for her past behavior. She wanted to speak, but she was held back by a lump in her throat. She brought the back of her hand to her mouth, as she struggled to keep from crying. She glanced at Romey, who was staring at her. She had not cried in front of him. She was afraid that the sight of her being upset would only add to his distress.

Immediately, Lula Mae attempted to gain Romey's attention so that Jesse Mae could have a moment to compose herself. "How's that toast, Romey?" She rubbed his upper back gently.

Romey had been watching Jesse Mae closely. When Lula Mae spoke to him he turned to her. His eyes met hers for an instant and then he looked away and focused on his plate. "It's good," he said.

Both women understood how confused Romey had to be feeling. They both struggled to hold back their tears.

Romey looked up from his plate. He looked at Lula Mae and then at Jesse Mae. "Where's Mama?"

"Oh Romey." Jesse Mae could not hold back the tears. She reached over and placed her hand on top of Romey's hand as her eyes began to fill.

Lula Mae stoically took the initiative. "You know that song that your mama liked to sing; the one about the undertaker and Jesus?"

Romey turned his attention to her. "Un-huh."

"Well, your mama has gone to meet Jesus."

Romey sat in silence looking at Lula Mae. He glanced at Jesse Mae, when she pulled her hand away from his and began wiping the tears from her cheeks. He then turned back to Lula. "Is she coming back?"

"No Sweetheart; your mama is not coming back." Lula Mae's hand remained on Romey's back. She understood how important human touch was in times of deep sorrow. It was a natural instinct of hers, and she could tell that it helped Romey. She watched him to see if she could tell whether or not he understood what she was saying to him. It seemed to her that he did.

Romey dropped his head and stared at the half eaten slice of toast covered with Mary's plumb jam. "Oh."

Lula Mae looked at Jesse Mae who had managed to somewhat regain her composure. The three sat in silence for a moment. Then Romey picked up the toast and bit into it. Lula Mae took her hand away from his shoulders and leaned back in her chair and continued to watch him. Jesse Mae also watched him as she lifted her coffee cup to her lips and sipped. The two women felt comforted as they could see that he was beginning to accept the situation, and come out of his depression.

Frank, Guy and Harold sat at the kitchen table while Louise stood at the sink, washing dishes. The men's plates, containing half eaten portions of eggs and sausages rested on the table in front of them. None of them had spoken for a while. They all stared in silence at nothing in particular.

Harold looked up from his plate and said to his father, "Papa, I want you to go to the mortuary with us."

Frank looked at his oldest son. "I told you all I didn't want to go. You kids can handle everything."

"I don't want to handle everything."

Frank looked at Guy. "Then Guy and Jesse Mae can handle it."

Guy shot back, "I don't want to handle it either."

"Well, god-damn-it! You're both going to. I don't want to hear no more about it."

"Mama was your wife," said Harold.

Louise moved to Harold's side and rested her hand on his shoulder in an effort to keep him calm. Harold had Rheumatic Heart Disease, and Louise feared that if he got too agitated or upset, he would run the risk of a heart attack.

"Don't tell me what your mama was to me!" Frank pushed his plate away. He opened his mouth as if he were going to say something more, but stopped abruptly, with tears forming in his eyes. He lowered his eyes and reached for his coffee cup. He wrapped his fingers around the cup, but did not lift it off the table. Quiet filled the kitchen again.

After a moment, Guy sighed heavily and said, "What are we going to do about those pigs?"

Frank hesitated before he responded. He turned his head and looked out of a window at nothing in particular. "You and Harold can help me dig a hole and we'll bury them." He turned back to Guy. "That is; when the god-damned sheriff says we can."

The faint sound of an approaching car could be heard from the road. They all listened when it turned onto the property and started up the drive, coming to a stop outside the house. The car door slammed shut. Louise looked out of the window above the sink. "That's the sheriff."

Frank, Guy and Harold got up and walked out onto the back porch. They watched as Tony and Sheriff Files stood next to the sheriff's car; talking. After a moment the sheriff pointed towards the barn and the old root cellar. Tony nodded his head and the two of them walked to the back of the car and continued their conversation with their bodies half turned away from the others.

Gary and Scotty came back into the dining room where Lula Mae, Romey and Jesse Mae still sat. Gary walked to his mother and put his arm around her shoulders. Scotty sat in one of the empty chairs. Lula Mae responded to Gary's hug by putting her arm around his waist. "Why don't you and Scotty go out to Romey's playhouse and read some funny books?"

"I saw a ghost last night," said Gary, glancing at Scotty. Gary had told Scotty about the light in the hole and the dark figure that he saw climb out of it, and Scotty had convinced him that he should tell his mother.

"Oh Gary." Lula Mae usually encouraged Gary's stories. She felt that it was good for him to use his imagination. But she was not in the mood and she felt that the moment was inappropriate. "Not now, Son. Go on outside."

Gary looked at Scotty as if to say, 'I told you so.' He dropped his head and said, "Okay." Then the two boys, talking quietly between themselves about ghosts and other supernatural phenomenon, walked through the kitchen, disregarding Louise; and continued out the back door past their fathers and grandfather and made their way to the playhouse.

The sheriff and Tony walked towards the men standing on the back porch. The sheriff touched his hat. "Morning all."

He was met with solemn greetings from Guy and Harold, but Frank was hurting and angry at the world and he did not feel like making small talk. His face revealed his attitude as he waited in silence for the sheriff to say what he had to say. The sheriff was not offended by Frank's attitude; he had some serious business to take care of and it was fine with him if they skipped the pleasantries and got to it.

"Frank, I need to talk to you. Why don't you come out to my car for a minute?"

"Why?"

"Why what?"

"Why do you want me to come out to your car?"

The sheriff registered a look of consternation. "I'm merely being considerate of your privacy, Frank."

"I don't have any privacy. Say what you have to say."

The sheriff hesitated for a moment and then stated flatly, "The coroner found conclusive evidence that Mary was murdered."

The father and two sons stood motionless as they absorbed the remark. They had all suspected as much after the evidence of the body being dragged, but they had hoped for some other explanation.

Louise stepped onto the porch and put her arm around Harold's waist. She said nothing as she waited along with the others for more information. All the youngsters had also gathered around as the sheriff continued.

"Her lungs were punctured by what the coroner suspects was a pitchfork." He looked at Frank who stood in stunned silence. "Do you have a pitchfork around here?"

Frank had difficulty speaking. The image of Mary's suffering triggered his emotions again. His struggle was obvious as he forced out, "There's one down at the barn."

The sheriff turned to Tony. "Tony, go down there and see what you can find. I'll be down there shortly." Tony left the group and headed toward the barn. The sheriff turned back to Frank. "And that's not all."

Frank's face took on a look of aggravated agony as he looked at the sheriff and waited for him to continue.

The sheriff scanned the faces of the group, trying to determine if everybody's reaction to the distressing news was legitimate or feigned. He had learned over the years how to read people this way. He focused on Frank. "That skeleton that these boys found down there wasn't no ancient relic. The people at the college cleaned off all that caked on clay that was all over her hands and feet." He hesitated a moment, and again scanned the faces. "They found a wedding ring." He paused again. "It had two names and a date inscribed on the inside of it; *'Elmer and Rena 1928'*. Looks like there's been two killings on your land."

"What?"

The group on the porch all turned to see Jesse Mae and Lula Mae standing just inside the kitchen behind the screen door. Jesse Mae opened the door, and moved past Harold and Louise. Guy and Frank were blocking her way, so she put her hand against Guy's back and gently pushed as she prompted him and Frank to move before her, and they all stepped off of the porch, and stood on the ground next to the sheriff.

"What did you say?" Jesse Mae faced the sheriff squarely.

The sheriff was intrigued with Jesse Mae's response to his news. "I said there's been two killings on your papa's land."

"No; about the ring! What was inscribed inside of it?"

"A couple of names and a date."

Jesse Mae did not try to hide her impatience. "What were the names?"

"Oh…uh, Elmer and Rena. Why?"

"I used to know a girl named Rena." Jesse Mae looked around at the others and then back to the sheriff. "Her husband's name was Elmer. I didn't know him. He had already run out on her before I moved in. She left her family in Oklahoma and moved here with him. She still wore her wedding ring. She said that's all he left her with." She turned to Frank. "Papa, that was the girl that I stayed with when…I was sick."

"She just up and left town after you came back home," said Guy. "We all thought that she had gone back to Oklahoma."

Nobody spoke as they all exchanged glances; thinking about the fact that Rena's body had been buried in that cellar all this time and that most of them had been so close to it so often.

"That necklace…" said Jesse Mae, under her breath. She turned and looked at Louise and Lula Mae. "I thought that necklace looked familiar. That was Rena's necklace. Now I remember seeing it at her house. She said that her new boyfriend gave it to her."

"What are you talking about?" asked Sheriff Files.

"Right before we all went to the lake, Mama came into her bedroom, wearing a turquoise and silver Indian necklace. She said that Johnny had dug it out of the clay down at that old root cellar. I didn't think much about it, but I remember; it seemed familiar."

"Where is this necklace now?"

The family members all looked questioningly at one another. Jesse Mae turned to the sheriff and said, "Maybe in her bedroom."

"I'd like to see it. Would you go get it for me, please?"

Jesse Mae hesitated. Her mother's bedroom had been closed up since her body had been removed the day before, and the thought of walking in there again and seeing the blood covered bed was making her feel very anxious. She realized that she would go in the bedroom eventually, but she had not counted on it being so soon. "Uh...sure."

Picking up on Jesse Mae's hesitancy, Lula Mae said, "I'll go with you."

"Me too," said Louise.

Lula Mae, who had remained standing in the doorway to the kitchen, turned to Romey, who was standing behind her. "Romey, why don't you go outside with the kids for a while?"

"Unh-uh," said Romey, shaking his head and backing further into the kitchen.

Lula Mae could see that he was frightened. He had not been outside the house since the incident. She moved to him and put her arm around him. "It's okay; nothing is going to hurt you."

"It's okay Romey," said Jesse Mae, as she and Louise left the others outside and entered the kitchen. She gently put her arm around Romey's shoulders, pulling him away from Lula Mae and embracing him. She looked at the other women. "Why don't Romey and me go to the front porch, while you guys look for the necklace?"

Louise and Lula Mae agreed that this was the best course of action, and headed to Mary's bedroom. Jesse Mae was relieved at being spared the task of going with them. She started to the porch with Romey, but hesitated when she heard Sheriff Files talking to Frank.

"I'm going to need to talk to Romey," said the sheriff.

"You leave Romey alone," said Frank. "He's not feeling good."

"I need to know what he knows." The sheriff looked up at Jesse Mae, who had sent Romey to the front porch and was now standing in the kitchen doorway.

Jesse Mae was annoyed with the sheriff, but she could understand his position. She made an effort to be civil. "I'm keeping a close watch on Romey. He's coming around. When he's feeling up to talking to you, I'll let you know. It won't be long."

"Fair enough," said the sheriff.

Lula Mae and Louise entered Mary's bedroom through Romey's bedroom. The doors had been closed and left unopened since the time that Mary's body had been taken away. The bad smells lingering in the room convinced the women that it would have to be cleaned today.

In an effort to begin airing out the space, Louise opened the door leading to the living room. The door was only a few feet from the screen door leading to the front porch. Louise could see Romey now sitting in the porch swing. She decided to leave the door closed; a barrier between the family and the memory of what had taken place there. She closed the door quietly and turned to Lula Mae, who was already at the dresser.

"Any luck?"

Lula Mae opened a second drawer. "Nothing yet."

The two women continued looking through the dresser drawers, and then through the drawers in Mary's bureau. They found no sign of the necklace. Louise let her eyes wander about the room. "What do you suppose she did with it?"

Lula Mae was rearranging Mary's underwear in the last bureau drawer where she had pushed the items to the side in search of the necklace. "I don't know." She closed the drawer. "I can't think of where else she might have put it. Do you think she hid it?"

"Why would she?"

They decided to conduct a more thorough search of the room. They looked through boxes that were stacked in the closet, and those under the bed. They looked under folded clothing, in the pockets of hanging garments, through purses; still nothing. They stood for a moment looking around the room, trying to think if they had missed any areas, which might be a hiding place.

"Now why on earth would she hide that necklace?" said Louise.

Lula Mae walked back to the dresser. She picked up a few pieces from the jewelry box. "These pieces are as nice as that necklace; they

197

might even be more expensive. Why would she go to the trouble of hiding it and nothing else?" She put the items back in the box.

"Maybe she was wearing it."

"And somebody stole it from her?"

Louise shrugged her shoulders. "Maybe."

"Well…" said Lula, "Let's go tell the sheriff that it's not here."

When they returned to the back porch, everybody was gone. They looked around and saw their husbands and father-in-law with the sheriff, followed by the youngsters, walking down towards the barn. Lula Mae knew that Louise would not make the trek down through the pasture, so she volunteered. "I'll go tell them that we can't find it."

CHAPTER FOURTEEN

Jesse Mae sat next to Romey in the porch swing with an arm around his shoulders. She pushed gently against the floor of the porch, making the swing travel back and forth slowly. "You don't have to be afraid of anything, Son. I won't let anybody hurt you."

"The devil pig got Mama."

Jesse Mae stopped the swing from moving and turned toward Romey. She took hold of his shoulders and pulled him around to face her. She looked into his eyes. "No Romey. There is no devil pig. Mama fell into the pigsty and hit her head. Those pigs didn't hurt her. They were just snorting around her, trying to wake her up; that's all."

Confusion filled Romey's eyes as he returned Jesse Mae's stare.

"Now that's the truth, Romey. I'm your big sister, you know I wouldn't say it if it wasn't true."

"There's not a devil pig?"

"No, there is no devil pig! That's just a made up story to scare the kids."

"Oh." Romey turned to face the front of the porch. "That's what Roger said."

Jesse Mae also faced forward and resumed pushing the swing. After a moment, she said, "Romey...have you told anybody about Roger?"

Without looking at her Romey replied, "No."

"Good; let's just keep Roger a secret. He'll be our secret. We won't tell anybody else; okay?"

Romey had always liked having secrets. He was very good at keeping them to himself. "Okay," he said, without asking why.

The next moment Louise walked onto the porch from the living room. "We couldn't find that necklace."

"Did you look through all her drawers?" asked Jesse Mae.

"We looked everywhere."

"Hmm…She must have been wearing it."

"That's what Lula Mae thought."

"What do you think?"

"Well, I think you guys are probably right."

"Where is Lula Mae?"

Louise looked toward the barn and gave a slight upward jerk of her head as she moved toward the rocking chair, which was facing the swing. "She's going down to tell the sheriff that we couldn't find it." She pulled the chair a little closer to the swing and sat down. "So, how are you doing, Romey?"

Romey gave a sideways glance to Jesse Mae and then faced Louise. "I'm okay, Louise."

Louise patted the top of his thigh. "That's good. That's real good." She looked at Jesse Mae for confirmation that Romey was doing okay as she leaned back in the chair and began to rock back and forth.

"He's going to be alright," said Jesse Mae. She ruffled his hair. "I'm going to be with him from now on. I'm going to take care of him."

Romey smiled sheepishly and looked at the floor.

Jesse Mae looked toward the barn and the group around the old root cellar. "I wonder what they're finding down there."

Lula Mae approached the old root cellar. On one side, the youngsters were gathered together, and on the other side were: the sheriff, Frank, Guy, and Harold. She could hear the sheriff speaking to Tony, who was down in the hole.

"Well, it's officially a crime scene now." The sheriff was snapping pictures with his flash camera.

Lula Mae was surprised when she looked over the edge and into what had been the cellar. Where the shelving had been pulled away from the wall, the recess where the skeleton was initially found had been dug out substantially; leaving a large hole, going back about four feet into the earth; with mounds of loose dirt piled here and there.

"If there was anymore evidence buried down there, it's gone now." The sheriff leaned over the edge of the hole and handed the camera to

Tony. "Go ahead and use up the roll of film while you're down there. I have enough of the scene up here. Get some good pictures of those footprints in that soft dirt." He stood upright and turned toward the blood covered pitchfork that Tony had found, which was lying on the ground a few feet away. "Bag that spade after you photograph it. I'll bag this pitchfork." He leaned over and carefully picked up the farm tool. "Other than those footprints, these are our only pieces of evidence. I hope we can get some fingerprints off of them." He spotted Lula Mae. "You got that necklace?"

"We couldn't find it anywhere. We looked through everything."

Gary moved next to Lula Mae. "Mama."

Lula put her arm around Gary's shoulders, but kept her eyes on the scene before her. "What Son?"

"Remember, I told you I saw a ghost last night?"

"Gary." The weariness was evident in Lula's voice.

"It was in this hole."

"What?" said Lula Mae, feeling a little guilty for not paying more attention to what Gary had tried to tell her. "You saw somebody down here last night?"

The attention of the whole group was suddenly on Gary. "I saw it! It came up out of this hole." Gary was excited to think that all eyes were on him. He enjoyed being in the spotlight. His first instinct was to embellish the story, but he understood the seriousness of the situation and restrained himself.

"What came up out of this hole?" Guy looked at Gary with a stern expression.

Gary looked up at his mother. His father's attitude told him that this was not to be his shining moment, and he now wished that all eyes were not upon him. "The ghost," he said softly.

In an effort to divert the attention away from himself, he blurted out, "I told Johnny." He pointed his finger at his brother.

Johnny was now the focus of the group. "Oh he didn't see anything." Johnny shot a menacing glance at Gary. "He's just making things up."

The impulse to prove himself overrode Gary's fear of his father's threatening attitude. "I am not! There was a light in the hole and then something crawled out of it."

"Well, I didn't see anything," said Johnny with an air of finality.

201

"Somebody was in here," said the sheriff. "That's for sure. They dug up any other evidence that might have been down in this hole."

"There was a murderer roaming around here last night?" said Geneva.

The sheriff turned to Frank. "Was anyone unaccounted for last night?"

"Don't start that bullshit again, Karl," said Frank. "You know god-damned well none of us had anything to do with any of this."

The sheriff hooked his thumbs behind his belt and looked into the hole at Tony, who was tying up the spade in a gunny sack. He sighed deeply. "Yeah, I know, Frank, but I have to ask; I wouldn't be doing my job if I didn't." He looked back at Frank. "I need to talk to Romey."

"Romey?" said Lula Mae.

"He was alone here with his mama for all that time," said the sheriff, defensively. "He might have seen somebody, or heard something."

"He didn't know where she was. I asked him," said Frank. "He thought she was down here digging."

"Well, I believe you Frank, but I need to file a report and the report has to have his testimony in it, so I need to talk to him."

Frank dropped his head and slowly shook it from side to side. Under his breath he said, "God-damn…" Then he looked up. He turned to Lula Mae. "How is he, Lula Mae? Do you think he's okay to talk to the sheriff?"

Jesse Mae and Louise watched the members of the group as they walked back toward the house. After crawling through the fence, they separated. The youngsters went to the back yard while the adults came to the front porch.

"What did you find?" asked Jesse Mae as they approached.

The sheriff looked up at Romey and then at Jesse Mae. He did not want to upset Romey, so he chose his words carefully. "Oh, just an old pitchfork and a garden spade." He pointed to the bagged tools as Tony laid them on the lawn next to the porch. "Looks like somebody's been doing a lot of digging down there."

Frank climbed the steps of the porch and sat in the swing next to Jesse Mae. Harold followed behind him and took a chair next to Louise. Guy and Lula sat on the steps and leaned their backs against the railings, so that they faced the others. The sheriff and Tony said a few words to one another while standing at the foot of the steps, and then Tony took his notebook and pencil from his shirt pocket as the sheriff came up onto the porch.

Frank looked at Jesse Mae and then at Louise. "The sheriff here needs to ask us all some questions." The two women showed no objections to this as they turned their attention to the lawman.

Sheriff Files faced the group as he leaned against the porch railing; half standing and half sitting. Tony remained on one of the lower steps of the porch with his pad and pencil; ready to take notes. The sheriff began his questioning. "What time did you all leave for the river?"

The family members looked around at one another. Nobody had been designated to speak for the group, so each waited for someone else to speak. Then Frank spoke. "They left a little past nine."

"Who all went?"

"They all did," said Frank. "Harold, Louise, Guy, Lula, Jesse Mae, and all the kids."

"And did everybody leave together?"

"Yeah, they took three cars and they all left at the same time."

"And, Frank why didn't you and Mary and Romey go with them?"

"Well, I had to go collect the rent money from my sharecropper and Mary didn't want to go and she didn't want Romey to go."

"And Frank how long after the group left for the river did you leave?"

"Why do you keep saying my name? I know who you're talking to?"

"That's so that when Janice types up the notes that Tony's taking I will know who said what?"

"Oh…well, I left about the same time."

"So only Romey and Mary were left here?"

"That's right."

The sheriff turned his attention to Romey. "Romey, did anybody come to visit your mama yesterday?" Everybody looked at Romey. Nobody spoke as the seconds ticked by in silence. Romey looked at Jesse Mae and then at the sheriff. He shook his head and looked down. Jesse Mae was relieved that the sheriff had not asked Romey if anybody had come to visit him.

"No…Did your mama go anywhere?"

Romey looked in the direction of the barn. "She went down to that old root cellar."

"How long was she down there?"

"She was gone a long time." Romey looked about at the others.

"Can you be more specific?"

Romey looked at the sheriff with confusion.

"Was she down there as long as it takes the big hand to go around the clock?"

"You mean and hour?" said Romey.

The sheriff was taken aback. He realized that he had misjudged Romey's intelligence and he was embarrassed by it. "Uh…yes, an hour. Was she down there longer than an hour?"

"Yeah, a lot longer."

"And Romey, did you see anybody else down at the old root cellar with your mama?"

"No."

The sheriff turned his attention to Frank. "Now Frank, what time did you return?"

Frank sighed deeply, remembering the chain of events. "I got back here about twelve-thirty or one o'clock."

"And what did you do?"

"Well, I found Romey in his bedroom with a fan on him. It was the heat of the day; that's when him and Mary always take their naps…But Mary wasn't in her room."

Frank's breathing became deeper. It was a struggle for him to remain composed. Nobody spoke for a moment; then he continued. "I asked Romey where his mama was. He told me she was down at that old cellar, said she had been down there a long time. I went looking for her down there, but she wasn't there. I came back up here and went to look in the henhouse. Thought she might be in there…" Frank paused again and took another deep breath. He continued, "I saw part of her dress hanging over the side of the slop trough in the pigsty…Everything is a little fuzzy after that. I got her out of there and put her in her bed." Frank's head dropped forward and he stared at his feet. Jesse Mae put her arm around him.

Sheriff Files glanced at Romey. "And where was Romey when you found Mary?"

"What?" Frank lifted his head. He had a hint of agitation on his face. "I don't know." He looked at Romey. "I guess he was in the house. He must have come outside when he heard me yelling at those pigs to get off her."

The sheriff looked at Romey. "Romey, do you know how your mama got in that slop trough?"

The porch erupted with protestations. The sheriff lifted both hands in front of him with his palms pushing down. "Calm down. Calm down; all of you." The group grew quiet. The sheriff dropped his hands. "Everyone here, including me, has Romey's best interest at heart. These are standard questions. They need to be asked." The group remained quiet. The sheriff looked back at Romey. "Romey, do you know how your mama got into that slop trough?"

Romey looked at the sheriff and then at Jesse Mae and back to the sheriff. He shook his head again.

"No. And you didn't hear anybody or see anybody snooping around?"

Romey shook his head again and spoke almost inaudibly, "No."

"No," repeated the sheriff for the benefit of Tony, who was scribbling rapidly on his note pad. "Thank you folks. I'm going to head on back to the office. I would like for Tony to spend one more night with you all if you don't mind. Just in case..." He looked at Frank.

Frank looked at Tony. "Fine," he said and dropped his head again.

"Would you like some breakfast before you go, Sheriff?" Louise stood up from the chair where she had been sitting. "We've all eaten already, but I could fix you some sausage and eggs."

"Thank you ma'am, but I need to get back. I appreciate the offer though."

Louise nodded her head, "You're welcome."

The sheriff and Tony walked to the sheriff's car and spoke for a while. The family members remained on the front porch.

Louise looked around at the others. "Well, I guess I'll go clean up the dishes."

Lula Mae stood up from where she had been sitting next to Guy on the porch step. "I'll help." The two women went into the house, leaving the family alone.

After a moment of silence, Guy looked up at his sister. "Jesse Mae are you going to go to the mortuary with me and Harold?"

Jesse Mae sat between her father and Romey on the porch swing. She still had her arm around Frank's shoulders. "I think I'll stay here with Papa and Romey. Whatever you and Harold decide is fine with me."

Guy looked at Harold. "You ready to go then? We might as well get started."

Harold stood up. "I'll just run to the outhouse for a few minutes and I'm ready." He left the others, making his way through the house.

"Take her navy blue suit with you," said Jesse Mae.

"Why?"

"She'll need it, Guy. They'll put it on her in the mortuary."

"Oh." Guy had no experience with funeral arrangements, and it had not occurred to him to provide a dress. "I don't know where it would be."

"I'll get it for you." Jesse Mae stood up.

"She'll need her locket too," said Frank.

"Papa, don't you want to keep that?" Jesse Mae was surprised that Frank would want to bury the locket that he had given to Mary before they were married. It was a heart shaped locket, containing two small photographs; one of Mary and one of Frank; taken when they were dating.

"She loved that locket." Frank looked up at Jesse Mae.

Jesse Mae paused for moment. Her first instinct was to argue the point of burying the locket, but she realized that it was an act of love for her father to request it. "Alright," she said, and went into the house. She opened the door to Mary's room and hesitated. She looked through the doorway at the blood stained bedspread and pillows. It reminded her of the bed where she slept in Rena's house; the bed where she had given birth to Romey.

Conflicting emotions were vying for dominance in Jesse Mae's mind. She was indeed grieving for her poor slain mother; but she was also dealing with the long felt resentment, which was ingrained in her heart. The pain of losing her mother would overcome her soon enough; but for the time being she found that if she concentrated on the resentment, she could forestall the catharsis, which she felt building within her. Right now she needed to get a grip on her emotions and go into the room and get her mother's things.

Mary's only dress suit was hanging in the closet, covered by an old bathrobe in order to keep it clean. It was what she had always worn for special occasions, such as weddings and funerals. It seemed appropriate that this was the outfit she should be buried in.

Jesse Mae looked at the shoes that went with the suit. Mary would not be needing them. The matching bag, a large blue leather bag, lay on the shelf above. That too could stay behind.

A thought began forming in Jesse Mae's mind. Mary had had that bag and those shoes for as long as Jesse Mae could remember. When Jesse Mae was around ten years old, she had discovered a secret compartment in the bag. She was playing dress-up with her little friend. What a surprise to find money in the hidden pocket of the bag. For a few weeks, she was a little rich girl, until her mother found out that she had bought some candy when she went into town with her father.

Frank asked Jesse Mae where she had gotten the money and she lied that Mary had given it to her. When they came home Frank made an offhand remark to Mary that she should not be giving the children money. Before she could respond to Frank, he walked out of the house to do his chores.

Jesse Mae had resisted telling her mother where she had gotten the money until Mary went to Frank's room and came back with his large leather belt. In an effort to escape a whipping, Jesse Mae finally confessed to discovering her mother's secret hiding place and stealing part of the cash.

That secret compartment in that purse was Mary's only place that she felt confident in keeping things from Frank. Her first inclination was to spank Jesse Mae severely for ruining it for her, but then she reasoned that there was a way to keep Frank from knowing about it still. If she made Jesse Mae a co-conspirator, then maybe Jesse Mae would keep her secret. Mary told Jesse Mae that if she promised to never tell anybody about the secret compartment that she would be spared a whipping from her and Frank. Jesse Mae was so pleased not to be punished that she agreed never to mention the compartment to anyone. Over the years, she had almost forgotten about it.

Not once had she looked in that bag since that incident. She now ran her finger under the undetectable flap and lifted. The compartment held several bills; nothing larger than a ten...and also the necklace from the old cellar.

Jesse Mae pulled the necklace out and held it up. She examined the silver and turquoise. It was Rena's necklace, she was now sure of it. She remembered seeing Rena wearing it around her house. She could not remember Rena ever going out at night or getting dressed up to go anywhere that would call for wearing jewelry; but she did remember thinking it was strange when Rena would put on the necklace to go out for her noontime walks.

Jesse Mae held the necklace and thought for a moment. 'That sheriff doesn't need this necklace. He knows that the skeleton was Rena. I'll keep it. Mama wanted it so badly; I'll keep it for her.' She slipped the necklace into the pocket of her sundress.

Guy was waiting by his car when Harold came back up from the outhouse and went into the house to wash his hands. Mary's dress suit was folded in the back seat with the locket lying on top of it. Guy had all of the windows rolled down and the doors open in order to cool the car down a little. It was only a little past nine a.m. but the day was already heating up.

The sweet smell of Honeysuckle blossoms wafted through the open windows of the car and a dust cloud rose behind it as Guy and Harold made their way along the dirt road leading away from the farm. After a few minutes, Guy steered the car onto the paved road and accelerated, quickly escaping the dust and leaving only the sweet smell of the flowers, which grew in profusion around them and permeated the air with their perfume.

For several minutes, the two men were silent; lost in their own thoughts. Guy momentarily shifted his eyes from the road ahead and looked at Harold. "I hope you're not still bothered about Mama and Papa before you were born."

Harold glanced quickly at Guy and then back at the road in front of them. He thought for a moment and sighed deeply; then he turned back to Guy. "It doesn't matter anymore. None of that seems important now."

"Good," said Guy, his eyes back on the road. "We need to decide how much we're going to spend on the casket." Guy was struggling with his sorrow over his mother's death, but he was also a pragmatist. Having four children had put him in a position where he was constantly concerned with finances. He made a decent living as a chef in a country club, and Lula Mae worked at a lunch counter in the five-and-dime, but their combined salaries were barely enough to make ends meet.

"Well," said Harold. "We don't have to go overboard, but I want Mama to have a nice one."

"Yeah, me too."

The men were quiet again. Then Harold looked at Guy and opened his mouth as if he were going to speak, but then he turned away and remained silent.

"What?" Guy said, dividing his attention between the road and his brother.

Harold began fidgeting with the knobs on the radio, although it was not playing. "Do you think Papa had anything to do with all this?"

"No; we talked about that," said Guy, a little crossly.

Harold looked out the side window and began playing with the knob on the window roller handle.

"Do you think he had anything to do with it?" asked Guy; all animosity gone from his speech.

"I don't think so...but who else would have done such a thing? And why is Sheriff Files acting so suspicious?"

The sound of the wind whipping around them was the only sound as the two brothers contemplated the possibilities.

"And Mama always said that he and Jesse Mae tried to kill her," said Harold.

"Yeah, but everyone knew that was just bullshit. You know Mama didn't mean that."

"Yeah," said Harold as he leaned back in the seat and closed his eyes.

They were quiet for the rest of the ride to the mortuary.

Guy pulled his car into the small parking lot next to what looked like a well kept older farm house. It had obviously been built before the

209

rest of the town, which had grown up around it. The small front yard was heavily planted with rose bushes and was enclosed by a low picket fence. On the gate of the fence was a wooden sign, almost the width of the gate, which read, *BENSON'S MORTUARY.*

The two brothers walked through the front door and into a modest parlor. A swamp cooler protruded through a side window, and hummed softly as it blew cool air into the room. There was a desk to the right of the entry door, with two chairs in front of it and one chair behind it. On the left side of the room was a settee, which faced two upholstered arm chairs. The settee and chairs were separated by a coffee table, on which rested a box of tissues and a large book. On the desk were: a vase filled with flowers, a bell, and a small sign that read, *Please Ring For Service.*

Harold grasped the handle of the bell with two fingers and shook it once, sounding a high pitched tinkle. He set it back down on the desk and he and Guy waited for somebody to appear from another room. After a moment of standing and waiting, guy said, "Ring it again."

"Just wait," said Harold. They found themselves inclined to whisper. The room was silent except for the hum of the cooler. There was a heavy, sweet smell coming from the vase of flowers on the desk.

A door opened on the back wall of the room and a man, who looked to be about forty years old entered. He had a full head of curly blonde hair and large blue eyes. His thick mustache and long sideburns gave him just enough of a masculine appearance to keep him from seeming pretty. Pulling off a pair of rubber gloves, he extended his right hand. As he shook hands with Harold and Guy he introduced himself.

"Hi, I'm John Benson. Are you with the Austin family?"

The two brothers introduced themselves, and the mortician led them into another room. The room was filled with six available caskets, all of varying designs and materials. After about fifteen minutes, they settled on a casket, which fell into the mid-price range.

The three men went back to the front office and Guy began filling out all of the necessary forms, while Harold went out to the car and collected Mary's suit and the locket. Meanwhile Mr. Benson called the pastor of the church and arranged to have Mary's service at ten a.m. the following morning.

Mary's suit lay on the desk in front of them. The mortician placed a hand on the folded fabric and looked from one brother to the other.

"I think it would be best to have your mother wear a hat with a heavy veil. I will do what I can with make-up, but there was severe damage to her face. My wife will be happy to pick one out if you would like, and I will just add the cost of it to your bill."

Harold and Guy looked at one another. They were both struggling with their emotions and it was difficult for each of them to speak. "Okay," muttered Harold, quietly.

The grieving brothers drove to the cemetery, following behind Mr. Benson who was driving his own car. The only thing left for them to do was pick out a plot for Mary's grave. They walked through the cemetery with the mortician and finally found a place underneath a large oak tree that the brothers both agreed their mother would have liked. Mr. Benson noted the number of the plot in his notebook and then pounded a small sign into the ground at the site where the grave would be. He then said good-bye to Guy and Harold and returned to his car.

As the brothers walked back to Guy's car, Guy turned to Harold and said, "I could use a beer."

Harold was not much of a drinker, but the circumstances being as they were, he found his brother's suggestion very appealing. They got into the car and headed for *Sally's Honky-Tonk,* just on the other side of town.

CHAPTER FIFTEEN

"I TOLD HAROLD AND GUY TO ARRANGE TO have the funeral at ten tomorrow morning," said Jesse Mae. "After the service in the church we will go to the cemetery and have the preacher say a few words next to the grave." She tapped the cake pan and the round layer of cake fell out onto the plate. "I think we should begin the wake around seven. What do you guys think?"

"I think that will be okay. What do you think Louise?" Lula Mae was peeling and cutting potatoes and dropping them into a large pot.

Louise laid strips of dough over precooked seasoned apples, which filled the unbaked crust in the pie tin. "That should be fine. It should be cooled off a little by then." She turned to Jesse Mae. "Do you think four pies will be enough? You know your mama had a lot of friends."

"That should be enough. Everybody will be bringing something." Jesse Mae began mixing frosting for the cake. "Lula Mae, if you need a dress for the funeral, we could probably find something of mine for you. We're about the same size."

Lula Mae stopped peeling potatoes and looked Jesse Mae up and down. "Thanks, but I think your dresses might be too small for me."

"Oh they might be a little short, but I'll bet you could wear them." Jesse Mae stopped mixing the cake frosting and began unbuttoning her dress.

"What are you doing?" said Lula.

Jesse Mae looked about the kitchen. "What? Romey is asleep and Papa and the kids are down in the pasture." Jesse Mae unbuttoned the buttons on her sundress and slipped it off. "Try this on. I'll bet it fits."

Lula Mae stood with the peeler in one hand and a half-peeled potato in the other. She looked at Louise, who gave no indication of an opinion as to what she should do. She put the potato peeler and potato down and untied her shirt from around her ribs. She slipped the shirt off and placed it on the kitchen table. She took the dress from Jesse Mae and slipped it on. The fit was a little snug as she buttoned it up, but it was not uncomfortable. Turning to Louise, she said, "How does it look?"

"It looks fine." Louise carried the unbaked pie to the oven.

"Let me see." Jesse Mae motioned for Lula Mae to turn around and show her how the dress fit. "It looks nice. Go into Mama's room and look for yourself."

Lula Mae turned and walked toward the dining room. She unconsciously slipped her hands in the pockets of the dress and immediately pulled something out of one of the pockets. She stopped and turned to the other women, extending her arm toward them; holding in her hand the turquoise necklace.

Jesse Mae drew in a short breath. She had forgotten about putting the necklace in the dress pocket earlier.

Without speaking, Lula Mae looked from one woman to the other, still holding the necklace out in front of her.

"What's that?" Louise advanced toward Lula Mae.

"It's Mama's necklace," said Jesse Mae.

"The one from the cellar?" Louise reached for the necklace.

Lula Mae allowed Louise to lift the necklace from her open hand. Louise examined it and then she and Lula Mae both turned to Jesse Mae for an explanation.

"I found it in the closet. It was in her purse."

"I looked in her purse," said Lula. "It wasn't there."

"It was in a secret pocket inside the purse lining. I've known about the pocket ever since I was a kid. I knew where to look."

Louise and Lula Mae looked at one another again.

"Why didn't you give it to the sheriff?" asked Louise.

"Because I decided that he didn't need it." Jesse Mae reached out for the necklace. "Mama really wanted this old necklace, so I'm going to keep it for her."

Louise handed it to her. "Was it…what was the Indian woman's name?"

"Rena, Rena Two Eagles. Yes it was Rena's. I remember seeing her wear it when I stayed with her." Jesse Mae touched two silver hearts on the necklace. "She said these two hearts represented her and her lover; the man who gave it to her. I never met him.

"Her husband ran out on her just a few months after they moved here from Oklahoma. She was only nineteen years old; just five years older than me."

"Why didn't you tell us you found it?" asked Lula Mae.

"Because I knew that if I told anyone, you'd all want me to give it to the sheriff, and he doesn't need it. He already knows that was Rena buried in the cellar." Jesse Mae handed the necklace back to Lula Mae. "Now put it back in the pocket and go see how well that dress fits. If you can wear this one, then you can wear one of my other ones at home." She turned around and went back to frosting her cake.

Louise moved to the cupboard and opened the doors. "I'm going to set the table for dinner. Guy and Harold should be back soon, and Frank and the kids should be back up here any time now."

"Gary, why don't you and Scotty go up and see if your mamas will give you some lemonade to bring down to us?" Frank stood next to the intended gravesite for the slain pigs and wiped his forehead with his bandana. He and Tony and the youngsters had been digging the hole for more than an hour. The five dead pigs were grouped together about ten yards away. One pig was still in the wheelbarrow, which had been used to carry it and the others from the pigsty.

"Okay," said Gary as Scotty and he sprinted up the pasture towards the house. They were both bored with digging and were glad to get away from the whole process.

"Those pigs stink!" Johnny stood at the bottom of the hole, which was now about six feet wide and seven feet long and two feet deep. He was leaning on his shovel, looking at the pigs.

From the other end of the hole, Loretta said, "You stink." She tossed a shovelful of dirt out of the hole. "And quit resting. My side is twice as deep as yours."

Frank tucked his bandana into his back pocket and reached for his pickaxe. "Alright you two, get out of there and let me loosen up some more dirt so that Geneva and Tony can have another turn."

215

Frank had planned on Guy and Harold helping him bury the pigs, but he wanted to get on with it, so he enlisted the help of the youngsters. He thought that they could use a diversion as much as he. There were only two shovels, so he instructed the kids to dig in pairs; first Tony and Geneva, then Gary and Scotty, and then Johnny and Loretta. He began the process by breaking up the dirt with a pickaxe and then letting them shovel the loosened dirt out of the hole. When they would reach solid earth, he would repeat his action with the pickaxe, and then let the next pair into the hole to shovel.

Johnny and Loretta eagerly climbed out of the hole and let their grandfather climb in and plunge the digging tool into the soil.

Loretta looked toward Geneva and Tony, who were sitting together in the shade of the barn about thirty yards from the hole with their backs against the wall. "Geneva! It's yours and Tony's turn to dig." She walked toward them. "Quit smooching and get up and do some work."

"Shut up Loretta." Mary's death had touched Geneva more deeply than it had her siblings and cousin. Being the oldest, she had been emotionally closer to her grandmother than the others. When she was born, she was the only granddaughter, so the adults had made quite a fuss over her and lavished her with attention; establishing a bond with her that was missing with the other children.

Loretta plopped down next to Geneva. Geneva hit her lightly on the shoulder as a gesture of disapproval. "Loretta, quit being such a smart-mouth around Grandpa. Don't you know he's feeling bad about Grandma?"

Loretta had a habit of speaking without thinking. Geneva's remark made her feel ashamed of her insensitivity. "Oh I didn't mean anything. I was just teasing."

"I know," said Geneva. "But when somebody is sad, you're supposed to show that you care by behaving yourself."

"Oh alright." Loretta looked toward the house where she saw Gary and Scotty, who were about halfway between the barn and the house. "I'm going to go help Gary and Scotty with the lemonade." She was up and gone in an instant.

Tony watched Geneva as she turned her attention to Johnny, who was walking around the pile of dead pigs, poking a stick at them. She shook her head in embarrassment over the behavior of her brother and sister. "They're just kids," said Tony. "Nobody is paying any attention to them."

Just then, Frank plunged his pickaxe into the dirt, stood upright and called to his grandson. "Johnny, get away from them pigs! They'll make you sick."

Geneva smiled up at Tony. "Oh yeah?"

Johnny walked away from the pigs, swinging his stick through the tall pasture grass in search of anything, which might be of interest to him, while Frank went back to his chore of breaking up dirt.

Tony, seizing on the moment alone with Geneva, and unnoticed by the others, reached over and took her hand in his. "I'm really sorry about your grandma. I know it must be difficult for you."

Geneva squeezed Tony's hand. "Thanks." She looked at the ground in front of her. "It's not that bad though." She looked up at Tony. "Not that I don't care. It's just that...I don't know...I guess I feel bad because I don't feel that bad. Does that make any sense?"

"Yeah, I guess."

"I loved my grandma, but we only saw her every two years. And that's just for two weeks. After we go back home, I don't suppose I'll even miss her."

"I understand. I had an uncle who was killed in Korea. My mother was really sad, but I had never been around him very much, so I didn't feel hardly anything. And I liked him. We just weren't close. I wanted to feel more, so what I felt most was guilt for not caring."

"Yeah."

Frank stepped up out of the hole and wiped his face again with his bandana. The pickaxe and shovels lay at the bottom of the hole. "Geneva, you and Tony come on up to the house. It's getting too hot to be out here digging." He looked across the pasture at Johnny who had found a rabbit hole and was sticking the stick into it. "Johnny, come on up to the house. We'll dig some more after dinner." He then proceeded to walk toward the house as Johnny, still whacking at the tall grass, followed behind him.

Geneva and Tony remained seated against the barn, watching the others walk away. They turned and looked at one another, bringing their lips together in a tender kiss. Geneva remembered her mother's advice, but quickly put it out of her mind. All she wanted to think about now was how nice it felt to have this moment alone with Tony before they would have to follow the others.

It was so warm inside the house; the women decided to make bologna sandwiches for Romey and Tony and the kids and let them eat outside on the front porch. Frank however was used to having a cooked meal for dinner; no matter what the temperature, so they set the dining table and prepared fried chicken and mashed potatoes.

Dinner for the adults however was delayed, while they waited for Guy and Harold, who were way overdue. Everything was ready and the women sat at the table sipping iced tea, while Frank sat on the back porch.

Jesse Mae looked at the clock. It was past one p.m. "Well let's eat," she said, getting up from her chair and walking to the back porch. "Come on Papa, let's eat. They can eat when they get back."

Frank joined the women at the table. One oscillating fan moved the warm air around the room giving some relief from the heat. They all ate very little. The meal was more of an attempt to re-establish a normal routine rather than a means of relieving hunger, which none of them really felt.

Jesse Mae fanned herself with a hand held fan. "Papa, do you want me to buy you a new suit for the funeral?"

"No Sister; that would just be a waste of money."

A lump formed in Jesse Mae's throat. Her father had not called her that since she was a child. Sister was his pet name for her. "Okay," she said.

The table was understandably quiet. Nobody felt the need to make casual conversation. They had discussed the funeral and the wake and everybody was at a loss for anything more to say.

Louise poured iced tea into Frank's glass. She set the pitcher down. "What's going to happen to Romey now?"

"What do you mean?" asked Frank.

"Well, you know Mary did a lot for Romey. Who's going to do those things now?"

"Well..." said Frank. He looked at Jesse Mae.

Louise looked at Jesse Mae and then back to Frank. "Are you going to put him in that school?"

"No," said Jesse Mae. "Not now. He needs to be at home for a while. I'll take care of him."

"Are you sure, Sister?" said Frank. "It's a lot of work."

"I'm sure. If I need to, I'll hire someone to help me out."

The sound of a car coming up the drive could be heard. "There they are." Lula Mae rose from her chair and headed to the back porch. She had been worried about Guy and Harold being gone so long. She stood on the back porch and watched the two men get out of the car. Louise opened the screen door and stepped out onto the porch next to her.

Guy got out from behind the wheel and stood wobbly-legged next to the car with the door open. He looked at the women for a moment and then leaned over and said something to Harold who was still sitting in the car. The two men talked for a moment and then Guy stood upright and shut the door. Harold remained in the car.

"Now Honey, don't be mad. We just had a couple of beers." Guy ambled up to Lula Mae. He stood on the ground next to the porch and put his arms around her waist and laid his head against her bosom.

"Harold drank beer?" Louise was watching her husband sitting in the car. "In the middle of the day?" She could not believe it. Harold very seldom drank alcohol. She had never known him to drink at anytime other than some festivity; and then it was very little.

"It's my fault." Guy still had his arms wrapped tightly around Lula Mae's waist. "I talked him into it."

"Well, why isn't he getting out of the car?" asked Louise.

"He's not feeling too good." Guy turned his head and joined the two women as they watched Harold open the car door.

The next instant, Harold disappeared from view and they could hear the sounds of retching as he vomited onto the ground next to the car.

"Oh good Lord." Louise stepped quickly off of the porch and walked briskly to the car. She stood at a safe distance from her husband, watching him. She did not want to get splattered with vomit. When the retching stopped, Harold looked up at her and began bawling like a baby. Louise moved quickly to him and helped him out of the car, being careful where she stepped. She walked him to the back porch and sat him down and then went into the kitchen and got a cool wet cloth for his face. She came out, took his arm and guided him to Romey's playhouse. She did not want Scotty or the other children to see him like this.

Meanwhile, Guy and Lula Mae had gone to the dining room. Guy sat at the table and Lula Mae filled his plate with food. She then went into the kitchen and quickly returned with a cup of strong black coffee. "Here; drink this," she said. She then sat in the chair next to him.

"Did you get everything taken care of?" asked Jesse Mae.

"Yes." Guy ate his food without looking up. He could feel his father's disapproving eyes on him.

"What time is the funeral?" continued Jesse Mae.

"The preacher said he could do it at ten, just like you wanted."

"And you picked a plot?"

Guy dropped his knife and fork on the table next to his plate and looked up. "Yes, Jesse Mae; everything is taken care of." He glanced quickly at Frank and saw that his eyes were indeed fixed upon him. He knew that his father did not approve of excessive drinking and he suspected that he was angry with him. He lowered his eyes and focused on his plate of food again; hoping to avoid criticism.

Lula Mae had one arm around Guy's shoulders and was quietly encouraging him to eat. She knew that food was the best way to counteract the effects of too much alcohol. She had learned this by seeing how her mother had dealt with her older brothers in similar situations. Guy picked up his utensils and resumed eating, as everyone fell silent for a moment.

Then Jesse Mae asked, "Did you see her?"

Guy stopped cutting the food on his plate and held his knife and fork in his hands. He looked up at his sister. His face was sullen and sad looking. "No," he said and the tears began to flow down his cheeks. He dropped his head and began crying softly. Lula Mae pulled him to her and rested his head on her shoulder.

Frank stood up from his chair. "Why don't you go lay down in Romey's room. It's the coolest place in the house." He left the dining room and walked to the back porch. There was no shade there at this time of day, but he did not care; he just needed a minute to be alone. He sat on the edge of the porch, with his feet on the ground and his elbows resting on his knees. He was close to crying himself, but was determined not to let it happen. He felt that there had been enough tears shed for the time being. Right now there were tasks, which needed attending to.

After a few moments, Frank stood up and walked around to the front porch where Romey, Tony and the youngsters were still gathered. As he walked past the front porch, continuing on toward the fence, he said, "Anyone who wants to help bury those pigs, come on. It don't look like your daddies are going to be any help."

The youngsters were unaware that their fathers had come home drunk, so they did not give their grandfather's comment another thought. They just assumed that they did not want to help with the pigs.

Loretta, Johnny, Gary and Scotty jumped from the porch, full of energy. The ninety degree temperature did not seem to bother them. They were eager to get back to the bizarre undertaking, and ran ahead of Frank as he walked slowly toward the barn.

Geneva and Tony remained seated in the swing with Romey. "Romey, do you want to go down and watch us dig?" asked Geneva.

"No," said Romey, shaking his head.

Geneva was not surprised at Romey's reaction. She understood that he was still afraid to go near the dead pigs. "Well," she said. "We're going to go help your papa. You just sit here and keep cool, okay?"

"Okay," said Romey, obviously relieved to be excused from going with them.

The fan moved the air around Romey's bedroom, giving very little relief from the heat of the summer's day. Lula Mae sat on the edge of Romey's bed next to Guy as he leaned forward with his elbows resting on his knees. She gently rubbed his upper back and shoulders as he struggled to control his sobbing. Lula Mae did nothing to discourage his crying; she knew that he had to let out the pain he was feeling.

"Why?" muttered Guy. "Why would anybody do that to Mama just for some god-damned necklace?" Earlier, Lula Mae had shared her suspicions with Guy that Mary might have been killed for the necklace.

"Oh," said Lula Mae, as her hand rested, motionless on his shoulders.

"What?" Guy looked up at her through his tears.

"We were wrong about the necklace. It wasn't stolen."

Guy sat upright. He wiped the tears from his eyes. "What?"

"Jesse Mae found it. It was in your mama's purse."

"I thought you and Louise said you looked everywhere for it."

"We did…we said that…and we did look everywhere."

"But not in the purse?"

"Well, yes; I looked in the purse, but I didn't see it. Jesse Mae said it was in a secret pocket."

A look of disbelief came over Guy's face. "Secret pocket?"

"Yeah; the purse has a secret pocket or something in it."

"Wouldn't you have felt something like a silver and turquoise necklace in it?"

Lula Mae shrugged her shoulders. "Well, I was in a hurry and I wasn't expecting anything to be in the lining of the purse."

"Humph." Guy leaned into Lula and put his head on her shoulder. The discussion of the necklace had helped shift his mood and dry his tears.

Jesse Mae was at the kitchen sink washing the dishes. She had watched Louise walking from Romey's playhouse, where she had left Harold. When Louise walked through the back door, Jesse Mae asked, "How's he doing?"

Louise picked up a dish towel and a plate and began wiping it dry. "Oh, he'll be okay. He's not used to drinking, you know." She placed the plate in the cupboard and reached for another one to dry. "How are you doing?"

Jesse Mae focused on the glass that she was washing. "Oh…okay." She looked at her sister-in-law and forced a sad smile. "We have to get through this."

At that moment a familiar car horn sounded from outside. Jesse Mae looked out the window. Due to the angle of the drive, she barely caught a glimpse of the mail truck coming towards the house. "There's Bobby Dean." She dried her hands and walked out to meet the postman.

The truck came to a stop and Jesse Mae saw Bobby Dean lean over and begin rummaging through his mail bag. She approached the mail truck. "Hi Bobby Dean."

The postman did not bother to get out of his truck. He just handed Jesse Mae a bundle of cards through his open window. "Hi Jesse Mae. Me and the wife was real sorry to hear about your mama."

"Thanks." Jesse Mae took the cards and began examining them.

Bobby Dean nodded his head towards the cards. "There's one from us in there."

Jesse Mae did not feel like saying thanks again, so she just nodded her head.

"I've been carrying a lot of cards like that today."

"Oh?" Jesse Mae looked up at him.

"Yeah. Roger Crawford died yesterday. Seems he had cancer."

Jesse Mae felt as if her heart stopped for an instant. She caught her breath and tried to think of something to say that would not indicate that she and Roger had renewed their friendship. Finally she just said, "Oh," once more.

"Well." Bobby Dean shifted into reverse. "We'll see you at the funeral tomorrow. The pastor already has the notice up on the church's board."

"Okay," said Jesse Mae as the truck backed up. She watched as the postman turned his truck around and drove back to the road. She slowly walked to the back porch, removing the rubber band, which held the sympathy cards together. She bit her bottom lip, struggling to hold back the tears. First her mother and now Roger. Granted, Roger's death was expected; it was just that she did not think it would be so soon. She had hoped to see him again.

"Sympathy cards?" said Louise as Jesse Mae entered the house.

"Yeah." Jesse Mae walked across the room looking at the return addresses on the envelopes. "Do you mind if I let you finish the dishes? I'd like to show these cards to Romey."

"No, I don't mind," said Louise. "You go ahead."

Jesse Mae stood behind the screen door to the front porch and looked at Romey as he sat in the porch swing. She wondered what he was thinking with his head down and his feet, unmoving on the enamel painted floor boards of the porch. Ordinarily he would be pushing the swing back and forth and looking around, taking in the day.

She opened the door and walked onto the porch. Romey turned to look at her. She could see the uncertainty in his eyes. Having no formal education, it was difficult for Romey to express himself. He had never attended school. He could not read or write, but Jesse Mae knew that he was more aware of the complexities of life and relationships than anyone else suspected. She sat next to him and put an arm around his shoulder.

"We got some cards from Mama's friends."

Romey looked at the cards in Jesse Mae's hands. Jesse Mae sat for a moment, looking at Romey. "You don't have to be afraid, Romey. I'm going to stay with you."

Romey's eyes met Jesse Mae's.

"You and I are going to live together," she said. "I will never leave you again."

Pain filled Jesse Mae's heart as she saw the tears forming in Romey's eyes. She felt her own tears rolling down her face and she pulled him close to her and he began to sob. Through the haze of tears and emotions, Jesse Mae was vaguely aware of the cards as they slipped from her lap and scattered across the floor of the porch.

CHAPTER SIXTEEN

L
ULA MAE WALKED INTO THE KITCHEN AS Louise pulled a large baking pan from the cupboard. Louise had finished with the dishes and she was ready to resume preparing food for the wake.

"How's Harold?" said Lula as she walked to the pail of water sitting on the counter. She lifted the dipper out of the water and took a drink.

"Oh he's okay." Louise spread flour on the table where she was preparing to knead dough. "How about Guy?"

"He'll be alright. He just needs to sleep it off. What are you making?"

"Peach cobbler. I think we'll have enough food with this."

The two women had taken it upon themselves to assume the household duties at this difficult time for the family. They were used to helping Mary anyway, so they knew everything that needed to be done. Being homemakers and caregivers, this all came naturally to them.

Lula Mae sighed and looked toward the front of the house where Mary's bedroom was. "I think I'll go ahead and start on Mary's room. I'm going to take the bedspread and sheets down there to Frank and let him bury them with those pigs. Those bloodstains will never come out. Where's Jesse Mae?"

Louise continued the ritual with the dough. "She's on the front porch with Romey. The letterman delivered some cards that she wanted to show him."

Lula Mae walked into the living room and stood just inside the screen door, listening to Jesse Mae as she read the cards to Romey.

She did not disturb them; she felt that they needed some time alone together; also, she did not want to draw Romey's attention to what she was doing.

She quietly opened the door to Mary's bedroom and went inside, closing the door behind her. She gathered up the bedspread, sheets, and pillowcases, which were stained with dried blood, and rolled them tightly together, making as small a bundle as she could. She then carried the bundle through Romey's bedroom and into the kitchen where she and Louise exchanged a silent glance before she went out the back door.

Small beads of sweat were popping up on Lula Mae's forehead as she approached Frank and the youngsters. The afternoon sun was strong and the bedding was heavier than she had expected. She heard Frank tell the boys to go help her; and Gary, Scotty and Johnny ran to relieve her of her burden. The boys reached for the linen, but Lula Mae would not let them take it from her.

"What have you got there, Lula Mae?" asked Frank, when she and the boys reached him.

Lula Mae dropped the bundle next to the pit and pushed her hair back from her face. She hesitated a moment, and looked at the children; reluctant to remind them of the image that she knew they must have in their minds of their dead grandmother, but she knew the matter had to be addressed. "It's the bedspread and linen from Mary's bed. The stains will never come out. I thought we could just bury them with the pigs."

Frank did not say anything. He looked at the bundle on the ground and then looked at Lula Mae and nodded his head. He looked into the pit, which was now almost four feet deep. "Tony, you and Geneva come on up. I think it's deep enough."

Geneva and Tony tossed their shovels up and out of the hole and then they climbed out. Tony lifted the ladder out of the hole and carried it towards the barn. Everybody was hot and tired, so there was not a lot of talking.

"Okay Johnny," said Frank. "Go get them and start dumping them in." Johnny had asked his grandfather earlier if he could push the pigs over in the wheelbarrow and dump them into the pit.

Loretta, who had been resting in the shade of the barn, joined the group around the hole. They all watched as Johnny ran to the pile of pigs and lifted the legs of the wheelbarrow off the ground. The one pig that had been left in the wheelbarrow was the heaviest; about one-hundred-twenty pounds. The others averaged between eighty-five and one-hundred pounds each. Johnny's legs were a little shaky as he struggled to keep the wheelbarrow balanced on his way back to the pit.

He dumped the first pig and went back for another one. Tony had to help him get the other pigs into the wheelbarrow; both of them being careful not to touch the carcasses with their hands. Tony would sink a meat hook into the flesh, and Johnny would position the wheelbarrow on its side next to the pig. Tony would then pull and lift with the meat hook, while Johnny turned the wheelbarrow upright with the pig inside.

Once all of the carcasses were in the bottom of the pit, Frank unceremoniously kicked the bundle of linen in after them. He stood for a moment, nearly faltering in his attempt to remain stoic. He felt that he was on the verge of loosing his composure as he thought of the blood of his dead wife so near to him now; and the feeling of finality that covering it with the earth would bring. He took a deep breath and cleared his throat. He looked at Gary and Scotty who were standing, each with a shovel in his hands; anxious to shovel the first bit of dirt back into the grave. "Start shoveling," he said and stepped back to give them room.

The eagerness of the youngsters as they began to fill the hole helped Frank momentarily divert his thoughts away from Mary. The activity was a distraction for them all; and they temporarily put aside their feelings of sadness, and concentrated on the task at hand. Johnny and Loretta began kicking dirt into the hole with their usual competitiveness; not waiting for their turn with the shovels. Eventually, each of the youngsters took a turn with the proper tools. When the hole was filled they all walked on top of the dirt to pack it down flat over the carcasses. The excess dirt was spread around the area so that the visible reminder of what had happened was now practically unnoticeable. The troop of gravediggers put away their tools and made their way back up to the house.

Louise had placed the bathtub behind Romey's playhouse and filled it with water. The summer sun had heated the water to a temperature that was comfortable for bathing. The plan was for Johnny, Gary and Scotty to share the tub of water by standing next to it and pouring bucketfuls over one another after lathering up.

After the boys were finished, the girls could each have their own tub of fresh water for proper bathing. Louise had chosen the area behind Romey's playhouse because it was out of view from the main house and it was close to the caldron where the water was being heated. She felt that it would be too much work to carry enough water down to the bath shed to fill three tubs.

"Harold and Scott and I are going home tonight," said Louise as she and Lula Mae stoked the fire. "You and Guy can come and bathe at our house tomorrow before the funeral if you want to."

"Thanks," said Lula Mae. "But I think we'll go ahead and bathe here. I don't mind bathing in this tub; besides, after today, I need a bath before going to bed. I'll wash my hair and bathe tonight and then just freshen up in the morning."

"Okay." Louise placed another log on the fire under the caldron.

"You're staying for supper aren't you?"

"Yeah, we'll stay for supper. I just need to go home and take a bath. That little tub isn't quite big enough for me to feel comfortable in." Louise looked toward the playhouse. "Well, look who's up."

Harold stood inside the playhouse, looking out from behind the screen door. His hands were at his sides and his head was bent forward as he squinted against the midday light. "What's going on?" he said; bringing one hand up to his head in a reaction to the pain caused by talking.

"It's bath time," said Louise. "How do you feel?"

Harold pushed open the screen door and stepped out into the sunshine. He was barefoot and wearing a pair of slacks and a sleeveless undershirt, which he had just slipped on before coming out. "Like crap."

"Are you hungry?" Louise watched him as he walked toward her.

"Oh no," he said, shaking his head. "But I would like some iced tea."

"Jesse Mae and Romey are on the front porch. She has a pitcher."

Harold slowly made his way around the house to the front porch.

Tony was sitting in his car, which was parked in the shade of the oak tree down by the road. His door was open and he had one leg out of the car. Lula Mae and Louise could hear the occasional static coming from his radio and the indistinct sounds of his voice and somebody on the radio talking back to him. After a few moments, Tony left his car and walked up to Louise and Lula Mae. "The sheriff thinks it will be okay for me to go home for a couple of hours," he said. "He doesn't think anyone will be in any danger this afternoon. I'll be back after supper."

"You're welcome to join us for supper," said Lula Mae.

"Thanks, but I have some business to attend to. Will you tell Geneva that I'll see her tonight?"

Lula Mae repeated her characteristic move of brushing back her hair from her forehead as she stood in the hot sunshine. "Sure, I'll tell her." She knew that Geneva would be glad that Tony was not going to be around when she was bathing. Geneva had an immense dislike for the whole hygienic situation on the farm.

"I'm sorry for not going with you and Guy," said Jesse Mae as she poured a second glassful of tea for Harold. She looked at Romey, who was sitting next to her; his eyes dry of tears and focused on the sympathy cards in his hands, which Jesse Mae had been reading to him. "I just thought I should stay with Romey."

"Yeah, I guess you were right. Anyway, everything is all taken care of now. We found a nice plot under a big tree." Harold lifted the glass to his lips and drank. Setting the glass beside him on the porch rail where he was leaning, he said, "It was a little expensive though."

"Don't worry about it. I know you and Guy have a lot of expenses; what, with your families and all. I'll talk to the funeral director tomorrow. I'll write him a check for the expenses and we'll work it out later." Harold started to thank Jesse Mae, but Jesse Mae cut him off. "Oh, here's a pretty one Romey." She held the card up for Romey to see, and then she turned to Harold. "Isn't this pretty?"

"Yeah," said Harold. He was touched by the expression of tenderness and consideration for others from his little sister. Over the years she had developed a hateful disposition and had become increasingly difficult to get along with. Her attitude now reminded him of when she was a

229

young girl; before she had come down with TB. The time that she had spent quarantined in that Indian woman's house had changed her.

After recovering from the illness and going back to school, there was a notable difference in her personality. Instead of the open, friendly girl, which she had been before; she became withdrawn and guarded. She stopped hanging out with her old friends at school, and never brought any girlfriends home. All through high school; she did not date. She spent most of her free time at the school library, studying or at home with her mother and Romey.

She did, however improve her grades and worked hard to earn a scholarship to college. She was planning on becoming a high school teacher, but then; during her third year in college, she wrote home to let everyone know that she had married and dropped out of college. Her new husband was a professional man; Eugene Burns. He was a successful attorney, he owned his own home, and he was twenty-five years older than Jesse Mae.

Only once did Eugene visit the farm. It was a very brief visit. He and Jesse Mae were newlyweds and he wanted to meet her family. During the encounter, the mood was strained but cordial. He invited Frank, Mary and Romey to visit Jesse Mae anytime they wanted. On the occasions that they did visit, he would either be at his office in town; or busy in his office at home. He was also amicable towards Guy and Harold and their families; but they too, saw very little of him.

Harold could not help but wonder if Jesse Mae felt a sense of liberation with Eugene's death. While he was alive, she had presented the image of the respectful, devoted wife; but after he died, she seemed younger and happier; with less social airs about her. Little by little he had noticed her changing; she seemed more like her old self again.

The screen door opened and Guy stepped onto the porch. Like Harold, he wore a pair of Khaki pants and an underwear shirt, and he squinted in reaction to the bright daylight. "I hope you don't feel as shitty as I do," he said to Harold.

"Have some iced tea," responded Harold. "It helps."

Romey looked up from the cards. "Guy, you know you're not supposed to be talking like that." Mary had conditioned Romey to censure anybody who cursed in his presence.

With anybody else, Guy would have brusquely defended his right to speak as he pleased, but with Romey, he was much more compliant. "Oh...okay Romey. You're right." He turned to Harold. "Any more glasses?"

"You'll have to get one out of the kitchen," said Jesse Mae. Romey's criticism of Guy's language pleased her. She felt that it was another sign that he was coming out of his depression and adjusting to Mary's absence.

"What's that?" Guy was referring to the cards, which Romey was holding.

Jesse Mae glanced up at Guy. "They're sympathy cards. Bobby Dean brought them earlier. Go get yourself a glass and come back and read them with us."

Guy looked at the closed door to his mother's bedroom as he passed through the living room on his way to the kitchen. He passed by it quickly and tried not to think about what had taken place there. He hated the memory of that awful scene. He knew that eventually the door would be left open during the daytime as it had usually been in the past. The layout of the house was conducive to good air circulation when all of the doors were left open. With this heat, circulation was crucial to everybody's comfort, but for the time being he was thankful that the door was closed.

In the kitchen the glasses were varied in size and style. There were no more than two alike in the whole group. Matching eating utensils and dishes were not important in the Austin household and Frank and Mary could never see the sense in investing good money in them. In fact there were a few canning jars in the cupboard amongst the glasses. Guy picked one of the jars from the cupboard. As he held it in his hand it gave him a sense of connection with his mother's spirit. He sighed deeply and shifted his thinking. He did not want to start blubbering again.

Out of the kitchen window, he caught a glimpse of Lula Mae. She was carrying a pail of water from the cauldron to the pigsty where his father was scrubbing the slop trough with an old broom. Lula Mae hesitated for a moment at the trough. Frank moved out of her way and she splashed the bucketful of hot water into the trough. Then Frank stepped back up to the wooden feedbox and began scrubbing again.

Lula Mae had told Guy earlier that his father and the kids were going to bury those pigs. He realized that they must have done so already. Soon all of the remaining signs of the horrible tragedy that had taken place would be gone. He watched his wife and his father. He was impressed with how they each had taken it upon themselves to get the job done, and he was reminded of how much he respected them both. He felt ashamed of himself for breaking down and getting drunk. He resolved that he would pull himself together and be more helpful; but not just yet. Right now he really needed a glass of iced tea.

The time spent on the front porch, talking and looking at cards was bittersweet for the siblings. They reminisced about their younger years together and about their parents. They had not spoken to one another this intimately for years. Their grief renewed the bond, which they had shared when they were younger.

Some time later, the screen door opened and Frank, who had walked through the house from the backyard, stepped out onto the porch. Guy and Harold tensed; they were both prepared for their father to reprimand them for getting drunk.

"I buried them pigs," said Frank. He carried a chair from the dining room, which he positioned next to the end of the swing where Romey sat. "Louise and Lula Mae are straightening up your mama's room. It's time to open it up. We'll need the circulation tonight." He sat down on the chair and reached into his pocket for his pipe. The porch was silent for a moment as he pressed tobacco into the bowl of the pipe.

"I'm sorry we got drunk, Papa," said Guy.

"Yeah, me too," added Harold.

Frank struck a match and put it to the tobacco in his pipe. He inhaled and the tobacco glowed red with fire. He shook the match until the flame was extinguished and then he threw the match into the yard. He took the pipe away from his lips, all the while staring out over the front yard. "That's okay; your mama would have understood."

"We got some cards, Papa." Romey held the stack of cards in his hands.

Frank turned and looked at Romey. "Well let me have a look, Son."

The others were quiet while Frank read the cards aloud to Romey. After a while, Lula Mae and Louise joined them on the porch.

Louise walked over to Harold and leaned on the porch rail next to him. "We've opened up your mama's room," she said as she put her arm around his waist.

Frank handed Lula Mae several of the cards and she joined Louise on the railing and they looked through them. "Mary had a lot of friends," said Louise.

"Yeah," said Frank. "We've been in these parts all our lives. We know just about everybody in town."

"How many people do you think will be at the wake tomorrow?" asked Lula Mae.

"Oh, I'd say near on to a hundred." Frank handed Lula Mae a few more cards. "You girls don't need to fret over it though. The womenfolk will all bring food and drink and their husbands will bring tables to set up outside. That's how it's done around here when somebody dies in the summertime."

Just then Gary came running around the corner of the house, followed closely by Scotty with Johnny right behind them. When the boys saw the adults, Gary and Scotty quickly positioned themselves on the steps and sat quietly. Johnny slowed his pace and casually positioned himself with one foot on the bottom step and leaned against the rail, as if his intention had been to do nothing but join the group. He shot a quick threatening glance at the other boys as they put on their most innocent looking faces and turned to the adults as if they were interested in what was being said.

"Did you boys finish your baths?" asked Lula Mae. All three boys were wearing only denim pants. They all answered with a simple, "Yeah."

Lula Mae looked at Johnny. "Johnny, don't you and Gary go getting dirty again." She knew that he was waiting for the chance to roughhouse Gary and Scotty as soon as he got them away from the adults.

"You neither, Scott," said Louise. "We're going to go home tonight, but I don't want you to have to take another bath."

"Okay," said Scotty, eying Johnny as he sat down between Gary and him and dug his elbows into the ribs of the younger boys.

"Why don't you guys spend the night?" asked Guy.

"Harold and I both need a bath and a change of clothes," said Louise. "We'll stay for supper, but then we have to go. We'll meet up with you all at the church tomorrow."

A half hour later Geneva stood at the screen door, dressed in a flannel robe with a towel wrapped around her head like a turban. "We're all through," she said; meaning that she and Loretta had finished bathing. She then went upstairs where Loretta had gone before her.

"Who's next?" asked Lula Mae. She looked around the group.

"Romey told me that he wants to take a bath," said Jesse Mae. "He's not afraid anymore. Guy would you and Harold help Romey with his bath?"

"Sure," said Guy.

Harold stood up from the porch railing. "Of course we will. Come on Romey, let's get you cleaned up."

"I'll help him," said Frank. "He's used to me. Come on Romey, let's go take a bath."

Romey was still like a child when it came to bath time. He especially liked bathing out of doors when the weather was nice. In actuality, he was capable of bathing himself, but the bathing ritual had been unchanged since his childhood. In his whole life, he had never bathed alone. He followed Frank down the steps and around the corner towards the back yard.

"We'll help with the water, Grandpa," said Johnny, following closely behind. Gary and Scotty looked at one another and apparently deciding that it was safe, followed behind Johnny.

Louise moved from the porch railing and sat in the swing with Jesse Mae. "So what happens now?" she said as she looked from one sibling to the other.

"What do you mean?" Guy was facing the others, sitting on the floor of the porch with his back leaning against the wall.

Harold moved from the rail and sat in the chair where Frank had sat. "She means who's going to take care of Papa and Romey. They're used to Mama doing for them. I don't think Papa would be very good at taking care of Romey. A bath is one thing, but Mama was with Romey twenty-four-seven."

"I'll take care of them," said Jesse Mae.

Harold was skeptical. "Are you going to leave that big house in town and live out here?"

"I don't know, Harold! I haven't thought it through; I just know that I'm not leaving Romey again."

"What does that mean? 'Leave Romey again'?"

Jesse Mae did not know how to respond. Of course nobody knew what she meant. They all thought that Romey was her brother. "Well we did, didn't we? We all left him. We all moved away and led our own lives without him."

Jesse Mae's words were perplexing to the others. Harold responded, "That's what brothers and sisters do; they leave home and pursue their own lives."

"Well Romey couldn't." Jesse Mae was nearly in tears again. The guilt she had always felt for leaving her child was welling up inside of her. This, coupled with the sadness of losing her mother and the added guilt she felt over her estranged relationship with her, had made Jesse Mae feel very vulnerable and defensive. She realized that her emotional state was making her careless. She had a strong desire to tell everyone that Romey was her child, but she knew that she could not. She grew quiet and reached into her pocket and pulled out her gold cigarette case.

After Romey had had his bath and put on clean clothes, it was evident to everyone that his spirits were improving; this made them all feel better. Toward suppertime, Jesse Mae had taken him out to his playhouse and convinced him to play some games with the youngsters. She had assured him that she was not going to leave; and she could see how this comforted him.

She realized, to a large extent, that what he was feeling, aside from the obvious trauma of losing Mary, was insecurity. She and the rest of the family were heartbroken and grieving the loss of Mary, but they did not have the added concern of an uncertain life ahead of them. They would all eventually get on with their lives; but Frank and Romey had depended on Mary so much that their lives were drastically changed forever.

Jesse Mae walked out of Romey's playhouse, leaving Romey playing cards with Loretta, Johnny, Gary and Scotty. Frank, Guy and Harold were gathered around on the back porch. Frank and Guy were smoking pipes and Harold was shelling nuts and eating them. Tony had had a change of plans and returned in time to have supper with them, and he and Geneva were on the front porch in the swing.

Jesse Mae entered the kitchen from the back yard. Louise and Lula Mae were busy preparing the meal. "What's for supper?" she asked.

"Leftover chicken, mashed potatoes, beans, and fried green tomatoes," said Lula Mae. She was slicing tomatoes and Louise was dipping the slices in a cornmeal batter and frying them in a large skillet.

"Can I do anything to help?"

"You can set the tables." Lula Mae continued to slice the tomatoes. "The adults in the dining room, the kids, Romey and Tony in here."

Jesse Mae got the table settings out of the cupboard and commenced the task. As she worked, she spoke to the other two women. "You two have really been a lot of help. I want to thank you."

"You don't have to thank me," said Louise.

"No, me neither," added Lula Mae.

"You all are our family." Louise transferred several tomato slices from the skillet onto a large platter. "I don't know what else we would do other than help you get through this."

Lula Mae nodded her head in agreement with Louise as she paused in her slicing and looked at Jesse Mae.

"Well, I appreciate it," said Jesse Mae.

Supper at both tables was quiet. The adults were dealing with their grief and the youngsters were trying their best to show respect for them. Even Scotty, the youngest and most rambunctious of the group was uncharacteristically subdued.

Jesse Mae dished some fried tomatoes onto Frank's plate. "Papa, I still have Eugene's suits in his closet. I think they might fit you. You want to wear one to the funeral tomorrow?"

"We'll see." Frank moved the tomatoes around on his plate. He cut a small piece of one and put it in his mouth.

Jesse Mae looked across the table. "Guy, you might be able to wear one too. I know you only have vacation clothes here. Lula Mae's going to borrow a dress; and maybe Geneva."

"Yeah, okay," said Guy, disinterestedly. "I hope Sheriff Files don't start asking any more questions tomorrow."

"He won't," said Frank. "Tony talked to him this afternoon. He told Tony that he had eliminated all of us as suspects. The fool even checked out my story about collecting rent from Bud Hoskins. He said that I was the only one who was alone yesterday. The rest of you was all together."

"Except for when Guy and Lula Mae and Jesse Mae went to the hospital," said Louise. "But they were together, so I guess he was right."

Guy and Lula Mae both glanced at Jesse Mae and then they looked at each other. They were both thinking of how Jesse Mae was gone longer than they had expected her to be. They glanced back at Jesse Mae and could not help but wonder why she was not correcting Louise. Why was she keeping quiet about going shopping by herself?

Jesse Mae was looking down at her plate as she broke a piece of cornbread on it. She raised her head and looked first at Lula Mae and then at Guy. "I'm sure he doesn't suspect any of us. He was just asking questions because it's his job."

As the meal progressed, the conversation tapered off. After a while, the family members began excusing themselves from the tables and moving to different areas of the house. Frank went up to his room. Harold went to the living room to read the newspaper. Romey was now in the living room listening to the radio as Gary and Scotty played a game of checkers next to him. Loretta and Johnny had joined Geneva and Tony on the front porch.

Louise pushed her chair back from the table and stood up. "Well, I'm going to start on these dishes." She collected dishes and utensils and carried them into the kitchen.

Jesse Mae, Guy and Lula Mae sat in silence at the table. They had spoken very little since the remark about the sheriff not suspecting anybody. Jesse Mae glanced quickly around to make sure the three of them were alone. She leaned toward the others and said in a whisper, "What are you two thinking?"

"What do you mean?" Guy kept his voice low.

"I saw the way you both looked when Louise said that none of us were alone."

Guy and Lula Mae said nothing.

"What are you thinking?" Jesse Mae repeated.

"Why didn't you say that you went shopping?" asked Guy.

"Why? Why would I? I don't have to prove anything."

"Why didn't you give the sheriff that necklace?"

Jesse Mae's jaw dropped a little. She looked at her brother and his wife. "I don't believe this. You...you actually suspect me of killing Mama?"

"No," protested Guy. "Of course not." Now he looked around to make sure they were alone. He looked at Lula Mae.

Tears began flowing from Jesse Mae's eyes. "Oh this is great. My mama has been killed and my brother and sister-in-law think that I did it."

"Oh Jess." Guy reached for his sister's hand.

"Leave me alone!" Jesse Mae stood up and grabbed her cigarette case from the table. She tried to compose herself as she passed through the kitchen where Louise was washing dishes.

"Are you okay?" asked Louise when she saw the tears.

"I just need a minute. I'm going to Romey's playhouse for a smoke." She exited the house and made her way across the back yard to the small structure.

After a brief moment Louise saw the glow from the lantern coming from inside the playhouse. Lula Mae entered the kitchen with some dirty dishes.

"Is everything alright?" Louise took the dishes from Lula Mae and put them in the sink.

"Yeah; Guy just hurt her feelings. He didn't mean to."

Guy walked through the kitchen and out the back door. He opened the screen door to the playhouse and stepped inside. Jesse Mae was sitting on a small chair, holding a lit cigarette between her two fingers. She covered her face with her hands to hide her tears.

Guy stood for a moment just inside the door. He could feel his emotions building up. He tried to say, "I'm sorry," but what came out was unintelligible sobbing.

For a moment the small building was filled with the sounds of their shared anguish. Slowly the crying subsided; replaced with sniffles and short breaths. Jesse Mae took her hands away from her face and put her cigarette to her lips. After a long inhale and exhale, she pulled another chair next to her. "Sit down," she said.

Guy sat on the chair and motioned for Jesse Mae to give him a cigarette. He lit the cigarette and took a long drag.

The light from the kerosene lantern gave off a yellow-orange glow as the brother and sister sat, averting their eyes from one another. Then Jesse Mae turned to Guy and spoke.

"I want to tell you something, but you have to give me your solemn promise that you will never repeat it to anyone."

Guy hesitated for an instant. He shrugged his shoulders and said, "Okay."

"Say it."

"Say what? That I promise?"

"Yes."

"Okay, I promise that I won't tell anyone what you're going to tell me."

"Not even Lula Mae."

"No, no one."

Jesse Mae sat erect in her chair and looked out the door as she took another drag of her cigarette. She exhaled deeply and then said, "I never had TB."

Guy's first sense was to question how this had anything to do with what was going on now, but in the next instant he was hit with the weight of Jesse Mae's statement just the same. He remembered that she was in that house for months. "What?"

She turned and faced him. "I never had TB."

"Of course you did; you were quarantined."

Jesse Mae looked intently into Guy's eyes. She wanted to make sure that she caught his first reaction to what she was about to say. "I was pregnant."

"Pregnant?" Guy was stunned. "You were fourteen years old."

Jesse Mae looked at Guy without saying any more.

Guy, realizing what she was actually telling him, said, "What happened to the baby? Did it die?"

"No."

"Well...what did you do with it?"

Jesse Mae was silent. She puffed on her cigarette and looked at the floor. "It's Romey."

"Romey?" A number of questions flooded Guy's mind. 'What happened to his mother's baby?...And why would she raise Romey as her own child?' This made no sense to him. He could not accept what his sister had just told him. "Romey is your brother."

Jesse Mae stood up and opened the screen door a few inches and flipped her cigarette outside. She turned to face Guy. "Romey is my son."

"Jesse Mae…" Guy was having difficulty taking Jesse Mae's statement as fact. He knew that she was upset, and for a brief moment he wondered about her mental state. Then he realized that she was not delusional or making this up for some reason. The gravity of her revelation sank in and he was speechless.

CHAPTER SEVENTEEN

J ESSE MAE TURNED AND WENT BACK TO the small chair. She sat down and picked up her cigarette case from the floor and began to rotate it in her hand. "I was here yesterday when you and Lula Mae thought I was shopping," she said, keeping her eyes on the cigarette case.

Guy did not speak. Her statement barely registered in his mind. A thousand questions were racing through his mind. How could Romey be her child? Was she saying that their father...?

"I brought Romey's father here to meet him. I told Romey that he was just a friend. His father was Roger Crawford."

With the immediate relief of dispelling the suspicion that his father had been an incestuous child molester, Guy was simultaneously shocked at the news that Jesse Mae and Roger Crawford had been involved romantically. "Roger Crawford?" Then Jesse Mae's use of the past tense hit him. "What do you mean 'was'?"

Jesse Mae stopped fidgeting with the cigarette case and looked at Guy. "He died yesterday. I dropped him off at the hospital after we were here and he must have died shortly after that. Bobby Dean told me when he brought those cards today."

Guy did not know what to say to Jesse Mae. He was not good at condolences, and he also was not sure how she felt about Roger, but he thought that he should say something. He started to say 'That's too bad,' but Jesse Mae continued before he could.

"That's where I ran into him yesterday; at the hospital, when I was getting coffee. He said that the doctor had told him he could go at any time. He wanted to meet Romey before he died.

"He didn't even know about Romey until a couple of years ago. His mama had kept it a secret from him. She knew that Romey was my baby. She told Roger that she suspected I was pregnant shortly after she sent him away. Then when I was out of sight for four months, she was certain of it. She told him that when she accepted the fact that he wasn't going to have any more children, she decided to tell him that Romey was his son.

"When Roger found out that he had terminal cancer, he decided that he wanted to know if Romey was really his son or not. He contacted me about a week ago, and I told him that he was. He said that he wanted to meet Romey. I wanted him to meet Romey, and I wanted Romey to meet him, even if he didn't know that he was his father.

"When Roger and I got here, Romey was alone on the front porch. He said that Mama was down at the barn. I was glad that she wasn't here. I was nervous about lying to her. She could always tell when I was lying. If she had come up while we were here, my story was going to be that Roger and I had run into each other at the hospital, and that I had to pick up something here at the house, and he just came along for the ride. She never showed up though, so I was relieved. It never occurred to me that something might be wrong. Anyway, Roger and Romey visited for a while and then we left. I never saw Mama."

The brother and sister looked at one another for a moment; Jesse Mae, wondering what Guy was thinking, and Guy trying to think of something to say to all of this. Then Jesse Mae turned her eyes back to the cigarette case and began fidgeting with it again.

"Mama never knew who Romey's father was. I wouldn't tell her. I didn't even know that I was pregnant. Mama noticed that I wasn't menstruating and she started watching me, to see if my stomach was growing. When she realized that I was actually pregnant she was furious. She said that it would ruin my life and hers if anyone ever found out.

"When I started showing so much that it was hard to hide, she came up with the plan of faking a visit to the doctor and claiming that I had TB. Papa dropped us off at the doctor's office and then waited for us at the general store. We never even went into the doctor's office. We walked over to the church and waited there about a half hour, and then went over to meet him. Mama made up the story that the doctor had told her I had TB, and had to be quarantined.

"She knew that Rena needed money, so she made a deal with her to keep me in her house, out of sight. It took nearly all of Mama's savings. Papa never had a clue that she was lying to him.

"She wore bags of rice on her stomach, so that she would look like she was pregnant and her stomach was getting bigger with time. I had Romey early one morning before daylight. Rena came here and told Mama, but Mama couldn't come and help me until you boys and Papa went to the fields. By the time she got over to Rena's, Romey was born. She and Rena brought him back here and used chicken blood to stain the sheets and make it look like she had given birth.

"I got a bad infection and really was sick for a while. I suspect that that has something to do with why I never had any more children. Now that Mama's gone, and Rena and Roger; you and me are the only people in the world who know the truth."

"What about Papa?"

Jesse Mae turned to face Guy. "What about him?"

"Does he know?"

"No. Mama never told him."

"But…he has a right to know."

"You want me to tell him that Romey is not his son?" Jesse Mae paused for a moment. "What…what if he stopped loving him?"

"He wouldn't do that." Guy had spoken before really thinking through the possibilities. He immediately questioned his statement in his mind.

"How do you know? What if you found out that one of your children wasn't yours? Would you still love him?"

"Of course…" Guy realized that this too was an automatic response. He searched his heart. "I love all of my children. I already love them for who they are; not for what part I had to do with creating them. Of course the fact that they are flesh of my flesh makes a difference, but I will never stop loving any of them." He looked intently at Jesse Mae. "I think you should tell him."

Jesse Mae looked at the cigarette case in her hand. She opened it and pulled a cigarette out of it. Then she closed the case and placed it on the small table next to her. She kept her eyes on the cigarette as she rolled it to and fro between her fingers. She stopped this action and looked at Guy. "I've wanted to tell Papa for years. I've always felt so guilty for helping Mama trick him like she did." She looked away from Guy. "But Romey could never know. He wouldn't understand."

"Let's go tell him."

"What…now?"

"Yeah; he's up in his room, alone. This is a good time. I'll stay out of it if you want me to."

"No, I want you to go up there with me." Jesse Mae dropped the unlit cigarette on the table next to the gold case. She stood up and walked out the door, followed by Guy.

The two of them made their way up to their father's bedroom; saying nothing to Lula Mae and Louise as they walked past them in the kitchen. The women continued their cleanup in silence, but could not help but wonder what was going on.

Frank was lying on top of the sheets on his bed, watching the fan as it hummed softly and moved the hot air around the room. He looked toward the open door when Jesse Mae and Guy appeared; saying nothing as they walked in. Jesse Mae sat on the edge of the bed and Guy pulled a chair next to the bed and sat down. Frank remained silent as he waited for them to explain why they were there.

"Jesse Mae has something to tell you Papa," said Guy.

Frank turned his attention to Jesse Mae. "What is it?"

"Uh…" Jesse Mae looked at Guy for an instant and then focused her attention on her father. "Remember when I had TB?"

Jesse Mae recounted what she had just revealed to Guy. When she finished there was a long moment when the only sound in the room was the gentle hum of the fan blades cutting through the air. None of the three made eye contact with one another.

"I thought your mama had been with another man."

Jesse Mae and Guy looked at their father. His statement was confusing to them. Then he continued.

"All these years," said Frank. He sat up and pushed himself back against the headboard of the bed. Neither Jesse Mae nor Guy spoke.

"I knew Romey wasn't my son!" Frank clinched his fists as they pushed against the bed. "She tried to fool me; that crazy woman." Frank raised his hands and then brought them down hard on the mattress. "All these years!"

He dropped his head, and was still for a moment; then he raised his head and looked, first at Guy and then at Jesse Mae. His ranting had been at himself, not them. "She got me drunk one night. Gave me so much whiskey that I passed out. The next morning she told me that we had…you know." He waved a hand in the air in a motion to indicate that the details were understood. "Well I knew better." He glanced at Guy. "A man knows certain things." Then directing his words to both of them, he continued, "Me and your mama hadn't done those things since you were born, Sister. I didn't mind…about not doing it anymore I mean. It was time; your mama and me both figured that three kids was enough.

"A few weeks later she told me that she was with child. I accused her of awful things, but she denied it. I told her that I knew that the child wasn't mine." Frank's head dropped. "We never slept in the same bed again.

"When we came in from the fields and she had Romey in her arms, I almost left her. But you kids was still too young to leave. Then I looked at the innocent little baby in her arms and I thought how he was you kids' brother. She put him in my arms and when I held him I knew he needed a papa. I still loved your mama…but," Frank looked away again. "we never was like a husband and wife again."

"And you loved Romey anyway?" said Jesse Mae.

Frank turned back to Jesse Mae and Guy. "Well, like I said, the baby needed a papa. When we found out that he…that he wasn't right, that made me love him even more. I didn't care that he wasn't mine."

A sad joy crept into Franks eyes. "But then, he was mine all along. He's my grandson; flesh of my flesh."

"This has to be our secret," said Jesse Mae. "If Romey ever heard any of this, he would be all mixed up. He wouldn't understand any of it."

"I know that Sister. Nobody else needs to know any of this." Frank dropped his head. "I wish your mama would have told me."

Jesse Mae put her hand on her father's hand, which was lying on the mattress. "Well…I guess we'll let you be now. Get some sleep, Papa." She leaned over and kissed Frank on the cheek.

"Good-night, Papa," said Guy. He and Jesse Mae walked toward the door.

"I'll be needing one of Eugene's best suits tomorrow," said Frank. Jesse Mae and Guy turned to look at him. "I need to pay proper respect to my wife."

The siblings stood for a brief moment looking at their father. He had a sad smile on his face. He brushed a tear from his cheek. "Good-night, Papa," said Jesse Mae. She and Guy turned and left their father with his memories.

Downstairs, Harold was sitting and listening to the radio. Guy joined him on the sofa and sat quietly. Jesse Mae went to the kitchen.

Harold looked over at Guy. "What's going on?"

"Oh," said Guy. "We're trying to get Papa to wear one of Eugene's suits tomorrow."

"Oh." Harold went back to listening to his radio program.

The looks from Lula Mae and Louise told Jesse Mae that they wanted to know what was going on. Jesse Mae pulled a fresh dishtowel out of a drawer and began helping Lula Mae dry dishes and put them away.

"We've been talking to Papa about Romey," Jesse Mae volunteered. She appreciated the fact that she was able to give such a general explanation and that the other women would assume that they knew what she meant. She did not want to lie to them. She was feeling enough guilt without adding that to the list of her misdeeds.

"Are you going to put Romey in that school?" asked Lula Mae.

"We haven't come to any conclusions yet."

Louise and Lula Mae were satisfied with this simple explanation from their sister-in-law. The conversation turned to the next day's funeral.

Guy looked at Romey as he sat a few feet away from him. Romey was playing a game of checkers with Gary while Scotty watched. Occasionally, in spite of Gary's objections, Scotty would whisper into Romey's ear, obviously advising him on his next move.

Guy examined his feelings toward Romey. His mind told him that he should feel differently toward him, now that he knew that he was his nephew instead of his brother; but Guy's feelings had not changed. Romey still seemed like his little brother. He had watched Romey grow up. He had taken care of him. He had played with him. Nothing had changed except that he had learned the truth about Romey's birth.

Louise came into the living room from the kitchen. She walked to the sofa and sat between Guy and Harold. "Are you ready to go?" she asked Harold, putting her hand on his knee.

"Whenever you are." Harold placed a hand on top of Louise's hand.

Louise turned to guy and lowered her voice, so that Romey would not hear her. "So, what do you think about Romey going to that school?"

"What school?" said Guy.

Harold had not heard anything about Romey going to any school. He directed his attention from the radio program to the conversation.

Louise shifted her weight on the sofa in order to face Guy. She looked at him with curiosity. Had she misunderstood Jesse Mae? "Weren't you and Jesse Mae talking to your papa about putting him in that school in town?"

"I don't know anything about any school."

"But Jesse Mae said…" Louise stopped herself. She realized that there had been some misinformation put forward. "Oh, never mind."

Harold looked at Louise. "What's all this about a school?"

"Come on, let's go home." Louise rose from the sofa. "Come on Scotty, we're going home."

"Wait," protested Scotty. "We have to finish this game."

"Well hurry up then." Louise went to the kitchen.

"Do you know anything about a school?" Harold asked Guy.

"No."

Harold turned his attention to his son. "Hurry up Scott."

Lula Mae and Jesse Mae were sitting at the kitchen table, each with a cup of coffee in front of her. They were discussing which dress Lula Mae might wear to the funeral. "Are you leaving?" asked Lula Mae when Louise rejoined them.

Louise sat down next to them. "As soon as the boys finish their game of checkers."

"I have a navy blue dress that's lightweight," continued Jesse Mae. "I don't think it would be too warm…"

Harold walked into the kitchen. "What's this about a school for Romey?"

Jesse Mae was taken off guard. She stopped in mid-sentence. "What?"

"Louise said that you and Guy were talking to Papa about sending Romey to some school."

Jesse Mae looked at Louise. She felt a tinge of anger, but mostly frustration. The last hour had been very taxing on her and she did not want to get into any discussions about anything weightier than what she and Lula Mae had been discussing. "Uh…no. We weren't talking about sending Romey to school."

A look of surprise registered on Lula Mae's face. This statement contradicted what she had understood Jesse Mae to say earlier.

Jesse Mae looked around at the little group. She realized that she would have to embellish her story in order to appease their curiosity. She addressed Harold, "Oh yeah, we did say something to Papa about sending Romey to a school that I talked to Mama about. It's a special school for people like him."

"Guy said he didn't know anything about a school."

For a moment, Jesse Mae was at a loss for words. She felt like she had been ambushed. "Well I guess he forgot, Harold. What do you want me to say?"

"What's going on?" Harold pressured.

"What do you mean?"

"You and Guy are sneaking around talking in private, and then you go upstairs to talk to Papa, and then lie about what you're talking about."

Jesse Mae started to speak but she could not think of what to say. She could not deny what Harold had just said. She looked around and saw Guy standing in the doorway looking at her. She knew what he was thinking. He wanted her to tell them. She turned and took them all in. They were waiting for an explanation.

She wrapped her hand around her coffee cup and focused her attention on it. She thought for a moment; she knew that Guy would eventually tell Lula Mae, and Lula Mae would eventually tell somebody else, and sooner or later, it would get back to Harold, and he would feel angry and alienated. She sighed and came to the conclusion that she might as well tell them. She turned to Harold. With a nod of her head she motioned to an empty chair on the other side of the table. "Sit down."

A few minutes later Jesse Mae's story had been repeated again. Harold was holding Jesse Mae's hand from across the table. Lula Mae was wiping tears from her cheeks and Guy and Louise sat quietly.

"Now I mean this," said Jesse Mae. "None of this is ever to be repeated to anyone."

The others all agreed not to breathe a word of her story; for Romey's sake.

"When you were here with Roger," said Harold. "Did you notice anything out of the ordinary?"

"No, but then I wasn't looking for anything. I thought Mama was being foolish for digging down there in the mid-day heat, but I was relieved that I didn't have to make up some story to explain why I had brought Roger here." Jesse Mae looked around at the others. "Believe me; I've racked my brain trying to remember anything that might give us a clue as to who was here."

"You need to tell the sheriff that you were here," said Louise.

"Why? What good would that do?"

"It might help him determine the time...that it happened."

Jesse Mae sighed deeply. "I've thought about that. I know she wasn't in that pigsty when I was here, so whoever put her in there did it after Roger and I left. I couldn't tell the sheriff before, but I guess I can now." She clenched her fist on the table. "God!...If only I had gone down to that cellar to get her; I might have saved her life."

"It don't do no good to think that way," said Guy. "You could have been killed too if you had gone down there."

"Are you sure you didn't hear anything unusual from the pigsty?" Louise refilled Jesse Mae's coffee cup. "Any loud snorting or squealing or anything?"

"No, nothing. I stayed on the front porch while Romey and Roger were visiting in Romey's playhouse. I didn't notice anything unusual when I went out there to join them. I'm sure I would have noticed if she had been there."

The group was quiet for a moment. Then Jesse Mae said, "You're right. I'll talk to the sheriff tomorrow."

The young undertaker stood just inside the entry door of the small Baptist Church. He greeted the mourners as they arrived and directed them to their seats. The front pew was reserved for the family, all of who were already seated; having arrived earlier through the rear door.

The preacher gave the eulogy and a member of the choir sang *Amazing Grace*, followed by *Undertaker Take It Easy*; a special request from the family. Mary's body was laid to rest by noon and the family was back home by one-thirty p.m.

At around five p.m. a couple of horse drawn wagons came up the drive to the back of the house. Four cars had pulled onto the drive behind them, but the cars stopped and parked under the shade of the oak tree at the entrance to the farm.

Several women and men got out of the cars and walked up to the house and joined the drivers of the wagons. Louise met them all in the back yard. These were friends of Louise and Harold's from the church, which they belonged to. It was common practice for the congregation to take over the duties of setting up for the wake when a members' loved one had passed on.

Louise had made arrangements with the head of her ladies' group the night before, and the group had organized everything for them. The wagons held; a large canvas, poles to support the canvas as a makeshift tent for shelter from the sun, fold-up tables and chairs, kerosene lanterns, dishes and utensils, and barrels of ice and food. The ladies also had extra food in their cars. The other guests who would arrive later were also expected to bring food and drinks with them.

Louise instructed the men as to where the tent should be erected and then she went back inside. Traditionally, the family of the deceased was not expected to do any of the heavy work in setting up for the wake. It was the general understanding that they should be allowed to gather together before the wake to comfort one another in a quiet, restful atmosphere.

The men went to work driving stakes into the ground, while the women began setting up the folding tables and chairs to be placed under the canvas after it was up.

Gary, Johnny, Loretta and Scotty all sat on the ground at a good distance away from the activity and watched the men work. Lula Mae and Romey watched for a while and then returned to the front porch where the other family members had gathered, away from all the ruckus, and out of the sun. They were reading more sympathy cards, which people had given them at the church.

Everyone had dressed down after they had returned to the farm. It was just too hot to keep on the clothing worn at the funeral. The men had removed their coats and ties. Guy and Harold were in their undershirts. The women had removed their shoes and nylons. In a couple of hours, when the majority of the guests were expected to start arriving, the women would put their shoes back on, but the coats and ties had been hung in the closet to stay.

Loretta jaunted quickly around the corner of the house. "The sheriff's here!" she said, then immediately retreated back to her spot on the grass to view all the activity.

Jesse Mae walked through the house to the back porch. While at the cemetery, she had told the sheriff that she needed to talk to him in private. He agreed to arrive early for the wake, so that they could do that. His wife had joined the church ladies as he approached the house.

"Hi," said Jesse Mae as she opened the screen door. "Come on in."

"How are you Jesse Mae?" Sheriff Files stepped through the doorway.

"Oh...you know...coping," said Jesse Mae, walking toward the kitchen table. She motioned to one of the chairs. "Have a seat. Can I get you a glass of tea?"

"That would be nice." The sheriff pulled out a chair from the table and sat down.

Jesse Mae took a pitcher of iced tea from the refrigerator and poured him a glassful. She put the pitcher back and sat in a chair across the table from him. She plucked a cigarette from a pack that was lying on the table. The sheriff sipped his tea quietly while she lit the cigarette and inhaled deeply. She exhaled and said, "I was here around the time Mama was murdered."

She told the sheriff the whole story; beginning with the part about getting pregnant and having Romey, and ending when she found the necklace in her mother's purse. "I'll get you the necklace. I'd like it back though."

"That's not necessary. It obviously wasn't a motive for killing. Just keep it safe, in case I need it for evidence."

Jesse Mae nodded her head to indicate her agreement to do as the sheriff asked.

"I'm sorry to have to keep asking you and your family all these questions. You've been through a lot and I sympathize with you, but I do have a few more."

"Ask me anything you want." Jesse Mae tapped her cigarette on the edge of the ashtray, knocking the ashes off of the end of it.

"How long were you and Roger here?"

"Oh…I'd say about half an hour; maybe a little longer."

"Did you spend all that time together?"

"No; I spent most of the time on the front porch alone."

"And Roger was with Romey all that time?"

"Yes. I wanted to give him time alone with Romey."

"Why do you think Romey lied to me about Roger when I asked him if anyone had been here?"

"Romey didn't lie to you. He doesn't even know what it is to tell a lie. You asked him if anybody came to visit Mama. He didn't consider me a visitor and I brought Roger here with me. We were visiting Romey." Jesse Mae paused for a moment. "Besides, I told him not to tell anybody about Roger. I told him that it would be our secret. I don't want anybody else to know about my connection with Roger Crawford. Chances are it would never be mentioned to Romey, but you can understand how confusing it would be to him to suddenly find out that his sister is really his mama."

"Everything you've told me about your personal life will be held in confidence. I'm sorry about Roger. Were the two of you close?"

"No. I pined over him for a few months after his mama sent him away. But after a while we both got on with our lives. He wouldn't even have contacted me if he hadn't been dying."

"I heard that there wasn't any service for him. He's already been cremated and the ashes put in the vault."

"Yeah, he told me that he had arranged for all that when he found out that he was going to die soon. He was a very sad, lonely man."

"Well, Jesse Mae, thank you for telling me all of this. I'd better go see if Thelma needs me to help the ladies with the setup." Sheriff Files pushed his chair back and stood up. "Remember tonight that there's still a murderer roaming around. We didn't get any prints off that pitchfork or spade, so I still have no idea who killed your mama, or why. At least I do know that it wasn't to steal that necklace, though."

"He'd be a fool to try anything tonight, what with all these people around and with me and Tony here. Just the same, if you or anyone else see anything suspicious, you let one of us know."

"We will Sheriff." Jesse Mae remained seated as the sheriff left the house through the back door. She sat for a few moments, appreciating the solitude. She felt exhausted from constantly being around a lot of people. Granted, it had been comforting being with her family during this time of mourning, but she missed being at home in her own house.

She thought about how it would be to live with Romey. She looked around the kitchen and imagined living in this house again. She had grown up here and at the time it seemed adequate, but it had been very easy to adjust to living in her husband's big house in Pine Bluff. She could never live here again.

Romey and her father could move in with her. It would be an adjustment for them, but she remembered how easy it was for her to get used to living with modern conveniences; especially running water and a bathroom.

By seven o'clock the guests began arriving in a steady flow. Frank, Harold, Guy, Jesse Mae and Romey had positioned themselves for receiving them outside under the canvas. The sun was getting low in the sky and the canvas cast a long shadow where they stood. Friends and acquaintances of the family filed by and paid their respects before mingling with the other guests and settling in for a night of food, drink and reminiscing.

As the guests arrived, they brought with them, a variety of prepared food and cold beverages. Louise, Lula Mae and Geneva helped the ladies from the church as they set out the provisions on the tables to be served buffet style. Individual groups began forming in the back yard and in the area between the house and the gate to the property.

Loretta, Johnny, Gary and Scotty sat on the edge of the back porch, each with a plate of food and a glass of iced tea. They were still enjoying being spectators of the event.

By eight o'clock the lanterns were being lighted and the grounds were filled with clusters of people; some milling about, others sitting in the folding chairs, talking to one another. A man sitting with a group not far from the serving tables began strumming on his guitar. After he had played for a few moments, a lone female voice lilted softly through the twilight singing *Undertaker Take It Easy*. The guitar player picked up the melody and began accompanying her. Shortly another voice from a group in a different area began singing harmony with the first woman; followed by an increasing number of voices, which were scattered throughout the crowd. In a touching tribute, the members of the choir from the church filled the evening with a gentle performance of Mary's favorite song.

Frank had slipped away from the crowd a few minutes earlier and he now sat in the swing on the front porch, listening to the music. He appreciated the guests paying their respects, but he was tired and sad and he just wanted to be alone.

The light from the living room spilled out onto the front porch. Next to Frank, on the swing, lay what he took to be the Sears Catalog. He absentmindedly picked it up and began thumbing through the pages. Something did not seem right with the catalog. He had been receiving it for years and there was always a familiarity about it. He closed the book and looked at the cover. Montgomery Wards was printed in bold letters. He could not remember receiving the Montgomery Wards Catalog. He turned the book over in his hands, wondering how it came to be here.

"Hi." Jesse Mae walked up the steps. "It's a nice gathering, isn't it?" She sat in the swing next to her father.

"Yeah," said Frank. He was still holding the catalog. "Look at this."

Jesse Mae looked at the book. "What? It's the Sears Catalog."

"That's what I thought. But it's not. It's the Wards Catalog."

Jesse Mae did not know what her father was getting at. "Okay, it's the Wards Catalog."

"I never ordered it."

Jesse Mae was not interested in the catalog. She gave a little push with one foot on the floor and started the swing moving back and forth. She took Frank's hand. "Papa, I want to talk to you about Romey."

Frank laid the catalog on the swing next to him and looked at Jesse Mae. "Okay."

Jesse Mae put her foot on the floor and stopped the swing from moving. She turned her body to face her father by hooking one foot beneath one leg. "I want him to come and live with me; and I want you to come and live with me too."

"You mean live in town?"

"Yes. You can sell this place and live with me and Romey in my big house in town."

"Oh, I don't know, Sister."

"Papa, you can't take care of Romey by yourself. Hell, I can't take care of Romey by myself. We need each other 's help now."

"I've never lived in town."

"It's real easy to get used to. You've seen my big back yard with all those trees. You can sit on my veranda and smoke your pipe. We can build Romey a playhouse."

"Well...that sounds real nice, Sister."

Lula Mae and Romey rounded the corner of the house. They climbed the steps of the porch. "Romey's getting tired," said Lula Mae. "He wants to go inside and listen to the radio."

"Thanks Lula Mae," said Jesse Mae. "I guess we're all a little tired."

Lula Mae opened the door to go inside and Romey was following right behind her.

"Romey," said Frank. Romey stopped and looked back at Frank. Lula Mae went on inside to turn on the radio. Frank held up the catalog. "Do you know where this Wards Catalog came from?"

"That's the Sears Catalog, Papa."

"No Son; you see these letters?" Frank pointed to the name on the book. "That says Montgomery Wards."

Romey looked at the book. "Oh."

"Do you know where it came from?"

"Bobby Dean brought it."

"When?"

"A couple of days ago."

"Did your mama know about it?"

"No; she was down at that old cellar."

CHAPTER EIGHTEEN

F RANK LOOKED AT JESSE MAE. SHE WAS as shocked by Romey's statement as he was. Frank turned back to Romey. "Go on inside Son. Lula Mae is tuning the radio for you." Romey turned and went inside the house.

"Bobby Dean was here," said Jesse Mae.

Frank picked up the catalog and looked at it. He looked up at Jesse Mae.

A glimmer of optimism sounded in Jesse Mae's voice. "Maybe he saw something."

"But why wouldn't he say something to us."

"Well, nobody questioned him, Papa. He could have seen something; like a car parked out back or something, and never gave it a second thought."

"Yeah...you're right. I'm going to go ask him."

"Well, let's go tell the sheriff first. He'll want to talk to him anyway."

Sheriff Files was sitting at one of the tables with his wife, eating fried chicken and potato salad.

"Karl," said Frank, as he and Jesse Mae approached.

Sheriff Files ripped a piece of the chicken thigh off of the bone with his teeth. "Frank?"

Frank sat in the chair next to the sheriff and Jesse Mae stood next to him. "Bobby Dean was here when Mary was down at that cellar."

The sheriff's wife instinctively turned away from the men, and began talking to a woman sitting next to her. She was accustomed to allowing her husband privacy when he was talking business. She knew that if she asked him later he would tell her what was going on. Besides, the fact that Bobby Dean had been on the premises did not seem very intriguing to her.

The sheriff put the half eaten chicken leg back on his plate and leaned toward Frank with a sense of confidentiality and spoke softly. "Are you sure about that?"

"Yes."

"How do you know?"

"Romey told me. Bobby Dean brought the Wards Catalog to him while he was waiting for his mama to come back up from that cellar."

"Why didn't Romey tell me that?"

"Oh, I don't know Karl. Romey don't always see things the way we do. He thought it was another Sears Catalog. I never get the Wards Catalog. I guess Bobby Dean just brought it by cause he had an extra one. Romey didn't think it was something you'd want to know about. Let's go talk to Bobby Dean."

The sheriff raised his hand in a motion to keep Frank in his chair. "Now hold on." He lowered his hand and looked around the crowd. "Let me think about this for a minute. Bobby Dean's probably drunk on his ass. You know he's been drinking all day long. Mary was his friend, and he's mourning her passing. I don't think we need to start questioning him tonight. Let's just let him be and I'll go by his house tomorrow and talk to him."

Frank looked up at Jesse Mae and then back at the sheriff. "Well... okay. I guess you're right." He nodded his head a couple of times and stood up. "Okay," he said again and turned back to Jesse Mae. "I'm going to go listen to the radio with Romey."

"I'll come with you," said Jesse Mae.

Geneva felt guilty for thinking of Tony at her grandmother's wake, but she just could not keep from it. He was first and foremost on her mind as she stood in front of the mirror that was above the bureau in her and Loretta's bedroom. She loosened the black satin ribbon from her hair, which had held it up in a ponytail for most of the day. She bent forward at the waist and let her hair fall forward in a profusion of brunette waves. After a few brush strokes to give it fullness, she stood up and tossed her head back the way she had seen Rita Hayworth do in the movie she had just seen. With the addition of a couple of imitation pearl earrings and some soft pink lipstick, she was ready.

She could not wait to kiss Tony again. She did not know how she was going to get him alone or where that would be, but she was going to do her best to make it happen.

Lula Mae was in the kitchen when Geneva entered through the dining room, on her way to the back yard. "Oh good," said Lula Mae. "Help me with this lemonade. You take a pitcher and I'll take one. Careful not to spill it on the floor."

Geneva picked up the pitcher and followed her mother out the back door. A lot more people had arrived since she had excused herself and gone to her room to freshen up. She had not seen Tony since the funeral and she was very anxious about seeing him tonight.

"There's another table down that way." Lula Mae pointed towards a table in the direction of the entry gate to the farm. "Go put that pitcher on it."

Geneva walked past people who were standing around talking to one another. Most of them had drinks of one kind or another in their hands. Some of them held plates of food. She saw several individuals standing around a table with food on it. As she approached the table she saw that one of the individuals was Tony. He looked at her and smiled as she walked toward him.

Just as she reached the group and started to say hello, a young woman; a little older than Geneva, turned from the table and rested her hand on Tony's shoulder. The young woman looked at Geneva and said, "Oh lemonade; I'd love some." She held up a glass for Geneva to fill. Geneva looked at Tony and then at the young woman. She forced a smile onto her face and poured lemonade into the glass.

"Thanks," said the woman. She turned to Tony; her hand still on his shoulder and said, "You want a sip?"

Geneva felt humiliated. She told herself that the woman was obviously *with* Tony. She stood there with the pitcher in her hand, feeling like she wanted to throw it down and run.

"No thanks," said Tony with a quick glance to the woman and then back to Geneva. "You look nice." He reached for the pitcher and moved away from the woman, causing her to remove her hand from his shoulder. "Can I take that for you?"

Geneva handed Tony the lemonade. Tony, holding the pitcher, said to the woman, "Arlene, this is Geneva, one of Mary's granddaughters."

Arlene extended her hand to Geneva. "I am so sorry about your grandmother."

Geneva accepted Arlene's handshake. "Thanks," she said, taking advantage of the opportunity to avert her eyes from Tony. She looked around the yard and then turned back to Arlene. "Well...It's nice to have met you." She looked at Tony. "I'll see you around." She turned and walked away into the crowd.

Tony turned quickly to the table and placed the pitcher on it. "Excuse me," he said to Arlene and then hurried after Geneva. He was about to catch up to her when he heard someone speak his name. He turned to see Sheriff Files.

The sheriff motioned for Tony to follow him as he moved a short distance away from the crowd. Tony glanced at Geneva's back as she walked briskly away, then he turned and followed his boss.

"Frank just told me something very interesting," said the sheriff. "It seems that Bobby Dean was here around the time that Mary was murdered."

"The mailman?"

"Yes. He gave a Montgomery Wards Catalog to Romey. He had already been here earlier that day to deliver the mail; he shouldn't have been here again. And Frank also said that he never gets the Wards Catalog.

"I want you to keep an eye on him. Right now he's down by the gate there drinking whiskey. Don't let him know you're watching him."

The sheriff walked away and joined some people at a table. Tony stayed where he was for a moment. He could barely make out Bobby Dean, standing by one of the cars, which were parked by the gate.

"Hey you."

Tony turned at the sound of the voice behind him. "Hey."

Arlene was carrying two folding chairs. "I saw you standing here all alone. I thought maybe you'd like some company. We can sit here and look at the stars. I need a break from Barbara and Sandy, anyway." She unfolded the chairs and placed them side by side.

"Sure," said Tony, taking a seat in one of the chairs. Arlene sat down and took his hand, while resting her head against his shoulder.

Geneva was embarrassed and hurt. She walked through the crowd, hoping to be unnoticed. She did not want to talk to anybody right now. She fixed herself a plate of food and made her way to Romey's playhouse where she could be alone.

Loretta, Gary and Scotty, having each finished off two plates of food and a piece of chocolate-layer-cake, were now coming back to the table where the desserts were for their second piece of cake.

"Scotty, how many pieces of cake have you had?" Louise came walking up to the table where one of the women from the church was cutting the cake for the children.

"I'm pretty sure this is just his first," said the woman with a wink to Scotty.

"Well okay then." Louise turned from Scotty to the woman. "I'm sorry I didn't get to say hello to you in church today, Ruth."

Ruth was Bobby Dean's wife. She and Louise had known each other on a casual basis for a number of years.

"Oh pshaw," said Ruth, waving her hand. "Don't you give that a second thought. You've got enough on your mind."

"Well...you're very kind." Louise looked around. There were three other women standing close by. Louise was acquainted with all of them through her church. "Has anybody seen Harold?"

"I believe he and his brother are with Bobby Dean down at those cars parked under the tree." Ruth pointed to a group of men gathered under the oak tree at the entry gate. "Somebody brought some whiskey."

Loretta stepped up and held out her plate for a piece of cake. Ruth cut the cake and started to place it on the plate. She stopped; holding the sliced cake suspended in the air. She was staring at Loretta. Loretta gave her a look as if to say, "Well?"

Ruth slowly lowered the cake to the plate; all the time staring at Loretta. "Sweetheart, what's that you have around your neck?"

After the funeral, Loretta had asked her aunt Jesse Mae if she could try on the necklace that had belonged to Rena. Jesse Mae told her how nice it looked on her, and that if she wanted to, she could wear it for a while. Loretta had almost forgotten that it was around her neck. "Oh." She held it up away from her chest. "It was my grandma's."

Ruth took hold of the necklace and was bending over to get a closer look at it. She picked up one of the kerosene lamps on the table and held it close to the piece of jewelry. "My Lord," she said slowly, as if her mind were somewhere else.

"What's the matter?" said Loretta, gently attempting to pull away from the woman. The woman continued to hold onto the necklace, encouraging Loretta to stop pulling away, and allow her to examine it.

"I used to have a necklace just like this one. I was told that it was one of a kind; made by an Indian woman in Santa Fe, New Mexico. Bobby Dean bought it for me before we were married. I still have the matching bracelet." She turned the necklace over and looked at the back of it. "I swear it looked just like this one. I lost mine some twenty or thirty years ago. Where did your grandma get hers?"

"My brother found it." Loretta was growing impatient. She wanted to go sit down and eat her cake.

"Found it? Where?"

"Down in that old cellar where they found the skeleton."

Ruth let go of the necklace. She straightened up and put the lamp back down on the table. She turned her attention to the other women; and found that Louise was the only one who was paying any attention to her examination of the necklace. The others were talking amongst themselves.

It was common knowledge that the skeleton in the cellar was the remains of Rena Two Eagles. What was not known to anybody except Ruth and her husband, Bobby Dean, was that Bobby Dean had been involved with Rena before she had disappeared. Ruth suddenly began putting pieces together. She feared that there might be a connection between Rena, the necklace, and Bobby Dean. She quickly tried to downplay the fact that the necklace looked like hers.

"Well don't that beat all," she said to Louise. "All these years I thought I had a one-of-a-kind bracelet. I guess there are more of them too." Ruth picked up the knife and cut a piece of cake for Gary, who had been holding his plate patiently. As soon as he got his cake he rushed after Loretta and Scotty who had gone to the front porch with theirs.

Ruth cut another slice of cake and put it on a plate. "I'm going to take some cake down to Bobby Dean," she said to Louise. "Do you want me to tell Harold to come back up here?"

"No, that's okay. Let him be. I just hope he doesn't drink too much." Louise turned her attention to the other women, while Ruth walked away.

Ruth approached the men who were gathered around a car. Bobby Dean wondered why she was coming down to him as he watched her approach. When she got close to him he said, "Hi Hon."

"Hi," said Ruth to her husband. She nodded to the other men. "Hi fellas." The men greeted her and fell silent. They all waited to see what was up.

"I brought you a piece of cake." Ruth held the cake in front of Bobby Dean.

This seemed odd to Bobby Dean. Why would his wife think that he would want cake with whiskey? "Well…thank you." He took the plate from her.

Ruth put her lips to his ear. "I need to talk to you."

Bobby Dean shot a quick glance at the other men. They had all lost interest in him and his wife, and were continuing with their drinking and talking. He walked with Ruth a few yards away from the other men and she stopped. "What is it?" he asked.

Ruth looked at her husband in silence for a moment, struggling to compose herself. She moved closer to him, wishing that the light was better, so that she could see his face. In the pale moonlight; she was barely able to see his eyes. "How is it that my necklace; the one that I lost almost thirty years ago, has turned up in Rena Two Eagles' grave?"

Bobby Dean backed away a half step. He sighed deeply. "How did you know that?"

"Mary's granddaughter is wearing it. She said that it was dug up with that skeleton that turned out to be Rena Two Eagles. Now, answer my question."

Bobby Dean held out his free hand as if he were going to hold Ruth. "Ruthie…"

Ruth slapped his hand away from her. "You gave her my necklace, didn't you? You gave your whore my necklace." Ruth wanted to hit her husband. Her anger was bringing tears to her eyes. "You said that you lost it. And all that time you knew right where it was."

Ruth hesitated a moment; afraid to ask another question, which was torturing her. Suspicion had edged its way into her mind when she heard that the skeleton was Rena, but she had been unable to bring herself to ask her husband what she now had to ask him. "Did you kill that girl?"

Bobby Dean was silent.

"Oh my God!" Ruth took hold of Bobby Dean's hand. "Did you kill Mary?"

Bobby Dean did not know what to say. He was not even sure that he could speak. He felt dizzy and his throat was tightening up on him. He had feared this moment for twenty-five years. He had hoped that the past would stay buried along with Rena. For all this time, he had lived with the guilt of his affair with her, and for accidentally taking her life in a fit of rage. He never meant to kill her. His mind raced back:

He remembered how he had met her as she was walking along the road that was on his mail route. He offered to give her a ride to her house, and she accepted. As they visited in his truck, he felt an instant connection with her. She never received mail, so in order to see her; he began taking her any magazines that were undeliverable.

When he would deliver the magazines, she would walk out to her mailbox and talk to him. She told him that her husband had left her, and she was all alone. She did not work and she had no transportation, so he figured that she had very little money or food. Soon he was taking the periodicals to her door, along with a few things like milk, bread, and coffee; and he refused to take any money for them. The gifts became a daily occurrence, and grew to include a variety of groceries and household supplies.

Finally one day his good deeds paid off and she invited him in for lunch. That is when they began sleeping together. He would visit every day at lunchtime up to the day when Jesse Mae moved in with her. From then on Rena would meet him on a side road and they would make love in his mail truck. He fell in love with Rena and he wanted to buy her something nice to show her how much he loved her.

Unfortunately, he could not afford to buy her anything very nice; but then a lucky opportunity presented itself. One day the clasp on

Ruth's necklace broke, and she told him to take it into town and have it fixed. He had it fixed, but then he gave it to Rena and told Ruth that he had lost it.

He told Rena that, for the time being, she must not let anybody see her wearing it because it was one of a kind, and if the sales lady that sold it to him heard that she had it, she would know that he had bought it for her instead of his wife.

Ruth was upset with him; thinking that he had lost her prize piece of jewelry; but she quickly got over it and the incident was forgotten.

Inevitably; after a few months, Ruth began to suspect that he was seeing someone because he seemed to have lost interest in her. Everybody knew that Rena had been deserted by her husband, so it was not difficult for Ruth to figure out what was going on. When she accused him of having an affair, and suggested that the woman was Rena, he admitted it. He told her that he was going to leave her for Rena.

By this time, Jesse Mae had returned home, so Bobby Dean went to Rena's house and told her that he had left his wife and that he wanted to marry her. Rena seemed surprised by this; she told him that he had made a mistake and should go back to his wife. He saw her packed suitcase and she told him that she had saved enough money to go back to Oklahoma. She told him that she was leaving that day.

He could not believe what she was saying to him. He became insistent that she must be in love with him; as much as he was with her. She became verbally abusive to him and told him to leave; but he would not. He tried to force himself on her, and she fought him. He was much stronger in those days and one blow from his fist knocked his unwilling lover across the room, causing her to hit her head against the iron kitchen stove, which ended her life.

Distraught and confused, Bobby Dean's first instinct was that of self preservation. He knew that Ruth would know that he was the killer if Rena's body was found; so he had to get rid of the body. He remembered that Frank Austin had an old abandoned root cellar that was a good distance from his house and easily accessible from the road.

If he were to bury Rena's body, along with her things in that cellar, chances were that his crime would never be discovered. With his truck parked out of sight beside the road, he waited until nightfall; and under the cover of darkness, followed through with his plan.

Just before dawn; after all the evidence of his evil act had been buried, he went home and begged his way back into Ruth's life. He swore to Ruth that he and Rena had done nothing but talk that night, and that he had told Rena that he really loved his wife, and that he was not going to see her anymore. Ruth believed him when he told her that Rena had decided to go back to Oklahoma; she believed him and took him back. For twenty-five years he had felt confident that his crime would never be discovered.

When he had heard the news of the skeleton being found in Frank Austin's cellar, Bobby Dean had felt panic; but he was at a loss as to what he should do. He prayed that the suitcase that he had buried with her would not be found. When he saw the necklace around Mary Austin's neck, he realized that Rena must have had it in the pocket of her dress. He felt like such a fool for not remembering it before he buried her. The necklace would be incriminating enough; but he feared that since it had been found, then her suitcase would most likely be found too. The luggage had contained her personal items; one of which was her writing tablet that she used as a journal.

Rena had hoped to someday be a professional songwriter and she said that her life experiences were what she would write her songs about. She had shown Bobby Dean the tablet containing a written account of the events in her life, and also her song lyrics. There were several entries referring to her affair with him. Although his name was not mentioned, one song was called *The Letterman and the Maiden*. He knew that if this were found, he would be linked with her, and suspected of killing her.

When he went to the site of the cellar to dig up the evidence, he looked into the pit and discovered that Mary was there and had already found it. She was looking through Rena's things.

He watched as she put everything back in the suitcase and started climbing the stairs. He quickly ran to the edge of the barn and hid behind the corner. At one point, Mary almost caught glimpse of him peeking around the corner and he moved back a step and almost tripped on the pitchfork that Johnny had dropped there.

Mary continued toward him with the suitcase. She was heading for the road. He could not let her show those things to anybody. He reached down and grasped the pitchfork. When she came around the corner, he thrust the prongs into her belly.

She dropped the suitcase and looked at him with terror in her eyes. She looked down at the iron prongs as Bobby Dean gripped the wooden handle; and with one forceful jerk, pulled the farming tool, turned murder weapon from her flesh.

The movement pulled Mary toward Bobby Dean. She grabbed for him as she fell to the ground, but Bobby Dean stepped back and let her fall. He stood for a moment in a state of disbelief of what he had done. Then he composed himself and tossed the pitchfork aside. He bent over and pulled Mary over onto her back. Her eyes were open…she was watching him. She lay there holding her stomach, struggling to speak.

Bobby Dean knew that he had to keep her quiet; he had to finish her off. He glanced around him; toward the house, then to the road. Nobody was in sight. He stood, trying to think of a way of disposing of her; then it came to him; the urban legend of the voracious pigs that attacked the old farmer's wife.

He took hold of Mary's arms and dragged her to his mail truck. Then he drove her back up to her house. He knew that everybody but Mary and Romey was supposed to be away from the farm for awhile. He pulled up next to the house and used the excuse of delivering the Montgomery Wards Catalog to Romey to look around and make sure that nobody else was there.

While Romey was alone on the front porch he dragged Mary to the pigsty and put her into the slop trough. The look in her eyes as she fell into the trough, unable to speak had disturbed him greatly, but his will to survive was stronger than his sense of morality. He stood back and watched as the pigs began to snort about his old friend. He watched as she lay helpless; opening and closing her mouth; struggling to breathe, and watching in horror as the pigs began to taste her blood.

Bringing his focus back to the present, Bobby Dean now pleaded with his wife. "I've been faithful to you for twenty-five years, Ruthie." He threw the cake to the ground and grabbed her hands.

Ruth stared at her husband. "Oh my good Lord, Bobby Dean." Who was this man standing before her? "What have you done?"

Bobby Dean did not answer her. He dropped his head. She glanced at the other men. They were not paying any attention to her and her husband. "I can understand Rena." She looked back at Bobby Dean. "But why Mary?"

Bobby Dean continued to look at the ground. "She was digging around down there. She found Rena's writing tablet. It would have exposed me." He raised his head. "I had no choice! I did it for us...I love you Ruthie. I've repented, and the Lord has forgiven me. Won't you forgive me too?"

"Oh, Bobby Dean."

"You're my wife, Ruthie! In the eyes of God, you're my wife. I need you now."

The two were silent for a moment; just holding one another's hands and searching the other's face in the pale moonlight. Then Ruth spoke. "Go on back to the men. Act as if nothing is going on. I have to think about what to do."

"You're not going to tell the sheriff are you?"

"No, I'm not going to tell anyone."

"What about the necklace?"

"What about it?"

"Can you get it from that girl?"

"No, Bobby Dean. How do you think I could do that?"

"People saw that necklace when you used to wear it. Remember, you used to wear it all the time. They've all seen you wearing that bracelet that's just like it. If that girl's wearing it around, somebody is bound to notice it. They'll know it's yours. They'll know that we...that I had something to do with it being buried."

Ruth looked toward the house, where she had last seen Loretta. "I have to think about what to do."

Bobby Dean took Ruth in his arms and held her, burying his face in the curve of her neck. Ruth's arms remained limp at her sides and she stared out into the darkness. With silence between them, Bobby Dean released his grip on her and then turned and went back to the men. Ruth picked up the plate from the ground and went back to the women.

It was almost ten p.m. Geneva had gone up to her room and was reading. Jesse Mae had helped Romey get to sleep, and then she and Lula Mae had rejoined the guests. Frank had gone to his room for a short break.

While their parents were commiserating with Mary's friends, Loretta, Gary and Scotty were sitting on the front porch telling ghost stories.

Loretta was sitting in the swing, and Gary and Scotty were sitting in chairs, facing her. The lamp from the living room gave the front porch just enough light to create a spooky feeling for the children.

Loretta was in the middle of telling her story when she suddenly stopped. The light was behind her, so Scotty and Gary were not able to see her eyes too clearly. After a brief moment, they realized that she was looking past them and into the darkness, which surrounded them. The boys turned their heads to see what she was looking at.

Panic grabbed them and they both jumped onto the swing and cringed with Loretta. After an instant of shock and terror, the three realized that the source of their fear was Johnny. He had draped himself with cheesecloth and was holding a flashlight under it to illuminate his face as he walked toward them from the tall grass in front of the house.

"Ah-hah, I scared you," sang Johnny, pulling the cloth off his head. He walked up the steps of the porch, followed by two boys. The boys had a hound with them, which remained in the yard, running about sniffing at everything. The boys were strangers to Loretta, Gary and Scotty.

"Who are you?" asked Loretta.

"That's my sister, Loretta," said Johnny. He pointed to Gary and Scotty. "And this is my brother, Gary and cousin, Scotty."

The two boys were about the age of Gary and Johnny. The older one spoke. "I'm Homer and this is my brother Jimmy Ray."

"Hi," said the boy named Jimmy Ray."

"Why are you carrying guns?" asked Scotty.

"We're going coon hunting."

With these brief introductions, the boys were immediately accepted as friends.

"Homer and Jimmy Ray want to see where we found the skeleton." Johnny flashed the flashlight on and off. "I'm going to take them down there. Who wants to come?"

"Not me," said Gary and Scotty in unison.

"Oh you little scaredey cats." Johnny looked at Loretta. "Are you chicken too?"

"No," said Loretta, defiantly; her voice rising to a higher pitch than she had planned. She was afraid to go down to the old cellar in the dark, but she could not let these new acquaintances see that. And her ongoing rivalry with Johnny would not let her back down from a challenge from him.

"Good." Johnny and the other boys turned their flashlights on and started down the steps. Loretta hesitated for an instant and then hurried to catch up with the boys and stay close to them so that she could see where she was walking.

Gary and Scotty sat on the porch and watched the dancing circles of light on the ground getting smaller as Johnny and Loretta led their new friends down the dark pasture; on their way to show them the site of the gruesome burial. The boys turned and looked at each other. "I'm going to tell," said Gary. "Yeah," said Scotty. They jumped up and scampered to the steps of the porch.

"You boys want the last two pieces of that chocolate cake?"

The voice out of nowhere frightened the easily spooked youngsters. They stopped on the steps and turned quickly to find the source. Ruth stood just inside the screen door. She had been eavesdropping on the children as they told their ghost stories; trying to figure out how she could get the necklace from Loretta without anyone knowing. "Huh?" said Gary, recognizing the lady who had given them slices of cake.

Ruth pushed the door open and walked out onto the porch. "There are only two pieces of that chocolate cake left. If you promise not to tell your mamas, I'll go get them for you and bring them back here."

Gary and Scotty looked at one another. They immediately forgot about their previous intentions. The thought of another piece of cake pushed all other thoughts from their minds. "Okay," said Gary, as Scotty confirmed with a nod of his head.

"You both wait right here for me. It might take me little while, but I'll bring it to you. I don't want your mamas to see me. They said that you had both had enough cake."

Gary and Scotty moved to the swing and sat down. They both told Ruth that they would wait there for her to return. Ruth walked back into the house and went to the kitchen. She picked up a pot of hot coffee that she had been heating on the stove. The coffee was to be her excuse for being in the house; should any of the others find her there. She carried the coffeepot outside and made the rounds of the guests, offering them coffee; eventually coming to Bobby Dean, who was now sitting close to the guitar player and some of the men he had been drinking with earlier.

"Any of you fellas want some coffee?" said Ruth as she looked about the group. They all declined her offer. "How about you Hon?" Ruth poured coffee into the empty cup that she had brought with her. She leaned over and put her lips close to Bobby Dean's ear when she handed him the cup. "That girl with the necklace and her brother and two other boys have gone down to that old cellar. She's wearing the necklace. In a little while you tell these men that you're sick and we're going home. Walk down toward the car and slam the car door loud, so that people will think you're in the car. Then run down the road to the cellar. Be sure to put your bandanna around your face so that they won't recognize you. Snatch that necklace and run to the car. I'll be waiting for you on the road with the motor running."

Ruth pulled away from Bobby Dean and stood upright. She spoke to him in a voice that was audible to the others sitting next to him. "Maybe the coffee will make you feel better. When you finish it, go on to the car and lay down. I'll be down in a bit and we'll go home."

Bobby Dean looked into his wife's eyes, which reflected the orange flicker of the burning lanterns surrounding the group. The look that passed between them told her that he understood and agreed to her plan. She rubbed his upper back for a moment and then walked away.

Johnny directed the beam of his flashlight into the open pit that used to be the old root cellar. "See how the side is all dug out? That's where we found it."

"And it was a whole skeleton?" asked Homer.

"Yeah. It was an old woman that used to live in that old house that's in the bayou. You know the one by the road?"

"She wasn't old," said Loretta. "Not when she was killed. She's been down there a long time."

"How do you know?" said Johnny, sarcastically. He did not like being corrected by his sister when he was telling his story.

"Because Aunt Jesse Mae knew her. She disappeared a long time ago."

"You're aunt knew her?" asked Jimmy Ray.

"She lived with her." Loretta remembered that she was wearing Rena's necklace. "This was her necklace." She lifted the necklace and stepped into the beam of the flashlight so that the boys could see it. When she did this; the edge of the pit where she stood gave way and crumbled beneath her. With a scream, she dropped into the hole. Her body landed on the dirt below, prompting cries of pain.

The three boys shined their flashlights into the hole and focused on Loretta. Johnny's automatic response was to deny that anything was wrong. "Oh stop your crying; you're not hurt."

"I am too," lamented Loretta; her annoyance with her brother playing a close second to the pain, which she was feeling in her ankle.

"What's wrong?"

"I hurt my leg." Loretta was righting herself to a standing position. "Oww…!" When she put her weight on her foot she experienced more pain in her ankle. She quickly leaned against the side of the pit and stood on one foot.

"We gotta go," said Homer as he and his brother began moving away from the pit. "If our mom and dad find out that we're out of the house, we'll get into a lot of trouble." The two boys disappeared into the darkness.

Johnny kept the light shining on Loretta. Now that there was nobody else around, he did not have to act so tough. "Come on up out of there."

Loretta tried to take a step toward the stairs and stopped. "Ow! It hurts."

"Is it broken?"

"I don't know." Loretta began to cry. "Go get Daddy," she said between sobs.

Johnny stood for a moment; not sure of what to do. "Are you sure you can't walk?"

"Yes! I'm sure…It hurts!"

"You won't be afraid here all alone?"

Loretta looked up at Johnny. She had been concerned with her immediate predicament when the other boys had left and she did not know they were gone. "What do you mean alone? You don't all have to go."

"Those other guys left. They were afraid their mama and daddy would find out that they were out of the house."

"Oh no! I don't want to stay down here all alone."

Johnny was already descending the stairs. "Okay, I'll help you out of here and we can go back up together." He reached Loretta and handed her his flashlight. "Here. Now put your arm on my shoulder." He then put his arm around her waist and walked forward with her.

When Loretta put weight on her foot, she cried out in pain and immediately lifted her foot off the dirt floor.

"You've got to walk. How else are you going to get out of here?"

"I can't!" Loretta pushed away from Johnny and hobbled back to the edge of the pit for support. "Go get Daddy."

"Alright." Johnny held his hand out.

"What?"

"Give me the flashlight."

"No, I don't want to stay down here in the dark."

"How do you expect me to see where I'm walking? You want me to step in a gopher hole and break my leg too? Then we'd both be stuck down here."

"I'm not going to stay down her in the dark."

Johnny looked around the pit and found the kerosene lamp. "Here." He went to the lamp and picked it up. "This will give you some light." He retrieved his box of matches from his pocket and lit the wick. "There." The lamp flooded the pit with a soft orange glow. "Are you okay now?" He set the lamp in the hollowed out area in the wall of the cellar.

Loretta looked about the old cellar. Handing him the flashlight, she said, "Yeah, but hurry up. I still don't want to be down here alone."

Johnny climbed the stairs and disappeared into the night. Loretta stood against the dirt wall with the lamp next to her. She looked around the hole and at the darkness above her. She was frightened. All of those ghost stories that she was always so fascinated with were now coming back to haunt her. She heard something that sounded like an owl; or was it the call of a dead Indian? She could barely make out the tones of the guitar playing back at the farmhouse. Then she remembered the devil pig and pressed her back closer to the dirt beside her.

She stood in silence, looking about and listening to the night. Then she heard something odd; a rustling noise from above. She looked up and searched the upper perimeter of the cellar. She now felt that there was not enough light. She wanted to be able to see more clearly. She reached for the knob at the base of the lamp and began to turn it in order to raise the wick and create a larger flame, which would give off more light. Unfortunately, she inadvertently turned the knob the wrong way, pulling the wick down and extinguishing the flame.

A little squeak escaped her throat as she gasped in horror at what she had done. "Stupid!" she whispered. She had no matches to relight the lamp. She stood in silence with the darkness engulfing her. After a moment she realized that she could make out the edge of the hole above. She could see the contrast between the earth and the night sky, which was filled with stars. To her dismay, the moon was too low on the horizon to shine its light into the hole. However, her eyes soon adjusted to the darkness and she was able to make out shapes around her.

Then she heard it again; that rustling noise.

Ruth moved quickly about the crowd pouring coffee for people. When the coffeepot was empty, she walked to the table where the desserts were. She cut two slices of cake and put them on a plate. The other women were busy talking and paid no attention to her actions. She carried the cake with her as she returned to the house with the empty coffeepot.

"Here you go boys." Ruth walked onto the porch where Gary and Scotty stood at the rail engaged in a competition of who could spit the furthest. The boys immediately turned their attention to her.

"I only got one plate and one fork, so you'll have to share them," she said, handing the plate to Gary, who had his hands outstretched. "That's all I could carry, and I didn't want to ask anyone else for help. We don't want your mamas to know."

"We won't tell," said Scotty as he followed Gary into the house. "Let's get some milk to go with it."

Ruth stood for a moment, watching the lights down at the old cellar, and then she turned and went back inside the house. "Enjoy your cake boys," she said as she left the kitchen for the back yard area.

Meanwhile, Lula Mae was watching Guy from where she was sitting at one of the tables. There was a group of choir members sitting in a circle with several lanterns scattered about them. Guy was sitting on a folding chair next to the man playing the guitar. His head was bowed as he leaned forward with his elbows resting on his knees and his hands clasped together in front of him. Harold was sitting next to Guy. Lula Mae could see that Harold was talking to him. Guy shook his head, looked up at Harold and said something and then resumed his forlorn position.

Harold rose from his chair and walked slowly to where Lula, Louise and Jesse Mae now sat together. "You better go get Guy, Lula Mae," he said as he approached the women. "He's about to fall out of that chair." Harold stood in front of Louise. "I'm going to go lay down for a while. I don't feel so good."

"Do you want me to come with you?" asked Louise.

"No, you stay. I'll be alright." Harold began walking unsteadily away from Louise. "I'm going to lay down in Romey's playhouse."

"Okay," said Louise as she watched him stagger to the small cabin.

Lula Mae rose from her seat and walked over to where Guy sat. She put her hand on his shoulder and he looked up at her. She could see the tears rolling down his cheeks in the light form the lanterns. He pulled her to him, wrapping his arms around her waist and pressing his head against her.

"Come on, Honey." Lula Mae took hold of guy's shoulders and lifted, helping him to his feet. She pulled his right arm across her shoulders and wrapped her left arm around his waist. They walked to the house this way and Lula Mae opened the screen door and helped Guy into the kitchen.

Gary and Scotty looked up from the checkerboard that rested on the table between them as Guy and Lula walked in. Their half eaten pieces of cake were next to the checkerboard, along with two glasses half filled with milk.

Passing through the kitchen, Lula Mae looked at the boys. "Where'd you boys get that cake?"

"That cake lady gave it to us," said Scotty, hoping to be exonerated of any responsibility for going against his mother's orders.

Lula Mae proceeded with Guy through the kitchen; the two of them, making their way to their bedroom. "You boys are going to make yourselves sick."

They were almost out of the kitchen when Gary said, "Johnny and Loretta went down to that old cellar."

Lula Mae stopped abruptly, forcing Guy to stop, causing him to stagger and almost pull her over. She struggled to right herself and him. "They what? When?"

The boys looked at one another and then back to Lula Mae. Gary shrugged his shoulders. "A while ago."

"Why didn't you tell me?"

Gary looked at his plate. "I was going to…"

"You two stay right where you are until I get back down here." Lula Mae, with her balance regained, continued with Guy through the living room. "I mean it Gary; you and Scotty stay there."

She got Guy up the stairs and into the bedroom. She guided him to the bed and as soon as she let go of him, he fell back on top of the sheet and passed out. Lula Mae knew it would do no good to try and wake him. She pulled off his shoes and pants and let him sleep.

In another moment she had slipped out of Jesse Mae's dress and pulled on a pair of denim jeans, tennis shoes and one of Guy's shirts. She grabbed the flashlight off the small table next to the bed and hurried down the stairs. She walked quickly through the kitchen. "Now Gary, I mean what I say. You and Scotty stay inside this house until I get back up here. I don't want to have to hunt you down too."

Ruth saw Lula Mae as she exited the house through the back door. She watched her walk quickly to the fence, and climb through, on her way down the pasture.

Ruth figured that Bobby Dean had had just about enough time to get down to the cellar. She walked over to Louise and Jesse Mae where they sat with several other women. "Louise," she said. "Bobby Dean has done drunk his self sick. He's down in the car waiting for me to take him home." She turned to Jesse Mae. "Please forgive me for running out like this; and again, our condolences to you and your family."

"Thank you," said Jesse Mae. "You don't give it another thought. Go on and take care of your husband."

Ruth looked around at the group. "Well okay then. Good-night all."

The group acknowledged Ruth and she walked to her car, which was still parked down at the entrance to the farm.

Sheriff Files walked up to Tony, who was sitting with several young women. He tapped Tony on his shoulder and motioned for him to follow him as he walked a short distance away from the women. Tony got up and followed the sheriff. The sheriff stopped and leaned towards him. "Where's Bobby Dean?"

Tony looked over at the spot where Bobby Dean had been sitting with the group of men. Bobby Dean was not in his chair. "He was just there Karl; I swear I've been watching him all night."

The two men looked around the crowd, searching for the mailman. There was no sign of him. "Find him," said Sheriff Files. Tony nodded his head and they both walked in opposite directions searching for the suspect.

CHAPTER NINETEEN

SUDDENLY A LIGHT FLASHED IN LORETTA'S FACE. She screamed and put her hand up to shield her eyes.

"What are you doing down here in the dark?"

Loretta pulled her hand from in front of her eyes. "You scared me."

"Where's the lamp?"

"It went out. Why aren't you getting Daddy?"

Johnny was now coming down the stairs. When he got to the bottom, he crossed to Loretta, shining the light on the ground. "I was going up the pasture and I turned around to make sure you were alright and I thought I saw something moving down here."

"What?" Loretta hoped that Johnny was putting her on and trying to scare her, but he was not a very good liar; therefore the seriousness in his speech convinced her that he was sincere.

"It looked like something walking around down here; but when I shined my light down this way it was gone. Maybe I was too far away and the light didn't reach it. I don't know if I just thought I saw something or if there was really something down here."

With a last attempt to expose Johnny's ruse, Loretta punched him lightly on the arm. "Oh you. Quit trying to scare me."

"I'm not trying to scare you. I really thought I saw something. That's why I came back."

Loretta gave up her attempt to expose any ploy to scare her. Her own intuition told her that her brother was on the level. She felt a fluttering sensation in her stomach as her fear mounted. "I heard something a while ago."

"What did you hear?"

"I don't know what it was. It just sounded like something moving up above."

"Well, you need to come on up to the house with me. I'll help you. We can't wait for Daddy to come down and get you."

"Okay," said Loretta. She put her arm on Johnny's shoulders for support and began hopping toward the stairs. When they got to the stairs, Loretta stopped. "How are we going to do this? I can't get up the stairs by myself."

They stood for a moment, contemplating a strategy. The stairs were very narrow; only about two feet wide. "We can get up them together," said Johnny, handing Loretta the flashlight. "Here, you take this." Loretta took the flashlight and Johnny tightened his arm around her waist and took hold of her hand, which was still across his shoulders. They both felt awkward; this blatant act of kindness from Johnny was throwing Loretta off her game and also leaving Johnny feeling vulnerable to attack from his lifelong nemesis, but they both realized that the situation was serious and that this was not a game.

Loretta could barely see her brother in the dim light cast by the flashlight, which spread out around them. If he was pulling a prank on her, she would not be able to detect it by reading any facial expressions. She did, however feel that he seemed solemn and genuinely concerned. She decided to trust him and go along with his plan. She did not care if he was going to play some kind of trick on her. She was frightened and she just wanted to get back up to the house as soon as possible.

Holding their bodies together, they made their way up the stairs; Loretta hopping and Johnny lifting. In a moment, they were out of the hole and making their way toward the house.

The sheriff walked up the steps of the front porch. He doubted that Bobby Dean would be in the house, but he always made a practice of investigating every potential scenario. It was possible that Bobby Dean had gone into the house to visit with Frank or another family member. The living room was quiet as the sheriff entered. There was one lamp lighted next to the large window facing the front porch. He passed quickly through to Mary's bedroom and into Romey's bedroom. There was a dimly lit lamp next to Romey's bed where Romey slept peacefully.

The sheriff could hear Gary and Scotty talking about space movies and aliens as they sat in the kitchen. He went back through Mary's bedroom and up the stairs to the second story of the house. He saw a light coming from under Geneva's bedroom door, and he knocked softly.

"Who is it?"

"Sheriff Files. Can I speak to you for a minute?"

Geneva opened the door. She was still dressed in the dark dress, which she had borrowed from her aunt. She stood looking at the sheriff, waiting for an explanation for the visit.

"I'm just checking to make sure you're alright," said the sheriff.

"I'm okay," said Geneva with an air of suspicion about her. "But what's going on down at that old cellar?"

"What?"

Followed by the sheriff, Geneva turned and walked to the bedroom window where they had a clear view of the pasture and the barn. She pointed in the direction of the barn. "Right before you knocked, I was looking out the window, and I saw lights down there."

She stood to one side so that the sheriff could move to the window and look for himself. He saw the beam from a flashlight halfway between the house and the barn. The light was dancing around on the ground, as if someone were walking quickly toward the barn. He saw another beam, close to the barn, moving slowly toward the house.

Without a word, the sheriff turned and hurried out of Geneva's room, leaving her clueless as to what was going on.

Suddenly, something hit Johnny in the back of his head and he fell forward, landing face down on the ground and remaining there. Loretta screamed at the top of her lungs as she was pulled backwards by her hair; landing solidly with her back on the ground. She saw a dark figure standing over her and screamed even louder. A large hand came toward her and she struck out hysterically with the flashlight and her empty hand. The attacker grabbed the flashlight and threw it a few feet away. Next the man grabbed both of her hands and held them together, rendering her unable to defend herself. She felt a pain at the back of her neck, and realized that the man had a hold on her grandmother's necklace with his free hand and was pulling on it.

"Loretta!" Lula Mae's voice carried through the night as she sprinted towards her children and this monster, who was assaulting them. With a full body slam, she hit Bobby Dean, who had stood upright and released his grip on the necklace at the sound of her voice. His two-hundred-twenty pound form tumbled to the ground and Lula Mae was on him in an instant. She pounded him violently with the flashlight she was carrying, while her other hand formed into a fist and matched each blow of the light, finding a target anywhere she could.

Bobby Dean managed to land a punch to the side of Lula Mae's head, stunning her for a moment. With difficulty, he got to his feet and headed toward the road. Just then the beam from another flashlight passed across his face, which was half covered with a bandana. Then another beam zigzagged about him as he dodged and weaved to keep out of the light.

He realized that he could not go to the road or his pursuers would see that Ruth was waiting there for him. He reversed his course and ran toward the woods. He had a head start of a couple hundred feet, and although he was overweight, his legs were still strong and carried him well. He disappeared into the darkness amongst the trees.

Pursuing the unidentified assailant into the night, Sheriff Files called out to Tony, "Check on the girl!"

Tony got to Loretta seconds after Lula Mae got to her. Lula Mae was holding her hysterical daughter; trying to be heard over her fearful screams. "Where's Johnny?" she said as she frantically shined her retrieved light around through the grass. Before Loretta could respond with anything other than gasps for air, and sobs; Lula Mae and Tony spotted Johnny lying on the ground a few feet away. "Johnny," cried Lula Mae as she lifted Loretta to her feet and rushed toward him; pulling the frightened child along with her.

Tony was the first to reach Johnny, who was lying face down. He laid his flashlight on the ground and dropped to his knees. "Johnny!" he said as he rolled the boy onto his back. By this time Lula Mae was on the ground next to them. Loretta had calmed herself somewhat, and was anxiously standing by as the others tried to get a response from Johnny.

Suddenly Johnny began swinging his arms and kicking his feet. "It's okay! It's okay!" said Tony, grabbing Johnny's hands. When Johnny realized that it was his mother and Tony beside him, he relaxed and ceased trying to defend himself.

"What happened?" said Johnny, sitting up and holding the back of his neck near the base of his skull where Bobby Dean had hit him with his fist.

"A man tried to kill me!" Loretta knelt down next to the others.

Seeing that Johnny seemed okay, Lula Mae turned her attention to Loretta. She embraced her and held her close. "You're alright now. Mama's here. You and Johnny are both alright."

Tony looked around for Sheriff Files. He saw the beam from the sheriff's flashlight at the edge of the woods. The light was traversing the thick underbrush and trees. Tony turned his attention back to the others, struggling against his instincts to follow after his fellow lawman to assist him in the manhunt. The sheriff had told him to help Loretta, and he knew he should get Johnny and her into some light to see if they had any serious injuries.

"Let's get them up to the house," Tony said to Lula Mae. Then he looked at Johnny. "Can you get up, Johnny?"

"Yeah," said Johnny, scrambling to his feet.

Geneva had watched from her window as Sheriff Files and Tony hurried down the pasture. She could not tell what was happening as the flashlights dropped to the ground. She could barely make out the movement of figures in the darkness. When she saw the two beams from the flashlights coming up the pasture, she hurried downstairs and waited on the front porch to find out from the sheriff what had happened. She had no idea that her mother, brother and sister had been the cause of all the commotion.

"What happened? What's going on?" Geneva stood on the front porch as the others approached the steps to the porch. "Mama?" she said as they climbed the steps and into the light from the living room.

Lula Mae ushered Johnny and Loretta up the steps, with Tony right behind her. Johnny's nose was dripping blood from his impact against the ground when he was knocked out by Bobby Dean. Lula Mae's hair was disheveled and one side of her face was already swelling. Loretta was limping, but her leg was already much better. She was covered with dirt and her hair was also a mess.

"Come inside, Geneva," said Lula Mae, placing one arm around Geneva's shoulders. She opened the screen door and guided Loretta and Johnny into the house before her.

Without hesitation, Geneva followed her mother's directions and walked with her through the doorway. They all went through the living room and into the kitchen. Gary and Scotty sat at the kitchen table with their eyes growing wide and their jaws dropping at the sight of the others.

Lula Mae sat Johnny and Loretta at the table and then she pumped water into the tea kettle from the pump at the sink and placed it over a burner to heat.

Tony had not disclosed the sheriff's suspicions of Bobby Dean to Lula Mae as they came up the pasture, so she was still unaware of the identity of the man who had attacked her children. "I'm going back down there to see if I can help Sheriff Files," he said. He turned to Geneva. "Why don't you find your pa and your uncle and tell them what's happened? Then stay in the house and lock the doors. I don't think that Bob…that the man will bother you here, but you never know."

Geneva rushed to the kitchen door and closed it, securing it with its barrel bolt. Then she followed Tony into the living room and locked the door to the front porch after he left. She quickly returned to the kitchen. She was frightened and did not want to leave her mother to go looking for her father and uncle right now.

On the trek up to the house, Loretta had calmed down somewhat, but when Geneva came back into the kitchen and once again asked what had happened, Loretta's tears resumed. She jumped up and moved to stand next to her mother. "Somebody tried to kill me!"

Lula Mae pulled Loretta close and wrapped her arms around her.

"What?" asked Geneva; "Who?"

"A Man! He hit Johnny and then he tried to kill me."

Geneva looked at her mother. "Tony thinks it was the man who killed Grandma," said Lula Mae. "Sheriff Files is chasing after him. He ran into the woods."

Everyone was silent for a moment. The reality of the situation was sinking in. Then Louise's voice came from the back porch. "Scotty, are you in there? Who locked this door?"

Scotty jumped up and ran to the door and opened it. "There you are..." Louise's words trailed off as she walked into the kitchen and Scotty wrapped his arms around her. She was stunned at the sight of Lula, Johnny and Loretta. She immediately looked down at Scotty. Seeing that he seemed okay, she walked to the table with Scotty staying next to her. "What's going on?"

"A man tried to kill me!"

Louise pulled Scotty closer. "My Lord." She looked at Lula Mae.

"Her and Johnny went down to that old cellar and somebody tried to get them," said Lula Mae.

Louise looked at Loretta and Johnny. "Are they okay?"

"I think they'll be alright." Lula Mae directed Loretta to a chair and sat her down in it. "Tony and the sheriff chased him away. They're after him right now. I think he ran into the woods." Lula Mae then went to the counter where she poured hot water into the enamel basin. She dipped a wash cloth into the water, wrung it out and walked over to Johnny. She began washing his face. "I think it's stopped bleeding," she said as she wiped the blood from beneath his nose.

"Where's Guy?" said Louise as she walked over to Loretta and brushed her hair back from her forehead and wiped her tears.

"He's upstairs in bed," said Lula Mae.

"I'll go get him." Gary jumped up from his chair and headed towards the dining room. He was frightened and he wanted his father around.

"No Gary; leave your daddy alone," said Lula Mae.

Gary stopped at the dining room door.

"Come back here and sit down. Daddy's sleeping. I'll go up and tell him in a little bit."

Gary returned to his chair and Lula Mae finished wiping Johnny's face. She went back to the wash basin and rinsed the wash cloth, and then turned her attention to Loretta. "How does your leg feel?" she said, now wiping Loretta's face.

"Better," said Loretta; her tears subsided.

Geneva walked to the back door and closed and bolted it again. "Tony said we should keep the doors locked."

Louise looked around at the group, still a little addled with the situation. "I'm going to wake up Harold." She started for the door, but stopped when she heard her father-in-law.

"What's all this ruckus?" said Frank, entering the kitchen. When he had gone up to his room, he had fallen asleep. Now all the talking had awakened him.

"A man tried to kill me!" Loretta started crying again.

"What?"

Lula Mae filled Frank in on the details of the incident. When she finished, Frank walked to his gun rack on the wall. "Where's Guy and Harold?"

"Guy's upstairs and Harold is in Romey's playhouse," said Louise.

"Well get them!"

"They're...asleep," said Lula Mae.

"You mean they're drunk?"

Lula Mae looked at her children. She hated for them to know that their father was passed out from drinking.

"Papa?" Romey stood in the doorway to his bedroom. The talking had awakened him also.

Frank turned and looked at Romey and then at the others. He started to tell Romey to go back to bed when he heard Jesse Mae's voice from the back porch.

"What's going on? Why is this door locked?" While sitting at one of the tables outside, Jesse Mae had seen the group in the kitchen and become curious.

Frank stepped to the door and opened it. As Jesse Mae walked in, he picked up a box of shotgun shells off a small table. "That god-damned Bobby Dean just tried to kill your niece and nephew."

Jesse Mae looked at the group. "Johnny and Loretta?" she said when she saw their condition.

"Bobby Dean?" said Louise.

Lula Mae said at the same time, "The mailman?"

"Well," said Frank, calming a little; realizing that he had no proof. "I've been thinking about it. It had to have been him." He checked the contents of the box.

Just then Sheriff Files, followed by Tony walked through the doorway from the back porch. "Now Frank, we don't know that for sure."

Frank looked at the sheriff and placed the box of shells back on the table. "You didn't catch him? What happened?"

"What the hell is going on?" said Jesse Mae.

Ignoring Jesse Mae's query, Sheriff Files walked past Frank and crossed to where Lula Mae was standing next to Johnny and Loretta. "How's everybody doing? Tony tells me that nobody was seriously hurt."

Lula Mae still stood next to Loretta as she sat in the chair. She rubbed Loretta's shoulders affectionately. "I think we'll be alright."

"He hurt my neck," said Loretta.

"Your neck?" Lula Mae pulled Loretta's hair back to look at her throat.

"In the back," said Loretta. She lifted her hair and turned so that her mother could see the back of her neck.

Lula Mae ran her hand between the necklace and Loretta's neck and lifted the necklace. "He was pulling at this necklace?"

"Yes," said Loretta. "I thought he was going to choke me."

"Bobby Dean?" said Jesse Mae. She looked at Frank.

Sheriff Files looked down at the necklace around Loretta's neck. "He was after this necklace."

Jesse Mae walked over to the group around the table. "Why would Bobby Dean want this necklace?"

The sheriff looked at Jesse Mae. "We don't know for sure that it was Bobby Dean." He turned to the others. "Now I don't want any of you telling anyone that it was."

"Well then why was his name mentioned? And what the hell happened?" Jesse Mae looked around at the group for an explanation.

"Ruth was really interested in that necklace," said Louise. "I heard her say that she used to have one just like it. She said that she lost it twenty or thirty years ago."

"So that's it," said the sheriff. "This necklace connects them to Rena Two Eagles." He looked at Tony. "This thing goes deeper than we realized."

"Wait a minute," said Louise. "That couldn't have been Bobby Dean. He got sick and Ruth took him home about thirty minutes ago."

"About the time of the attack," said Sheriff Files. He turned and walked to the screen door. "Tony, you stay here with these folks. I'm going to Bobby Dean's house to see how he's feeling."

At that moment the echo of a shotgun blast and the baying of a hound not far away carried to the farm. The sheriff stood at the screen door and listened for an instant.

"Someone got a coon," said Romey. This was a common response from Romey when gunfire was heard from the woods at night. He looked around at the other family members.

Frank stepped next to Romey and put his hand on his shoulder. He realized that the night's events were frightening Romey and that he was attempting to establish some normalcy. "Yeah, Son; someone got a coon."

"Frank," said Sheriff Files. "Why don't you go ahead and tell folks that the wake is over and that you all need to get some rest. A lot of them have already gone home. I'd just as soon have the place cleared out. I'm pretty sure that Bobby Dean is our man, but you never know. It'll be best if your family is alone."

"Yeah, I'll tell them," said Frank.

"You don't want me to come with you, Karl?" asked Tony.

"I want you to stay here with these folks. I can handle Bobby Dean. Keep the doors locked." The sheriff turned to Frank. "I want him to spend the night again."

Frank nodded his head in agreement.

"I'll need that necklace now," said the sheriff to Jesse Mae. "I'll make sure you get it back."

Jesse Mae reached behind Loretta's neck and unhooked the clasp of the necklace. "Keep it," she said as she handed it over. "I don't want it anymore."

The sheriff took the necklace and put it in his pocket. "I'll see you folks in the morning."

Almost an hour later, the last of the guests drove away from the farm. All the food had been picked up and taken away. The chairs were stacked next to the tables. The horses that pulled the wagons were tethered to the backs of the wagons so that they could not wander off during the night. The next morning, a few men would come back and take down the canvas, load up the tables and chairs and haul everything away.

Louise did not want to spend the night at the farm. She roused Harold up and got him into their car without telling him what had happened. He was still so drunk that he could not stand up on his own. She would tell him what had happened the next morning. She and Scotty said their good-nights to the family and she drove home.

Tony left the main house and walked to Romey's playhouse where he would spend another night. It was still quite warm and he was wound-up from all the excitement. He knew that he would not be able to sleep for a while yet, so he went over and got one of the stacked chairs and opened it up. He put it next to the playhouse, and sat, looking at the sky.

The night was still and quiet. Tony could hear dogs baying in the distance. Raccoon hunting was very popular on summer nights. He heard the screen door open and he looked toward the house. Geneva stood on the porch for a moment and then stepped down into the yard and walked toward him.

"Hi."

Tony stood up. "Hi."

"Got an extra chair?"

Tony moved the chair toward Geneva. "Take this one. I'll get another one." He quickly got another chair, placed it in front of Geneva and sat down facing her.

They looked at one another for a moment and then Geneva said, "Is Arlene your girlfriend?"

"No," Tony said quickly. "I mean…we've dated a couple of times, but it's nothing serious."

"Oh."

"I like you a lot, Geneva."

"I like you too." Geneva smiled a sad smile. "But we have to be realistic. My mama was right when she told me not to get serious about

289

you. We're going home in a few days and you and I will probably never see each other again. But I'll always remember you."

"Oh? Why's that?" Tony took Geneva's hands in his.

"You know."

"I'll always remember you too. You're a fast learner." Tony leaned towards Geneva and kissed her lightly on the lips. Geneva did not pull back. She leaned towards him and their lips met again. They kissed for several seconds, and then finally broke apart.

Geneva could not believe that she was being so sophisticated. It was much easier than she had imagined it would be. She felt happy. In spite of her grandmother's death and the inevitability of not seeing Tony again; she felt good about herself. She stood and pictured herself as Ingrid Bergman in the movie Casablanca. She squeezed Tony's hands. "Good-night, Tony."

"Good-night." Tony hated to let Geneva go. He sensed that he had been touched by her much more deeply than she, by him. He let go of her hands and watched as she walked into the house.

Lula Mae and Jesse Mae were sitting at the kitchen table drinking coffee when Geneva came back into the kitchen. Lula Mae had told Geneva that she could go out and say good-night to Tony, but she must not stay too long.

"Good-night," said Geneva, distractedly as she passed through the kitchen on her way upstairs. As she entered the bedroom, she found Loretta fast asleep. It was obvious that Loretta's ordeal with the attacker had exhausted her. Geneva changed into her nightgown and lay on the bed on top of the sheets. The movement of the bed startled Loretta.

"It' alright; it's just me," said Geneva. She patted Loretta's shoulder and Loretta went immediately back to sleep.

Sheriff Files approached the Brown's residence and pulled his car in behind Bobby Dean's car, which was parked there. The lights were still on inside the house, but he could not see any movement through the drawn curtains. He killed the engine and turned off his headlights. He sat quietly for a moment with his windows down. The house sat back from the road and there were no other houses for at least a quarter of a mile. He heard no sounds coming from the house. He climbed out of his car and went to the front door.

"Sheriff?" said Ruth when she answered his knock at the door. "What is it?"

The sheriff visually searched the room behind her as she stood in front of him. "Hello Ruth. I just stopped by to tell you and Bobby Dean that there was an incident out at the Austin's farm right after you left." He made it obvious now, that he was looking past her. "Where's Bobby Dean?"

"He's in the bathroom. He don't feel too good." Ruth remained in the middle of the doorway, blocking as much of the living room as possible. "What kind of incident? What happened?"

"A couple of Frank and Mary's grandchildren was roughed up down by the old cellar where those bones were found."

"Roughed up? By who?"

"I don't know. It all happened in the dark in the middle of the pasture. Looked like a big man when I shined my light on him. He had a handkerchief over his face."

"Why on earth would a man be after those children?"

The sheriff pulled the necklace out of his pocket. "It seems that he was after this." He held it up in front of Ruth. He thought that he noticed a flicker of fear in Ruth's eyes when she saw it.

Whatever was in Ruth's eyes, she concealed it in an instant. Her demeanor remained calm as she reached out and took hold of the body of the necklace; turning it over, looking at the back, and then turning it up again; all while the sheriff continued to hold onto the chain. "This is the necklace Mary's granddaughter was wearing tonight. I used to have one similar to it."

"Is that so?" The sheriff lowered his hand, gently pulling the necklace out of Ruth's grasp. "What happened to it?"

"Oh, I don't know, Karl. You know how things get misplaced or given away over the years. I haven't seen my necklace for almost ten years."

"Ten years?" said Sheriff Files. "You sure it was in your possession that recently?"

"What kind of question is that?" Ruth looked intently at the sheriff. She was an intelligent woman and she was not easily intimidated. "What are you getting at?"

"Nothing, Ruth; just trying to put a few pieces together." Sheriff Files tried his best to read Ruth's expression, but she was very good at concealing her feelings.

"Well, it's late…" Ruth put her hand on the door to signal to the sheriff that their little chat had come to an end. "…and I need to check on Bobby Dean. Thank you for letting us know what happened. I hope you catch the monster that attacked those children."

"Good-night, Ruth," said the sheriff, just before the door closed in front of his face.

Keeping out of the sheriff's line of vision, Bobby Dean quickly made his way around to the back of the house as the sheriff walked back to his car. He listened to the car engine turn over and heard the tires moving on the gravel as the sheriff pulled out of the drive.

When he was sure that the sheriff was gone, he began pounding on the back door of the house. Ruth pulled back the curtain on the window next to the door and saw him standing there.

"Good Lord, Bobby Dean! What happened to you?"

Bobby Dean rushed into the house and closed and locked the door behind him. One of his shirtsleeves was soaked with blood and he had more blood smeared on his face and other areas of his body. He had a few scratches on his face from running through the brush and his shirt had several tears in it.

"Somebody shot me!" Bobby Dean went directly to the bathroom, followed closely by his wife. Ruth helped him out of his shirt and began to wash the blood from his arm and shoulder.

"Oh my Lord," said Ruth as she examined the injury. "They took a piece out of you!" She was looking at a cleft in Bobby Dean's arm a quarter of an inch deep, a quarter of an inch wide, and about two inches long. It made a horizontal line along the outside of his shoulder where a bullet had grazed him.

Bobby Dean cried out in pain as Ruth dabbed the wound with the wet cloth. "God-damn woman! Just pour some alcohol on it and get a bandage over it. I have to stop this bleeding."

Fifteen minutes later the couple went into the kitchen. Ruth poured Bobby Dean a cup of coffee as he sat down at the table, wearing only a robe. The scratches on his face were cleaned and Ruth had bandaged his shoulder and managed to stop the bleeding.

Ruth told Bobby Dean about the sheriff showing her the necklace. They were both aware that they were under suspicion. "Remember when the sheriff asks you about that necklace; that I told him it turned up missing about ten years ago. That being the case; mine could not be the one found with Rena's...remains." Ruth sat down in the chair facing her husband. Suddenly she slapped him across the face. "God-damn you Bobby Dean," she said and began to cry.

With his right arm, Bobby Dean pulled her toward him and held her close while she cried.

CHAPTER TWENTY

LULA MAE POURED HOT COFFEE INTO JESSE Mae's half filled cup. She put the coffeepot back on the stove and sat down at the table. "So, what's going to happen now?"

Jesse Mae put a spoonful of sugar into her coffee and stirred it. "I want you all to come to my house tomorrow. That way Papa and Romey won't feel so misplaced if you guys are all around. Louise said that she and Harold and Scotty will come over too.

"I want Papa and Romey to move in with me right away. We all need to get away from this place. You and Guy and the kids can finish out your vacation there. I have five bedrooms, so there's plenty of room." She took a sip of coffee and then smiled. "Plus I have a real bathroom."

Lula Mae reached across the table and touched Jesse Mae's hand. "I'm sorry for being hateful to you in the past, Sis. I never had any idea how hard your life has been. I always thought you had it so easy."

Jesse Mae turned her hand over and held her sister-in-law's hand. She was touched by Lula Mae's sincerity. For most of the eighteen years that they had been acquainted, they had both been superficial and cool to one another. "I haven't always been so nice to you either. I don't know why I'm so mean sometimes." She paused a moment. "I guess I've been pretty selfish."

"No..." said Lula Mae, meaning to deny the fact.

Jesse Mae cut her off. "If you want to know the truth, I was glad when Mama took care of Romey for me. I didn't really want to be a mother at that time. And by the time I got old enough to want children it was too late for me to take Romey. He had already gotten used to Mama being his mama. I couldn't take her away from him or him away from her.

"When I got married and tried to get pregnant, it just wouldn't happen. I finally went to a doctor to be checked out; he said that I would never have another child."

Lula Mae squeezed Jesse Mae's hand. "You'll make a good mama for Romey."

"I'm going to try." Jesse Mae let go of Lula Mae's hand and picked up her cigarette case. She gave her sister-in-law a cigarette and they both lit up.

Lula Mae inhaled deeply and then exhaled. She picked tobacco from her lip and then had another sip of coffee. "What was it like living with that Indian woman?"

Jesse Mae tapped her cigarette on the edge of the ashtray. "Oh it wasn't so bad. She was really nice. It was just boring. I had to hide in that house for months. I couldn't even go to the outhouse. I used a chamber pot. I had to keep out of sight so that nobody would see my big belly and guess that I was pregnant. I used to sit out on the front porch at night though."

"Well how did she ever get together with that awful letterman?"

"They met each other before I moved in. Rena told me that he had been coming to her house in the middle of the day, when his wife thought he was working. Of course, I didn't know who it was that she was seeing. She wouldn't tell me.

"After I moved in, she would go out somewhere almost every day to meet him. She would always come back with food or something she needed around the house; stuff he had given her. I was glad she was seeing him. We ate well.

"She told me he was really mad that she was letting me stay with her, cause he couldn't come there anymore. I would watch her through the window when she would go out, but I never saw her meet him." Jesse Mae shook her head. "And all the time it was Bobby Dean.

"I remember how he would always stay on the porch talking to her when he would bring her those free magazines that didn't have addresses on them. She never got any real mail. If I had had any sense back then,

I would have guessed it was him. She always went out shortly after he came by."

"And she didn't mind that he was married?"

"No, she didn't seem to care. In fact, I think she liked it that way. She told me that she had enchanted him with a magic spell. She sneaked his house key from him and used it in a charm. She really believed in magic."

"What kind of charm?"

"It was this thing she had made out of a willow tree branch. It was sort of pretty. She twisted the branch into a circle and then stretched thread from side to side, making it look like a spider's web. She hung feathers, and dried flowers, and his house key, that she had stolen from him, on the thing and then hung it in her window. She knitted a little doll over his key so that he wouldn't know what it was when he saw it. She said that as long as she kept that charm in her window, he would always come back to that house.

"After she told me she had a lover, she showed me that necklace. She was really proud of it. She said that it was the nicest thing she owned. She told me that she wasn't really in love with him, but he gave her food and stuff. She was saving up the money that Mama was giving her, and she didn't want to spend it on food, so she didn't tell him that she had it. She said that she also just needed the company of a man after her husband left her. Of course, I didn't understand what she was talking about then."

"I just don't see how a woman can have anything to do with another woman's husband."

"She wasn't a bad woman, Lula Mae. She had that one problem, but she was still a good woman."

"Did you see her anymore after you came back home?"

"Yes; a few days after I came home, she came here to get the last of her money from Mama. That was a Sunday, I think. She told Mama and me that she was going back to Oklahoma the very next day. The reason that she had agreed to let me stay in her house all that time was so that she could get together enough money for a bus ticket. We thought she had left the next day. Nobody ever suspected anything was wrong.

"Mama knew about her having a lover and she asked Rena if he knew she was leaving. Rena said no, he didn't. She said that she knew he wouldn't want her to go, so she was just going to leave without telling him. She said that she had thrown that charm in the potbellied stove and burnt it up; hoping that he wouldn't come back.

"Mama said that he probably wouldn't come back. She said that once a man gets the milk, he doesn't have anymore need for the cow. Rena just laughed at that."

Jesse Mae noticed Lula Mae looking at her in a peculiar way. "What?" she said.

"Did you say that that charm had his house key on it?"

"Yeah."

"And that Rena put it in the stove to burn it up?"

"Yes…What, Lula Mae? What are you getting at?"

"I don't think a key would burn up."

"So?"

"It might still be in that stove."

"Sis, you're not making any sense. So what if a key wouldn't burn…?" Suddenly Jesse Mae realized what Lula Mae was thinking. "If the key is still there, and her lover was Bobby Dean, that key would open Bobby Dean's front door."

The sheriff's wife, Thelma, was dozing on the living room sofa when she heard her husband's car pull up in front of their house. She glanced at the grandfather clock against the wall opposite the sofa; it was almost twelve-thirty a.m. She sat up when he let himself in through the front door.

"Hi Hon," said the sheriff as he entered the living room. "What are you doing still up?"

"Oh, I couldn't sleep, so I laid down here to read." She picked her book up from the floor next to the sofa. "Looks like I could sleep after all." She said with a smile.

Sheriff Files sat down on the sofa next to his wife. She placed the book on the end table and turned to him. "So what's going on, Karl?"

The sheriff leaned back on the sofa and exhaled. He turned to his wife. "I think that was Bobby Dean that attacked those kids."

Thelma did not seem surprised. "I figured he was your main suspect from what little I heard between you and Frank Austin."

The sheriff reached into his pocket and pulled out the necklace. He held it up towards Thelma. "You ever see Ruth Brown wearing this necklace; say about twenty-five years ago?"

"Twenty-five years? Good Lord Karl, I have a discerning eye but I don't think I would remember a piece of jewelry somebody wore…" Thelma took the necklace out of Karl's hand. "Wait a minute." She held the necklace under the lamp next to the sofa. "I don't remember seeing her wear this necklace, but I sure have seen her wearing a bracelet that looks just like it."

The sheriff sat upright. "Are you sure?"

"Of course I'm sure. She wears it a lot. It looks just like this necklace."

"That's the necklace that was found next to Rena Two Eagles' skeleton. It connects one or both of them to Rena at the time that she was put in that cellar."

"My Lord, I just can't believe that they would hurt anyone. We've known them since we were all kids, Karl."

Sheriff Files shook his head. "I know; it just don't seem possible. But Ruth sure looked guilty tonight when I showed her this necklace. And I don't believe Bobby Dean was in that bathroom being sick. He might've been in the bathroom, but if he was, he was hiding so that I wouldn't see that he was out of breath and messed up from running through the woods."

"What are you going to do?"

"Well, I'm not sure; I need to find some proof. Unfortunately, testimony about the similarities in a bracelet and a necklace from the wife of the arresting sheriff would not be enough to convince a jury that those two was involved with Rena's death. I know what you say is so, but those people wouldn't know you; they might think that you was just siding with me."

"Well, I'm sure that a lot of people have seen Ruth Brown wearing that bracelet."

"Yeah, I guess you're right. Still, it's weak evidence. I need something more." The sheriff put his hand on his wife's knee. "Come on, let's sleep on it. I'm tired as hell."

Guy's head felt like it had swollen to the size of a watermelon and was being squeezed in a vice as he eased his way down the stairs. There were no sounds of anyone else being up as he stepped into the living room. The house was still dark, but he could see the glow of dawn through the windows. He could also see light shining through the open spaces around the door leading from the dining room into the kitchen. When he had woken up and found that Lula Mae was not in bed, he assumed that she was already up and making breakfast. He pushed the door open and was surprised to see his wife and sister, both with their heads lying on the kitchen table, fast asleep.

"What the hell?" croaked Guy; barely able to get the words out due to the pain in his head.

The sound of his voice roused the women from their slumber, and Lula Mae immediately got up from her chair and went to him. "How do you feel?" she said.

"Did you two stay up all night?"

"Is it morning?" asked Jesse Mae; lifting her head from the table and looking around the room.

Lula Mae put her arm around Guy and looked back at Jesse Mae. "I guess we fell asleep."

"What time is it?" Jesse Mae lifted her arms and stretched in an effort to relieve the stiffness in her back.

They all three looked at the wind-up clock on the counter. "It's almost five o'clock," said Lula Mae as she guided Guy to a chair.

Guy sat down in the chair that Lula Mae pulled out for him. "What time did I go to sleep?" he asked.

"A little before ten," said Lula Mae. She walked to the stove where the coffee simmered over a low flame. She filled a cup and set it in front of Guy. She filled Jesse Mae's cup and topped off her own. She put the pot back on the stove and sat down at the table. Guy noticed the two women looking at one another. "What's up?" he said, carefully sipping the hot coffee.

"There was a little trouble last night," said Jesse Mae.

Guy looked at Jesse Mae and then at Lula Mae, still sipping his coffee. "Somebody get into a fight?"

"Somebody tried to hurt Johnny and Loretta," said Lula Mae.

Guy held his coffee cup away from his lips. "Who? Who tried to hurt them?" He was not sure if this was something serious or just another juvenile scuffle.

"Some man attacked them down by that old cellar." Lula Mae turned her face toward Guy at an angle that made her cheek visible to him for the first time since he had come downstairs; exposing the bruising there.

Guy's cup hit the table, splashing coffee over the edge of the cup. "Some man? What the hell are you talking about? And what happened to you?" Guy stretched his arm out and held Lula Mae's chin in his hand, examining her cheek.

"The sheriff thinks it was Bobby Dean," said Jesse Mae. "He tried to get that necklace off Loretta's neck."

"Who the hell is Bobby Dean? Where are the kids?" Guy rose from his chair.

"They're alright," said Lula Mae, also rising. "They're still sleeping." She took hold of Guy's arm. "Sit down and drink your coffee."

Guy slowly took his seat at the table. He reached up and gently touched Lula Mae's cheek as she sat next to him. "Did he do this to you?"

"Your wife beat the hell out of him," said Jesse Mae.

"Who was it…and what was going on?"

"I told you, Bobby Dean." Jesse Mae realized that Guy did not know who she was talking about. She elaborated. "The mailman. You saw him the morning we went to the lake remember? He drove up just before we left."

"Where the hell is he? I'll beat the shit out of him."

Lula Mae turned to her sister-in-law. "Now Jesse Mae, remember the sheriff said he wasn't positive that it was Bobby Dean. He told us not to go around saying that it was."

"Well the evidence is certainly pointing in his direction."

"Where is he?" insisted Guy.

The two women proceeded to fill Guy in on all the details of the previous evening. Guy was ashamed and upset that he had been too drunk to protect his family. He held Lula Mae's hand and told her how badly he felt for not being able to protect her and the kids.

301

"Never mind," said Lula Mae, squeezing his hand. "You just lost your mama; you had a right to get drunk. None of us knew anything like that was going to happen."

"We think we might know how to find out who it was for sure," said Jesse Mae. She told him about Rena and the charm with the key that she had thrown into the stove.

By six-thirty, the sun was up and so were the other family members and Tony. During breakfast, Johnny and Loretta were unstoppable in talking about what had happened to them the night before. An hour later, Guy, Frank and Tony had finished breakfast and were on the front porch discussing what to do about Bobby Dean. Guy had filled Tony and Frank in on the details concerning the house key.

"Sheriff Files said that he was going to try to get more evidence," said Tony. "When we talk to him we'll tell him about that thing that the Indian woman made and put in the stove to burn up. If there is a key in that stove and it fits Bobby Dean's house, then I think that's got him."

By eight a.m. the breakfast dishes were washed and water was being heated in the cauldron for baths. Tony and the youngsters were in the back yard tending to the fire. The adults, including Romey were sitting on the front porch, discussing what needed to be done before they would leave for Pine Bluff.

When the sheriff arrived, Tony met him at his car and they spoke briefly before going to the front porch to talk to the family.

"Morning folks," said the sheriff as he climbed the steps of the porch. He was greeted by the others and offered a seat, which he declined. He preferred to stand after the ride in from his office. He filled them in on his conversation with his wife about the necklace and once more cautioned them all not to discuss their suspicions about Bobby Dean to anyone outside the family.

He also told them that he had had a call earlier that morning that a couple of boys who had been hunting raccoons nearby the night before thought that they had accidentally shot a man that came running out of the woods. They thought he was a bear. The man did not fall, but he staggered backwards and cried out; then he ran away. Unfortunately, the boys did not get a good look at him; just a few quick glances as they shined their lights in his direction. They did say that he was a big man, but he turned his face away from the light. The sheriff said that if that man was Bobby Dean, that he would be wounded and that would be one more piece of evidence against him.

"There might be a more surefire way to catch him," said Jesse Mae. She proceeded to tell the sheriff about the charm that Rena had made and claimed to have burned in the stove. "If that key is still there, and if it fits his door, then it will prove that Bobby Dean was her lover and that he probably killed her."

The sheriff was quiet for a moment, thinking the thing through. "Well, it will *suggest* that he was her lover; now whether a jury would determine that it was proof of him murdering her...I don't know. But it's a damn good piece of evidence. I just wish there was some way that I could get him to confess that he murdered Rena and your mama."

"What if he tried to get to that key before you could?" said Jesse Mae.

The sheriff finally sat down. "Go on."

"We need to somehow let him know that the key is in that stove and that it could be used as evidence against him." Jesse Mae looked around at the others. She needed a little help in coming up with a plan to get Bobby Dean to go after the key. For a short while they all sat in silence, trying to come up with a plan.

"What happens to all those notes that Tony is always writing down?" asked Jesse Mae.

The sheriff was not sure what she was getting at. "My secretary, Janice types them up and files them."

"I don't know if you know this Sheriff, but Louise tells me that nothing goes across that woman's desk that most of the town doesn't hear about."

The sheriff frowned, but said nothing. He was aware of his secretary's loose lips.

Jesse Mae tapped her cigarette on the edge of a jar lid that she was holding in her hand and using for an ashtray. "Make sure that she knows all about the key in the stove. That will be just too juicy of an item for her to sit on. I'll bet she'll be on the phone telling several women in no time. It's sure to get to Ruth within an hour after you give it to her."

"That's good," said the sheriff. "But Bobby Dean won't go anywhere near that house if he knows that I'm watching him."

"Then we have to get you out of the picture; you and Tony too." Jesse Mae flipped her cigarette butt into the yard and put the jar lid aside.

The sheriff was reluctant. "But we don't want him to really be able to get it. And I'm not going to let anybody else get mixed up with him."

"They won't have to," said Jesse Mae. "You'll just pretend to be out of town."

Frank leaned in towards the sheriff. "Don't you have a daughter in school in Little Rock?"

"Yeah." The sheriff waited for Frank to elaborate.

Jesse Mae picked up the thought. "What if she was in a car wreck and you went to see her?"

The sheriff nodded his head. "Un-huh…Go on."

"That would leave Tony in charge." There was another pause as the group continued to speculate on a possible method of fooling Bobby Dean. Jesse Mae snapped her fingers. "There's a movie playing in Pine Bluff that everybody is wanting to see; *East of Eden*. We're all going to Pine Bluff today. Tony can say that he's coming over to take Geneva to the movies tonight."

Guy looked at Lula Mae. "I don't want Geneva going out tonight."

"She won't really be, Guy," said Jesse Mae. "And neither will Tony." She turned to Sheriff Files. "Be sure to let your secretary know that you've given Tony the day off so that he can go to Pine Bluff. When we get to my house, I'll call your office and tell your secretary that I'm a nurse at the hospital in Little Rock and that your daughter was just brought in; in critical condition. Make sure your wife knows that it's all a setup so that she won't hear about it and get scared. Your secretary will tell everyone she knows. If that key is Bobby Dean's, then I'll bet he'll try to get it out of that house as soon as he can. You and Tony can be there in the house tonight waiting for him."

"That might work," said the sheriff, "But how do we know that Janice will get the word out?"

"The church ladies," said Lula Mae. They all turned to her. "We can tell Louise to tell the ladies that she knows at the church all these stories and you can be sure that it will get back to Bobby Dean's wife."

The sheriff considered these plans for a moment. "I think it might work..." His words trailed off as he and the rest of the group looked toward the road in front of the house.

They all saw Bobby Dean driving his mail truck along the road in front of them; obviously on his way to Frank's house. "That son-of-a-bitch," said Guy, standing up."

"Now Guy," said the sheriff, also standing. "You stay away from him. I'll handle this. I want to keep him guessing whether or not I really suspect him."

"He attacked my kids, Sheriff!"

"I mean what I say, Guy." The sheriff looked at Frank. "Frank, tell your boy to settle down and keep away from Bobby Dean."

Frank waved his hand at Guy, motioning for him to sit down. "Sit down Guy. This is a matter for the law."

Guy remained standing.

"God-damn-it! I said sit down!"

Guy turned towards his father. The tone in Frank's voice told him that this was a nonnegotiable issue. He looked around at the group and took his seat with a sullen look on his face.

"Now I want you all to stay right where you are," said the sheriff. "I'll go talk to Bobby Dean."

Bobby Dean pulled his truck up to the house and put it into neutral gear. He and the sheriff locked eyes as the sheriff approached the truck. "Morning Sheriff."

"Morning Bobby Dean."

Bobby Dean looked past the sheriff towards the house. "Where's Frank?"

"Frank's not feeling too good. I told him that I would get the mail for him."

"Well, I don't have no mail for him." Bobby Dean leaned over and picked up a pie from the other side of the seat. "But Ruth baked this pie for him and his family. Would you tell him that we just want to show our respects for him and his?" Bobby Dean handed the pie through the truck window to Sheriff Files; using his right hand. The sheriff noticed Bobby Dean wincing a little as he turned.

The sheriff took the pie. "Sorry you weren't feeling so good last night. I imagine Ruth told you what happened to Frank's grandkids."

"Yeah she told me. I could hear someone talking last night when I was in the bathroom, but I wasn't in no condition to come out and see who it was. She told me it was you."

The sheriff looked Bobby Dean over. "How you feeling this morning?"

"Well, I don't feel so great, but I'll survive. It ain't the first time I had too much to drink."

"Something wrong with your arm?" Sheriff Files was referring to Bobby Dean's left arm, which he was hardly moving.

"Yeah, the damnedest thing; I must have slept on it wrong last night. Either that or just my old rheumatism acting up."

The sheriff held up the pie. "Well I'll be sure to give Frank and his family your regards. I know they'll be grateful for the pie; especially Romey." He started to turn away and then turned back to Bobby Dean. "Oh that reminds me; Romey says that you brought a Wards Catalog to him the other day."

"Yeah, I did. I remember that. It was in the post office and it didn't have no address on it, so I thought he might like it. I know he likes the Sears Catalog."

"What time was that?"

"Oh I don't know, sometime around noon."

"Did you see anything unusual while you were here?"

"Unusual?"

"Yeah." Sheriff Files did not elaborate; he merely stared at Bobby Dean.

"Well…I guess it was unusual that Mary was down at that old root cellar. I asked Romey where she was and he told me, and then I left. Other than that, there wasn't nothing unusual."

The sheriff nodded his head. "Oh by the way; Frank and the whole family are going over to Pine Bluff today to stay at Jesse Mae's house. They won't be here for a while, so why don't you just forward their mail to her. I can call you later with her address. Frank might be giving up his farm."

"Oh." Bobby Dean nodded his head. "We'll miss them." He put his truck in reverse and pulled away from the house. The sheriff stood where he was and watched as he drove away.

CHAPTER TWENTY-ONE

SHERIFF FILES AND TONY EACH PUSHED AN oar into the mud at the bottom of the bayou, maneuvering through the murky water between the trees, shrubs and fallen logs. Due to the density of the vegetation; using the oars as poles was much easier than trying to row through the overgrown marshy area next to the old house.

The route behind the house, which they were taking, gave them plenty of cover. The space in front of the house was much too open for their approach. It had only a few reeds and tree stumps scattered throughout the water. The men were coming up behind the house in order to insure that they would not be observed by any passersby on the road.

With the groundwork laid for their sting operation; the gossip about the key in the stove, and the cover story about them both being out of town; they were hoping that Bobby Dean would fall for their trap and return to the old house in an effort to find his key.

Before dawn, Tony had hauled his rowboat to a spot next to the bayou that he and Sheriff Files had agreed on. He left the boat there and then returned to town and went into the office as he usually did on a workday. When Sheriff Files came into the office around nine a.m. Tony asked him, in front of Janice, if he could take the day off and go to Pine Bluff to take Geneva to a picture show. The sheriff agreed that Tony could take the day off, and as Tony left the office he told Janice that he would tell her all about the movie the following day. She and her friends had heard a lot about the movie and she was anxious to get his opinion on it.

In the early afternoon, Jesse Mae had called the sheriff's office and told Janice that she was a nurse at the hospital in Little Rock and that the sheriff's daughter had been seriously injured in an auto accident. Practically in tears, Janice radioed the sheriff in his car and told him about his daughter. The sheriff told her that he and his wife would be leaving immediately for Little Rock.

Before leaving town, the sheriff and his wife had received a phone call from Louise. Louise told Thelma that she had already gotten calls from two different ladies who had gone into every detail about the key in the old house, and how Tony and the sheriff were out of town for the night. She said she asked one of the women if she thought Ruth had heard, and the woman said that she had just finished speaking to her about it.

After Louise's phone call, Thelma had driven the sheriff out of town, so that the residents would see them leave. When they were a few miles out, she changed her course and drove to the spot at the side of the bayou, where Tony was waiting for them. She said her good-byes to her husband and wished both men good luck and then she drove on to her sister's house in Pine Bluff where she would wait until her husband called her and told her to come home.

The two lawmen had enough food and water to last them the rest of the day and that night. The plan was for the sheriff to hide out in the house, hoping to catch Bobby Dean when he came for the key, and for Tony to wait in his car until the sheriff called him on his walkie-talkie to tell him to bring the boat back for him; at which time he would haul Bobby Dean out of the bayou in handcuffs.

Now they moved the boat up to the back of the house. The water in this part of the bayou was only about two feet deep, so its surface was just below the floorboards of the building. When the house had been built, the owner knew that this was a flood area; therefore he had built it on stilts so that the interior would rest above the level of the frequent floodwaters.

Tony tried the back door, but it would not open. They brought the boat around to the side of the house, being careful to keep out of view from anyone who might be on the road. Tony reached through a small broken window pane and turned the latch that had the window secured. With a lot of effort, he soon succeeded in raising the window. Sheriff

Files steadied the boat against the outside wall as Tony hoisted himself up and crawled into the house.

The inside of the building was damp and clammy. When Tony jumped down into the room, his feet slipped on the moss covered floor, and he fell backwards, landing hard against the wall.

"What happened?" The sheriff called from outside.

"I just slipped, that's all." Tony was mindful of the slippery floor as he walked carefully to the door, which was blocked with a wooden plank resting in two supports on either side. He lifted the plank out of the supports and pulled the door open.

Sheriff Files handed his supplies through the doorway and Tony placed them to one side. Tony then grabbed one end of a rope, which was attached to the boat, and he tied the rope to the doorknob. The sheriff reached up to Tony. "Give me a hand," he said. Tony took the sheriff's hand and pulled as the sheriff stepped out of the boat and into the house.

"Careful on this floor," said Tony "It's slick with moss."

"Yeah, yeah." Sheriff Files ignored Tony's warning as he looked around at the old house. They were in the kitchen, which had only one window. Even with the door wide open, the kitchen was still dark. There was a table with two chairs next to it, a wood burning kitchen stove covered with rust, and something that looked like it used to be an icebox covered with moss and several sprouts of some kind of weed.

They walked through the rest of the house, which consisted of a living room and a bedroom. In the living room was an old sofa that had weeds growing out of the seat cushions, a rocking chair, a small table with a kerosene lamp on it, and the potbellied stove. The bedroom had an iron bedstead and a bureau, which had fallen over after its legs had rotted.

After determining that there was no one else in the house, they went to the potbellied stove in the middle of one wall in the living room. With some difficulty, the sheriff got down on his knees and opened the door of the stove. There was not enough light coming through the two windows in the living room for him to see into the stove clearly. "Get me my flashlight from the kitchen," he said to Tony. Tony quickly got the flashlight and the sheriff shined it on the ashes inside the stove. Using his free hand, he sifted through the ashes until he touched something that felt like a key. He grasped the key with two fingers and lifted it out from the belly of the stove.

"We got him," said Tony, eying the key.

"Looks like it." The sheriff wrapped the key in his handkerchief and handed it to Tony. "Put this in your pocket. Don't wipe the ashes off of it. It'll be more convincing during the trial with them still on it."

"So you think there'll be a trial?"

"I don't know. I'm going to do my damnedest to talk him into a confession when he sees he's been found out; but if he don't confess, then…yeah, there'll be a trial."

The sheriff took hold of the stove and pulled himself up to a standing position. He looked around the dismal old house. "I guess the bedroom is the best place for me to hide and wait for him." He picked up the rocking chair and both men walked into the bedroom. The sheriff put the chair down and shined his flashlight into the corners of the floor. "I hope there aren't any cottonmouths living in here."

There was no sign of snakes or anything else that might go scurrying around the room, so the sheriff went to the kitchen and got the bag with his things in it. His supplies consisted of a flashlight, a jug of water, an apple, some dried beef, a box of cookies, a candle, a paperback novel, and a roll of toilet paper. He began taking the items out of the bag. "You go on back to your car now; and remember to leave your walkie-talkie on."

"I'll remember, Karl. You call me if you need anything." Tony was genuinely concerned for his superior's welfare. He had offered to stay in the house with the sheriff, but the sheriff insisted that he could handle Bobby Dean.

"I'll call you when I have that son-of-a-bitch in handcuffs. You go on now."

Tony climbed back into the rowboat and pushed away from the house. Sheriff Files replaced the plank across the rear door of the house and went back into the bedroom. He picked up his paperback novel and pulled the rocking chair next to the window where there was light enough for reading. In a few moments he was absorbed in a story of the Old West.

Bobby Dean slowed his truck down as he drove past the house. It was after midnight and there was little chance that anybody else would be on the road at this hour, but he was not about to start getting careless again. He had fallen for all of the fabricated stories about the sheriff and his deputy being out of town, and he was determined to get that key before they returned.

His eyes scanned the house and the surrounding area and he saw no signs of anybody in the vicinity. He continued up the road a short distance and then doubled back. A little ways from the house, he pulled his truck into a turnout behind some low hanging trees where he was sure that it would be out of sight, should anybody drive by.

He made his way to the edge of the bayou and pulled his waders over his feet, legs and hips. He picked up his large heavy duty flashlight and a pole about five feet long that he would use to help him with his balance while walking through the water.

For the most part, the pole was an advantage, but it was also cumbersome as it would sometimes get stuck in the mud as he sloshed along on his way to the house. Amongst the rocks and dead branches under the water, he could see things moving about as he disturbed their nighttime shelters. He kept a sharp eye out for alligators. He did not think that there were any in this water, but he was still a little spooked by the possibility.

The heat of the night and the exertion of wading through the mud and water had proven a little more difficult than Bobby Dean had anticipated. His injured shoulder was hurting him, and he was afraid that the wound had started bleeding again. The thought that this would be a quick *grab the key and run* job helped him continue on.

Before he got to the house, he had to stop for a moment and catch his breath. He wiped the sweat from his brow with his shirtsleeve and looked in the direction of the house. "God-damned witch," he muttered under his breath. At that instant a flash of green swamp gas ignited next to him, causing him to jump away from it and almost lose his balance. Something bumped against his leg and he shined his light into the water; glimpsing a large snake swimming away from him.

Annoyed with the whole situation, he grumbled under his breath and proceeded to the house, where he had difficulty finding the steps to the porch, which were submerged under the dark water. By feeling around with his pole, he was able to locate them toward the middle of the long porch.

Beneath the water, the three short pieces of wood were slick with algae, and his feet nearly slipped from beneath him before he managed to step up onto the floor of the porch. It was covered with moss and weeds, which had grown out of the cracks between the planks.

He leaned his pole against the side of the house next to the door and reached for the doorknob. Beside the door was a pile of rotting, decomposing firewood. There was a piece of wood in front of the door and Bobby Dean kicked it aside, knocking it into the stacked logs and causing the whole pile to tumble and scatter. When he kicked the wood, his foot slipped on the wet moss and he dropped his flashlight and grabbed the doorframe in an effort to keep from falling. As he righted himself, his flashlight lay on the porch illuminating several large dark colored snakes scurrying from the area where the woodpile had been.

With the protection of his waist high waders, Bobby Dean began kicking violently at the snakes, propelling them off the porch and into the water. With the last snake off the porch, he picked up his flashlight and scanned the porch with its beam just to make sure there were no more to bother him.

"God-damned cottonmouths." Bobby Dean opened the door cautiously and shined his light into the room. His heavy waders protected him against snakebite, so he did not have to worry about being bitten; but the serpents had still rattled his nerves and he wanted to make sure that there were none inside the house.

Feeling sure that there were no more crawling about, he quickly walked to the potbellied stove to retrieve the key. He squatted on his haunches and pulled the iron door open and shined his light into the inside of the stove. He stuck one hand inside the stove and scattered the ashes about, trying to find the key. After sifting through the ashes several times, he was beginning to think that the key had never been placed there. "God-damned...Rena," he said aloud with an air of disgust in his voice."

"Looking for something, Bobby Dean?" With these words, the sheriff flipped on his flashlight, flooding the area around Bobby Dean and the potbellied stove with a powerful beam of light.

Startled by the unexpected presence of another person, Bobby Dean twisted his body around to see who was there. He lost his balance and toppled backwards, sitting down hard on the damp wooden floor. He quickly gathered his composure and pointed his flashlight in the direction of Sheriff Files. "Sheriff! What are you doing here? I thought…"

The sheriff approached Bobby Dean as he sat on the floor. "I'm looking to catch a murderer, Bobby Dean. The more pertinent question is; what are you doing here?" The sheriff stood next to Bobby Dean, shining his light directly at Bobby Dean's face.

"I…" Bobby Dean realized that anything he would say would be useless. It was obvious that he had been set-up.

Before Sheriff Files had surprised him, Bobby Dean's fingers had been buried in the ashes in the stove. Without thinking consciously to do it; he had grasped for something to prevent his fall backwards, and closed his hand around a fistful of ashes, which he still held. Now as the sheriff stood over him, Bobby Dean swiftly brought his hand up and threw the soot and ashes towards the sheriff's face.

The ashes hit their mark and filled the sheriff's eyes. "Aghh!" The sheriff dropped his flashlight and bent over, holding his hands over his eyes.

Immediately, Bobby Dean brought his heavy flashlight up and hit the sheriff on the side of his head with a powerful blow. The sheriff stumbled sideways, almost losing his balance; struggling to overcome the effects of the blow to his head and the grit and soot in his eyes. He staggered backwards, trying to open his eyes, unable to focus his attention on his assailant. This gave Bobby Dean the opportunity to get to his feet and hit the lawman repeatedly with the light.

Bobby Dean continued to strike the sheriff about the head until the sheriff dropped to his knees. With the advantage of being able to exert more force from above, Bobby Dean hit the sheriff once more, causing him to waver. Then as the nearly defeated lawman swayed back and forth, trying to regain his equilibrium, Bobby Dean swung the light again.

A cracking sound came from the instrument and the light went out, spreading darkness across the side of the room where the two men had struggled. Bobby Dean saw the vague outline of his adversary fall to the floor, and everything was silent.

For a moment, Bobby Dean stood unmoving, hearing nothing but the sound of his own heavy breathing and the sheriff's low moans. The flashlight in his hand no longer worked, so he tossed it to the floor and hurried to pick up the sheriff's light, which was lying on the floor with the beam directed onto the opposite wall. He picked it up and pointed it towards the sheriff, who lay on the floor moving slightly, in a state of semi-consciousness.

Fear and uncertainty was building in Bobby Dean's mind. He had been found out. This had been a setup to catch him. His legs were telling him to run, but he knew that the sheriff was the only person who knew that he, Bobby Dean was the one who had come for the key. And where was the key? He had to finish the sheriff off and get that key from him. He walked over to where the lawman was lying on the floor, and he reached down for the sheriff's gun, which was strapped to his side.

Before his hand touched the weapon, a sudden flash of green light burst from the floor somewhere between him and the sheriff. There was a force behind the light and it knocked Bobby Dean backwards, causing him to stagger. Terror filled his mind as he regained his balance and stood in the middle of the room trying to deny what he thought he had just seen.

With panic building in him, he turned in circles, shining the light around the room, searching for anyone else that might be there. He began backing up, making his way towards the door; wrenching violently around and twisting in spasmodic jerks, as he searched the dark corners of the room. "Rena?" he heard himself mutter.

His plan to find the key and murder the sheriff had been forgotten. All he wanted to do now was get out of that house and back to his truck on the road.

His back touched the closed door and he reached behind him for the doorknob. His free hand closed around the knob as his other hand waved the flashlight, shining the beam frantically through the dark interior before him; his eyes searching for what his mind told him could not be there.

In a desperate attempt to escape, he twisted violently; jerking the door open and bolting out of the house. Suddenly his feet flew out from under him and he landed hard on his back and skidded across the porch to its edge.

His balance pole had somehow fallen across the threshold of the door and he had slipped on it. For a moment, he lay there in a daze looking up at the darkened underside of the porch's roof, trying to catch his breath, which had been knocked out of him with the impact from his fall. He slowly became aware that his legs were hanging over the edge of the porch; his feet in the water. With difficulty he pulled himself up into a sitting position. Suddenly there was another flash of green light from behind him and he felt a powerful force hit his back, propelling him face first out into the dark water of the bayou.

The wetness closed around him and in the next instant he felt several sharp pains against his neck and face. Wrapping around his arms and going under his shirt, he felt the serpentine shapes of the cottonmouth snakes, which he had kicked from the porch. He knew in that instant that he would never make it out of that bayou.

Sheriff Files slowly became aware that he was still lying on the floor of the old house. He opened is eyes slightly and winced with the pain in his head and his eyes. Barely managing to keep his eyes open, he looked around the room, trying to get his bearings. He had to get to his walkie-talkie and call Tony. His head throbbed when he sat up and looked around. His recollection of the conflict with Bobby Dean was coming back to him. Then he remembered what he knew must have been a hallucination. "Swamp gas," he said to himself as he thought about the green light, which he had seen just before losing consciousness.

He pushed the uncertainties of the night out of his mind and got to his feet. In the dim early morning light, he practically had to feel his way to the bedroom, where he found his walkie-talkie. "Tony," he said after making contact with his deputy and waking him up. "Come and get me. But be careful. Bobby Dean was here last night. I don't know where he's gone to."

The spacious back porch of the large Victorian style house seemed very comfortable to Frank as he sat there wondering what it was going to be like; living here with Romey and Jesse Mae. The fact that Jesse

Mae called the porch a veranda seemed odd to him, but that was just one of several things that he felt he could get used to.

He leaned forward in his rocking chair and picked up his pipe. He pressed tobacco into the bowl of the pipe and placed the stem to his lips and lit the tobacco. After several short puffs to get the fire going, he shook the match in his hand until the flame was extinguished and then dropped it into the large crystal ashtray that Jesse Mae had placed, just for him, on the table next to his chair. He was quickly growing fond of his new surroundings. He had decided to accept Jesse Mae's offer to make this house his and Romey's new home.

Jesse Mae walked out onto the veranda, pushing a cart before her, which held sandwiches and a chocolate cake. She was followed closely by Lula Mae and Louise. "Lunch," she called out.

"Be right there," responded Guy. He pounded a large nail into the frame made of two-by-fours that Harold, Johnny, and Romey were holding in place. "Okay," he said to his helpers. "That'll hold it till we get back." The other three let go of the frame and began walking towards the house.

Geneva, Loretta, Gary and Scotty had already abandoned their viewing position on the lawn next to the half-built playhouse and were eagerly keeping a pace ahead of the others in order to have first choice of seats at the two small tables on the veranda, which had been set up for Romey and the youngsters next to the larger dining table for the adults.

"How's it coming?" asked Jesse Mae as the men climbed the stairs behind the youngsters.

"It's great!" exclaimed Romey. He was adjusting quickly to his new environment. When Harold and Guy had offered to build him a new playhouse, he smiled broadly and, of course said yes. The men and youngsters had been working on it all morning.

"It's coming along good," said Guy, pulling his chair up to the table. "We'll have it finished by tomorrow."

Loretta, having secured her eating place, pushed her chair back from the table, making a noise as the chair legs scraped against the wooden floor. "Nobody take my place." She gave the other youngsters a stern look so that they would know she meant what she said.

"Where are you going?" asked Lula Mae.

Loretta looked at her mother and then she glanced around at the others. She stood up. "I'm going to wash my hands." She walked into the house as the others glanced around at one another, acknowledging the obvious homage to Mary. Then the tray of sandwiches began making its rounds and Louise and Lula Mae poured iced tea and lemonade.

After a few minutes, Loretta returned to the veranda. "Mama," she said as she approached the tables. Lula Mae looked towards Loretta and saw Sheriff Files walking next to her.

"Afternoon folks," said the sheriff, touching the brim of his hat that he had neglected to remove. For a moment, everyone at the tables stared at the sheriff without speaking. His eyes were still red and swollen and he had several cuts and bruises on his face. Following the initial shock, they all greeted him and Jesse Mae convinced him to join them at the table.

The sheriff declined Jesse Mae's offer to have lunch with them, but he eagerly accepted a glass of iced tea. He took a long drink from the glass, almost emptying it. He set the glass on the table and looked around at the group. "Well, Bobby Dean's dead."

Louise and Lula Mae both shot a quick glance at their respective children out of concern for their responses to this statement. The youngsters did not seem disturbed; in fact, they sat with rapt attention.

Sheriff Files continued. "He came to that old house last night just like we thought he would. He went straight for that potbellied stove. That's when I surprised him. Unfortunately he surprised me too… with a handful of ashes from the bottom of that stove thrown in my eyes. While I was temporarily blinded, he knocked me out with his flashlight."

"That must have been some flashlight." Frank examined Sheriff Files' face from across the table. "Looks like he pounded you good with it too."

"Yeah, he got the best of me. I thought he was going to do me in, but something happened."

The family sat in silence as the sheriff took another long drink of iced tea. Louise picked up the pitcher and refilled his glass and they all waited for him to elaborate.

"Well…what, Karl? What happened?" asked Frank.

"I'm not sure; something strange."

With this statement, the family became even more intent on the sheriff, and they waited in silence for him to continue.

"There was this flash of green light."

"Swamp gas." Frank took a bite out of his sandwich; satisfied that he had provided a logical explanation to what the sheriff had called strange.

"Well, that's what you'd think. Now granted, I had ashes in my eyes and I was half out from him beating on my head with that flashlight, but I could have sworn that I saw someone else in that room."

The only sound was that of the sparrows in the tree next to the house. All eyes were on the sheriff as he took another drink of tea. This time Jesse Mae picked up the pitcher and filled his glass after he replaced it on the table. "Who do you think you saw?" she asked.

"That green light in the room didn't look like no swamp gas. It looked like a woman with long hair."

"Aw, that's crazy," said Frank.

"I know, I know," said Sheriff Files. "And I'm not saying that that's what it was. I'm just saying that that's what I thought I saw at the time." He looked around at the others. "Of course it was swamp gas."

The youngsters all looked at one another, remembering their night at the bayou watching the glowing *swamp gas.*

"So, what happened to Bobby Dean?" asked Guy.

"I guess he must've stumbled or tripped on a underwater log or something when he was trying to get back to the road. He had his waist high waders on. Those snakes couldn't of got him if he had stayed standing up. Anyway, when Tony and me got back there after the doctor cleaned my eyes out; we found him floating face down. His head was swollen so bad, we could hardly recognize him. He even had a cottonmouth inside his waders; it almost bit Tony. Anyway, I left Tony there with the body, and went back to my office to call the coroner. He should have the body back at the morgue by now.

"Then I went to tell Ruth that we had found him. After she stopped crying, she told me that it was Bobby Dean that killed Mary...and Rena too. She didn't know anything about it until yesterday at the wake."

"What's going to happen to her?" asked Louise.

"She's in jail in Dumas right now. She's an accessory. A deputy from Little Rock is coming to pick her up and take her to jail over there. They'll keep her there for her arraignment."

The sheriff pushed his chair back from the table and stood up. "Well, thank you kindly for the tea. I best be getting back to my office. I got a lot of paperwork to do."

"Thank you Karl," said Frank. He stood up and walked the sheriff to the front door. When he returned to the table, the family was quiet and introspective. The ordeal had come to an end. It had been a summer that would be talked about for many years to come.

Manufactured By: RR Donnelley
Breinigsville, PA USA
July, 2010